DANGEROUS GAMES

James Courtney loved to play high-risk games. Games of the flesh, with hungering females, hypodermic needles and gold coins all part of the unspeakable pleasure. Games of deception, blinding the world's press to a past and a present linked to a Nazi Germany that had never died. Games of power, in savage competition with the other multinational megacorporate heads of the earth. Games of death, to remove any man or woman standing in his way.

Now James Courtney had plunged into the ultimate danger game, as he moved the pieces in New York, Paris, Venice, London and the Middle East—and waited for the greatest prize of all to fall into his ruthless hands. . . .

THE PLUNDERERS

THE PLUNDERERS

Jonathan Black

A SIGNET BOOK
NEW AMERICAN LIBRARY
TIMES MIRROR

To Joan, with all my love.

PUBLISHER'S NOTE

This novel is a work of fiction. Names, characters, places, and incidents either are the product of the author's imagination or are used fictitiously, and any resemblance to actual persons, living or dead, events, or locales is entirely coincidental.

SIGNET TRADEMARK REG. U.S. PAT. OFF. AND FOREIGN COUNTRIES
REGISTERED TRADEMARK—MARCA REGISTRADA
HECHO EN CHICAGO, U.S.A.

SIGNET, SIGNET CLASSICS, MENTOR, PLUME, MERIDIAN AND NAL BOOKS *are published by The New American Library, Inc., 1633 Broadway, New York, New York 10019*

FIRST PRINTING, JULY, 1983

1 2 3 4 5 6 7 8 9

PRINTED IN THE UNITED STATES OF AMERICA

I

1

James Philip Courtney traveled extensively, but found travel itself both tiresome and tiring. In-flight sex vanquished boredom and served as an energizer, and his bedroom aboard the private DC-10 had been furnished and decorated accordingly. The bed was king-size. Bulkheads were sheathed with mirrors made of a remarkable shatterproof glass developed by a subsidiary of his giant holding company, CVI—Courtney Ventures International. The floor was carpeted with jaguar skins, a touch that never failed to arouse the cupidity of the women he chose as traveling companions. They assumed this was a hint they could earn furs of their own and were inspired to give virtuoso performances.

Eileen Marsh was not impressed. As James Courtney's current mistress, she had already won an array of costly gifts. And she was suffering from a hangover. Although she was only twenty-one, the aftereffects of too much Taittinger *blanc de blancs* served to blear eyes, coarsen lovely Miss Universe runner-up features, and destroy enthusiasm for lovemaking. In any event, Eileen no longer felt it necessary to outdo herself and, having undressed, lay down on the bed and made a vapid, patently spurious show of desire.

"Hurry, Jim, I don't want to wait," she murmured. Miracles of soundproofing held the DC-10's engine noise to a muted, distant whisper; there was no need to raise her voice. "Please . . . I'm drenched."

"Bullshit." James Courtney, fully clothed in open-necked sports shirt and white linen slacks, lowered his lean, five-foot-eleven frame into an ecru leather armchair bolted to the floor. A man of almost sixty, his thick auburn hair graying only at the temples and his scarcely lined aquiline face belied his age by a decade. His pale blue eyes fixed on the girl, who sat bolt upright, her expression now one of genuine dismay—and fear.

"Jim . . ."

"Save it." Courtney spoke in a low, even tone, but he was clearly issuing orders. "I'll talk. Give me any arguments and it will mean just that much less for you."

James Philip Courtney, invariably identified in the news media as "the expatriate American billionaire" and "flamboyant entrepreneur," believed there were only two kinds of women. Those a man paid to stay with him, and those he paid to go—and stay—away. Eileen Marsh had been in the former category for almost three months, and was about to be shifted into the latter. A sex-object souvenir acquired during another business visit to New York, he had taken her back to his estate on the Spanish Costa del Sol, installed her there as his resident mistress.

Unfortunately, Eileen overestimated her own worth. She had grown increasingly greedy and troublesome. For Courtney, the end had come the night before, when they attended a party given for Bjorn Borg at the Puente Romano Regine's. Eileen got drunk, created a scene, and when they returned home to Courtney's mansion, went to bed and passed out. He had shaken her awake in the morning, announced that she was to go with him to New York. Brain still champagne-fuddled, the girl took this as another sign that Courtney was infatuated with her, firmly hooked. An hour after the plane took off from Málaga airport, he led her from the amidships lounge compartment to the bedroom—to have sex, she thought. But now it was evident that he intended to discard her—as he had an endless procession of her predecessors.

"Please, Jim—my God, I'm sorry!" It was an anguished plea. Eileen Marsh suddenly realized that she might not be a permanent fixture, after all. She had reveled in her exalted status as the billionaire's live-in mistress and the luxuries of life at Montemar, his Cabo Verde *finca*. She dreaded the thought of losing either. "I'll do anything you say from now on. I swear it."

"You have no choice but to do exactly what I say." Courtney fingered the old diagonal scar on his right cheek, and his tone was harsh. "Once we land, you're on your own. I'll give you a fifteen-thousand lump-sum payment, then two thousand a month for a year. Provided you behave, make no waves—"

"Wait a minute!" Rage replaced dread. "My jewelry, clothes—everything's in Spain."

"Correction. Everything is in the cargo hold. The servants packed your belongings while we were having breakfast and put them aboard at Málaga." Courtney laughed. The laugh infuriated Eileen. Others would laugh, too, when they heard that she had been summarily discarded.

"You son of a bitch! I'll get even—"

"Indeed?"

"I know plenty about you. Plenty. I made sure I learned!"

"Is that an implied threat?" Courtney asked. He stood up, moved toward the door.

"Call it any fucking thing you want." Eileen swung off the bed and stood, glaring hatred at him. "I can cause you trouble, Jim. Big trouble."

He paused at the door. "Perhaps. But then the money would stop." He held the doorknob, spoke over his shoulder. "And it's not beyond the realm of possibility that you might be stopped, too. Permanently."

Eileen took a step forward, but he left, closing the door behind him. She stared at the door, her look vengeful, vindictive. She knew there were sure, safe ways to hit back and more than even the score. She was determined to use them all.

The office compartment was deserted save for a stewardess, trim in an aqua uniform with the CVI monogram embroidered on the jacket lapels. She was surprised when Courtney entered. His sexual stamina was legendary. When he went to the bedroom with a woman during a flight, he stayed for hours. Today he had emerged after less than twenty minutes.

"The usual, Anita." Courtney smiled, sat down on a port-side sofa. "Then please tell Eberhardt and Paco I'd like to see them—in that order."

"Yes, sir." The stewardess went to the compartment's mini-bar, poured aged Jerez into a Baccarat glass, served it, and hurried off to the forward cabins. Courtney took a sip of the sherry.

Tom Eberhardt, a thirtyish American and minor-grade administrative aide, appeared. "You sent for me, Mr. Courtney?"

"I sure as hell did." Courtney was grinning. His decision—too long delayed, he now realized—had been made, and he was in good humor. "Miss Marsh is being put out to pasture—upon arrival."

Eberhardt repressed the urge to offer his employer congratulations. Like everyone on Courtney's payrolls who had contact with Eileen Marsh, he disliked her intensely as a selfish, conceited, and troublemaking bitch. He waited until Courtney told him to draw a fifteen-thousand-dollar check on a Swiss bank, payable to Eileen, then left. Paco—Francisco—Figueras came in a moment later. A burly, fiercely mustachioed former member of the Spanish Guardia Civil, he served as an assistant security chief. Although he spoke fluent English, Paco habitually reported to his *patrón* in Spanish, addressing him as "Don Jaime."

"Message our New York security people," Courtney said. "I want a couple of men to help Miss Marsh off the plane and escort her to the St. Regis Hotel. Add that she's to be placed under twenty-four-hour surveillance until further notice."

Paco Figueras heaved an inner sigh of relief. The ill-tempered *puta* was going at last. Of course, she would have a successor—and soon. It was April 30, he reflected, and made a mental wager that Don Jaime would have another in-house *cortesana* within a week. Whoever he chose, she would be an improvement. He all but ran to carry out his orders and spread the good news to the others in James Courtney's airborne retinue.

The DC-10 landed at Kennedy Airport shortly after ten A.M., local time. Courtney, Tom Eberhardt, and Figueras were the first to disembark. After clearing immigration and customs, they went to a waiting Cadillac limousine and were driven to the World Trade Center in lower Manhattan.

The three men returned and boarded the plane again at six-fifteen. By all rights, James Courtney should have been elated. His quick trip to New York had been completely successful. The officers of Globe-Aarco Metals, the giant mining combine, had met his sign-by-five ultimatum. The resulting agreement meant a $25-million instant profit for Courtney Ventures International. As an added bonus, he was told that Eileen Marsh had taken her check and, accompanied by a pair of private detectives, left the plane without creating a scene.

But Jim Courtney was accustomed to dealing in millions, and he had rid himself of unwanted mistresses many times before. Besides, he had an appointment to keep more than 3,500 miles away, at his home in Cabo Verde on the Spanish Sun Coast. The meeting would be the first move in an intricate scheme that involved sums—and risks—of a magnitude awesome even by his standards.

"Take off ASAP, Ed," he told the pilot, glanced at the five stewardesses, nodded at the one named Anita. "You come along with me. I'm going into the office section—don't want to be disturbed." He strode aft. Reaching the office compartment, he dumped himself down on the sofa he had used earlier.

"Double whiskey for a change, Anita," he said.

His eyes followed as she went to the bar jutting from the damask-covered forward bulkhead. The girl was young, sultry, and moved with supple grace. She returned to him, drink in hand. He took it, said:

"I'll ring for you later."

He swallowed whiskey, set the glass down, and fingered the scar on his right cheek. It was a familiar gesture—and reassuring, a reminder of reckless gambles taken and won in the past. The odds to be overcome in the next weeks and months would be exponentially greater than any before, he mused. Much—everything—was at stake. He felt a twinge of uncertainty, almost fear, shook it off.

There were no uncertainties—or almost none, Courtney told himself. He had first begun to formulate the game plan in the autumn of 1981, when it became apparent that Reagan, Thatcher, and Mitterand economic policies were disasters that could be exploited. The game plan called for an ultimate coup, global in scale. Since then, the plans had been refined, honed to zero tolerance, a complex apparatus assembled. All in utmost secrecy. And the secrecy was guaranteed. Those party to the scheme—and they were a highly select few—knew the consequences of any secrecy breach could be fatal, literally was well as figuratively.

The billionaire had calculated and recalculated foreseeable risks to irreducible minimums, but they were still formidable. As for the unforeseen and unforeseeable? He thrust the question aside. Contingencies would be dealt with when they arose. As they had always been dealt with in the past. Swiftly. By whatever means necessary.

". . . estimate arrival at oh-seven-fifty hours, local time."

The pilot's voice over the loudspeakers brought Courtney back into the here and now, and he scowled. The hours of flight across the Atlantic would seem endless, intolerable in their monotony, and he was already spooled up, the need for release an imperative. The scowl faded. He pressed a call button. The stewardess materialized seconds later. Her presence induced the beginnings of an erection.

"Yes, sir. Care for another drink—or dinner?"

"Neither, Anita." He got to his feet, blue eyes glowing and saying the rest. He started aft. She followed, unbuttoning her uniform jacket as she went.

Grasping and wholly self-oriented from childhood, Eileen Marsh had made grave miscalculations during her three months as James Courtney's favorite. She thought her youth and beauty would ensure at least a year's tenure at Montemar—perhaps longer. Ego bloated, she had treated everyone on Courtney's staff as underlings, with contempt. The affair had ended—or rather, had been ended—abruptly, without warning. But Eileen could not bring herself to believe she was at fault, and her woman-scorned rage had intensified during the day. She vented some of it on the bellmen who brought the mounds of luggage up to her suite.

"Now get out of here," she rasped when they were finished. "You can put your tip on the bill."

Courtney had arranged that she was to have use of a CVI suite at the St. Regis for two weeks. Two weeks, no more. Instead of being grateful, Eileen boiled at the knowledge that a time limit had been imposed on her free stay. Fury rose even more when she began opening her Vuitton bags—like their contents, gifts from Jim Courtney. They had been packed every which way by servants at Montemar. It was impossible to guess what was where, and by six-thirty in the evening she had given up trying.

She used the sitting-room telephone, called the manager's office, and demanded that maids be sent to unpack for her. Told it was impossible until morning, she slammed down the receiver.

Eileen was about to lift the receiver again, make another—an outside—call, then remembered. The suite was leased on a yearly basis by Courtney Ventures International. She had learned that CVI had many such suites in various large cities around the world. They were used by executives of CVI subsidiaries or the people with whom they dealt. Rooms and telephones in them were always bugged.

Eileen left the suite, took the elevator downstairs, found the pay telephones, picked one at random. Luckily, Evan Gerlach was at home. Gerlach, a man of dubious origins and even more dubious occupation, had been Eileen's lover in what she thought of as her B.C.—Before Courtney—period.

"Well, I'll be damned!" Evan Gerlach was delighted. Eileen was magnificent in bed. "In town on a vacation from billionaire-balling?"

"The mother dumped me. Today."

"Sorry for your sake—not for mine. I'm not doing anything tonight. Come on up—grab a cab."

"I'll do that—and tell you a lot of stories. They're worth money, Evan. Aren't you glad I thought of you first?"

"I'm not so sure I want to hear. Courtney swings weight. He's not a guy to mess around with."

"There won't be any problems. He'll pay—and plenty."

"Give me a ball-park figure."

"Half a million . . . a million, depends on how you handle it, Evan."

"Holy Christ! You've got to be kidding!"

"I'm not, believe me. Now, are you willing to listen while we fuck?"

"Like I said, grab a cab."

2

Arrival at Málaga airport was on the original ETA dot: 0750. It being May 1, a holiday in Spain as in other European countries, there was even less airport activity than usual at that hour. The DC-10 taxied to the main terminal building, a glass-and-concrete structure gleaming in the early-morning sun, parked on the apron near a Bell helicopter. Like the Douglas jet, the copter had the legend "Courtney Ventures International" emblazoned on its fuselage.

The DC-10's engines were switched off. A boarding ladder was maneuvered against the fuselage by coveralled Spanish ground personnel. The forward door opened. Paco Figueras, mustaches freshly waxed, stepped out of the plane, stood for a moment surveying the scene, then descended the steps.

James Courtney came after him. Two hours with the stewardess Anita and four of sleep had eased his tensions, energized him. He was casually dressed in short-sleeved sports shirt and white linen slacks. He moved jauntily and was smiling, as though delighted to be home again, even though he had been gone less than a full day. Men in the ground crew waved, called out greetings:

"*Buenos días, Don Jaime.*"

"*Como está usted, Señor Courtney*?"

It was not surprising that they recognized him. *El billonario norteamericano* made frequent use of the airport and was the most famous of all foreign expatriates living along the 225-mile length of the Sun Coast. Many Andalusian Spaniards good-naturedly referred to him as "*El Rey de la Costa del Sol*" in recognition of his wealth and power. He was much liked by the majority of Spaniards. He provided employment for many, gave generously to charity, respected Spanish pride, traditions, and customs. And, unlike most *extranjeros*, he spoke Spanish fluently, with a flawless Castilian accent, and was aways willing to exchange pleasantries, as he did now, while striding across the apron to his helicopter.

Courtney and Figueras did not have to undergo immigration and customs formalities. Shortly after the billionaire—then only a millionaire but an important personage nonetheless—had settled in Cabo Verde, officials of the Franco government showed gratitude for various favors he had done. They extended freedom of the port to Courtney and any one *guardaespalda* who might accompany him. That had been more than two decades before. Generalissimo Francisco Franco was long dead, the Spanish Government long a constitutional monarchy, but no one had thought to rescind the privilege.

Courtney boarded the copter. Figueras took a last look around him, followed. Minutes later, the craft lifted off. The cabin was luxuriously appointed. James Courtney, reclining in a modified clam-shell seat, gazed through the large square window next to him at a rapidly spreading panorama he never tired of seeing.

The city of Málaga lay below, an expanse of red-tiled roofs with great islands of verdant parks. Modern high-rises jutted skyward, discordant and vulgar. The city hall was a massive, soothing confection; the bullring, near the waterfront, a sullen, almost menacing perfect circle. Beyond, there stretched the blue sweep of the Mediterranean, the calm sea dotted with sails and, here and there, roweled by the wakes of engine-powered pleasure boats.

Banking right, the copter began to follow the multilaned Carretera de Cádiz coastal highway. Fertile lands were cradled against the sea by foothills of the Sierra Ronda. Ancient houses clustered together in centuries-old villages. Courtney grew pensive. He could remember when Andalusian villagers drew their harsh *tinto* from barrels, danced flamencos, and sang malagueñas. Now their wine came in snap-cap liter bottles purchased at *supermercados*; the young danced in sleazy discotheques, and transistor radios blared hard rock. Although anything but a romantic, he frowned, grumbled aloud. Paco Figueras, seated opposite him, leaned forward. His jacket fell open, revealing his shoulder-holstered nine-millimeter Beretta.

"Never mind," Courtney said above the thwack of rotors. "I was talking to myself, Paco." He turned back to the window. Miles of beaches, once glorious, now overbuilt and lined with garish hotels, were visible. Eyesore extremes were achieved around Torremolinos and Fuengirola. The towns had grown rich—and ugly—from catering to low-budget package-tour vacationers, Courtney mused, then thought: What the hell. CVI's Spanish subsidiaries had earned healthy profits from the construction boom. Fuengirola was left behind, Marbella loomed ahead, and he felt better. Marbella had managed to become a thriving city and still retain much of its old picturesque quality. He peered down at the old town with its narrow, always spotless streets, enclosed squares, and white houses. Minutes passed. Beyond Marbella were the five-star hotels, marina enclaves, the mansions and *fincas* of the rich and superrich—the fabled segment of the Sun Coast where the Beautiful People lived and played.

A sleek oceangoing yacht was nosing into Puerto José Banus. Courtney recognized the *Avila*, made a mental note to give a dinner party for whichever members of the Belgian royal family were aboard. Royal families. Association of ideas brought memory of a party he had given a few years before in honor of Prince Bernhard of the Netherlands. He chuckled. The prince had received his door-prize envelope; a CVI company had received Dutch contracts that netted millions in profits.

Cabo Verde, the town that James Courtney regarded as his private fiefdom, lay dead ahead. The Cabo Verde *puerto* was busy. Al Medani's *Myrna* was berthed at its usual place. There were numerous other large pleasure craft, motor and sail, tied up along the quays. The helicopter slowed, swung right. For a moment the distant bulk of the Rock of Gibraltar loomed in the window, then vanished as the pilot eased the chopper around farther and descended to the helipad at Montemar, Courtney's home and the nerve center of CVI.

Newspapers and magazines were wont to describe Montemar as "baronial" or "sumptuous," and with justification. The estate covered a thousand acres. The main house was a seventy-two-room Moorish-style mansion surrounded by expanses of lawns and gardens that sloped gently down to a private beach. An enormous sweet-water reflecting pool was a glistening carpet spread in front of the house. Elsewhere on the grounds there were indoor and outdoor swimming pools, tennis courts, a nine-hole golf course, riding stables, woodlands, and orchards. Tucked behind the H-shaped mansion and screened from it by trees and bushes was a compact two-story building, the "office annex" where some forty CVI administrative employees worked. All lived in Cabo Verde; those without cars were shuttled back and forth by CVI minibus. But it was a holiday; the office annex was deserted. However, there was a golf cart on the helipad to take Courtney and his bodyguard-companion to the front entrance of the mansion.

Leslie Grenville was an unusual type to be a butler. Although English to his Kentish core, he spoke several languages. Although a superb butler aware of his station, he had attended a public school and spent a year reading economics at Magdalen

College. Although gentle in appearance—his face even had a lamblike quality—he had trained as a commando in the peacetime British Army and then fought, for whichever side paid most, as a mercenary in various strife-torn African countries.

Leslie Grenville's free-lance military career had been ended by an Angolan Popular Front shell splinter that tore away his genital organs. Released from the hospital, he went—for no particular reason—to Spain, found work as a valet to a tax-exiled British millionaire who lived in Estepona. James Courtney hired him away in 1978, made him his butler-majordomo at Montemar. Some months later a Basque terrorist intent on killing Courtney eluded security guards and managed to make his way into the main house. The terrorist carried an Uzi submachine gun. Grenville accidentally encountered him in the corridor leading to Courtney's study-office—and proved that even though he was a eunuch, he could still stand up to a man firing an Uzi and put a .357 Magnum slug squarely between his eyes.

"Habit, I suppose," he had explained when asked why he had been carrying the Magnum.

Courtney offered him a choice of more prestigious jobs within the CVI organization, but Grenville knew that CVI executives had little real authority, were hired and fired at Courtney's will—or whim. He refused the offer, asked to stay on as majordomo, saying:

"It's a more permanent post and at the center of things, as it were. I can make myself quite useful, sir."

The message between the lines was clear. Grenville's emasculation had led him to desire security. Yet he remained a mercenary soldier at heart, eager to remain close to the seat of power, unflinching in loyalty to whoever wielded the power and paid him.

"I think you can be very useful," Courtney agreed, and since then Grenville had enjoyed a degree of power himself. He was in full charge of the thirty-strong Montemar domestic staff, enjoyed special status, and was Courtney's household confidant—an extra pair of eyes and ears.

Grenville, resplendent in lightweight butler's regalia, opened the huge iron-bound doors to the mansion. "Welcome back, sir. I trust all went well."

Jim Courtney stepped into the atrium/entrance hall. "Better than well, Grenville. Swept the board clean." He nodded to Paco Figueras, who hurried off to lose himself in the east-wing reaches of the great house. Courtney saw that the butler's right eyebrow had risen a fraction of an inch, read the question, answered it: "I left her in New York." He grinned. "She's not, repeat not, returning."

"May I offer congratulations?"

Grenville looked like a ferociously triumphant lamb, if any such thing was possible, Courtney thought, and said, "Sure, and I'll accept them—with thanks." Grenville had often tried to warn him that Eileen Marsh was a problem that required solving but he had not listened until very recently. "Oh, I expect a visitor at around eleven. I'm not to be disturbed for any reason until he's gone."

Courtney turned and strode down the long, high-ceilinged corridor that led off the atrium to his left. Great masses of fresh-cut flowers from the gardens of the estate were in bowls on antique tables and chests. Paintings from his famed art collection hung on the walls: a Vandyke, a Murillo, works by lesser masters. He ignored them. His mind was sharp-focused elsewhere.

James Courtney called his private office in the mansion "*el estudio*"—the study, a misnomer that erred on the side of gross understatement. Spaniards who worked at Montemar called it "*la jefetura*"—the headquarters of the chief, which came somewhat closer to the truth, for it was an extravaganza of space, splendor . . . and anachronisms and incongruities.

Walls mahogany-paneled to a height of eight feet soared ten more to a vaulted ceiling. Rare Persian carpets seemed no larger than throw rugs on the expanse of mosaic floor. A fireplace caliphs might have used to roast oxen whole served a purely decorative purpose, for the house was climate-controlled. Chairs and sofas were functional modern; tables and cabinets were museum-quality antiques. Courtney's desk was a huge writing table originally crafted for French King Louis XV, but telephones, closed-circuit TV sets, and other ultramodern paraphernalia were arrayed across its marquetry top.

Courtney seated himself at the table. The electronic devices ranged within easy reach of his spatulate fingertips were mute and dark. They would remain so, and not only because it was a holiday on the European continent. He had no interest in stock- and commodity-market quotations. Not today. There were other, infinitely more important matters that demanded attention—and much thought—before his visitor arrived.

Courtney gave himself over to a few moments of reflection. Bernard Rechstein was due in a little over two hours, provided his Air France flight from Paris landed at Málaga Airport on schedule. It had been years since they last saw each other, but he knew that Rechstein was still the perfect instrument: anonymous in appearance, totally reliable, and above all, icy-nerved. Who else was better suited for the task to be performed? Grenville perhaps. Even probably. But at present, Grenville was not expendable. There would be other special work for the ex-soldier of fortune to do, and soon. Very soon.

A thick folder lay on the tabletop. It contained an inventory of Courtney's art collection. He broke off his musings and, eyes narrowed, angular features sharp-set, opened it and thumbed through the pages to one headed:

VELAZQUEZ, DIEGO
Horse and Rider
Oil on canvas
121 × 183 cm

Courtney stared at the heading as though at a prism through which he could see into other dimensions of time and space—and, in a sense, it was. It served as an immediate reminder that final and irrevocable decisions had been made, and that a far-reaching train of events was about to be set into motion. He hesitated for a second, then, with a swift, almost furtive motion, removed the page from the file and fed it into the document shredder that stood beside his chair.

He closed the folder, lost himself in thought.

Bernard Rechstein was ushered into the study at 11:05. He had not changed much since their last meeting, Courtney mused. He was fatter, and there was even less hair on the round skull. Otherwise Rechstein looked the same. As though he had come off an assembly line that mass-produced flabby bottom-rung civil-servant types complete with loose jowls, horn-rimmed glasses, and rumpled off-the-peg brown suits.

They shook hands and greeted each other as old friends will. Then Bernard Rechstein lowered his dumpling body into a quilted-leather Barcelona chair. Refusing offers of food, drink, a cigar, he said:

"Better we get down to business and I move on." He spoke American English with a trace of Brooklyn-Jewish inflection. But Courtney knew he could switch languages and accents as easily as he changed identities, and this prompted him to ask:

"Mind telling me who you are today, Bernie?"

Rechstein chuckled. "I came in as Alcide Guyot, *citoyen* of France. Going out, I can be Brit, Swiss, West German, or

Israeli. I've got the spare passports in my pocket, Jaypee." There was mocking emphasis on the "Jaypee."

Courtney felt a trace of annoyance. One niche in his compartmented brain held a miscellany of half-believed superstitions, among them a notion that some names carried a magic ring of their own. His initials—J.P.—were the same as those of yesteryear tycoons Morgan, Warburg, Getty. He liked his close associates to address him as J.P., but Rechstein's "Jaypee" sounded almost like a jeer. He shook off the annoyance and said:

"Use whichever you want. You'll be leaving for Tangier this afternoon by boat, and—"

"Boat?" Rechstein scowled. "I hate boats. Why not by plane?"

"Because Velázquez was a Spaniard." Courtney spoke with exaggerated patience, as if to a child, getting his own back. "His works are classified as national treasures here in Spain, and there are security checks at airports. They won't be a problem anywhere else, but going through Málaga . . ."

"Yeah, somebody might inspect and want to see export permits."

"Bravo, you're with it at last." Courtney relented, smiled. "It's a risk we can't afford, Bernie. In 1972 the Velázquez *Juan de Pereja* sold for five and a half million. *Horse and Rider* is worth a very great deal more—or do I have to remind you?"

"I know." Rechstein's face underwent remarkable transformation. No longer blurred, nondescript, it had turned brutally hard. "Next to you, who knows better?"

Courtney went to his Louis XV writing table. An aluminum cylinder about four feet long and eight inches in diameter and with screw caps at both ends was propped against it. He took the tube, walked back to Rechstein, gave it to him.

"Christ, it weighs," Rechstein grumbled, hefting the object before laying it on the floor beside him.

"Veláquez always laid on heavy paint," Courtney said, tone and expression sardonic. "That's why he's always been one of our favorite artists—right, Bernie?"

"Sure. A genius. What next?"

Courtney handed him a sheet of blank paper. "Next, details about those spare passports. Nationalities, numbers, the names."

"Not afraid I'll run off with the masterpiece, are you, Jaypee?"

"No. Just aware of who you'll be dealing with. You're to call me twice daily—shoot for ten and ten, Spanish time. If twelve hours pass without a call, I'll know there's been trouble and start tracing your movements. Which I can't do unless I know who you're supposed to be."

Rechstein gave him a long look from behind thick eyeglass lenses. "If there's trouble, you'll be tracing my corpse, not me," he said in a grim tone, but began to write. He finished, gave the paper to Courtney. "Okay, what next?"

"One of my chauffeurs will drive you down to the *puerto*. A charter-boat operator named Harkness is waiting for you there."

"How much does he know?"

"Only that I'm paying him to take someone to Tangier."

"Harkness? What is he, a Brit?"

"American. Showed up on the Costa in 1973."

"Another expatriate?"

"Sort of. He was on the run after being disbarred—"

"Hold it. I suddenly don't like what I hear. Lawyers are bad enough. Disbarred lawyers? They're poison."

"Usually, yes. In this instance, no."

"You trust the guy?"

"It goes beyond trust, Bernie."

"That means you own him."

"Of course. What else could it possibly mean?"

When Rechstein left, James Courtney settled into his desk chair and gazed at the picture hanging on the wall directly opposite him. It was a Frans Hals portrait of a chess player holding a black queen in midair and about to checkmate an unseen opponent. Hals had endowed his subject with a shrewd, cynical, and supremely self-confident expression. Here, the master was saying, is a man who consistently outwits and outmaneuvers his adversaries, at chess and all else. Courtney liked to look at the portrait. He and the chess player were of the same breed, he thought. Two of an unbeatable kind.

3

"Cabo Verde" designated an eighteen-square-mile area that lay between Marabella and Estepona and was renowned as one of the Costa del Sol's havens for wealthy expatriates and pleasure-obsessed Beautiful People.

It was not always thus. In the mid-1950's Cabo Verde proper had been just another Andalusian village situated astride the then still-wretched Barcelona-Cádiz coastal highway. *El puerto*, the portion on the seafront, was where local fishermen landed their catch, moored their boats, mended their nets. *El pueblo*—with its seventeenth-century church, unpaved streets, and tiny commercial center—was on the inland side of the highway. Beyond were farmlands, and beyond them, the foothills of the Serrania de Ronda.

Spain was poor, its economy moribund, the need for hard currency desperate. The Franco government offered foreigners preferential treatment, immunity from taxes, promised to hold prices and wages low. The Andalusian coast added its own lures: the guitars-matadors-mantillas romance of Old Spain, superb beaches, magnificent scenery, ideal climate. Foreigners came in great numbers. Many established residence in and around Cabo Verde, and their convertible currencies fueled a boom. The village itself had grown into a thriving town. There were luxury-class resort hotels on the *playas*. Mansions, villas, high-rise apartment blocks stood on what had been farmlands. An elaborate marina—Puerto Cabo Verde—had been superimposed on the lower-case *puerto*; it vied with Puerto José Banus as an "in" port-of-call for the international yacht-set.

Limousines are commonplace sights in Costa del Sol marina enclaves, as much part of the *ambiente* as the yachts tied up at the concrete quays. Noontime drinkers and diners sitting under colorful table umbrellas in the outdoor cafés lining Puerto Cabo Verde's waterfront ignored the chauffeured Mercedes. It turned onto the Muelle Soriano, drove past Bar Espada, George's Pub, and Restaurante Las Olas, stopped near a long dock that jutted from the mole. A sign in English read:

BERTH 21
NEIL HARKNESS
SKIPPERED CHARTERS

The chauffeur held a passenger-compartment door. Bernard Rechstein, transmogrified into Wilhelm Fischer by the Swiss passport in his breast pocket, got out. Holding the heavy aluminum tube in both hands, he peered at a boat moored some fifteen yards away, the name *Deirdre* painted on its stern. It was a sleek, steel-hulled vessel, larger and sturdier than he had feared it might be and he was pleased. But there were four people on the afterdeck, not just one, as he had expected. This made him suspicious, uneasy. He started sorting out the people.

A sandy-haired giant leaped to the dock. Six-feet-three, about thirty-five, Rechstein noted. Wearing white T-shirt and faded khaki slacks. Face and arms burned dark by sun and wind. Undoubtedly Harkness, he thought, and the two burly Spaniards hurrying toward the foredeck were crew members. The fourth figure defied classification, rang alarm bells. A woman. Apparently in her mid-twenties. Wearing a bikini top, jeans, and leaning against the rail.

Rechstein scowled. Women deceived and betrayed. They were dangerous. The only use he had ever found for them was sexual. He wanted no female traveling companion. Least of all on this voyage.

The big man came up to him, confirmed that he was Neil Harkness and said, "Sorry, but J.P. didn't tell me your name."

"It is Fischer." The accent was German-Swiss. "Wilhelm Fischer."

"Ready to go aboard, Mr. Fischer?"

"No." Rechstein saw the chauffeur carrying his suitcase to the boat—and the girl still leaning against the afterrail. "Who is the woman?" he demanded, tone sharp.

None of your damned business, Harkness thought. He had taken an instinctive dislike to Wilhelm Fischer. But he could not afford to antagonize anyone sent to him by James Courtney, and said, "A friend of mine," and, as if offering bona fides, added, "She works for J.P."

"She is to accompany us?"

Neil busied himself lighting a Celta. He had acquired a taste for the cheap brand of *negros* cigarettes when, a frame-up having ended his legal career in New York, he first came to Spain. The Celtas were like a reminder of how far he had gone—up or down, depending on the viewpoint—since 1973. He exhaled acrid smoke and answered the question.

"Nope. You're the only passenger."

"Then what is she doing here?"

"It's a fiesta, May Day." Neil smiled, baring strong white teeth. The cross-examination was beginning to irk him. "The masses march in parades—or visit friends on boats." He cranked the smile down, called to the girl. She joined them moments later.

Rechstein registered impressions. A pert face, long-lashed eyes—hazel—an uptilted nose. Pretty rather than beautiful. His uneasiness increased. Pretty women were the most dangerous. Men felt comfortable, safe, with them, and let down their guard . . .

". . . to meet Miss Sybil Pearson."

He heard Harkness finish making introductions, bobbed his almost hairless head to acknowledge them—and snapped alert. The woman was staring at the metal cylinder in his hands.

"Something is the matter, Miss Pearson?" he rasped.

"Matter? Oh. It's just . . . well I ordered that tube through Vivian Dixon's gallery. See?"—Sybil Pearson pointed a finger; Rechstein felt as though she was pointing a gun at his midriff—"there's the label. Galerías Vivi."

"So what's the big deal?" Harkness shrugged.

"Odd, is all," Sybil said. "Only last week, Mr. Courtney made a point of telling me he'd used it to send off some blueprints."

Rechstein activated mental computers. The woman was intelligent, perceptive. However, her accent was upper-class Home Counties English. Britons of that sort were usually credulous, imagination having been trained out of them. Usually. Not always. He would have to test.

"*Ach!*" he exclaimed, faking a smile intended to show that understanding had dawned. "A matter of verb tenses. Jaypee has given me the blueprints to deliver personally." He silently cursed Sybil for being there, James Courtney and himself for failing to notice and remove the tiny sticker label. Such coincidences and oversights were the stuff that bred disasters.

"Must be the answer," Sybil said. Her employer had a security obsession, often sent documents by courier rather than trust them to the mails. "Well, I'll run along. *Adiós*, Mr. Fischer—*buen viaje*." She looked up at Harkness, who towered over her by more than eight inches, winked. "*Hasta luego*, Captain Bligh. I'll see you tonight." She smiled, turned, walked away.

Rechstein glared after her balefully. Glance, wink, and bantering tone told him she was sleeping with Harkness. This gave rise to fresh concern. Men and women who shared beds also shared what they saw and heard, and were liable to assemble fragments into discernible patterns.

"What is the woman's—Miss Pearson's—work for Jaypee?" he asked.

"Sybil's his private secretary."

And she respects and admires the son of a bitch, Neil thought sourly. He hated the billionaire, and there was ample reason for the hatred. But he was helpless. Courtney could make him jump, do tricks, stand up and beg. On command. Or else.

"Indeed?" Fischer persisted in his interrogations. "How long has she worked for him?"

"Over three years."

Bernard Rechstein felt better. If the woman had been in Courtney's employ that long, it meant he owned her, too.

The chauffeur, suitcase-carrying done, stood beside the Mercedes. Rechstein dismissed him and waited, watching owlishly, until the limousine made a U-turn on the quay and drove off.

Neil chafed, eager to get under way. He and Sybil were invited to a party being given that evening by Kenneth and Vivian Dixon. Kenneth was an author. Vivian owned the Galerías Vivi art gallery in the Cabo Verde pueblo. He liked them both, their parties were fun, and he did not want to be late. He knew from much experience that the actual trip down the coast, across the Strait of Gibraltar, and then back, would take only about five hours. Much less if *Deirdre*'s powerful twin diesels were run at full speed. But allowance had to be made for the inevitable delays when entering and leaving the haphazardly managed port of Tangier.

"Okay if we go now, Mr. Fischer?" Harkness reached out a hand. "Here, I'll take that thing for you."

"Keep away!" Fischer leaped aside with surprising agility for anyone of his ponderous bulk. "You are not to touch this!"

Brief—but bitter—experience as a lawyer had taught Neil that things were seldom what they seemed and that straight paths led nowhere. The lessons had been reiterated in his years of operating skippered charters in Mediterranean waters. The largest profits came from transporting dubious passengers and cargoes. He had carried many of both for James Courtney—for the profit and because Courtney left him no other choice—but Wilhelm Fischer was the most dubious of the lot, Harkness thought, and, shrugging, said:

"Sorry. Only trying to be helpful." He turned, walked rapidly to his boat. Vaulting up on the foredeck, he began issuing orders to his two-man crew. Fischer followed, hauled himself aboard.

"I am a bad sailor," he confessed. "I must lie down during the voyage."

"Cabins are at the foot of that ladder," Neil said, pointing, and added, "Since you don't like being helped, help yourself."

The sarcasm was lost on Fischer. Clutching the metal tube to his body, he made for the ladder. Blueprints, my ass, Harkness reflected. But whatever's really inside, it's none of my business. He lit a Celta, inhaled, turned to the task of starting the engines.

Another vessel was being made ready for sea at the opposite side of the *puerto*. It was an ostentatious, overpriced cabin cruiser, a Chris-Craft of the type favored by many wealthy men who fancied themselves to be deep-sea fishermen but were not.

A red-white-and-blue Liberian flag of convenience hung limp at the stern. A man in bathing trunks sat cross-legged near the bow on the foredeck. He held a pair of binoculars to his eyes. The binoculars were trained on *Deirdre*.

Harkness saw none of this, would not have given a second thought if he had. Pleasure craft of all types and registries come and go on the Sun Coast; the people aboard them often use binoculars as toys, amuse themselves by scanning beaches, shorelines, other boats. It might have been different if Wilhelm Fischer had remained on deck. But Bernard Rechstein was below and, having dosed himself with Dramamine, already sprawled on a bunk.

Deirdre, making a steady fifteen knots through a slight chop, was off Playa de Arenas, midway between Cabo Verde and Gibraltar, when Neil first took note of the Chris-Craft. It was five hundred yards astern and apparently following. It was a floating jukebox, he mused, laughing to himself, owned by amateurs. Only amateurs would buy such a boat and feel the need to hang on the tail of another vessel on a clear, sunny day. The opinion seemed to be confirmed ten minutes later, when the gap had narrowed to three hundred yards.

If the cruiser wanted to pass, whoever was at the helm was an asshole, Harkness thought. The course taken would carry it within feet of *Deirdre*. Then another thought struck him. Amateurs loved to show off, play idiotic games akin to those of teenagers who played chicken with automobiles. He wanted none of it and grinned complacently.

The *Deirdre* was a YP-class 61-footer originally built for RAF air-sea rescue work, then refitted for civilian use, could travel at high speed, and was unmatched for maneuverability. Whatever the Chris-Craft could do, *Deirdre* could do faster and better. Even so, Harkness was in no mood for games, and simply opened the throttles. The big Cummings diesels responded. Speed rose to twenty-five knots. The pitch-and-roll effect of the chop increased; the cruiser not only hung on but closed another fifty yards.

"Shit!" Neil said aloud, took his boat to thirty knots. He doubted that the dilettantes would continue to hang astern, but they did, nosing into the foam of *Deirdre*'s wake. He changed course, turning farther out to sea. The cruiser stayed with him.

Neil's two crewmen made their way to him. They were curious. He explained in Spanish. Moments later, he had to explain again, in English, as Wilhelm Fischer emerged on deck. Sweat poured from his face, which had a greenish pallor, and he used the metal tube as a cane to steady himself.

"Good God, man! Slow down!" he croaked above the engine roar.

Harkness told him what he was doing and why. Fischer spun around, looked aft. The greenish pallor of his face faded to white.

"We must go back!" he screeched.

"Why?" Neil pushed the throttles to full. "I'll lose them . . ."

His voice trailed off. Obviously the Chris-Craft had souped-up engines. Instead of falling back, it was gaining.

"You do not understand! Turn back!"

Neil agreed that he did not understand. Why would amateurs goose up the power on a pleasure craft? He glanced at Fischer—and the tube. It's insane, he thought, but maybe they aren't amateurs and maybe . . .

The cruiser was on the port, the seaward, side of *Deirdre*, bow even with *Deirdre*'s stern. Harkness saw that there was no name painted on the vessel's bow, but there were three men on the afterdeck.

"They are after me!" Fischer yowled. To Neil's surprise, his face was regaining color, and that dropped many pieces into place. Fischer was a man accustomed to facing danger and regained composure when facing it. Clearly he—with all of us, Harkness realized—was facing it now. For whatever reasons. He stared across the mere twenty yards of water separating *Deirdre* from the cruiser, which had edged ahead a little and was running on a parallel course.

The men aboard the cruiser were busying themselves around a coil of steel cable. The cable had a curiously shaped, football-size metal object attached to its free end. Neil recognized the device as a Jansen interceptor line. The Jansen line had been developed by the Swedish Navy. Under ideal conditions, it was a remarkably effective, silent weapon that could stop a vessel dead so it could be boarded. The object at the end of the cable was a float hydrodynamically designed to be unerringly attracted into the churn of a boat's screws. Then the steel cable fouled the propellers or sheared their blades.

Neil's palms had begun to perspire. The Jansen line was not a toy. Anyone who used it was out to do damage—or worse. But the operative term in its employment was "under ideal conditions." Perhaps he could make the conditions less than ideal.

"Turn!" Fischer spoke again.

"I will—when I'm ready." Neil held a straight course. Two

men on the cruiser had lifted the Jansen float and were dangling it over the side. Neil ignored Fischer's continuing drumfire of commands and the puzzled babble of his crewmen, glued his eyes on the Chris-Craft and the men aboard it. His timing had to be right. Exactly right. He braced, waited.

The float was dropped into the water. Harkness counted one hundred, two hundred, three hundred to himself, bit into his lower lip, and spun the wheel. *Deirdre* responded instantly, turning to starboard almost on her own axis. Fischer lost his footing, fell to the slanting deck—but clung to the aluminum tube.

Deirdre's stern was now broadside to the cruiser. Neil chopped power, opened the throttles again, said a blasphemous prayer that the maneuver would work. It did. The surging backwash of *Deirdre*'s screws deflected the Jansen float, drove it back toward the cruiser's own wake—and it was then sucked in by the propellers. He could see the men on the Chris-Craft rushing aft. One stopped, held an arm up as if pointing at *Deirdre*. What he pointed was a revolver—and Harkness chortled. Whoever the men were, they were amateurs, after all. Their boat lay dead in the water and *Deirdre* was far beyond range of any handgun. He eased off the throttles, turned from the wheel, helped Fischer to his feet, and asked, "Those people after you, the tin tube, or both?"

Fischer ignored the question—in itself a yes answer on both counts—and to Neil's surprise smiled. "You think fast. I feared you might use your radio and call Spanish authorities for assistance."

"Not a chance," Neil said dryly, remembering previous escapades and close scrapes. "Any man who wants to survive in this business doesn't blab in the clear over a ship-to-shore. Especially not if he's doing work for J.P."

"Very wise." Fischer nodded approvingly.

Harkness jabbed a Celta between his lips, lit it with a wooden match he struck with a thumbnail after turning away from the wind. He inhaled, blew smoke through his nostrils, indicated the cabin cruiser bobbing several hundred yards away on the water. "They're not going anywhere until somebody gives them a tow. What about us? Still want to head back?"

"No. Now that I see you are not a stranger to . . . ah, difficulties, we shall proceed to any destination."

"You sure, friend? Those clowns may be chatting to friends over their radio. How the hell do you know there won't be another boat—or a welcoming committee waiting for you at Tangier?"

"I do not think so. However, it is a risk we must take."

"*We* must," Neil muttered. Then his wide shoulders rose and dropped in a gesture of resignation. "Yeah, it is *we*. I don't have a clue as to what the fuck I'm into, but I'm in it. Deep." He gave Fischer a bared-fangs smile, turned back to wheel and throttles. He had stopped wondering if he would return to Cabo Verde in time for the Dixons' party. The question now seemed to be whether he would return at all.

4

Vivian Dixon's personal maid, Teresa, belonged to the Partido Comunista Andaluz and, extra-money *premio* or no, resented working on the *fiesta* set aside to honor labor and laborers. Particularly since she would have to work late and as an ordinary fetch-and-carry domestic like the other servants. Then, she felt that Kenneth and Vivian Dixon had committed sacrilege. The *pórtico* was decorated with Señora Dixon's charcoal-sketch caricatures of Marx, Lenin, Brezhnev, other gods in the Communist pantheon. Teresa thought it was a disgusting May Day party joke—made all the worse because there would be Spaniards among the guests, and they, too, would laugh.

Teresa stood at the door of Vivian Dixon's airy bedroom and, in a tone that matched her sour look, asked, "*Algo mas, señora*?"

"*Nada mas, gracias*." Vivian beamed a smile that would have captivated Marx or Lenin or the head of the KGB, but it failed to mollify the maid, who went out muttering under her breath.

Vivian locked the door, took off her ankle-length tailored robe, and tossed it on the bed. Her willowy body naked save for a narrow bikini strip of white silk, she went to the dressing table, sat, inspected her mirror-reflected image. Copper-red hair, already brushed to a glowing sheen by Teresa, fell to smooth shoulders. It framed a finely molded oval face that some described as patrician, others as sensual, and, all agreed, beautiful. Smoky eye makeup to emphasize great gray eyes and apricot lip gloss—the only cosmetics needed—had been applied minutes earlier.

The gray eyes held their reflection for a moment, then flicked down to an open jar of Estée Lauder cover-up cream on the table. The cream was the same shade as Vivian's suntanned breasts. Although she was thirty-three, the breasts remained firm and fresh, but now they were marred by bruises. She took some of the cream on her fingertips, spread it over the ugly discolorations, wincing a little as she did.

"It's past six." Her husband's voice came through the closed door to the adjoining bedroom. "I'm going downstairs."

"All right, Ken." Vivian knew he was still sober, but also knew that an entire evening stretched ahead. Like a Dali landscape, she thought. Great scenery for another episode in the ongoing romantic drama of Ken and Vivi, the crown prince and princess of the Costa del Sol. Her expression went bleak. She sighed and applied more cream.

Kenneth Dixon had come to Cabo Verde in 1967. He was then thirty-one and already world-famous as an author of blockbuster novels. He built a seventeen-room contemporary-style house on a plot of seafront land, named it "Broadmoor" after the Tulsa, Oklahoma, apartment-hotel in which he had lived while writing *Gusher!*, his first smash best-seller. There had been many Ken Dixon best-sellers since; they appeared at the rate of one every year, were translated into a score of languages, made into boxoffice-hit motion pictures.

In 1972 Dixon married Vivian Blascombe, also an American expatriate residing on the Sun Coast. He was then thirty-six, she twenty-two. To the dismay of foreign colonists from Málaga to San Roque, the marriage had lasted, and Vivian Dixon had become a prominent Costa figure in her own right after establishing Galerías Vivi in Cabo Verde. The gallery was the first of its kind, size and cachet on the Costa del Sol. It specialized in works by young—mainly Spanish but some few expatriate—contemporary artists who lived and worked in Andalusia. Previously, these sculptors and painters had been forced to sell their works to tacky tourist souvenir and gift shops at abysmally low prices. Or at informal outdoor exhibitions in public parks or on sidewalks, where the prices were scarcely higher and yowling brats smeared *helado* or *turrón* on their canvases and stray dogs urinated on their rickety display stands.

With the opening of Galerías Vivi, the better artists at last had a discerning, honest—and, above all, understanding and supportive—dealer. The gallery—thanks to Vivian's adroitly orchestrated publicity campaign—immediately began attracting clients who, if not necessarily connoisseurs of fine art, did have the desire and the money to buy. Success was swift—and continuing. Outside of Madrid and Barcelona, there were no others quite like it or quite as highly regarded in Spain.

As a result, Vivian had become a capital P Personage in her own right on the Costa. Indeed, if James Courtney was the Sun Coast's titular King, then Kenneth and Vivian Dixon ranked as its cultural Crown Prince and Princess. They were lionized by expatriate hostesses with cultural pretensions in foreign colonies from Málaga to San Roque—and points beyond. Invitations to their own parties at Broadmoor were sought after, prized. Rich expatriates came to mingle with The Exciting Creative People—many of whom attended in hopes of gaining patronage of the wealthy. Those on the outer—the impecunious—fringes of expatriate society came because excellent food and drink and first-quality pot and hash were always plentiful. Then there were those who simply liked Ken and Vivi and came to enjoy, to have fun.

Kenneth Dixon was on the portico, seated in a half-reclining position on a lounger, holding his now half-empty third iceless gin-tonic in one hand and staring sullenly out over the sea. Juan—the Dixons' de facto mayordomo—and Teresa, carrying laden trays, distributed bowls and platters of cocktail-snack tapas on portico tables that were covered with red cloths and had hammer-sickle emblems as centerpieces. They moved silently, warily. Señor Dixon was in his usual state of pre-party depression.

"Juan." Dixon held out his empty glass. "*Un otro*—like *pronto*." He was among the thousands of foreigners who had lived years, even decades, on the Costa del Sol and never learned to speak much Spanish.

"*Sí, señor*." The manservant hurried to take the glass, leaving Teresa to scowl at a caricature of Ronald Reagan offering jelly beans to picketing strikers. She thought it was Brezhnev, not Reagan.

Ken Dixon was well into his fourth drink when Vivian appeared, cool and beautiful in a creamy cotton jumpsuit tied at the waist with a multicolored sash.

"Happy May Day, comrade," she said.

Ken turned toward her. He had the kind of face readers like to believe that all worldly writers have—or should have: rough-hewn-masculine but jaded and sardonic. His eyes, deep-set and intense, focused on his wife. He mumbled something, turned away, and resumed staring at sky and water.

Vivian returned inside the house. She was concerned, worried. Kenneth Dixon always cheered up when guests arrived. Sometimes he drank too much—and then talked too much. She sensed it was going to be one of those nights. Normally his monologues were harmless. Tonight, if prompted by questions Vivian was certain people would ask, they could cause irreparable and incalculable damage. She would have to hover close to him, ready to avert or prevent catastrophe. It would be awkward. The Beautiful People resented protective wives. However, there was no alternative, Vivian told herself.

Ken's mood metamorphosis was noticeable by eight-thirty, when he had greeted a dozen or more early arrivals. It was complete two hours later, when some thirty guests danced in the disco room and some seventy others had clotted into small groups here and there. Dixon, intense eyes slightly glazed over, was again on the portico, this time standing, holding forth to a knot of admirers.

" . . . all fiction is based to some extent on fact," he was saying, oblivious of the stereo blare from the disco room. "My novels are more so than most." He paused to gulp down a drink.

García Aguirre, a painter whose minimals were the rage, wanted a special show of his works at Galerías Vivi and seized the chance to ingratiate himself with the gallery owner's husband.

"There were articles about your next book in the newspapers only yesterday," he said. "They claim it will be the most sensational yet."

"Didn't say what it's about, though," a florid-faced American grumbled. He was Clay Trager, erstwhile Dallas conglomerator who had fled to Spain after siphoning millions from his companies. The enormous diamond set in his Masonic ring was a glowing coal in the reflected light of the red lanterns. "Come on, Ken, give us a hint."

"You really must." That from Gloria Meese, the much-divorced expatriate breakfast-cereal heiress. As usual, she was grotesquely overdressed—tonight in a ruffled Ungaro gown. There are a hundred or more foreign, well over a score American, social and special-activities clubs on the Sun Coast. Gloria Meese was chairperson of the Marbella American-Spanish Friendship Society, most important of the lot, and she often invited Dixon to be guest speaker at club luncheons. "I insist."

Italian Count Ruggiero Pisani, who had arranged the much-publicized private audience with Pope Paul VI for Dixon, echoed the urgings. "My dear Kenneth, it is impossible for you to refuse."

Ken preened, finished his drink, held the glass high in the air. Juan materialized with a refill, exchanged it for the empty. Dixon struck a pose and, voice thick, began:

"Well, my last book, *The Golden-Hearted*, ripped into banks and bankers. Readers loved it and Sam Spielberg grabbed the film rights. So I had to top myself, and when I started my new book . . ."

Vivian had trailed after her husband and was sitting with some people at a table nearby. She leaped from her chair, rushed over to Ken, took hold of his wrist. "Sorry, everyone," she said, her smile apologetic. "I just remembered something." Pretending to kiss Ken, she whispered fiercely, "Shut up, for God's sake! Talk more, and you'll be committing suicide." He tried to pull free. She tightened her grip. He blinked, finally picked up her excuse cue.

"Hell, I forgot, too. Excuse me. Have to call my agent in New York."

Vivian released her hold. He thrust the hand into his trousers pocket quickly, before anyone could see the blood welling from four half-moon fingernail gouges in the flesh, and followed Vivian into the house. His abandoned admirers were disappointed.

Gloria Meese loosed one of the barbs for which she was noted. "Vivi keeps poor Ken a prisoner in the bedroom."

"Wouldn't mind being locked up there myself!" Clay Trager guffawed.

Count Ruggiero Pisani frowned distaste. García Aguirre took the hand of a blond British television actress who was vacationing on the Costa. He led the slightly stoned young woman toward the *sala*, where a servant presided over cut-glass bowls containing hashish and marijuana. From there it was only a few steps to the staircase that led down to the beach and the cabanas. He fondled the girl's buttocks.

"I'm into group sex," she said, chewing on a pinch of hash—a current fad on the Sun Coast.

"So are the people we're going to join," Aguirre assured her, a hand gliding over the fabric of her dress.

Sybil Pearson never worried if Neil Harkness failed to keep a date. Although their relationship had gone beyond the casual, it remained free, easy. Then, charter runs often took longer than anticipated. Besides, Sybil would remind herself, Neil was a superb sailor and had equipped his boat with every kind of communications and emergency gear.

She waited at her Cabo Verde apartment until ten, then taped a note to the kitchen fridge and went on to the Dixons' party alone, driving to Broadmoor in her vintage Seat 124 sedan. She squeezed the small car in between a Rolls and a De Lorean parked in front of the house and went inside. She knew many people at the party and enjoyed herself drinking white wine, dancing, and talking until midnight, when guests drifted—or lurched—off to the outdoor buffet tables. Sybil would have gone too, but Vivian Dixon drew her aside and into a deserted reception room.

"I haven't seen Neil—is he coming?" Vivian's gray eyes were troubled; there was a pleading note in her voice.

Sybil understood immediately. Kenneth Dixon considered very few men as his friends. When he was drunk and plagued by inner demons, the number shrank to one. Neil Harkness was the only person—male or female—he would allow near him. And Neil could nurse and cajole Dixon through the worst of his drinking bouts.

"Long John Silver's a bit overdue—he'll be along, though," Sybil said, bantering in an effort to raise Vivian's spirits. "I—"

They were interrupted by the Baroness von Ausheim, distant niece of Hapsburgs and an insufferable snob. "Vivian, darling!" she gushed, withering Sybil—whom she knew to be nothing but a secretary—with a superior glance. "You absolutely must join the Rothschilds and me—and I'll tell you about the exciting new artist I've discovered."

Sybil and Vivian exchanged weary glances. The Baroness von Ausheim was forever "discovering" studs who pretended to be painters or sculptors. But she was also the doyenne of Marbella foreign-colony society and formidably influential.

"Let me know when Neil gets here—please," Vivian murmured to Sybil, and reluctantly permitted herself to be dragged away.

It was almost twelve-thirty when Neil Harkness arrived. He had changed into sports shirt and slacks aboard the *Deirdre*. The leathery giant was a familiar figure on the Costa. Women found him extremely attractive, and many had found their way to his bed over the years. Men sought his company—probably in hopes that some of his emphatic masculinity would rub off on them. He had to stop and exchange greetings with numerous guests as he went through the house in search of Sybil.

He found her in the reception room where she had spoken with Vivian. She was curled into the corner of a sofa, gazing glumly into empty space. She looked up, instantly sensed that he was not his usual self, stood up, grinned when he rumpled her close-cut chestnut hair, kissed him, listened to his apologies for being late.

". . . a long—a very long—story," he said, obviously eager to narrate it to her. "I'll get us a couple of drinks and—"

"Tell me later," Sybil interrupted. "It's Condition Red here—and no May Day pun intended."

He cocked an eyebrow. "Ken?"

"Uh-huh. He's upstairs in his den. You'd best run, not walk." She sighed, the sigh dismal. "I'll give Vivi the news that the first-aid team of one is on the job."

Neil scowled. He was planning to spend an hour or so at the party, the rest of the night with Sybil—at her apartment, because she had to work the following day. And he wanted to be alone with her, recount all that had taken place. Now, instead of having a sympathetic listener, he would have to listen to Ken Dixon, play nursemaid. Until God only knew when, he thought. But Ken was his friend. The scowl faded.

"Okay, honey, so it's like hello and good-bye," he said, kissing Sybil's freckle-splashed nose, then her lips. "Guess I won't see you until tomorrow—uh, tonight—at around seven."

Neil Harkness never ceased to be amazed by Kenneth Dixon's den. He had always imagined that authors of prodigious output who periodically went on drinking sprees would work in cluttered, disordered surroundings. But the den was never anything but shipshape, pin-neat. Floor-to-ceiling shelves along two walls were filled with books arrayed in neat, precisely aligned rows. The Olivetti Praxis on a typing table was always squarely placed, sheathed. Such things as typing paper, ribbons, and other materials a writer needed were—presumably—stored in a metal cabinet whose doors Neil had never seen open. The top of a refined version of a U-slotted newspaper copy desk was always clear.

Except for times like the present, Harkness mused as he entered. When it was littered with bottles—Tanqueray gin, Schweppes tonic—bottle caps, openers, glasses . . .

"Got a drink left for me?" Neil asked by way of greeting.

Kenneth Dixon, his safari suit gin-tonic-stained, fixed bleary eyes on Neil. He managed a lopsided, sloppy grin, mumbled, "Fucking freeloader." He was sitting in an old-fashioned wooden swivel chair pushed into the U-slot. "Want gin? Sure you want gin. Pour me some, too, you goddamned sailor."

Harkness folded his six-three frame down on a plain-backed and also old-fashioned wooden chair, reached into the desktop welter for a Tanqueray bottle. He poured into two tumblers, added tonic to one, and pushed it toward Ken.

"When the hell are you going to start putting ice in your drinks?" he asked. It was a perennial question.

"Never. Want ice, yell downstairs for some."

"Too much trouble. Cheers." Neil emptied his glass in a single swallow, grimaced, poured himself another. "Nice party you and Vivi have going."

"Shit." Dixon took a large swallow of his drink. "Hey. You weren't here . . . er . . . earlier. Where in fuck were you?"

Neil was delighted by the question. Yarns of any kind fascinated Ken, and they were the best therapy when he was on a binge. They distracted him from liquor, grabbed and held his writer's mind. He would listen and become totally absorbed, improvising plots and subplots around what he heard. Neil had not hoped to have an opening quite so soon. And he did want to tell his story to someone, anyone—but, he realized, more to Dixon than anyone else, even Sybil. There were many elements in the rapport between Neil and Ken Dixon. Among them was their shared hatred for James Courtney, and the story did center around Courtney.

"I had a bad day—wild," Neil said, intending the throwaway lines to serve as bait, whet Dixon's curiosity. "I still can't figure what I got myself into—or out of. Maybe you can come up with answers."

"Me? Answers? Balls." Dixon showed no flicker of interest. He moved his glass in circles on the desktop.

Harkness tried again. "Would you believe attempted piracy ten miles off San Roque?"

"Nope." Dixon continued to make circles. "I wouldn't."

Neil went for his Achilles' heel. "You wrote a book once—"

"I wrote a lot of books," Dixon rasped, blood-streaked eyes glaring. He practically flung the glass to his mouth, drained its contents.

"The book about gold smugglers," Harkness went on doggedly. "There's a part where Dolan—I think the name was—takes his sailboat out from Miami, and the Coast Guard—"

"Sure." Dixon was pouring himself more gin, stopped, and seemed to brighten up. "*The Midas Engram.*" He chuckled.

"Wrote it in 1969. The character's name was Nolan, not Dolan. The Coast Guard sends a cutter out—"

"I don't have a sailboat, and it wasn't any Coast Guard."

Ken reached for bottle of tonic, pulled his hand back. "Huh? What the fuck're you talking about?"

"Me. My boat." Harkness swallowed straight gin, threw out more bait. "The passenger I was hauling for J.P.—"

"That cocksucker." Dixon glowered, but showed interest. "Wha' . . . what happened?"

Neil told him the facts, without embellishment. Drunk or sober, Kenneth Dixon had an uncanny instinct for separating truth from fabrication. The author listened silently for several minutes, not drinking.

" . . . so I get to Tangier and offload this guy Fischer," Harkness wound up his tale. "He hires a porter for his suitcase and takes off. Like five minutes later, the customs assholes descend, and they hold me there for hours, searching."

"They find anything?"

Ken was hooked, hadn't even reached for his glass, Harkness thought, lighting a Celta before he answered: "No, they finally gave up and cleared me to leave port. I'm sure they were looking for the same thing as those assholes on the Chris-Craft—"

"Sure." Dixon nodded. Interest in what Neil told him had a sobering effect. "That tube you said Fischer was lugging with him."

"Wonder what he was smuggling in it for our buddy J.P.?"

"How big did you say it was?"

"I didn't. About this size." Neil gestured with his hands.

Dixon grunted, leaned forward, swept his jacket sleeve across the desktop to clear a space in front of him. Dipping a forefinger into spilled gin-tonic, he began drawing geometric designs on the cleared surface.

Neil knew this was a certain indication that the author was emerging from his alcoholic fog, using his brain. Harkness watched in silence as an isosceles triangle took form.

"Papers, plans," Ken mused aloud.

"Fischer said blueprints," Neil reminded him.

"Blueprints? Could be. I used that gimmick a lot—years ago." He wet his finger again, started on a pentagram. "That's the trouble with the idea, Neil. Years ago. Not these days. There're nine million ways to get plans from here"—he drew a line—"to there. Microfilms, microdots—you name it, sailor."

"You've made a good point."

"Look. There are only two possibilities. The first is that he was carrying something that can't be photocopied or paraphrased. In other words, the object itself has to be delivered. Right?''

''Keep talking,'' Neil urged. The more Dixon talked, the less chance there was that he would turn his attention back to the gin.

''He probably did have some blueprints—to distract and divert,'' Ken declared thoughtfully. He dipped his forefinger into a puddle of spilled liquor with the elegant gesture of a Restoration dandy dipping a quill pen into ink and grinned. It was an indication that he was well along toward recovery—even of his sense of humor about himself. The finger began making almost perfect circles. ''Fischer had whatever was really being smuggled in his suitcase or on his person, anywhere but in that tube.''

''That much makes sense,'' Neil said. ''Nothing else does, though. Why would somebody like J.P. God Courtney have a meatball like Fischer—''

''No wonder you were disbarred.'' Dixon leered. ''You never would have made it as a conniving shyster. No imagination. What happened today stinks. Where there's a stink, there's a scheme. Where there's a scheme, there are two kinds of people. Fuckers and fuckees. Indubitably, sailor, Courtney is playing the fucker.''

He grew serious, shifted into plot-improvising gear.

''Good material. Just as it happened. Is happening. Boat, would-be pirates, everything. You—the guy, the hero—sniff the stink. The hero can't figure it. Goes to a me-type character. Together they nose around, find the answers. Then they throw in with the fucker's intended fuckees—and bring him down, like smash.'' Ken's expression changed; he might have been contemplating some sensually pleasurable vision. ''How'd you like to do that to Courtney?''

Harkness fired up another Celta. ''Nobody can bring God down—you and I know that. But go on, dream up the script. We'll both get kicks out of the fantasy.'' He knew that Dixon would go on—for an hour, two, even longer—and adjusted as well as possible to the idea he would have to sit where he was and listen.

5

The clock-radio switched on automatically at seven. A male voice announced *la apertura del emisión* of Torcal FM in tones that declared this to be the most significant event since the Creation. Sybil Pearson stirred, rubbed sleep from her hazel eyes. Another male voice took over, began to read the latest *noticias*. The first was a bulletin about a cabin cruiser that had been found floating in the sea off San Roque. It had been abandoned. Its *hélices* had been mysteriously fouled by steel cable. The dinghy was gone. Official sources theorized that those who had been aboard had rowed ashore. . . .

Sybil yawned herself fully awake, shrugged mentally. Pleasure craft operated by inexperienced and inept people were constantly having accidents of one sort or another.

"*Madrid. Manifestaciones en celebración del primo de mayo . . .*"

A report on May Day demonstrations. Sybil turned off the set. She swung out of bed and padded barefoot into her kitchen to make coffee. The note she had left for Neil was still on the fridge. She removed it, regretting that he had not been able to spend the night with her, wondering if he was still ministering to Ken Dixon. Sybil hurried through her bath and dressing rituals. Her employer was back from his quick trip to New York, and work always backed up over a *fiesta*. The day would be hectic.

Sybil parked her Seat in a space provided behind the Montemar mansion at eight-thirty, half an hour earlier than usual. A security man let her in by a side entrance; another was already on duty in her office, which adjoined James Courtney's *estudio*. The guard, normally a taciturn man and perpetually gloomy as some Spaniards are by nature, greeted her with a huge smile and a torrent of courtesies.

Taken aback, she responded warily with a simple "*Buenos días, Luis*" and puzzled over what might have precipitated such a personality change in him.

The minor mystery was solved minutes later, when Grenville, the butler, came into her office. They were both British, and they shared a bemused protective feeling for James P. Courtney.

Thus they were natural allies in the intramural intrigues and squabbles at Montemar, exchanging information freely—albeit often in a sort of private code.

"Good morning, miss." Grenville beamed; freshly shaven, he looked like a sheared but much pleased lamb. "The Witch of Endor has been banished permanently."

Sybil knew he meant Eileen Marsh. That explained Luis. He had doubtless heard the glad tidings over the domestic staff's grapevine. But it was obvious that Grenville wanted to impart some details, which were not for Luis to hear. She helped the butler, cluing him to code: "When and how were we delivered from evil?"

"Day before yesterday, on the spur, as it were. Witch, her goods and chattels, were flown to the New World."

"Hosanna. What's the weather forecast this morning?"

"Crackling fine on first reading." Grenville conveyed that he had found Courtney in excellent spirits and filled with get-it-done-now energy. "He'll be down shortly. Care to have me send you a pot of tea from the kitchen, Miss Pearson?"

"Lovely, thanks." Sybil nodded gratefully. Grenville vanished. She started to sort through telexes and correspondence piled on her desk, stopped when the multilined telephone rang. Bit early, she thought, probably a wrong number, and answered casually: "*Dígame*."

"I wish to leave a message for Mr. Courtney." A man spoke accented English; faint background whines indicated it was a direct-dial call from some second-string country. "Please take this down exactly."

Sybil frowned; voice and accent were vaguely familiar. "Yes, sir." She did not bother reaching for pencil and memo pad; a tape recorder had been activated when she lifted the receiver.

"There were certain nautical hazards to overcome. Do you have that? He will understand. Say also that I shall telephone again tonight."

"May I have your name, please?"

"Fischer. Wilhelm Fischer."

"Oh, hello! We met yesterday. This is—" But the line had gone dead. Sybil shrugged, replaced the handset. Sounds like we're into World Maritime Day, she thought, amused. Boats are abandoned, and now take-this-down-exactly nautical hazards. Amusement vanished; she nipped a thumbnail between her teeth. Neil had returned very late, with a "long story" he was unable to tell her. Perhaps Fischer was dissatisfied for some reason and wanted to register a complaint about Neil. . . .

" 'Morning, Sybil—lovely day, and you're looking fresh and rested. *Qué tal, Luis?*" James Courtney had made his appearance, and Grenville had been right—as usual. Courtney radiated vitality. His angular face glowed; his blue eyes seemed charged with electrical energy. He would make everyone around him jump today, Sybil reflected, and followed him into the study. She closed the door behind her. He sat down at the gadget-laden Louis Quinze writing table.

"You had a call a few minutes ago," Sybil said. "From—"

But he had leaned foward, punched a control-console button. The conversation with Fischer replayed over a box speaker. His face clouded as he listened, cleared, clouded again when he heard Sybil's reproduced voice say: "Oh, hello!"

The tape stopped. "How did you meet him?" Courtney demanded.

Sybil told him without hesitation. He knew of her relationship with Harkness—indeed, seemed to take an avuncular interest in it. But then, it would have been impossible to keep the affair secret on the Sun Coast, where gossip was the most favored pastime.

". . . and he explained about the tube," Sybil concluded.

"Oh." Courtney's face cleared once more, and his eyes shifted focus, fixing on the Hals chess player on the wall behind Sybil. "Find anything urgent on your desk this morning?"

"Not much very important, to my surprise. Seeley telexed wanting to know about the budget increase for the Capetown operation . . ."

"Reply that it's under consideration. I want him to dangle."

"Another telex from the CVI office in Paris . . ."

"I know what it's about. What next?"

"Everything else seems routine, for handling by the people over in the annex. I'll check through it all more carefully, though."

"Never mind." He patted a thick file folder that lay in front of him. Sybil recognized it immediately as the inventory of his art collection and smiled, the smile verging on the maternal. At twenty-five, she was neither naive nor impressionable. She knew that Courtney was ruthless in business and a difficult, demanding person at all levels. However, she preferred to view his redeeming qualities—which, in her opinion, were many and outweighed the negatives. Among the pluses was his love for art and for his art collection. It showed him to be a cultured, sensitive man at heart, Sybil believed, and was quick to argue the point with any who felt otherwise—even Neil Harkness.

"Have the drones in the annex make six stat copies of this," Courtney said, lifting the folder. "Destroy the old sets."

"All five?"

"All six. Our professor is due soon. I want fresh new sets before he gets here."

Sybil knew the billionaire had a phenomenal memory. Its rare lapses were always—as now—over trivial details. He would have to be reminded of the particulars, she thought, activating her own recall mechanism.

Courtney's renowned art collection, amassed since World War Two, was meticulously inventoried and documented, but had never been properly cataloged. In January he finally had decided to have the work done. He had turned to Wyler College in California for help—naturally, because he was a nostalgic. Sybil smiled to herself. She considered nostalgia a weakness, had—with reason—purged her own makeup of the trait, yet thought it endearing in her employer, an inner soft spot in a hard, ruthless businessman who could buy anything, anyone.

Born and raised in Los Angeles, James Courtney had attended Wyler College there for a few semesters before entering the U.S. Army in 1944. He had not graduated—thus Wyler was not truly his alma mater—but he remained loyal to it and contributed large sums toward the support of the famed Wyler College Museum of Art. And he had requested that the college send a qualified art historian to do the cataloging.

The museum curator had written in February saying that a Professor David Lippmann had been selected for the task. He would be given a year's sabbatical from Wyler, would arrive in Spain to begin work on the project on May 10. In the meantime, could Mr. Courtney furnish an inventory of the collection so that Professor Lippmann might acquaint himself with it.

"Afraid we have only five sets left," Sybil said. "We sent one to the museum—to Professor Lippmann—in California. Remember?"

"You *sent* it?" There was a sharp edge to Courtney's tone.

"Yes, of course, as you told me. I shouldn't wonder that it's slipped your mind. You were negotiating with the Saudi Arabian delegation that week, and—"

"Oh, Christ!"

It was a groan voiced in a hoarse whisper, and Sybil could have sworn that Courtney went pale. I'm hearing and seeing things, she thought. Must be hung-over or my period's early or something equally stupid. There's no reason for him to react like that—or react at all.

But the blood that had drained from Courtney's face did not drain far. It returned an instant later, and when he spoke again, it was in normal tones.

"I don't remember, but it's not important." The fingertips of his right hand stroked the scar on his cheek; he held the inventory file out to Sybil with his left. "Have Xerox copies made, and make sure the old copies are destroyed. Use a shredder."

Sybil assumed she was being dismissed for the present, took the folder, started toward the door. His voice stopped her. She turned to face him once more.

"Do you know where to reach Harkness?"

"Why, yes, of course—"

"I mean now, right away."

Sybil hesitated. She did not dare tell him that Neil might very possibly still be at Broadmoor, with Ken Dixon. It was understood that the names of Kenneth and Vivian Dixon were never—but never—to be mentioned in James Courtney's hearing.

"The Ancient Mariner could be in several places," she said, keeping it light as she dodged a direct answer. "I can telephone around." She wondered how to manage if she had to call the Dixons. The conversation, like any and all held over Montemar lines, would be taped, and Courtney sometimes played back tapes made during a given day. While he knew that she and Neil were friends of the Dixons', actually hearing Ken's or Vivi's voice would cause him to explode. "I'll start trying right away, Mr. Courtney."

"Do that. I want to see Harkness. Here."

Sybil went into her office. Luis, the security man, had returned to laconic normal. Someone had brought the tea promised by Grenville. A tray stood on her desk. She eased it to one side, sat, her forehead wrinkling in thought. Courtney had not said *why* he wanted to see Neil. Perhaps it had to do with Fischer and his "nautical hazards." She sighed. Neil had probably lost his temper—as he did, often—and said the wrong things to Fischer. But she had her instructions, reached for the telephone.

Harkness owned a condominium apartment in a Marbella *urbanización*, but more often than not, stayed aboard *Deirdre*. If he had gotten away from Ken Dixon, he would most probably be there—or at the Bar Espada, his favorite waterfront café. The *Deirdre* had a regular Cabo Verde telephone line; the line was unplugged when leaving port, plugged back in on return. Might as well start there, Sybil reflected. She dialed. The phone rang several times, and she was about to hang up when:

"Ummppff." Or so it sounded.

"Sybil, calling from Montemar," she said hastily to warn him against mentioning the Dixons. "Mr. C. wants you to come around, ASAP."

"Shit! I only got to sleep like ten minutes ago." A silence; then: "Tell him I'll be there, honey. In about an hour."

Sybil hung up, reached for the tea tray. The telephone rang. She answered. The Bauerkreditbank in Zurich. Herr Kloster, its head, wished to speak with Mr. Courtney. She manipulated intercom switches, ascertained that Courtney would take the call, put it through to him. Another call. Señor Gomez-Morante of the Trade Ministry in Madrid.

"*Quiere intentarlo de nuevo mas tarde?*" She asked if he would care to try later, adding that Señor Courtney was having an important conversation and would be occupied for at least fifteen minutes, perhaps longer.

6

James Courtney's mind was fully occupied as he talked with Heinrich Kloster of the Bauerkreditbank. Kloster was one of the men he sometimes—when in a whimsical mood—thought of as "The Anointed," privy to his master plan. Or rather, since he had broken the scheme down into "need-to-know" segments, familiar with that portion that concerned him.

The scope of the scheme was vast. So vast that each of the segments was in itself a major project. Kloster and his bank were to originate—and carry through—a daring diversionary move. Acting through a series of intermediaries to hide the identities of the actual originators, Bauerkreditbank was to launch a takeover feint against Chrysler Motors in the United States. The game plan called for information to leak—on purpose—that Arab oil money was behind the move. Whether James Courtney and CVI really succeeded in acquiring the ailing Chrysler Corporation did not matter. What did was that there would be consternation on Wall Street and in Washington—and, even more important to the overall plan, suspicion and distrust among the leading Arab oil-producing states.

Although Chrysler's automotive division was losing money (many observers believed it would have to be written off entirely before long), the division that produced battle tanks prospered. Chrysler was far and away the major tank manufacturer in the United States. Control of Chrysler would mean control of factories that could—and did—turn out great numbers of armored fighting vehicles. Each oil-rich Arab country would fear that another was trying to buy up Chrysler's technology—and tank-manufacturing capacity. One would question the next; denials would not be believed; and another bitter and potentially explosive element would be injected into the ongoing turmoil of the Middle East.

"The odd quantity should be apprised first," Heinrich Kloster was saying. His scrambler and Courtney's were not compatible, a lack Kloster was to correct within days. Until then, the two men were forced to rely on their wits to ensure telephone security.

The "odd quantity" was a reference to Israel.

"Agreed." James Courtney said. He was toying with an object on the tabletop, a cube of crystal-clear Lucite. Embedded in it was a gold medal, especially struck and awarded him by B'nai B'rith for "selfless work and great contributions to the Cause of World Jewry and Zionism." A very high honor to be conferred on the son of a California Baptist minister. He rolled the cube along his desk blotter, and with a cryptic smile said, "More than agreed, Heinrich. It's a must. Our friends will raise a cry of righteous horror—as well they should. The louder the roars of protest, the more attention will be drawn away."

"From the sound of mice nibbling at the foundations," Heinrich Kloster said. He delighted in conversations like these, so different from the usual in the banking world. They required an exercise of imagination to select euphemistic words and phrases that conveyed exact hidden meanings, yet revealed nothing to anyone eavesdropping on the line. And he knew there were myriad reasons—to say nothing of the seven or eight billion dollars involved—why countless people in a score of countries would want to eavesdrop on this particular conversation. Kloster reflected that he would regret the installation of a compatible scrambler; it would rob him of the fun. He said, "We have previously discussed the advisability of informing the odd-quantity people, J.P."

"Yes, during our meeting in London last month."

"We were in agreement—in principle. The . . . A moment while I find the American words. . . . Ah, yes. The mechanics of dissemination were not firmed. I have some ideas of my own but will naturally defer to your suggestions."

You'll defer, all right, Courtney thought, or the fifty-million bait that pulled you in will go into other pockets.

"Very simple," he said. "Your bank's representatives"—the front men—"start shopping"—buying Chrysler stock—"next week. They are to patronize the most heavily starred stalls" —brokerage houses with strong ties to the Jewish community and Israel, hence "starred," a reference to the six-pointed Star of David. "A few inadvertent remarks dropped here and there should do the trick."

"Yes, yes." A pause. "However, once the rumors begin to circulate, and they will immediately, should not there be a bit of"—once more a pause—"a bit of drama?"

"A good point, worth consideration." Courtney chuckled. "Give me ten seconds to consider it." He met and held the eyes of the Hals chess player, tugged at the scar on his cheek with the fingers of his free hand, reached a decision. "Listen and then choose your words with particular care, Heinrich," he said. "Think back to the September transaction and the intermediary who was used."

Heinrich Kloster, solidly emplaced in the dark oak-paneled bunker that was his office in the fortresslike Bauerkreditbank Building on Zurich's Bahnhofstrasse, grunted and activated his mental memory banks. The "September transaction" had been complex. It involved the purchase of heavy machine tools in West Germany. They were bought by a dummy company, purportedly for sale to Kuwait. The shipment, loaded aboard a 45,000-ton freighter—which it filled—had been diverted en route to Libya. Invoices and shipping documents had been conveniently lost. The Bauerkreditbank had netted nine million dollars in commissions and fees as its share of the proceeds, Kloster remembered with a gloating smile that became a frown when he tried to estimate how much James Courtney had made. No matter, Kloster thought, searching his memory further. The go-between among all parties concerned had been Sheikh Abdul al Amari.

Kloster frowned again. Himself staid, ultraconservative—as all good Swiss bankers should be and invariably are—he disapproved of the Omani Sheikh Abdul. Supposedly a former banker turned free-lance financier, the sheikh cut a flamboyant swath through international society, attracted attention to himself. Young, handsome, a graduate of Cambridge, he lived in New York, occupying two entire floors in the Olympic Tower (which Kloster, who despised Greeks and ultramodern architecture in equal measure, thought a hideous eyesore). A darling of New York society, frequent guest at the White House, escort of American motion-picture actresses—no, Kloster did not like Abdul al Amari, and chortled as he hit upon a perfect name for him.

"I have the transaction clearly in mind—and I am certain you mean the Vulgar Prince," he said into the telephone.

Courtney groaned. Heinrich Kloster was a superb intriguer and master of international financial manipulations, but otherwise a stodgy bore. "The label will do," he said, then spoke more sharply. "I have had no—absolutely no—dealings with him since that September transaction in 1979, which puts ample time between us. What about you?"

"The same. No occasion arose—and I despise the man."

"All the better that you do, Heinrich, because we will utilize him to provide that bit of drama you mentioned."

"J.P., wait—"

"Uh-uh. You wait, Heinrich. It was your suggestion, and I wouldn't want to deprive you of the pleasure." Courtney reached for the Lucite cube again, held it up, and stared at it as he spoke. "This is how I see the scenario. Some large, *very* large quantities of items"—Chrysler shares once more—"are to be bought in his name. It can be arranged easily enough . . ."

"But he will be informed."

"Not if the orders to purchase are given at a certain hour and the curtain rises on the drama minutes later. What words can be heard if there is no ear to hear them? And, conversely, ears can hear no words when there is no mouth to speak them. I trust you understand my meaning."

"What you want will require time." Kloster's voice was ragged at the edges. "By next week, it is not possible."

"You'll find that it's possible, Heinrich—if you put your mind and the facilities at your disposal to work."

There was a silence; then: "How do wish the drama staged?" Kloster's voice sounded as though he was perspiring, and he was.

"With sound, fury, and in a manner that will leave the critics arguing—violently, it is to be hoped—about who the playwright might have been and what message he was seeking to give the audience. Have I made myself clear?"

"Yes. J.P."

"Then keep me posted on your progress. Good-bye, Heinrich."

Jim Courtney replaced his handset, thin lips forming into a satisfied smile. The final loose end on that part of the plan had been tucked in, he reflected. He had given orders that no one could ever prove he had given. They would be implemented by

Heinrich Kloster—but he, too, would be several steps removed. Sheikh Abdul al Amari's death warrant would actually be issued and signed by the head of the Libyan breakaway faction operating out of Zurich—which, in turn, would . . .

But the mechanics that would produce Kloster's "bit of drama" did not interest Courtney. The aftermath of the drama's opening and instant closing did, and he gave it a quick mental review. Abdul al Amari worked only on behalf of Arab-country clients—whichever paid most at any given time. Immediately after his death, it would become known that Sheikh Abdul had purchased large blocks of Chrysler Corporation stock—purchased them the same day. Arab governments would accuse each other of being behind the buying or responsible for killing al Amari. The Israelis were certain to leap in, exploit the squabblings, and gain benefit from them.

That could do no harm, he mused, picking up the Lucite bauble, holding it between thumb and forefinger and studying it as one might a precious gem. There would be ample benefits to go around. For everyone. The takeover feint was not designed to succeed, but there was an outside chance that, given the dreary U.S. economic outlook, it might. If it failed, CVI would profit to the extent of a projected thirty-five million dollars from Chrysler stock manipulations. If it did happen to succeed, the figure could be multiplied a hundredfold. Even so, it would still remain a sideshow. The grand scheme would bring wealth and power on scales few men could comprehend, much less calculate.

All was going well, would go better, Courtney reflected. All but the odd business Bernard Rechstein hinted at when he telephoned in his Wilhelm Fischer avatar. He guessed it meant that Rechstein had been followed from Paris—or perhaps had been preceded to Cabo Verde by whoever followed him later. It was a matter for concern, but since Rechstein was obviously still alive and on the move, not critical. Not yet. However, it was evident there was a leak, a hole—somewhere within his organization, Courtney knew. It would have to be found . . . and repaired. And some changes would have to be made in Rechstein's itinerary.

He pressed an intercom lever. "Have you located Neil?"

"Yes, Mr. Courtney. He said he'd be here in an hour—that was about fifteen minutes ago."

"Bring him in immediately when he arrives."

Courtney neutralized the key. Harkness would give him a full account of Rechstein's—of Fischer's, he reminded himself—trip. And then he would send Harkness to meet Fischer, wherever he might be, and take him the rest of the way on his journey. Remembering how Rechstein hated sea travel and how easily he got seasick, Courtney laughed.

7

The flurries of morning telephone calls, mainly international, continued. Sybil screened them with ease born of long experience. James Courtney would consider speaking only with certain people and under certain circumstances (these could change from one day to the next, but there were standing criteria, and he had given no instructions to depart from them this morning).

Geoffrey Whitstone, senior partner of Whitstone, Bleecker & Sands, London brokers, was asked to leave the information he wished to give Courtney on recording tape.

Emerson Kent, indefatigable fund-raiser for the American Hospital in Paris, gasped with joy when Sybil told him that "Mr. Courtney is doubling his usual twenty-five-thousand-dollar contribution. I believe that a check for fifty-thousand dollars has been mailed by his accountants."

Arnalfo Frascati, who headed CVI's Italian operations, said it was urgent he talk to "J.P." Frascati was on Courtney's telephone-taboo list. Sybil made some excuse, asked the English-speaking Italian to tell her what it was. He breathlessly reported that the Italian lira was to be devalued another five percent on May 9. Poor Frascati, Sybil thought. He had committed mortal corporate sins. He had passed confidential information over an open line—and, worse, his figure and date were wrong. Courtney had already received an accurate tip from a high Italian government official. These blunders would enable him to fire Frascati (something he had been wanting to do) without paying him a lira more than the salary currently due on his $180,000-a-year contract.

Frascati went off the line; another light on the telephone base lit up. Sybil punched in on the line, started to answer, was overwhelmed by a flood of words. They were slurred, mouthed by a woman who was either very drunk or, Sybil thought, more probably stoned out of her head. She listened to a jumble of "murrerfuckers" and "cocksuckers" and realized it had to be Eileen Marsh, on a direct-dial call from New York. "Just a moment, please," she said, repeating the request twice, put the caller on hold, rang through to Courtney, told him.

"Don't put her on my line, but let her talk—be sure it all gets on tape," he said.

Sybil got back on the line, said, "Mr. Courtney is not in his study. May I ask who is calling?" The last was to help establish identity in the event there was ever need to use the tape.

"Me. I'm calling. Eileen, and—"

"I'm sorry, it's a very poor connection," Sybil lied. "I couldn't understand the name."

"Up your ass, Shy . . . Sybil. You know fucking well who I am. Eileen. Eileen Marsh."

"Goodness!" Sybil played the requisite role to the hilt—and took a degree of malicious enjoyment in it. "It's not even ten here—what's the time difference? Oh, yes. Six hours. Terribly early for you, isn't it?"

"Not . . . N-o-t early enough." The sound of the receiver being dropped. Sounds of it being recovered. "Wanna . . . want to tell that prick Jim . . . Huh?" It was obvious she had turned away and was listening to somebody near her speak. Seconds elapsed. "No difference. You tell him. He's gonna be in trouble. Big trouble. I'm goin' sue. Going to see D.A. and then sue hell outta him."

"I'll deliver the message, Eileen—but wouldn't you care to tell me more? I really am interested, you know."

The receiver slammed down at the other end.

Sybil thought it wisest to give Courtney the gist personally and without delay. There might be some substance to Eileen Marsh's threats. If there was, he would want to hear the entire tape, then call his Spanish attorneys immediately, send a telex alerting his New York law firm. She tapped on the study door, opened it. The *estudio* was completely soundproofed. When the door was closed, an entire symphony orchestra could play inside and not be heard beyond the walls. But when the door was open . . .

A full symphony orchestra was indeed playing, and a great chorus of voices singing—over Courtney's custom-built stereo. Sybil instantly recognized Carl Orff's overpowering *Carmina Burana*. James Courtney owned every recording—disc or tape—of the work ever made. He played it frequently, and at almost full volume, as he was playing it now.

Loudspeakers blared the primal energy of the song "In the

Tavern,'' in a Latin version: ''. . . *estuatis interius, ira vehementi . . .*''

Sybil had studied Latin in the excellent English girl's school she had attended and translated easily: ''Seething inside, with boiling rage . . .''

Sounds like Eileen Marsh's theme, she thought, amused. Courtney was standing in front of the fireplace, motionless. The rapt expression on his angular face was familiar to Sybil. It was the expression it always assumed when he listened to *Carmina Burana*.

''Mr. Courtney!'' she practically shouted. He stirred, looked at her, and moved across the room slowly, as though wading through the resounding music and voices that ended the first stanza.

''. . . *similis sum folio, de quo ludunt venti . . .*''

''I am like a leaf, tossed in play by the winds,'' Sybil translated to herself; thought: Well, that certainly doesn't apply to James P. Courtney. Neither winds nor anything else tossed him in play.

He had reached the stereo console and turned it off.

''Yes, Sybil?'' Courtney might have been awakening from a dream.

She told him about the telephone call from Eileen Marsh.

''Tell me again later—in the afternoon,'' he said, moving a hand in a gesture of dismissal, ''and I don't want to be disturbed for any reason until Harkness arrives. Bring him straight in when he does.''

Sybil withdrew. She closed the door slowly, but Courtney did not turn on the stereo again. She shook her head, wondering, as she often did, why Courtney had a hang-up on *Carmina Burana* and played it at the oddest times. It was just another James Courtney mystery, she told herself. There were many of them, and they made her employer seem all the more fascinating. A complex, multidimensional man, his wealth and success proof that he was superior, his generosity proof that he was sensitive, kindhearted, she thought. Little wonder that she loved working for him, felt fiercely loyal.

The telephone calls stopped—at least for the time being. Sybil drank the last of her tea, used the intercom to summon an errand-running prole from the CVI annex, laid the inventory original in a basket labeled ''For Pickup,'' and went to the filing cabinets. She dug out the inventory copies that had been made in February. They were as crisp as ever. A shame—a terrible waste—to shred them, she mused. Professor David Lippmann would never tell the difference. But Courtney might. And stat paper and the salary of whoever would operate the Xerox machine were his to squander as he pleased. Even so . . .

Sybil had been born into a land-poor aristocratic English family that had no choice but to rate thrift high on its list of virtues. Although she was self-exiled from Britain and alienated from her parents, early training left its mark. She could almost hear her father—the fifth Viscount Pearson, no less—and tweedy mother preaching the "waste-not-want-not" doctrines that circumstances forced them to follow.

There was certain to be need for additional copies after the art historian began his cataloging labors, Sybil reflected. It would be bloody stupid to destroy the five "old" sets and bloody damned good sense to keep them on hand. She opened the door of a corner stationery cupboard, stacked the folders on the bottom shelf. There, she thought with a satisfied smile, they would be available when required.

A girl, flaxen-haired and Junoesque, entered the office. She was from a CVI-annex steno pool, a relatively new employee. About twenty, and originally from Amsterdam, she was one of the thousands of attractive foreign girls who wash up on the Sun Coast each year. They come hoping to find work—or better still, wealthy men who will keep them. Few achieve the former ambition. Spain has a staggering unemployment rate; foreigners can obtain work permits only if sponsored by someone of influence. The rich-lover fantasy is even more difficult to realize. Moneyed Spanish and expatriate men on the Costa have sophisticated tastes. Epidemics of herpes and penicillin-resistant gonorrhea among young foreign females had made them even more discriminating lately.

But Kristin Verkerk had been fortunate. James Courtney saw her playing tennis at the Marbella Club one afternoon and struck up a conversation. He learned that Kristin spoke English and Spanish in addition to Dutch, could type and take shorthand, recognized that she had no sexual inhibitions. Always alert to acquire what he thought of as "ready spares," Courtney offered her a job in the CVI-annex steno pool on condition that she went first to the Policlínica Los Manantiales for a medical examination. She went, was certified free of venereal infection. Courtney arranged for her work permit, had put her on the payroll some weeks before. Thus far, she had been merely another prole—typing, filing, running errands. Hoped-for invitations to the master bedroom had not materialized.

"They sent me over," Kristin Verkerk said absently. Her Meissen-blue eyes were on the closed door to Courtney's office. Obviously this was not to be The Day either. Her eyes shifted to Sybil, whom she envied and disliked. Sybil Pearson was only five years her senior, yet held a key position as private secretary to the man who had the wealth and power. Worse still, Sybil—small and hoydenish—was considered exceptionally pretty by almost everyone. "I hear the bitch is gone," she said before Sybil could speak. News of Eileen Marsh's banishment had evidently spread to the annex. Kristin looked at the study door again hungrily.

Poor dumb kid, Sybil thought. In some ways, Kristin reminded her of herself as she had been four years earlier. Newly arrived in Spain, all ties with family and England severed, desperately wanting to stay, fearful that she might not be able to hang on.

"He'll be horny as hell," Kristin went on, speaking the Americanese learned from U.S. Air Force personnel who were stationed at bases in Spain and often spent leaves on the Costa del Sol. "Girl I know in Torremolinos balled him last year. She says he—"

"Kristin!" Sybil spoke sharply, wanting to save the girl from herself. Electronic eavesdropping equipment monitored conversations in the house. Although proud enough of his sexual prowess, James Courtney would not tolerate it being discussed. "Take that folder"—Sybil pointed to the inventory original—"and give it to whoever's operating the Xerox today. Mr. Courtney wants six copies."

"Can I bring them back to him myself?" Kristin asked, picking up the folder. When Sybil nodded, she left, and Luis, seated at the tiny table that served as his fixed sentry post, glared after her.

"*Ramera, puta*," he muttered.

Sybil heard, bridled at what she heard, and went to the girl's defense. Kristin and others like her were not harlots, whores. They were reaching, seeking, by the only means they knew. She tried to express this to Luis, but even though her Spanish was perfect, he did not—could not bring himself to—comprehend.

Luis was among the countless thousands of Spaniards who worked for *extranjeros*, yet—and with considerable justification—resented their presence in Spain. The foreigners were invaders and occupiers. All too many among them regarded Spain as a vassal state, its people as their serfs. And to the minds of such men as Luis, foreign women were just what he had said: *rameras, putas.*

Sybil gave up her effort, resumed sorting through the correspondence and other papers on her desk.

Summonses issued by James Courtney were imperial commands, and Neil Harkness swallowed pride along with bile whenever he obeyed them. Which he always did, and with minimum delay. But he made it a point to wear shipboard workclothes—old T-shirt, khaki trousers—when going to Montemar. The feeble gesture helped him maintain a shred of the illusion that he was an individual able to exercise freedom of choice.

Jim Courtney readily tolerated such trivial shows of independence in employees and people like Harkness, whom he considered wholly owned auxiliaries. The gestures were safety valves through which steam was vented in harmless wisps before there could be a buildup of sufficient pressure to cause rebellious explosion. Not that Courtney actually feared rebellion among his underlings, for he could crush any that arose instantly. He simply preferred to avoid them, keep operations running smoothly, even when that called for him to appear indulgent, lenient. As it did now, when Sybil Pearson ushered Neil Harkness into the *estudio*.

Courtney ignored the negligently worn work garb, dismissed Sybil with a grin, nodded Harkness into an armchair drawn up close to his Louis Quinze writing table.

Neil took a pack of Celtas and his Dunhill lighter from a trouser pocket and sat down. There was no doubt in his mind why Courtney wanted to see him. It had to do with Fischer and what had transpired the previous day. Courtney wanted a full report. But Neil was also eager to hear anything that James Courtney might have to say—directly or as inadvertent comment or remark. The all-night session with Kenneth Dixon had fired his imagination and curiosity. Together they had formulated broad-stroke theories. Courtney might provide pieces that filled some of the gaps—and if Dixon was up to it (a question for Vivian to answer later), he and Ken would try fitting the pieces together.

Harkness lit a Celta without offering the pack, for James Courtney had given up smoking years before, when the first cancer alarms were sounded. He blew a smoke ring toward the ceiling beams some eighteen feet above his head, waited for Courtney's opener.

It came, delivered in an offhand tone: "I heard from my friend Fischer this morning."

"That doesn't surprise me, J.P." Neil was determined to make the billionaire ask questions, dig for the answers.

"Apparently you encountered problems." Courtney placed his elbows on the tabletop, templed his fingers.

"Some." Neil's eyes, deep green, were steady and expressionless.

Courtney demolished the temple, freeing his fingers for other employment. Those on his right hand combed through his gray-streaked auburn hair. Those on the left hand toyed with a Lucite cube that had a gold medal embedded in its center.

"All right," he said. "Tell me about it. In detail."

"Sure," Neil said, began. While at Columbia Law School and later as a practicing attorney, he had won high praise for writing terse, concise briefs that presented all pertinent facts in a minimum of words. He narrated his account the same way, watching Courtney closely as he spoke, and concluded by saying:

". . . the morning news reported an abandoned Chris-Craft off San Roque. My guess is, it's the same one."

Courtney followed up with questions that were predictable and revealed nothing in their asking. Neil answered them honestly. No, he had never seen the cabin cruiser before. Nor did he obtain a good look at the men aboard it. Yes, the customs search at Tangier had been very thorough, and he did feel that the searchers were looking for something specific. No, he had no intention of making any reports to Spanish or Tangier authorities. No, he had no idea of what Fischer was carrying. But, wanting to jolt Courtney, Neil added:

"He said blueprints, J.P. Which is pure horseshit."

There was no jolt. The response was a mild-voiced, "What leads you to think that?"

Harkness recited the logical arguments about microfilms and the rest, not mentioning Ken Dixon, but stating them as his own deductions. When he finished, Courtney narrowed his eyes, said:

"Sound reasoning. It must have led you to some conclusion—or a guess—as to what Fischer had with him."

"I don't care or want to find out," Harkness lied, hoping to elicit some hint, but Courtney merely stared at him.

"Afraid the unknown boatmen might come after you?"

"Why should they? I told you the *Deirdre* was searched by customs police, and they found nothing, cleared me to leave port."

"Did you verify their credentials?"

Well, I'll be goddamned, Neil thought. There's an angle Ken and I never even considered. He added this new element in with the already-knowns, came up with an impressive total. It took organization, influence, money to mount a sea chase and, when it failed, have bogus customs officials waiting at the end of the line. And the Chris-Craft left to drift at sea was worth close to a half-million dollars, Neil estimated. And there had to be an intelligence network that knew in advance who Courtney would send when, where, and by what means. J.P. must be worrying about that more than anything else, he mused, lit another Celta, and said:

"The men who came aboard had badges and guns. I never argue with people who carry badges and guns. Anyway, it's all the better for me if they weren't legitimate. It means the bad guys found out for themselves that I was clean, just a truck driver who'd hauled a load from Point A to Point B."

He exhaled smoke, eyed Courtney through the blue mist.

"If they come after anyone, it'll be you, J.P."

Courtney laughed. "You'd enjoy that, wouldn't you?"

One of those times when God wants a moment of truth, Neil thought, and obliged: "Only if they came after your blood—and got it."

"Behold the candor of the beholden," Courtney jeered.

"Our accounts were squared long ago."

"The hell they were. You came to me in seventy-three, hat in hand. I made you a long-term proposal, and you leaped at it. We might say that constituted a contract. Not entirely legal, perhaps, but enforceable."

"Sure. Enforced your way. With threats."

"If you weren't vulnerable, the threats would be meaningless," Courtney said blandly. He picked up the Lucite bauble, studied it. "That truism aside, remember that you've done well for yourself."

"I've made some money, if that's what you mean."

"It is . . . and a good part of it from—or through—me."

"Not all that good a part. I could have gotten by without it."

"Really?" Courtney nailed Harkness with his eyes, now pale and cold as ice. "Aside from normal charters and work done for me from time to time, you've earned profits by running contraband."

Neil shrugged inwardly. Most commercial boat owners in the Med ran contraband. Tax-free cigarettes and liquor. Gold. Political refugees. On occasion, a little marijuana or hashish. Once in a while, guns.

"Ever wonder why you weren't caught?" Courtney asked.

"I've had my share of close scrapes."

"But no arrests." Courtney tossed the Lucite-encased medal down on the tabletop, leaned forward. "Not even in Piraeus, when you landed the ingots, although they got the man who was accompanying the shipment."

Harkness blinked amazement that Courtney knew.

"Not even when you took the assault rifles to Beirut." Courtney's smile was sharklike. "I won't bother citing other instances. Suffice it that I've had you protected all along."

Neil's throat had gone dry. The billionaire had been exerting influence, manipulating strings for his own purposes.

"You owe for past favors of which you were never aware," Courtney went on. "Favors done against a day when I'd require your"—a muted chuckle—"absolute blind loyalty. That day has come, and I'm presenting the bill. I want your services exclusively—for a month."

"I have advance charter bookings," Harkness protested, and instantly realized the protest was foolish, futile.

"Cancel them. You'll work for me—and be well paid."

"Suppose I refuse?"

"My security people have richly detailed dossiers on you, Neil. Various authorities here and there around the Mediterranean would be delighted to have them."

"I'd survive," Neil said, keeping his voice steady.

"Maybe," Courtney conceded, then said acidly, "But where—and as what?"

Harkness swallowed against a closed throat, wet his lips, and was about to make some response, but Courtney spoke again.

"You have until five this evening to make a decision. Either be back here by then with a yes answer or . . ." He let his voice trail off, depressed an intercom lever, called for Sybil. "Neil is leaving. Please come in." He did not want them talking together until later—until after Harkness had made a decision.

Neil got to his feet, went toward the door wordlessly. When Sybil entered, she found James Courtney leaning back in his chair, grinning at the Frans Hals painting on the wall opposite him.

8

The private road on the Courtney estate wound through acres of formal gardens, then orchards, and finally virgin woodlands, and was posted with signs limiting speed to forty kilometers an hour. Neil Harkness, intent on getting clear of Montemar and seeking advice from the only two people who might be able to give it, disregarded the signs. He took his Citroën Pallas around the curves at eighty and one hundred, tires screeching counterpoint to his inner bellows of rage.

Immense wrought-iron gates tended by a pair of uniformed guards barred access to the Carretera de Cádiz. Neil jammed the brakes. The Citroën skidded to a halt. A guard, primed to raise hell with the driver for speeding, recognized Harkness, grinned, and opened the electrically operated gates. Neil burned rubber, roared through, swung right onto the coastal highway.

Traffic was normal for a Costa del Sol morning: anarchic, berserk. A Sava *furgón*—a truck the size of an American freight car—cut in front of Neil without so much as a wink of its directional signals. But both directionals were flashing steadily on a tiny Seat 600 sedan, which—impossibly overloaded with six passengers—wallowed along, stradding a lane-divider line. A red Porsche with French license plates zoomed past, weaving in and out of lanes, with a Madrid-plated Alfa-Romeo Spyder close on its tail. A tourist bus limped; a burro-drawn Gypsy cart meandered from right to left.

On most days Neil would have taken it all in good-natured stride. Not today. He cursed, let loose with his illegal airhorn, and released some of his pent-up aggressions by pushing the Citroën to 120, 140, 160. After a few minutes of boring through channels opened in the traffic chaos by the blare of the horn, he slowed, eased the car into the inside lane. A road sign indicated that the cloverleaf turnoff to "Cabo Verde—Centro Urbano" was only five-hundred meters ahead.

The construction boom that began in the 1950's transformed scores of Sun Coast towns and villages into underplanned, overbuilt eyesores. Fast-money promoters and developers threw together imitations of the garish worst to be found in such places as Miami Beach, Jesolo, Brighton. Little thought was given to basics like water supplies and sewage facilities. The buildings were flimsy, hideous. Toilets backed up, cesspools overflowed, swimming pools and tennis-court surfaces crumbled.

However, there were exceptions. Saner, less avaricious heads prevailed in some areas: Estepona, Mijas, San Pedro de Alcántara, Cabo Verde, and others among them. The *pueblo*—or *centro urbano*—of Cabo Verde ranked high on this list. New construction, and there had been much, was kept away from the town center. The Plaza José Antonio—the very heart of the *pueblo*—retained its Andalusian character and, although refurbished, looked much as it had a century or more earlier.

There was a park at the center of the plaza; the grass was a luxuriant green, the flowering shrubs were carefully tended, the dozen or so orange trees seemed to be perpetually bearing fruit. One side of the square was taken up by the crenellated ocher-brick *ayuntamiento*, which dated from the time of Isabella II, and was still used as the town hall. On the left was the *iglesia parroquial*, the parish church noted in guidebooks for its seventeenth-century stained-glass windows and baroque altarpieces. The other two sides of the plaza were lined by a miscellany of old buildings—one, two, in a few cases three stories high. The ground floors of most were offices—a physician, a notary, two attorneys, a travel bureau; or shops—greengrocer, pharmacist, butcher, *perfumería*, hairdresser, and the like. The upper floors were used mainly as living quarters.

A building on the north side was more impressive than its neighbors. Three-storied, its double entrance doors were of thick plate glass; a polished brass plaque on the wall read "Galerías Vivi." Vivian Dixon had bought the building in 1972 and converted it to house her highly successful art gallery.

Neil Harkness wanted to talk with Vivian personally rather than by telephone and knew that, party the night before or no, she would be at work in the gallery. Since parking was prohibited on the Plaza José Antonio, he left the Citroën a few streets distant, walked toward the square, his spirits rising a notch as he did. But then, Neil reflected, a walk in a Spanish town on a sunny day was bound to have a cheering effect. Flowers bloomed in window boxes, scenting the air. A gentle breeze came down from the sierras. Although the *puerto* itself was not visible from the *centro urbano*, the sea beyond it was—the water calm and a lustrous blue in the bright sunlight.

Gaggles of preschool children played on the narrow sidewalks.

Their mothers, grandmothers, aunts, clustered in front of the shops gossiping, complaining about prices, commenting on the state of the world. Like all Spanish women, although merely out to do their morning marketing, they were neatly dressed. The parish-church bells began to toll ten. Despite himself, Neil grinned broadly. Church clock and bells were forty-five minutes late and had been as long as he could remember. Natives blamed it on the 1936 Civil War—some on Franco's Republican troops, others on Loyalist forces—saying the works had been damaged in a battle. All conveniently forgot that the Civil War had bypassed Cabo Verde and that, in any event, the electrical timing mechanism was not installed until 1956. However, the myths persisted, were accepted as fact, and provided yet another story to tell tourists.

Neil started to cross the park. A small boy, mouth full of sticky *turrón*, darted between his long legs. He stepped carefully to avoid tripping the child. A uniformed Cabo Verde *policía* whose main task was to chase stray dogs and would-be parkers out of the plaza recognized Harkness with a smart salute and an exuberant "*Hola, torero*!" The last was a reference to the time Neil had used a thrusting broomstick to pacify a mob of drunken American tourists rampaging through the Bar Estrella in the *puerto*. He had been a favorite folk hero of the town police force ever since.

Waving an arm in response, Neil continued on to Galerías Vivi, entered the main-floor showroom. Several people, obviously tourists rather than Costa residents, were gawking at pictures displayed on the burlap-sheathed walls. Harkness grimaced wryly. Vivian had an unerring eye for what was truly good in art—and an equally unerring instinct for what, good or not, would sell. She had recently opened a special exhibition of contemporary primitives painted by Andalusian Gypsies living in Granada. Neil thought they were raucous, god-awful, but the painted-by-Gypsies gimmick had an exotic appeal. The daubs had been selling briskly—and at prices up to 100,000 pesetas, more than a thousand dollars, apiece.

Neil was acquainted with all the gallery employees and especially friendly with Carlos Lozano, the young—twenty-seven—and earnest multilingual Spanish assistant manager. Carlos noticed Harkness and detached himself from a couple dressed in identical His-'n'-Hers print shirts, Bermuda shorts, and espadrilles. An exceedingly handsome man with coal-black hair and eyes, Carlos Lozano was at his best with female customers, to whom he could sell almost anything. Women were entranced by his earnest, burning look tinged with sadness. It suggested that he was hopelessly in love, and that the love was unrequited. As he was (secretly, he believed) with Vivian Dixon, his employer. Unfortunately, Carlos wore his feelings like a neon sign. The secret had long been common knowledge. But since he limited himself to arm's-length adoration and was, everyone agreed, *muy simpático*, he was treated gently.

"Hi, Carlos. Where's Mrs. Dixon?" Neil carefully avoided saying "Vivi" or even "Vivian." Carlos always seemed to wince—and wilt—a little when he heard a man use her first name.

"Señora Dixon is upstairs in her office," Carlos replied—with a discernible trace of a blush.

Poor guy's a basket case over Vivi, Neil thought. Can't say I blame him. Still, why the hell does he keep chasing after the impossible? He liked Carlos, had taken him on a few deep-sea-fishing trips, drunk bottles of *tinto* with him. He knew Carlos to be all-male and attractive to women. Damned fool should give up—and take his pick of the birds who swarm around him. Harkness, of course, had never known unrequited love—not since he was in the sixth grade in the Cutchcogue, Long Island, elementary school. Neil started toward the staircase. Association of ideas led him to think of Sybil Pearson. The relationship with Sybil was good, gratifying, and fun, he told himself, but a long way from being love. Certainly from being the kind of heavy "I-want-to-die-for-you" love that Carlos Lozano felt for Vivian.

Harkness reached the third—top—floor, found Vivian Dixon in her office studying a score or more of unframed canvases lined along the floor, leaning against the walls. She looked up, surprised to see him. She showed no signs of party wear and tear. Her loose red hair was a coppery mesh glinting light; her smile dazzled.

"Glad you dropped by, Neil. I want to thank you for being so wonderful with Ken and—" She would have said more, but he stopped her.

"He tell you what we talked about?"

"No. He went to bed after I did—without a gin bottle, according to the servants—and was sleeping like a baby when I left the house this morning at nine-thirty. All good signs. The best."

Neil went to an office window that overlooked the plaza, lit a Celta, and stared out at the parish church. "I'm in trouble, Vivi—or will be soon," he said, not turning. "I may need help. Much as I hate it, you and Ken are the only people I can ask."

"Hate it? Don't be absurd!" Vivian was already moving toward her desk. "My God, with all that you've done for Ken and me over the years?" She took a checkbook from a drawer, opened it. "Just say how much. If I don't have it all in the Galerías account, I'll take whatever you need from another."

"It's not money, Vivi. I wish to Christ it was." Neil turned now, faced her, his expression grim. "It's Courtney. He's pulled me into something—and is pulling me in deeper."

Vivian's face paled, her gray eyes went dead. She hurried to the office door, closed and locked it. She was greatly agitated and spoke rapidly. "Please, Neil. You know how I feel about Jim, how Ken feels about him—but not why. There's a long—a very long—history. You've never heard it—and won't. No one has." Her hands were trembling. "Ken and I don't want to get involved with Jim"—she hesitated before adding—"again. We can't."

Neil bit his lower lip. "I'm not asking that you involve yourselves with Courtney."

"Then what do you want?"

"Advice, suggestions, information . . ."

"If that's all, why from Ken and me?"

"Because no one else knows as much about God."

"God?"

"Ken and I were calling the bastard that last night—in recognition of his omnipotence."

Vivian stared at her hands, looked up at Harkness, said: "Sit down, Neil. Start from wherever you started with Ken and bring me up-to-date. I'll listen"—her voice turned bleak—"for whatever good that might do."

Harkness found a chair, sat. It took him fifteen minutes and three chain-smoked cigarettes to comply. When he was through, Vivian spoke in a flat, lifeless tone:

"Maybe you're aware of this, maybe not. Jim Courtney never lies or exaggerates when he makes a threat. If he claims to have something to break you, he has it—and more." She paused, shook her head as if shaking off the memory of a bad dream. "He won't hesitate to use what he has, Neil. He's"—she averted her eyes—"one kind of sadist. There are others. His is the worst, most vicious kind. I can't advise what you should do."

"I haven't any choice in the short term. I'll go back before five and agree."

Vivian's expression was one of puzzlement. "If you've decided, any further talk would be useless, Neil."

"I think otherwise. Look, he said he wanted me to work for him for a month. I say yes today, and I'll learn something more immediately, and more yet every day that passes. The three of us—you, Ken, and I—might be able to make some sense, find answers . . ."

"You want to pick our brains . . . and our memories."

"Yes, without actually getting you involved."

"I can't give you an answer myself. I have to discuss it with Ken first. Come over to the house after you've finished the session—or would 'confrontation' be closer?—with God. I'm not making any promises, but maybe Ken and I will decide to . . ."

"Thanks, Vivi. I'm grateful. I really mean that." Harkness stood up, ready to leave.

"Wait a moment," she stopped him. "Are you supposed to be seeing Sybil this evening?"

"Yes, around seven. Want me to bring her along?"

"No. It's exactly what I don't want. No matter what the three of us might say to each other, it mustn't go any further. Least of all to Sybil." Vivian moved her hands in a helpless gesture. "Please understand. Sybil's probably the dearest woman friend I have here—or anywhere else, for that matter. But she's like I was—once. Blinded by the dazzle. She believes Jim Courtney is wonderful—cultured, a great philanthropist, a business genius—I'm sure you've heard all that and more from her."

"Often, and I've tried to argue—"

"It's useless. Sybil will have to learn for herself"—Vivian Dixon's lovely patrician face seemed to sag, age—"just as I had to learn. She won't listen to you and would never believe any of what Ken and I could tell her." Vivian closed her eyes, opened them. "Sometimes I try not to believe it, to think I've merely had dreams, nightmares, but that holds for many of us, doesn't it, Neil?"

"Many? I'd be willing to bet it applied to most of us." Harkness said; thought: The common denominator shared by expatriates, wherever they're from, wherever they may be. Trying to hide—or hide from—the truth, always finding that it's impossible.

Vivian forced a smile. "We'll be expecting you—at whatever time you arrive."

Old cutlasses (their blades and points dulled), belaying pins (made of light, frangible wood and made to look old), seamen's pikes (their tips bent back), and other more or less related oddments decorated the walls of Bar Espada on the Puerto Cabo Verde waterfront. They were there for the benefit of tourists and transient amateur sailors who sought nautical "atmosphere" when they drank and ate. The prices shown on a list that hung beside a color-photo portrait of King Juan Carlos I behind the cash register were also for their benefit.

Regulars and owners of commercial vessels ignored both decor and price list. They came to Bar Espada because the wine and brandy were of the best and the *bocadillos*—crusty bread loaves sliced down the middle and crammed with serrano ham or manchego cheese or both—had no equal anywhere. They were charged less than half what the atmosphere-seekers paid. Beyond these considerations, Bar Espada was favored by the pros, Spanish and foreign, as a place to trade nautical shop talk, yarns (invariably much exaggerated), jokes, (invariably bawdy), and complaints (about every conceivable matter under the Andalusian sun).

Neil Harkness was a longtime Bar Espada regular and on excellent terms with the owner, Enrique, for whom he occasionally brought in cases of duty-free liquor. Enrique was a burly Spaniard with dark olive skin and massively developed biceps and forearms—musculature developed, he said, during three years of rock-breaking in a Franco-regime prison. The experience had not embittered him against governments or ruling establishments, however. He was an ardent monarchist, and whenever King Carlos' yacht, *Fortuna*, came into port, he decorated the outside of his bar with Spanish flags and served free drinks to any of the yacht's crew who came ashore.

Harkness entered the Espada shortly before noon. Enrique was behind the bar, near its center, talking in his fair-to-middling good English with a trio of visiting boatmen Britons, who were drinking Aguila beer, a pallid brew known to regulars as "gnat piss." Neil had no desire to be drawn into the conversation, propped his big frame at the far end of the bar, waited.

". . . the people are safe, I think," he heard Enrique say. "The—how is it in English—yes, the dinghy it was found on the *playa* . . ."

Neil fine-tuned in. The talk was obviously about the derelict Chris-Craft. Any scrap of information could be useful.

". . . no *cadáveres*—bodies."

"Who owned the cruiser—the big boat?" a Briton asked.

"*Qué sé yo*—how should I know?" Enrique spread his thick arms. "Nobody knows. There was no *matrícula*—license, registration . . ."

Neil tuned out. Apparently the mystery was still a mystery. It would remain so, he thought glumly. The entire affair had been well-organized—too well for the organizers to have left any loose, traceable ends dangling. Enrique noticed him, bustled over, eager to talk. Harkness blocked him as politely as he could, ordered a bottle of Viña Sol and serrano-ham *bocadillo*. He drank half the wine before the *bocadillo* was served, then washed the hastily eaten food down with the other half.

So much for food, he thought, giving Enrique the entirely valid excuse that he was tired and did not want another bottle of wine or a coffee or anything else. He went to the *Deirdre* and his cabin, stripped off his clothes, and slept four hours. He awoke scarcely less tired than before, showered, dressed in clean khakis and T-shirt, went to his car, and started for Montemar.

Neil drove at a speed barely more than a crawl at first and was oblivious of horns that blared from behind and cars and trucks that passed, their drivers shouting obscenities. Big jaw clamped tight, big hand clamped hard on the steering wheel, his mind elsewhere and churning, he sought to fit knowns together and guess what Courtney might demand of him. After a time, he conceded that the exercise was futile—and meaningless. Whatever the orders, they would have to be carried out. Harkness chewed at his lower lip in frustration, floored the accelerator.

Sybil was tidying her desk, ready to leave for home. "He's waiting for you," she told Neil with a pout and a nose-wrinkling that combined into an expressive moue. She was curious to learn what had transpired during his morning meeting with Courtney and the reason for this second visit, but could not ask openly. "And I'll be waiting for you later—"

"Don't," Harkness cut her short. "I'll be busy until late—possibly most of the night." That gave him clear time to spend with the Dixons. "I'll phone your place soon as I have an idea of the schedule." He counterfeited an easy, reassuring grin. Sybil's moue went from curious to disappointed. She sighed and said:

"Well, Mr. C. said you're to go straight in."

Neil grunted, went to the *estudio* door, paused, thought: The hell with it—and him—I won't knock. He turned the knob, entered, swung the door closed behind him.

Courtney was behind his desk, looked up lazily. "Glad you met the deadline, Neil," he said. "Take the same chair as before—and yes, do light one of your Celtas."

Harkness reached for his pack instinctively, stopped. He took another chair, one that was set at a greater distance from the desk.

Courtney chuckled dryly. "The record shows that you have a superior IQ and graduated from Columbia with honors—a brilliant, clear-thinking man. Yet, because you're surly and rebellious, you try to demonstrate independence and freedom of choice—how? By not smoking when I suggest you do. By sitting there when I invite you to sit here. Sorry, my friend. I find it all hilarious—and puerile."

Neil gritted his teeth, cursed himself silently for not having thought faster and better.

Courtney's angular features remolded themselves into a cast that was almost benign. "Well, no harm done." A small smile. "I take it that you've mulled and pondered and are now agreeing to be my employee for thirty days."

Harkness was silent, and his silence was affirmation.

"You'll start tonight." Courtney hiked his lean body forward, took a thickish airmail-letter-sized envelope from the tabletop, flipped it into Neil's lap. "Thirty thousand dollars in mixed currencies," he said. "For expenses. Use part of it for the two men in your crew. They're to be laid off for a month—with full pay."

"No way," Neil protested. "I can't operate the boat alone."

"You did when you brought it to Spain from England," Courtney said. "And you will again. Is that clear?" He did not wait for an answer. "The men are to be off your boat by midnight. I'll be sending one of my own men to the *puerto* then—at twelve midnight—to make certain they are off."

"Then what?"

"You're to fuel up and be ready to leave port at oh-six-hundred hours, bound for—"

Neil did not learn what his destination would be. Not then. A telephone on Courtney's desk rang. Evidently he was expecting it or had some way of knowing it was important, for he reached for the instrument with one hand, operated what Harkness recognized as a scrambler-device switch with the other, and said: "Yes. What is the situation as of now?" Then he listened, high forehead furrowing in concentration. He spoke only at intervals and then in phrases that meant nothing to Neil.

"No more money."

Courtney listened for a full minute.

"I refuse to consider it."

Another minute.

"If you're so damned insistent, I'll give you twenty-four hours."

Less than ten seconds.

"I said twenty-four hours. That's the absolute limit."

Five seconds.

"In that event, you go with the other option."

Two seconds.

"You decide the method. Good-bye."

Courtney hung up. He was still frowning—but with annoyance. The frown faded slowly. He pursed his thin lips, looked at Neil. "You'll receive the rest of your instructions later—from the man I'll send to the *puerto*. Now, if you'll excuse me, I have to take care of some other matters."

Neil was taken aback when he stepped from the *estudio* into the outer office. Not because Sybil was gone—he had expected that—but because there was no sign of a security man, and Leslie Grenville, the liveried Montemar butler, was sitting at Sybil's desk. But he sprang to his feet and said:

"Miss Pearson has left for home and Mr. Courtney asked me to take over for a bit, sir."

Neil disliked Grenville, recognizing him as an icily homicidal type and guessing that he was Courtney's in-house spy.

"Why? Because you're as good at handling telephones as you are handling guns?"

A lethal gleam came and went in the eunuch's eyes. "Afraid Mr. Courtney didn't say. Perhaps you'd like to ask him yourself."

"I'll leave that to you, Grenville. Tell me the answer the next time you see me."

"Of course, Mr. Harkness." The gleam returned, stayed. "That will be tonight. At midnight, I believe."

9

Grenville tapped on the *estudio* door, entered.

"I have doubts about Harkness," he said. "There's something about the man . . ."

"Nothing to lose sleep over," Courtney said. "I know all there is to know about him. Here"—he produced a dossier—"I had this out today. Sit down and glance through it while I finish some work, Grenville. You'll come to the same conclusion as I did years ago."

"What's that, Mr. Courtney?"

"Skim over the opening pages—then we'll compare opinions."

Grenville did as he was told, opened the dossier, and, by so doing, opened the cover on Neil's life story. He began to read.

* * *

Born and raised in Cutchogue on Long Island's Great Peconic Bay, Neil Harkness loved the sea from childhood. He worked aboard fishing boats and Caribbean cruise ships during high-school and college vacations, but chose a legal career because it promised security and status. After passing his bar examinations in 1970, Neil joined the prestigious Wall Street law firm of Pearce, Goulden & Detweiler. The practice of corporate law soon began to pall on the rangy, six-foot-three attorney. He found it boring, confining, and regretted his choice, but stayed on, outwardly competent and conscientious, inwardly frustrated and restive.

After three years with PG&D, Harkness yearned to be independent, own a largish boat, and somehow make his living with it. But he was twenty-seven and knew the wish was futile. There was no possibility—none—that he would have the time and money to realize it until he reached an age when the juices ran dry and it no longer mattered. Then the miracle came. On Friday morning, March 23, 1973. By an ugly and initially soul-shattering route.

Called to the office of Malcolm Pearce, number-one senior partner of PG&D, Neil entered smiling, for Pearce had taken an active interest in furthering his career. The smile was not returned. Malcolm Pearce curtly directed him to take a chair, declared:

"I must talk to you about United Masters."

United Masters Electronics, Inc., was an AMEX-listed company and a client of the firm. Some months before, Pearce had announced that Neil was to handle its legal affairs but continued to deal with company executives personally and spelled out the wording of every document Harkness prepared and signed. Neil had chafed but assumed this was Pearce's way of training him in the finer points of corporation law.

"The company will file bankruptcy sixty days from today."

Neil's expression reflected dismay. United Masters' financial statements showed the company to be solvent. Dismay turned to shock as Pearce recited specifics. Unauthorized use of corporate funds. Massive losses through currency speculations. Books falsified. Company officers had acted with full knowledge of accountants and legal representatives, Malcolm Pearce went on, and criminal charges would undoubtedly be brought against the executives, the accountants, and Pearce, Goulden & Detweiler . . .

". . . or rather, the attorney directly responsible."

Harkness comprehended the unthinkable, leaped to his feet.

"My God! I followed your instructions to the letter and—"

"And your signature is on all the appropriate lines." Pearce's eyes were invisible behind glinting bifocals.

Neil slumped back into his chair defeated—and worse, resigned to defeat. He could be certain that Malcolm Pearce, a leading figure in the New York legal establishment, had built an escape-proof trap.

"It's a matter of survival, Neil. *My* survival. However, whether you're prepared to believe it or not, I do have a conscience. No, hear me out. I can arrange to have you disbarred on some relatively trivial grounds before the bankruptcy." It ordinarily took months to crank up such proceedings, but Pearce, a force in the Bar Association, could do what he said. "I'll also ensure that criminal charges against you are dropped." He wielded enough influence to do that, too.

"Furthermore—call it blood money if you wish—I will give you fifty thousand dollars. Cash. More than three times your present net income." Pearce's voice softened. "Go abroad until the United Masters affair is forgotten. I recommend Spain. I have a friend there who can be of great help to you. Think it over, Neil."

Harkness was astonished to hear himself blurt: "You have a deal." Unconscious mind had perceived miracle, thrust perception up through the turmoil of the conscious. The rigged odds were insuperable. Only a fool would stay and fight. Then, he was a bachelor, his mother and father were dead. He had no family to support, no parents who would be crushed by shame at his disbarment. By selling everything he owned, he could realize perhaps ten thousand dollars. Added to what Pearce offered, the total was sufficient. He could strip off layered straitjackets, do as he pleased. Immediately. While the juices still ran and it still mattered. "You have a deal," he repeated.

By the time New York reporters started looking for the disbarred lawyer whose name cropped up in the developing United Masters Electronics scandal, Neil Harkness was in London and the bulk of his cash was in a Swiss bank. For a month he mixed sex, sightseeing, and general fun, then turned to the serious business of transmuting long-cherished dreams into reality. He shopped for a boat—the right boat—eventually found it in Portsmouth.

A steel-hulled 61-footer originally built for RAF air-sea rescue work, the vessel had been declared surplus shortly after completion in 1971. It was purchased by a retired Royal Navy officer who spared no expense converting the craft for civilian charter use, named her *Deirdre*—and then died of a kidney infection.

His widow wanted to sell *Deirdre*. Her asking price plummeted to forty-five-thousand dollars when Neil offered to pay one-fourth on the official record, the rest in untaxable cash.

The transaction completed, an exultant Neil Harkness took *Deirdre*—sleek, roomy, powerful—on a dawdling voyage down the continental coastline to the Strait of Gibraltar. He put into port often, spent several days ashore at each stop to obtain some feel of Europe and buff the roughest edges off rudimentary French and Spanish learned while working aboard Caribbean cruise ships.

Malcolm Pearce had kept his promise, written to his friend James Philip Courtney, and, once through the Strait of Gibraltar and into the Mediterranean, Neil made directly for Puerto Cabo Verde. The marina was new then. As yet, no charter boats operated from there. Foreign residents or vacationers wishing to hire crewed vessels could find none closer than Marbella. Harkness saw that the potentials were great, but the obstacles many. He went to Courtney. The titular American king of the Costa del Sol listened and offered to use his influence, slash bureaucratic red tape, arrange for Neil to obtain the necessary papers and permits, and open doors for him along the Sun Coast. But there were conditions:

"I'm a businessman, Harkness, and business requires quid pro quo. Every now and then, I will want to hire you and your boat—oh, I'll pay you, and liberally. However, it must be understood that I have first call on your services and that you ask no questions, none, but simply do what I tell you."

Neil's capital had dwindled down to a few thousand dollars, and he had no other prospects. He agreed fully and without hesitation.

That was on Wednesday, July 25, 1973.

Leslie Grenville had assimilated that much from the dossier and had reached the bottom of a page. He turned it. The next page was a cardboard divider labeled "July 25, 1973–   ." There was no second date. He started to turn the divider. James Courtney stopped him.

"Don't read any further," he said, held out a hand. "That's all you need to know about Harkness, at least for the present." He took the dossier from Grenville, laid it—cover closed—in front of him, and smiling sardonically, asked, "Well, having digested that précis, do you still have doubts about the man?"

Grenville's sheeplike features reflected scorn. "No. It's fairly obvious that Harkness is a born loser."

"A born *victim*. I'm sure you appreciate the difference."

"Indeed I do. A type ideally suited for your purposes."

"You say that with feeling, but I detect a reservation."

"Not to do with Harkness personally and directly, sir."

"Then with whom—or what—and how?"

"It's Miss Pearson. She's an entirely different sort, and she and Harkness are close. Perhaps too close for our—for your—comfort, sir."

"Odd, our thoughts must run on the same wavelengths." Courtney laughed. "Since Sybil is to play a part in our upcoming drama, I took her dossier out of the safe too this afternoon and went over it." He took another folder from the tabletop. "If you'd care to take a look—as with Harkness's, only the first part—you might be able to set your mind at rest that she's eminently controllable."

"Be glad to, Mr. Courtney."

Grenville opened the folder and began to acquaint himself with Sybil's past. Being English himself, he could relate closely to what was contained in the typed pages and easily read between the lines.

In 1978 Sybil Pearson was twenty-one. She had a keen, lively mind and was very much her own person. She was also attractive, with long-lashed hazel eyes, a complexion that glowed health, and a coltish (some called it lissome) body. By all rights, she should have been happy and content; because she saw Britain and her life in her own lights, she was neither.

Sybil felt squeezed in what (with her weakness for puns) she termed the "English vise." On the one hand, Britain's group-unconsciousness remained trapped in a Land-of-Hope-and-Glory time warp. On the other, welfare-state mentality programmed Britons into computer-printout ciphers. Or so she believed—and said, whenever occasion arose.

There were more immediate reasons, too. By prevailing English standards, her secretarial job with a London advertising agency was a plum. Sybil saw it as repetitious and dull. Even so, it was preferable to the ultimate dead end of marriage and mortgage. Thus, she avoided serious romantic involvements, kept her love affairs light, ended them when they threatened to become heavy. At twenty-one, Sybil had already given considerable thought to joining the exodus of people young and not-so-young who were leaving the United Kingdom and going to other countries that promised more opportunity. But she did not make the final, irrevocable decision until September 24, 1978—three weeks after the abortion.

It was a Sunday. Sybil had promised to join her parents for tea in the afternoon. After lunching with friends in London, she went by Underground to Waterloo Station, from there by fast train (a half-hour ride) to Guildford. From Guildford Station she took a taxi to her parents' dreary, poorly maintained country house—a slowly decaying relic of grander, richer times. She arrived at 3:35 P.M. The flaming family row erupted the moment she stepped inside—and was still going on thirty endless minutes later.

". . . intolerable—absolutely unbelievable . . ."

Roger, fifth Viscount Pearson, Sybil's father, paced the faded carpet of the small drawing room. Sybil, silent and brooding in a corner wing chair, followed his movements from half-lowered lashes and thought that he needed only period costume and side whiskers to epitomize the heavy mid-Victorian father.

". . . we bloody well scrimped to send you to good schools. For what? You've behaved like a common tart!"

Elizabeth, Lady Pearson, was Sybil's mother. For several minutes she had been holding a stricken pose on the Queen Anne settee that remained as one of the family's more prized heirlooms. She suddenly came to life—to the extent of choking back an anguished sob.

Sybil choked back her own impulse—to laugh. They're both museum-quality anachronisms, she mused.

". . . your mother and I tried to instill a sense of decency . . ."

Sybil glumly remembered one "try." She had been fourteen, went horseback riding with a boy, and returned late for dinner. The family physician was summoned. She was subjected to probings by his rubber-gloved finger until he nodded, turned to her mother, and announced: "Not to worry, Lady Pearson. Your little girl's membrane is intact."

A montage of memories. Membrane broken at last. At sixteen. After a party. By an inept youth. Slight discomfort, no pleasure. Subsequent experiments—more selective, less hurried—usually enjoyable.

". . . rebellious, threw everything away . . ."

At eighteen and an adult under the law, Sybil left home, took a job in London, where she shared a flat with three other young women. True, the job was dreary, the flat cramped, but she had her own friends, life, and life style. And she had her package-tour summer holidays abroad. A fortnight touring France the first year, another roaming Italy the second, and this year, during the last half of June and first week in July 1978, a holiday in Torremolinos on the Spanish Costa del Sol. There were sun, sea, sand, the colors and flavors of Andalusia, and Sybil had fallen in love with the Sun Coast. And she also met Derek, a young chemical engineer from Manchester, also on holiday, and they had a delightful, summer-fun affair.

Sybil returned to London and her job, forgot Derek—but could not forget Spain—and, at the end of July, missed her period. She missed again in August. A gynecologist determined that her diaphragm no longer fitted properly; tests confirmed that she was pregnant. Sybil made the necessary arrangements and on September 7 went to a National Health Service Clinic. She experienced no sense of guilt or remorse after the abortion, but she had unwittingly made a ghastly mistake. Patients at the clinic had to furnish "name and address of person to be notified in the event of emergency." She had given her parents' name and address—and some mindless clerk had mailed the routine postoperative paperwork to them

The envelope arrived Saturday, September 23. Roger Pearson naturally opened it, read the contents, and showed them to his wife. They knew Sybil was coming the next day. This gave them ample time to brew up the storm of moral outrage with which they greeted their daughter. The outrage stemmed less from the fact that she'd had an abortion than that it had been performed in a National Health Service facility.

"We would have found the money for private care somehow!" Roger Pearson bellowed, while his wife wailed, "People will find out—the disgrace will ruin Edward!"

She and her husband considered their son and only other child, a paragon of all virtues and, as a tyro broker in the City, a last hope of recouping some of the family's fortunes. Edward was, predictably, a prig, more hidebound than his father, and a closet homosexual. He was six years older than Sybil. They loathed each other.

". . . shock, disgust." Roger Pearson was running down.

Tolerance exhausted, Sybil broke her silence. "You left out 'horror,' Daddy," she said, stood up, soft mouth forming into a weary smile. "Afraid I must be off. Pax—Brittanica, what else?—be with you."

Sybil walked into Guildford. She would have liked a drink, but it was 4:55 on an English Sunday. The pubs were closed. She resigned herself to tea in the station snack bar. She waded through litter to a stand-up counter veneered with the day's accumulation of spilled liquids turned gummy, stirred sugar into her tea with a flimsy white plastic spoon, and studied the graffiti on a nearby wall.

Acrylic and felt-pen scrawls exhorted her to bash Pakis, support a misspelled Manchaster United, hang IRA terrorists, vote Labor, free Maze prissoners (also misspelled). Others demanded that various clinically explicit sexual acts be performed on Harold Wilson, Arabs, Joe Gormley, Jews, Margaret Thatcher, the National Coal Board. Sybil lit a Rothman's, ravaged her palate with a swallow of British Rail tea, and grimaced. The grim snack bar and moronic graffiti strengthened the decision made while her father ranted and her mother played the tragic muse. Luckily, the five hundred pounds left her by a maiden aunt was in a Barclays passbook account. But I'll go even if I have to swim, she promised herself.

Sybil arrived at Málaga airport on October 18, 1978. Friends had told her about a tiny but good hotel in Fuengirola. She went there, settled in, and took stock. If watched carefully, her money would last five months. To stay longer, she would have to find work. This would be difficult. Spain was plagued by unemployment. The Suarez government had tightened restrictions in the issuance of work permits to foreigners. During the next few weeks, she did nothing but eat, sleep, and study Spanish. Then she took a job as a barmaid-waitress—working "black," illegally—and for tips only in a replicated English pub owned by a blowsy widow from Liverpool. She listened to barroom talk for leads to better jobs, had experiences similar to those of most job-seeking foreigners on the Costa. A Mijas-resident American divorcée wanted a (lesbian only) social secretary. An English couple in Marbella needed a nanny for their three children, offered room and board, no pay. A Torremolinos "club bar" sought "*señoritas de buena presencia*" who spoke English to work as topless hostesses.

Sybil continued working at the Fuengirola pub. The holidays—Christmas, New Year's, Epiphany—came and went. Then one evening she overheard some pub gossip. James Courtney—"*el rey de la Costa del Sol*"—was said to be furious. His private secretary had quit without notice, clearing out of her apartment—and apparently out of Spain—over a weekend while he was away in South America. There was no one on his CVI office staff qualified to replace her.

Sybil took a taxi to Montemar the next morning. Her secretarial and language skills impressed Courtney, and being shrewd, he recognized qualities that would make her invaluable. She was awed by success and wealth, had the built-in Britons' belief that whoever achieved them was necessarily superior, a person to be admired, almost venerated. And she unconsciously hungered to hero-worship a rich and powerful surrogate for her ineffectual, hollow-headed father—who, like James Courtney, was in his late fifties.

Sybil began working at Montemar the following day: Wednesday, January 31, 1979, her residence and work permits assured.

Leslie Grenville finished reading the background portion of the "PEARSON, SYBIL" dossier, reached the cardboard-divider page beyond which, Courtney had warned, he was not to go. He closed the file, returned it to his employer, who asked:

"Satisfied that Sybil—like Harkness—is no threat?"

"Entirely satisfied, sir," Grenville replied with the faint trace of a smile, and rose to his feet. "They're prisoners of their own flaws—innocuous." He cleared his throat. "Anything else, Mr. Courtney?"

"Um. The girl. Christina . . ."

"Kristin," Grenville corrected, and anticipating the rest of the question, said, "She's been informed—and is ecstatic. I'll bring her to your suite after you've dined. Would you like anything special laid out beforehand?"

"A syringe, the gold coins, and the speculum."

"Then she'll be spending the entire night?"

"If she's good and has the stamina, yes."

"Excuse me, sir, but am I to infer that she may become Miss Marsh's successor?"

"Christ, no. And do us both a favor. Pretend that Eileen Marsh doesn't exist."

Grenville caught the odd note in Courtney's tone, and as he withdrew from the *estudio*, wondered if he was to infer that Eileen Marsh would soon cease to exist.

10

A fatalistic streak enables most Spaniards to accept whatever happens with resignation. *A lo hecho, pecho*—what can't be cured must be endured. This was the attitude of Neil Harkness's two crewmen when he gave them their wages to date and for the next thirty days and told them they would be free for a month.

Neil had gone directly to the *puerto* from Montemar. His men needed time to remove their personal belongings from the *Deirdre* before the midnight deadline set by Jim Courtney. He offered them no reason or excuse for the layoff because he could think of none that would sound convincing. In their turn, the two seamen asked no questions. Since they were being paid for the period they would be idle, there were no questions that could be asked without overstepping the bounds of propriety, appearing much too inquisitive. In any event, they lived in Cabo Verde and would spend most of the next thirty days hanging around the waterfront. They would be in close touch with Harkness when he was in port. They would have no trouble learning where he was headed and when he was due to return if he put to sea.

However, the layoff called for a drink in the Bar Espada. One led to another, and a third and fourth, and it was after nine before Harkness was able to get away. He drove from Puerto Cabo Verde to Broadmoor, arriving there at nine-thirty, and found Kenneth and Vivian Dixon alone. They had given their live-in servants the night off, Ken explained, leading his friend into the breakfast-room area next to the kitchen.

"We'll be talking a lot, and there's no sense having the hired help around to eavesdrop."

Neil saw that although Dixon was by no means drunk, he was a fair distance past being cold sober. But his mood was ebullient. Vivian was more subdued. She saw Harkness frown as he studied her face and said:

"What you see is a hangover—from playing devil's advocate. I've spent the last two hours advancing arguments why we should lock and bar the door against you, Neil." She spread her hands in a helpless gesture, and her expression softened. "None of it did any good. Ken's made up his mind to go all-out—and I'm sold, too."

She nodded toward the table. "We'll sit here. I'll bring something to eat when we want it. In the meantime, how about a drink?"

"A beer will do me fine, Vivi."

They sat at the table, Neil with a bottle of San Miguel, Vivi with a small glass of sherry. Ken had his unvarying usual—Tanqueray gin and tonic, no ice—and wanted to propose a toast:

"To the humbling of the capital-A Almighty, Jehovah P.—for Poison—Courtney."

Neil demurred, shaking his head and saying, "Sorry, but I'm

a lot less than amused by this whole damned business. It's getting darker and dirtier, and I'm being dragged in deeper and deeper.'' He told of his afternoon meeting with Courtney, the furloughing of his men, and concluded:

''I have to be back at the dock by twelve to get the rest of my orders from that eunuch Courtney has as a butler.''

Ken Dixon was undaunted. He drank, chortled. ''Great. Whatever he tells you should fill in our plot line beautifully.''

''Jesus, Ken, this is for real,'' Harkness protested. ''We're not collaborating on a novel.''

''Maybe not, but I have to think of it that way—or I can't think,'' Ken riposted. ''It's how we started last night, and I told you, there's a great book here, good as any I've ever written.''

Vivian shot her husband an odd cautionary look from under half-lowered lashes. He either failed to notice or ignored it, Neil could not be sure, but then his own attention was suddenly distracted. Vivian shifted position. The front of the blouse she was wearing fell away, enough to let him glimpse the tops of her breasts. They were covered with bruises. She saw him looking at her, straightened up abruptly.

''I've spent the day building on what you told me,'' Ken was going on. ''We have all the basic elements—''

''Ken.'' Vivian's voice was sharp. ''Neil is right. We're not talking about a book, and he's pressed for time.''

Dixon's glass was empty. He left the table with it, went into the kitchen, returned a moment later; the glass was full again.

''Truth is stranger than fiction,'' he declared—almost declaimed. ''And it's like I've said a million times. All fiction is based to some degree or other on fact. . . .''

Neil fidgeted. Vivian stared at her sherry glass, still almost full, did not touch it.

''My books've always been based solidly on fact—the more fact, the better the books. Here's to fact.'' Dixon raised his glass, drank some of the contents, set the glass down.

Harkness lit a Celta, smoked nervously, avoided looking at Dixon. The silence lasted two minutes, perhaps three, until Ken grinned foolishly and said, ''Oh, hell. I went off on a tangent.'' He glanced at his wife as if asking for forgiveness.

''It's after ten,'' she said. ''Neil will have to leave in . . . What?''

''An hour at the outside,'' Harkness said.

''Are you hungry?'' Vivian asked. Neil shook his head; the last thing he wanted was food. ''Then let's start somewhere,

Ken," she said to her husband. Her great gray eyes flicked to Neil. "Do you have any suggestion where that should be?"

"I have," Ken broke in. "It's like you and I said earlier. We know plenty about Courtney"—he had begun slurring his words—"but we don't know how much Neil knows. Hey, how's that for alliteration?" He drained his glass, stood up, and made for the kitchen.

It suddenly struck Harkness that something was wrong. Very wrong. Kenneth Dixon usually—hell, always, Neil reflected—stayed sober or, if drunk, sobered up when his mind was occupied with plots or with true stories someone was telling him. Just as he had sobered up, stopped drinking altogether, the night before. And now, they were simply picking up the threads where they left off, and while Ken had shown interest at first, he was losing it rapidly, drinking more. Neil was baffled, looked at Vivian. She averted her eyes.

"Is he okay? I mean, Ken's going heavy on the gin," he said.

Vivian spoke into her lap. "He . . . he has some problems of his own, Neil. I thought I'd talked him around to forgetting them. . . ."

"So what do you know?" Dixon returned, sat, slopped some gin-tonic from his glass onto the table. Vivian reached for a paper napkin, wiped up the liquid.

"Maybe we can still salvage something out of the evening, Neil," she murmured. "Start by talking about Jim. Let him—and me—follow your lead, fill you in."

"Sure." Harkness felt acutely uncomfortable, as though he had intruded in some kind of taut husband-wife situation. He drank a little more beer, said: "Well, I do know he's one of the richest men in the world—ever since Getty died in seventy-six, the richest American expatriate anywhere—"

"Hold it, whoa!" Ken interrupted. "You're going at this ass-backwards. Reel off what information you have chronologically, or you'll get yourself and us all fouled up."

"Well, he's from California—born there in 1923, I think."

"Los Angeles—and it was 1922," Ken interjected.

Vivian became aware of the telephone ringing, looked up. "I forgot the servants were off. They usually answer."

"I'll get it." Ken went to the kitchen extension. He returned a moment later. "For you, sailor. It's Sybil."

Harkness frowned, got to his feet. "I didn't tell her I'd be here. Did you?"

"Nope—but she must have found out somehow."

Neil went into the kitchen, picked up the handset Dixon had left lying on a counter.

"It's nice I've finally found you." Sybil's voice was chill. Harkness knew she was miffed because he had broken their date, irked because he had said nothing about going to visit mutual friends. "Mr. Courtney called me," she went on. "He gave me a message to deliver." There was no thaw in her tone. "You're to be at the *puerto* an hour earlier—eleven, not twelve. Considering what time it is now, I'd suggest you hurry."

She hung up. Neil replaced the receiver in its cradle, went back to the Dixons, told them he would have to leave. Ken mumbled something, went to make himself another drink.

"Please come by and see me at the gallery tomorrow," Vivian said, and Harkness noticed for the first time that she had dark shadows under her eyes. "Ken and I may be needing your help as much as you need ours."

The Puerto Cabo Verde yachting crowd preserved the Spanish tradition of late dining, and kept its own late hours. Waterfront bars and restaurants were busy. The quays were brightly lit, as were many of the moored vessels. Leslie Grenville, wearing an ordinary dark linen suit, was waiting on the bridge of the *Deirdre*.

"Good evening, Mr. Harkness." The politeness was patently bogus.

"Do me three favors, Grenville. Drop the butler act, tell me what J.P. wants—then get the fuck off my boat."

"Delighted to oblige, old boy." The tone had changed to one of acid insolence. "The schedule was advanced so you can take on fuel before the service facilities close at midnight. Once fueled, you're to leave for Venice."

"Without crew?" Neil made rapid mental calculations. A straight run across the Med to the tip of Sicily, some eight hundred nautical miles. Around Cape Passero, then the heel of the Italian boot and up the Adriatic, only a bit less. "J.P. must have slipped a cog. It'd take me the better part of two days—even if I push it. I'd have no sleep—"

"That's your problem. After arriving, you're to meet an old acquaintance, Herr Wilhelm Fischer. He'll be waiting for you, registered at the Hotel Gritti Palace."

Harkness could not suppress a laugh. A picture of flabby, slovenly-dressed Wilhelm Fischer staying at the elegant, exclusive Gritti Palace was amusing—hilarious. He let the laugh die away, asked: "What am I supposed to do after meeting Fischer?"

"Whatever he says—with no questions. Those are Mr. Courtney's orders." Grenville eased himself past Neil and stepped down to the dock. "Enjoy yourself, Harkness."

Neil checked his fuel gauges; the tanks were more than half full, but they would have to be topped off. He went below to his cabin, started disconnecting the *Deirdre*'s dockside telephone, paused, changed his mind. He dialed the Dixons' number first. After several rings, Vivian answered.

"Thought I'd better tell you," he said. "I'm leaving in an hour."

"Going where, Neil—or should I ask?"

"Venice, for starters—and while you asked, I didn't tell you."

"Oh." A short silence. "Can you hang on a couple of minutes, Neil? I've just had an idea." Vivian went off the line. The couple of minutes stretched to five, six. Harkness was nearing the end of his patience when he heard her voice again. "Neil, there are reasons why Ken should be out of Spain for a few days. He says he'd love to go with you. Will you—can you—take him along? He can fly back from Italy if necessary."

The request took Harkness by surprise. He snap-shifted mental gears, mulled it over. Kenneth Dixon was an excellent amateur sailor, and they had been on several cruises together. He would be handy aboard, take his turns at the wheel—if sober. But he had not been sober less than an hour before. Neil was about to say no, when he heard an extension phone being picked up and Dixon's voice:

"No booze, that's a promise." He was obviously aware of Neil's reservations. "I'll not only do my share of the work, but you and I can finish what we started tonight about Jehovah P."

Dixon sounded much less alcoholic, Neil mused, and he usually kept promises. But Courtney had been adamant that there be no crew aboard. Letter of law, spirit of law—two different things, Harkness reflected. Neither the billionaire nor his eunuch-butler-messenger-boy said anything about taking a friend along as a passenger. At least, that'll be my story if J.P. finds out. Which he shouldn't.

"I'll bring along everything I have on him," Dixon's voice continued. "We can go over the stuff together—"

"You've lost me, Ken. What stuff?"

Vivian fielded the question. "We didn't tell you. Should have, but we were waiting—don't ask me why, but we were. Ken once planned to write a novel based on Jim Courtney and gathered information—"

"There're notes, documents, tapes," Dixon broke in. "I'll bring everything. Vivi can drive me over, with time to spare."

Neil feared he would live to regret the decision but made it anyway. "I'll be at the service dock, fueling. Try to get there a little after midnight—the lights should be out by then. I'd rather not have anyone see you come aboard, Ken. And, Vivi, don't tell anyone. Least of all Sybil. *Hasta pronto.*"

Harkness next dialed Sybil Pearson's apartment number. She was cool to begin, warmed perceptibly when Neil said he was leaving and had no idea when he would return.

"I'll throw on some clothes and drive over to see you before—"

"No way," Neil said sourly. "J.P. wouldn't approve."

"Can't you tell me where you're going?"

"Croesus probably wouldn't approve of that, either. You might ask him in the morning and maybe—just maybe—get a straight answer."

"Your hate-Courtney moods are too much," Sybil said peevishly. "If it weren't for him—"

"Yeah, you've told me before. Often. He's brilliant, generous, the last of a great breed, et cetera. Keep holding the good thoughts, and I'll see you when I see you. Take care."

Neil tooled the *Deirdre* across the yacht basin to the service dock, took on diesel fuel. When he had signed the bill, the attendants locked up, extinguished the lights, and left. Some minutes later the Dixons arrived. They were being careful, using a Seat 124, the smallest and most inconspicuous of their three automobiles. Vivian was driving and pulled the car alongside the *Deirdre*. Harkness went to Kenneth's side of the sedan, but the author climbed out. He was, surprisingly, almost sober and took two suitcases from the rear seat, carried them aboard the boat. Vivian leaned across the front seat, spoke to Neil in a low voice—rather cryptically, Harkness thought.

"You're doing us a great favor. Very great. Ken may or may not tell you why, but he will tell you all about Jim. Bless you—and have a good voyage."

Harkness returned to the foredeck as Vivian drove away. Ken offered to help by casting off the lines. Neil shook his head.

"Stay below til we're past the breakwater," he said, adding, "Galley's stocked up if you want something—but lay off the liquor."

The *Deirdre*, built for work in all kinds of water and weather, had a spacious enclosed bridge. When thick glass panels were slid home in their steel frames, the bridge was sealed off from wind, spray, and all but a faint thrum of engine noise. The night being clear, the sea calm, Neil Harkness set an easterly course at an easy twenty knots and let George do it, allowing autopilot and interfaced steering computer handle the vessel. He lolled in a high-backed captain's chair, keeping an eye on instruments and sea nonetheless, and drank mud-thick bitter coffee Ken Dixon had made and brought up from the galley.

Ken disdained using a matching captain's chair set to one side of the helm. He sat on the deck, back propped against the after bulkhead. An open suitcase containing the material he had promised to bring lay between his veed-out legs. He sifted and shuffled through papers, keeping up a running commentary as he did. Neil could not help grinning; the world-famous author looked for all the world like a small boy rummaging in pieces of luggage he had found in the attic.

"You have to remember what Spain was like when I came to Cabo Verde in sixty-seven. Franco held that whip and used it to make a Promised Land for foreigners who had convertible currency. Christ, local wages were like thirty, fifty cents an hour. Good little villas sold for six, eight thousand—in dollars. I built my own house for twenty-five—it's worth over two hundred thou now. Food and liquor? They cost next to nothing—you could eat dinner in a good restaurant, have a bottle of wine, and get change for five bucks."

"It was still pretty good when I got here in seventy-three," Neil said, putting his coffee mug aside and lighting a Celta.

"Not nearly as good, though, believe me. People were pouring in from all over—Europe, the U.K., North and South America, you name it. They were living like kings—but I wasn't around long before I realized there was only one real king on the Costa. James Courtney—and damned if he hadn't been the biggest bigshot foreigner for years and years."

"You got acquainted with him soon?"

"After about three months. I wangled an invitation to his estate. I must say the guy impressed me. Montemar and all the art and antiques and the fifty-thou-a-shot parties he gave impressed me more. Well, in those days he wasn't a billionaire yet—just a centimillionaire—but any moron could see that he had his fingers . . . Did you ever notice how they sort of splay out at the tips?"

"Sure."

"Sailor, anybody could tell those fingers were in a million pies and pulling strings all over the damned world. He had his company—CVI—and it was big and some parts of it were visible. I felt that a lot of other parts—maybe most—weren't. Stood to reason. He was making too much noise about those that did show, and he seemed to have a compulsion about showing—and showing off. It didn't square with many of his other facets."

"For instance?"

"He had a security mania even then, and while he chased after publicity, there were certain questions he'd always dodge—things of that sort. Well, the public was getting its rocks about then from J. Paul Getty's autobiographical magazine articles and books that made super-rich entrepreneurs look like plaster saints. I got to thinking I could build a great novel around a character based on Courtney. You know, the American tycoon who runs an empire from abroad, is a ruthless manipulator, has much to hide.

"My literary agent felt it was terrific—my best idea ever for a future project. I had three novels out that were making a lot of money. He suggested I invest some of it and have researchers dig and scour up the details of Courtney's life story. Which I did, but first I drafted up a sketchy set of guidelines for myself."

Dixon extracted a sheet of paper from the suitcase. "I'll read you the opening: 'Feared and hated in some quarters'—I figured he must be—'and a folk hero in others'—which he is, don't ever kid yourself otherwise—'James P. Courtney is a flamboyant personality who delights in flaunting his wealth, women, and other possessions.' "

"I'll buy every word so far." Neil blew a smoke ring, scanned his instrument panel, looked back at Dixon. "What comes next?"

" 'But perhaps these displays are merely empty movement to distract others from the real action he must conceal.' "

"Is that all?" Harkness asked.

"God, no. The outline runs thirty pages, and you can see how much research—hundreds and hundreds of pages."

"You never wrote the book, though. Why not?"

"I'll get to that eventually. Right now, we have to start at the same point as we did at the house." Dixon suddenly looked apologetic. "Uh . . . afraid we didn't get very far."

"We got to the place and year of birth—L.A., California, 1922," Neil said with a grin. "After a few more gin-tonics, you might have come up with the month and day."

"April 2," Ken blurted.

"A great leap forward," Harkness needled. "What next?"

"He was a bastard."

"Was and is. What else is new?"

"I mean literally—in the sense that he was illegitimate."

"Lots of people are. I don't see how it's relevant."

"It is in this case. His father was a Baptist minister—the Reverend Wendell Courtney. To quote by memory from one of many news clippings that were gathered for me, 'Reverend Courtney is renowned for being the spiritual adviser to some of the most beautiful women in the motion-picture industry.' He made a fortune with the sex-and-religion gimmick in Hollywood. You know the gimmick. Fuck the preacher and be saved."

Neil lit another cigarette. "The preacher got one of his flock pregnant?"

"He did. He begat James P. and the first of the many mysteries in James P.'s life. The researchers I hired didn't find many of the reverend's contemporaries still alive, but there were a few. They advanced some far-out theories about the identity of the mother. Three claimed she was Theda Bara. Then there were votes for Dorothy Gish and Pearl White. No evidence, much less proof, of course."

"Hold it, Ken. There must have been a birth certificate."

"There was. I obtained a copy. James Philip was born in the reverend's house, delivered by a doctor whose name is illegible, and the mother's name is shown as Roxanne Courtney—no 'Mrs.' The preacher later told people she was his niece and died a week after giving birth. No record of any death certificate—in fact, no record that Wendell Courtney had any relatives at all."

Harkness shifted position, stared out at the dark expanse of the sea. "Was there a legal adoption or any formal acknowledgment of paternity?"

"Nothing. Made it rough for James when the reverend died. Wendell Courtney had money, real estate—left it all to a mistress. Our friend J.P. didn't get a dime . . . had to quit college. That's when he joined the Army."

"Back it up a little, Ken. The reverend—or Courtney senior, if you prefer—kept and raised the boy?"

"With the help of nurses, housekeepers, tutors, and so on. He could afford it."

Neil frowned. "Why? Any explanation?"

"None from James. In fact, he tells an elaborate story about a happy family life with a mother and father."

"Yeah, I've heard some of it from him. But if it's all bullshit, we're still left with the same question. What made preacher Courtney give the boy a home? Guilt?"

"My researchers got some wild answers. Some people who knew the reverend and were still alive told my researchers that he was a saintly man and did it for love of his niece. At the other end of the spectrum, a onetime chauffeur claimed that Courtney senior swung both ways and had a weakness for young boys and—"

"Kept the kid on hand for sexual use."

Dixon was startled. "Christ, but you came up with that fast—like you knew all along."

"You telegraphed it." Harkness yawned—because he had slept only a few hours in two days, not because he was bored. "Anyway, ask any shrink or juvenile-court judge. Homosexual incest between father and son isn't all that uncommon." He stifled another yawn, stretched. "Even so, the chauffeur might have been lying. Let's move ahead, Ken."

"Maybe we're ready to go into this." Dixon took a stapled sheaf of papers from the suitcase, studied it, his features tightening. He took a deep breath, released it. His expression relaxed a little.

"I'd better give you a short preface," he said. "As late as sixty-nine, I still thought a roman-à-clef novel based on James Courtney was a viable major project, and my agent was still cheering me on. So I boiled the mass of information that had been collected down into a chronological narrative—"

"You went that far and never wrote the book?" Neil interrupted.

"No." Dixon's face froze hard. He made it thaw, with evident effort. "No, I never wrote the book . . . but let's get back to this. It's a skeleton, bare bones—all fact or what people interviewed by the researchers related as fact, to the best of their knowledge and recollection. I didn't invent or elaborate much—hardly at all—but here and there I added a touch that was most likely true. I'll give you a quick skim—you can read and study it later. Okay?"

"Shoot." Harkness settled back, prepared to listen.

11

He was a precocious child. The impressions that were to form his earliest memories dated back to December 1923, when he was barely twenty months old.

Hollywood Boulevard was then a glamorous, glittering thoroughfare where members of the film colony shopped or merely strolled to be seen and to bask in being recognized by passersby. During the Christmas season it was renamed "Santa Claus Lane," lavishly bedecked with Christmas decorations. Each evening, a huge and elaborate Santa Claus float made its way along the length of the boulevard, and large crowds massed along the sidewalks to watch it pass.

Taking children to see the nightly spectacle was a Los Angeles area tradition—virtually a must. James Courtney—then, of course, "Jimmy"—was taken on the evening of December 20 by his nurse, Alice Truro, whom he called "Allie." She managed to find a choice vantage point in front of the H. B. Dyas Department Store on the corner of Vine Street, took Jimmy from his carriage, and held him in her arms.

He would always remember gazing in wonder at the bright lights and gaudy decorations festooning nearby lampposts and telephone poles and declaring that he wanted them. When Allie told him it was impossible, they were for everyone to see, he began to cry. The nurse could not make him stop.

A woman standing beside them reached out, patted his tear-stained face. Alice Truro was plain of face, dowdy of dress. The woman was radiantly beautiful, her clothes exquisite—Jimmy thought she must be an angel, at the very least, a fairy godmother. Alice recognized her instantly as Leatrice Joy, the motion-picture star (as she was to tell Jimmy much later), and was overcome with movie-fan emotion. She almost dropped the child. Leatrice Joy caught him in time, held him in her own arms, kissed and cuddled him. When she tried to return him to Alice Truro, he resisted fiercely, screaming and struggling, but the transfer was eventually made.

The flustered nurse put Jimmy back into his baby carriage, wheeled it away. He did not see the Santa Claus float that evening—but he did see the beautiful woman often. For many years in his dreams, when she was his loving mother—and afterward, again for years, as the image conjured up in his masturbatory fantasies.

Christmas Eve four days later provided the second indelible impression. The Reverend Wendell Courtney owned a nine-room "hacienda-style" house on Wilshire Boulevard in what was then an exclusive and expensive residential neighborhood. The house was staffed by a squad of servants, all—like Alice Truro—unattractive people. Jimmy would be only five years old when, being perceptive and precocious, he realized the reasons for this phenomenon.

The reverend, who taught Jimmy to call him "Da-Da" but was angry whenever he tried to say "Daddy," knew that homely—or better, ugly—people were likely to be insecure, afraid, and thus less demanding, easier to control. Then there were the women—lovely and temperamental—who came to his study for prayer sessions and counseling. Pretty women in the house would make them uneasy; handsome male servants might well distract them, for although Wendell Courtney had an interesting, aquiline face, he was rather less than a matinee idol in appearance.

On this Christmas Eve, Reverend Courtney had a short prayer service for his servants in the living room, in front of the ceiling-high Christmas tree. Jimmy was present—freshly diapered and in his stroller, watched over by Alice Truro. The other servants stood in a semicircle, their heads bowed. Da-Da spoke—Jimmy did not comprehend what he said—and was still speaking when the door chimes sounded.

Da-Da stopped. Someone went to the door and opened it. There was the sound of a shrill, demanding woman's voice, and then a woman did burst into the living room. She was weeping, carrying on hysterically. (Later in life, Jimmy would see photographs of Clara Bow and be certain he recognized her from that Christmas Eve). Da-Da spoke to her, said something to the servants, all of whom—including Alice, who carried Jimmy—hurried out and went into the kitchen. Once there, they began talking among themselves.

One remark caught the boy's ear—and fancy.

"He'll fuck the bejesus out of her."

Everyone laughed.

"Fuck bejesus," Jimmy repeated.

The laughter was even louder than before.

A male servant produced a bottle of bootleg liquor. It was passed around twice before it was empty. Alice took her turn drinking from it each time. Then another bottle appeared and made the rounds.

"Fuck bejesus," Jimmy said loudly to attract attention.

"He's going to be just like the preacher," someone said. Even those on the household staff who had reason to believe that Jimmy was Wendell Courtney's son were careful never to say so.

"Here—let's see the size of him," a gaunt man who worked as the gardener said, taking Jimmy and laying him on the kitchen table. He tickled the boy, who thought it was great fun. "Give us a look, Alice," the man said.

Alice Truro had drunk enough not to care. She laughed, unpinned Jimmy's diaper, removed it.

"Still bite-sized—but it looks cute enough to bite," a female voice said. "Go on, Alice, nibble at it!"

Others joined in, urging, cajoling.

Jimmy, lying on his back on the kitchen table, gurgled happily as something warm and moist closed around him and something flicked at him, tickling. It was a wonderful, comforting feeling. Alice Truro remained his nurse for another year. During that time, he would refuse to go to sleep until she did what she had done on Christmas Eve.

The Reverend Wendell Courtney had been ordained a minister through the good offices of the United States Post Office Department. He had sent fifty dollars and a filled-in form to a box number in Alabama in 1920, and received all the appropriate documentation—issued by a self-styled Baptist-splinter-group church—by return mail.

Wendell Courtney was ahead of his time, a man who had deep insight into the manners and mores of Hollywood. He mixed large measures of Oriental mysticism into the purported Baptist Christianity that he professed in public or when interviewed by the press. The mix had enormous appeal to many in the film industry—mainly, but not entirely, for females.

John Barrymore and Gilbert Roland were among the male stars who attended his "Inner Soul Search" meetings and sang his praises.

"Reverend Courtney is in harmony with human creative souls on the one hand—and the One Great Soul that created us all," a Los Angeles *News* columnist quoted H. B. Warner as saying.

Indeed, the blend had so many ingredients that such words as "reverend" and "minister" fell short, and the press began referring to him as "the noted clergyman, philosopher, and student of comparative religion." Wendell Courtney's "Soul-Search Center" on Fairfax Avenue looked like a church from the outside, and it was small, purposely so. Limited seating capacity made those who paid five hundred dollars annually for pews feel they were part of a privileged—and anointed—elite. There were also two "Total Meditation Chambers" in the building. They were identical save that the one in which he meditated with women followers was furnished with a huge lozenge-shaped couch; the other—for men—was not. Sessions in his study at home were reserved for very special people (mostly women), the "suggested offering" for communing there with self and Reverend Courtney was very high, and a curtained door interconnected with a bedroom.

Oddly enough, Wendell Courtney made no great effort to maintain religious facades when out of sight of his followers—and this was one of the paradoxes over which James Courtney would long puzzle. True, there were such gestures as the Christmas Eve prayer service for the servants, but these were few and far between. Indeed, Jimmy received very little religious training beyond being required to say his evening prayers. Even these were taught him and supervised by servants like Alice Truro.

But then, Wendell Courtney showed very little interest of any kind in the boy he claimed was the son of a niece (until a year before his death, when he told Jimmy and a few others the truth—to the extent of admitting paternity but refusing to divulge the name of the mother). For his first five years of life Jimmy shared a room with whoever was his nurse-governess, played only occasionally with other children, associated mainly with the servants, saw "Da-Da"—later "Uncle Wendell," later still simply "Wendell"—infrequently. And he had his nightly dreams that Leatrice Joy was his mother.

James Courtney reached the age of six in 1928. The Los Angeles school system had seized upon the relatively new and radical "intelligence-quotient testing" device as the ultimate educational panacea. Children were given Stanford-Binet tests to determine their "mental age" and were placed in schools (and often promoted through the grades) on the basis of the results they obtained.

Jimmy Courtney scored a genius-level 154 on his first IQ test. It was recommended that he start in the third grade at the Rio Vista grammar school, which had special "Opportunity A" classes for exceptionally gifted children. Wendell Courtney praised the boy, agreed with the recommendation, and Jimmy was chauffeured to and from the school daily.

The principle of "Opportunity A" teaching was to give pupils an almost entirely free rein. There was little formal teaching—the youngsters were supposed to become interested in subjects on their own, and largely learn by themselves. Jimmy Courtney, among children more or less his own age for the first time, was at a loss for weeks. Then he gravitated toward the clique formed by the more rebellious boys. Nature had endowed him with a lithe, excellent physique. He thought fast, moved fast, was good at outdoor games and sports—and had discovered that he wanted to lead rather than be led. This led to fights. At the beginning, he was usually beaten. Then, gradually, he learned how to win, and it was Wendell Courtney who taught him how.

Wendell took notice of Jimmy's bruises and—as it happened—black eye one day.

"Don't ever tell anybody, but I grew up in Hell's Kitchen," Wendell told him. "There we knew enough to fight dirty—the dirtier the better."

He spent a few hours with Jimmy over the next week, teaching him the rudiments of street fighting. Jimmy learned fast—and too well. Near the end of his second semester, he split another boy's skull with a piece of brick. Wendell took him out of school, hired tutors for him. They came and they went. James Courtney learned what he could from them, but he was already thinking ahead. Far ahead.

"Uncle Wendell, I'd like to go into your business."

It was April 2, 1935, James Courtney's thirteenth birthday.

Wendell Courtney did not know whether to laugh or be stern and angry. He compromised, spoke evenly.

"I am not in a business, Jimmy. I'm a minister of the gospel and the head of a religious group."

"Nuts! You're like the Ballards and Aimee—"

"Wait a minute, boy. Where did those ideas come from?"

"I read. I've gone to I Am meetings and other places that're supposed to be churches—"

"My God!" Wendell could not help but laugh now. The boy was bright and surprisingly mature. He felt a surge of pride (that he dared not show) that this was his son, so very like him—like he had been when the same age. "All right. Let's say, for the sake of argument, that it is a business. What do you like about it?"

James Courtney's features were already angular, and his eyes—blue like Wendell's, but even paler—were already capable of speaking volumes by their expression. They were shrewd, calculating now as he replied:

"I like the money. You make a lot—and it's easy, not the way it is for most people. Everyone's talking about the depression. You'd never know there was one around here."

"Just the money?" Wendell asked, sensing there was more and the boy was holding back. He was right.

"You get all the tail you can handle," Jimmy blurted.

"Well, I'll be damned!" Wendell threw back his head and guffawed. He laughed until tears came into his eyes. He dabbed them away with a white lawn pocket handkerchief, asked: "Have you gotten yourself laid yet?"

"No. Only fooled around, had the girls jack me off."

"Jimmy, much as I hate the goddamned Jews"—Wendell was a virulent anti-Semite in private, which he dared not be in public—"they're right about one thing. When a boy reaches thirteen, he's a man. I'm going to buy you an extra thirteenth-birthday present."

Wendell drove the big green Packard up Beechwood Drive into the Hollywood Hills. He stopped in front of a mock-Moorish palace complete with crenellated tower that was located between a mock-French château and a house that tried to be an imitation of nothing—or everything at once. He got out, started toward the door. Jimmy followed, his look at once eager and determined.

Wendell Courtney was obviously known to the madam, but she did not address him by name. But she saw the boy and instantly knew what was wanted. She led them into a sitting room. Moments later a trio of young women entered—they wore cliché negligees. Jimmy had an instant erection: the third girl, although her hair was dark rather than light, bore a faint resemblance to Leatrice Joy.

"I'd like you," he mumbled, nodding his head toward her—his manner that of a man who had been in whorehouses often before. "Okay with you, uh,"—he decided to omit the "Uncle"—"Wendell?"

"Sure. What's your name, honey?" He directed the question at the girl. She said it was Naomi, smiled at Jimmy, and held a hand out to him.

It was an expensive bordello; the upstairs bedroom was tastefully decorated and furnished, the turned-down bed large and inviting. James Courtney stood in the middle of the room, not moving, his pale blue eyes fixed on Naomi's face.

She smiled professionally, asked, "Want me to undress you?"

"Yes. While I'm lying in bed." Jimmy started toward it.

"Hey, your shoes."

"I want you to take those off, too."

"On the bed?"

"Please."

He lay down in the fetal position and hugged a pillow to him.

"Straighten your legs so I can get at the shoes," the girl said.

"You pull them straight and make me turn over." His eyes were closed, locked tight, and he spoke into the pillow.

"God, you're awful young to be kinky. All right, here."

She pulled his legs straight, eased him over on his back, removed shoes and socks, started to undo his trousers, stopped.

"I don't believe it!" she exclaimed, grasping his erect penis through the fabric of his trousers. "Your cock—it's huge."

"Take my clothes off."

She did, gently, tenderly, as though he was a small child, for she was now aware that it was what he desired. His sex, massive in its erection, throbbed and strained even larger in response. He had flung the pillow aside, but his eyes remained closed and his right hand, clenched into a fist, was pressed against his mouth. But the lips moved; he seemed to be mumbling. The girl leaned closer to hear, then gave up the effort, for it sounded as though he was repeating "Fuck Jesus" over and over, and she knew it could not be that. She slipped off her negligee, draped it over a chair. Her body was good, fresh. She sat on the edge of the bed, offered her firm breasts, their pink nipples sharp, by brushing them against his face. He shook his head in refusal. She got up on the bed, knees straddling his thighs.

She began lowering her body to impale herself on the rigid column of his penis. Again he shook his head. He reached out blindly with his hands—Naomi saw they were long, slender, but splayed at the tips—groped at empty air, finally found her lips, thrust and pinched at them. She understood, rolled away, twisted around on her haunches. Fondling his scrotum and testicles gently, she bent her head low.

Jimmy's eyes remained shut, but inner vision held a sharp-focused image of the woman who had taken him from Alice Truro and held him in her arms. Her figure was surrounded by an aura of multicolored light, reds and greens predominating, and she was reaching for him as she always did. He called her all the secret names he had for her, not aloud, but inside himself, reciting them over and over, savoring them, praying that she would . . .

She did.

Naomi took the boy's sex in her mouth, made of it a sheath that had a life of its own. He gasped, then groaned as if in agony and seized her head with both hands, forced it down farther, his exploding penis stabbing deeper, impelled by violent upward thrusts of his hips.

The groan subsided. His hands fell limp to his sides, his body slumped down in the bed. He opened his eyes slowly. That made the image vanish. He closed them once more. The image refused to return. He opened them again and saw the girl. She no longer resembled Leatrice Joy. She no longer resembled anyone. Not even herself, he thought, and was seized by a fear-filled fury he could not understand, did not try to understand, and his actions were reflexive, not governed by conscious will. He sat bolt upright, right hand clenched into a fist swinging back across his chest, then lashing out as if spring-loaded. The fist smashed into Naomi's mouth and chin, both still wet with his semen. She screamed, leaped off the bed.

Jimmy felt his stomach churn and the surging rise of vomit. It spewed from his mouth, over his body and the bedclothes. The girl screamed again, angrily now, cursing him, he supposed. He was still retching, and unable to stop, and he could hear the pound of running feet.

Wendell Courtney and the madam burst into the room. Naomi screeched out her story. Wendell seized Jimmy, dragged him off the bed, began to give him a vicious beating.

". . . damned pervert . . . sadist . . . should kill you . . ."

The women watched—and laughed. And hit Jimmy too.

Shame and humiliation planted the first seeds of paranoia. Jimmy sought shelter in his own ego by thinking that Uncle Wendell and the women had somehow conspired together, created the situation, made him do what he did, then taken enjoyment out of beating him—and, worse, out of making him an object of contempt and loathing.

The boy had never previously given much thought to how he felt about his Uncle Wendell. He guessed he had a liking for the man. After all, Wendell Courtney was his closest—his only—relative, provided a home, paid for food, clothes, tutors, all the rest. Now there was a change—sudden, radical, irrevocable. Jimmy knew that he hated his Uncle Wendell. The hatred was to grow over the years, and when Wendell, in the last year of his life, told the boy the truth, the hatred became poisonous, murderous.

Wendell made the servants keep Jimmy out of his sight for many weeks after the bordello incident. Although the boy would have dearly loved to be with a woman again, there was no way he could. Guilt-shame feelings kept him from resuming sexual experiments with girls his own age in the neighborhood. He was left to seek—and find—outlet, both physical and emotional, at night when he lay in bed in the fetal position, his eyes closed, alone with his fantasy-image Madonna.

Eventually Wendell Courtney relented, but only to a degree. He would talk to the boy. The conversations were always brief, devoid of warmth, impersonal, and never without Wendell's scorn and contempt for Jimmy showing through. This fed Jimmy's hatred, increased his sense of alienation, and intensified the conviction that Wendell was his enemy—a devious, treacherous enemy waiting for the first opportunity to hurt and debase him further.

Tutors changed every six months or so. Jimmy knew that each, during his tenure, made periodic reports to Wendell about the progress his ward/grand-nephew was making. The boy reasoned that if tutors reported about one thing, they talked about other matters that concerned him. This made them Wendell's allies, co-conspirators, spies. He was careful to make friends with none and avoided any extraneous conversations to prevent the informants from knowing how he really thought and felt. He concentrated on his lessons and excelled, learning at a rate that astounded those who taught him.

The servants, sensing their employer's continuing coolness toward Jimmy, feared that they might jeopardize their jobs by being too friendly with the boy and treated him with polite reserve. All but Harold Mitchell—whom everyone called "Mitch" —who had been Wendell's relief-chauffeur/general-handyman for less than a year. Mitch was young—in his mid-twenties—a rawboned former machinist who, because of the depression, was unable to find any other work. Harold "Mitch" Mitchell—physically tough, shrewd, cunning—befriended the youngster, called him "Jim" rather than "Jimmy," talked to him as a man rather than as a boy. He taught "Jim" about mechanical things, how to handle tools. In December, Mitch—using his Model A Ford for the purpose—taught Jim how to drive, then let him take the car for short drives by himself. James Courtney regarded the handyman-chauffeur with hero-worshiping adulation.

On a Saturday afternoon in February 1936, the boy helped Mitchell wax and polish the Reverend Courtney's Packard and Buick cars. Afterward they went to Mitchell's quarters above the garage. Mitch opened bottles of beer, gave Jim one, easily turned their conversation to women and sex. Having drunk a bottle of beer, Jim stammered out a confession of what had happened in the whorehouse. Mitch gave him a second beer, showed sympathy and understanding—and it all came tumbling out. About the Leatrice Joy fantasy. How she always appeared wondrously dressed and surrounded by an aura of multicolored light.

"You need another try with a dame," Mitch said. "I'll fix it."

Harold Mitchell occasionally took Jimmy to the movies at night. It was the pretext given a few days later—they were going to see a movie at the Carthay Circle theater. Instead, they drove to downtown Los Angeles, to the Mexican quarter around Olvera Street. The house, a few blocks from the phallic tower of City Hall, was old, small, one-storied, shabby—totally unlike the bordello in the Hollywood Hills—and there was only one woman inside it. Her face—what Jim Courtney could see of it—bore no resemblance to that of Leatrice Joy, but that did not matter. His penis sprang erect instantly.

"This is Lupe, Jim—an old pal of mine," Mitch said. He gave the Mexican girl an approving wink. Lupe had followed instructions exactly. She wore a colorful flamenco skirt, frilled blouse, and white lace mantilla. There were candles burning on a mantelpiece; she stood in front of them. The effect was to make her clothing seem iridescent, glowing with colored light.

"Go on with Lupe," Mitch said. "I'll wait out here."

He waited two hours. Lupe, now in a shapeless plum-colored rayon wrapper, emerged from the bedroom, lit a cigarette, grinned. The boy had made no violent moves—and was drained, she reported.

"He'll be okay now, I think—a big *toro*. He came five times—maybe six."

During the days that followed, Jim repeatedly begged Mitch to take him to the girl again. Mitchell would shake his head regretfully. Lupe charged five dollars. He had paid the first time, but could not afford to pay again. The boy went to Wendell with a contrived tale of needing ten dollars for books.

"You're lying," his Uncle Wendell said, and went on to point out that Jimmy received $1.50 weekly allowance, and his books could be bought on charge. "Now, run along—leave me alone." The reverend was anything but generous with money—except when spent on himself.

Mitchell commiserated and agreed to put up another five dollars. He said it was a strain on his finances—which was true enough, for in addition to the above-garage quarters and the privilege of taking meals with the other servants, he received only sixty dollars a month in pay.

Jim's second visit to Lupe was even more gratifying than the first. So much so that the olive-skinned young woman with high, prominent cheekbones supplanted Leatrice Joy in his masturbatory fantasies. He would have liked to visit Lupe twice, three times a week—every night—and said as much to Mitchell.

Over the ensuing weeks, Mitch guided their conversation to

the subject of Reverend Wendell Courtney and what Mitchell called "his religious racket." Jimmy had long since recognized it as a business, readily agreed it was a racket, an outright swindle that netted his uncle huge sums, and Mitch would remind him that:

"He fucks himself blind, too—gets paid for it. And he won't pop a lousy fin for you."

Jim Courtney was the first to mention the safe in the reverend's study—as Mitchell had hoped he would and intended he should.

"It's behind that altar he has," the boy went on, "and filled with cash that he doesn't want to deposit in banks."

"You've seen the dough?"

"I've been in there with him a few times when he opened the safe. Funny, he keeps it almost open—"

"How the hell can you keep a safe *almost* open?"

"The combination has three numbers. He just keeps the lock two clicks from the last number . . ."

The boy stopped, stared at Mitchell, his thin lips twisting into a knowing grin.

"Right or left?" Mitchell demanded, grabbing Jim's wrist.

The grin shaded from the knowing to the sly. "I can't remember, Mitch. I'd have to think." Jim extricated his wrist, and he did begin thinking. Now that the idea had been born and verbalized, he could do it himself. But then, it was far wiser to stay clear, let Harold Mitchell take the risks of being caught in the act—or identified and apprehended later. But there was an even better, more tempting, and, all things considered, entirely risk-free variation on the theme.

"Suppose I remember, Mitch? How much would be mine?"

"Well, kid, since I'll be taking all the chances . . . say, twenty percent—that'll give you lots of fives for Lupe."

"Half!" It was an animal growl, and Harold Mitchell was the first person ever to see the icy, menacing, wholly ruthless look with which James Philip Courtney would later intimidate—even terrify—his adversaries in business deals.

Mitchell did a double-take, grinned inwardly—the boy was not yet fourteen, he reminded himself—and said, "Sure . . . half. Even split." He had no intention of keeping the bargain. Once he had the money, he would leave—and leave the kid holding an empty bag. "You remembered yet whether it's right or left?"

"Not yet. I remembered something else, though. There's a big, heavy pickproof Diebold on the study door. He locks that all the way, Mitch, whenever he leaves the house.'' The boy was playing with Mitchell, who, of course, failed to realize it.

''Oh, Christ,'' Mitch groaned, his face falling. ''Can't bust the door down.''

''I know where he keeps a spare key.''

''Where?'' Mitchell blurted—and finally began to comprehend that the youngster might be his match.

''I'd be an asshole to tell you, now, wouldn't I, Mitch?''

''Hey, we're partners—you've got to trust me.''

''I will—when it's the right time to trust you.''

Southern California has always had an Easter Sunday hang-up, marking the day with Hollywood-style showmanship and fanfare. Each year, there were elaborate—according to traditional newspaper billing, ''star-studded''—Easter sunrise services in places like the Hollywood Bowl and on Mount Rubidoux near San Bernardino. All-night vigils and sunrise services on somewhat lesser scale were offered by hundreds of churches of every Christian denomination and by cult groups of all kinds. The Reverend Wendell Courtney's Soul-Search Center annually held services that began at midnight and continued through with ''Ethereal Introspections'' to a ''Resurrection Love Feast'' at sunrise.

In 1936, Easter Sunday fell on April 12. It was, Jimmy argued, the very best time. Ideal. Wendell would be gone from midevening Saturday until midmorning Sunday. He was certain to leave the safe ''almost open,'' because, returning to the house tired and sleepless, he would want to put the always-huge Easter collection into the safe before going to bed. As for the servants, all but one or at most two would go to their own Easter services, and those who remained home would be in bed.

''Too bad we can't get the Easter collection too,'' Mitch grumbled.

''Are you crazy? He'll be home. The servants will be back—and suppose with all that extra money in the safe, he locks the safe all the way.''

Mitchell grudgingly admitted that Jim was right—and in a burst of generosity drove him to Olvera Street and on to Lupe's, paying the woman's five-dollar fee.

Wendell Courtney and his regular chauffeur left for Soul-Search Center at nine-thirty on Saturday night, April 11, Harold Mitchell, having told everyone he was coming down with a cold, went to his quarters, stayed there. Other members of the household staff drifted off—to churches or bed. Jim Courtney waited until those who had gone to bed were asleep, left his room in the rear of the second floor, went to Wendell's bedroom. The spare key was where he knew it would be—tucked under a huge, ornate copy of Manly P. Hall's *Encyclopedic Outline of Masonic, Hermetic, Rosicrucian, and Cabalistic Philosophy,* which he had never opened, but kept lying flat under a pile of other books on a bookcase shelf.

In his stocking feet, Jimmy made no sound going downstairs. The large cloth sack he had acquired days before was neatly folded, thrust into his trouser pocket. He unlocked the study door, went inside, locked the door behind him. The Reverend Courtney's private altar—an intricately carved wooden piece with an assortment of crucifixes, ivory statuettes of Buddha, Kwan Yin, and other esoteric deities atop it—was at the far end of the room. Jim switched on one small lamp—like an electric votive light. It provided adequate illumination, for he knew his way.

The safe behind the altar was smallish, squat. Jimmy knelt on one knee, held his breath, and mentally crossed his fingers. Two clicks to the right—and here's hoping he hasn't changed it or decided to twirl the knob. He reached out, the splayed tips of his fingers touched the combination knob, held it delicately—then, hearing a sound he could not immediately identify, jerked his hand away and froze, heart pounding. The sound was that of a car backing out of a nearby driveway. He breathed relief, took hold of the knob again . . .

One right.

His hands had begun to sweat. He bit his lips.

Two right.

He tried the handle. It gave. The safe door swung open.

The money was in banded packets—fives, tens, twenties, even fifties. Jimmy pulled the sack from his pocket. He did not count—not then—scooped the money into the sack. All of it.

Then he reached back into the sack, and now he did count, taking out banded packets, replacing them in the safe. When he had returned three thousand dollars, he used his handkerchief to wipe metal surfaces clean, held the handkerchief over his hand while he closed the safe door and turned the knob two clicks to the left, wiped some more, stood up, carrying the sack in one hand.

He went out carefully, wiping everything he had touched—even the switch on the little lamp, which he left burning. He locked the door, returned to his bedroom, shoved the bulging sack between his bedspring and mattress, made adjustments so it would lie there flat and invisible. That done, he stood stock-still, listening. There was no sound save for a distant, muffled snore.

Jimmy grinned, once again went downstairs, through the house, and to a side door. He opened it slightly, whistled. Harold Mitchell had been waiting eagerly for the whistle and came out of his quarters—like the boy, in his stocking feet—sprinted across the concrete driveway, and slipped into the house.

"Here." Jimmy handed Mitch the door key. They went to the study together. Mitch unlocked and opened the door. They went inside. Jimmy kept his hands in his pockets. He saw Mitchell frowning at the small lamp, said: "He always keeps it on at night—says it gives a nice religious touch."

The lie held. Jim guided Mitchell behind the altar, pointed at the safe, put his hand back into his pocket.

"Go ahead, kid," Mitch growled. "Open the fucking thing."

"I'm afraid I might mess it up. Two right."

"You're sure about that. Two right?"

"Yes." The boy nodded vigorously. "Hurry, huh?"

Mitchell knelt as Jimmy had, muttered beneath his breath, turned the knob. "Click," he said hoarsely, "and click. God help your ass if this isn't . . ."

But he had the safe door open. He peered inside. The light from the lamp was dim, barely reached behind the altar. He took out the banded packets, peered further. Then he started pawing inside the safe. His hands encountered account books, files, packets of documents. He swept these all out on the floor, continued pawing.

"What's wrong, Mitch?"

"There!" Mitch jabbed a finger at the packets of money. "That's what's wrong, you stupid little shit! I figured there'd be twenty, thirty grand in here . . ."

"How much is there?"

"Son of a bitch!" Mitchell pawed through the bundles of currency, his face growing ugly, venomous. "About three thousand . . ."

"If that's all there is—well, it's still money." Jim braced himself; the next few seconds would be crucial. "Better than nothing. Just give me my half . . ."

He bent down toward Mitchell, hoping. His hopes were realized.

"Give you half?" the man snarled, and he slammed Jimmy's head against the steel frame of the safe. "I'll give you shit."

Jim Courtney knew he would have a large bruise, but thought a little blood would be better. "I want it. You promised!" He grabbed for a packet of twenties. Mitchell hurled him away. His cheek scraped against the angular edge of the safe door. The steel cut deep. He had his blood—it was running down his right cheek.

"Get out of my way!" Mitch rasped. He kicked Jim aside—and he was gone.

James Courtney stayed where he lay, counting off the minutes. He knew Mitchell had packed his belongings into the Model A Ford earlier—that was his plan, to be ready to clear out and keep going after "they" took the money.

At last he heard the distinctive sound of a Model A engine and Mitchell driving off. He stood up, went to the open study door, and shouted, "Help, I'm hurt," to awaken the servants who were sleeping in, returned to the study, picked up the telephone there, calmly dialed the Wilshire precinct.

"This is the Reverend Wendell Courtney's residence. The house has been robbed."

Police came quickly. The Reverend Courtney was an important personage who had many influential friends. Jimmy Courtney, blood pouring from his cheek, told the story he had rehearsed to himself—and would repeat many times that night and in later days.

"I was reading in my room and heard noises downstairs. I thought I'd better take a look around. Mitch—he's my uncle's assistant chauffeur—was in the study. He was going through the safe. I tried to stop him. I think he wanted to kill me."

A police ambulance rushed him to Georgia Street Receiving Hospital, where eleven stitches were needed to close the deep gash on his cheek. He insisted on returning home. A police car took him. By then the Reverend Courtney had been informed, and leaving his flock in the midst of their Ethereal Introspections, went to his house.

Police officers told him about the boy's courage and bravery. He seemed pleased by that, in somewhat of a quandary when asked how much money had been taken. Wendell could not admit that he, a minister of the gospel, was in the habit of keeping twenty-five thousand dollars—cash—in his safe.

"A few thousand—I'm not certain how much," he said finally. "You see, I have the money on hand to help parishioners or other deserving people in need. I give it out, don't keep very close track, I'm afraid. Now, if you'll excuse me, I must return to the Center—we're having Easter services."

Jimmy, face heavily bandaged, went to his room, slept soundly. The next morning he counted the loot—twenty-two thousand dollars—and hid it under pried-up floorboards in his closet. He was exultant. He could afford to visit Lupe—or any other whore—as often as he wished and still have a fortune left to be hoarded against the day when he would leave Wendell Courtney's house and strike out on his own.

Police had the description and license number of Harold Mitchell's Model A which the state highway patrol spotted and stopped near San Luis Obispo on Easter Sunday afternoon. Mitchell still had some $2,900 of the stolen money—and the key to the study door, which he had evidently dropped into his pocket and forgotten about. He was returned to Los Angeles, booked, questioned by detectives.

"The kid was in it with me," he tried to tell them. "He got the key, told me about the combination."

They refused to believe him and were infuriated by his attempt to implicate the boy. After several beefy patrolmen dragged him into an empty cell and worked him over for an hour, Mitchell realized it was wiser to accept full blame himself. Later, on the advice of a public defender assigned to his case, he pleaded guilty to robbery and assault with intent to kill and threw himself on the mercy of the court. Superior Court Judge Edgar Barish was not overly inclined to be merciful. He gave Harold Mitchell a 10-to-21-year sentence in the state penitentiary.

The stitches were removed from Jim Courtney's cheek. The wound healed, leaving a diagonal scar. Wendell Courtney offered to pay for a plastic-surgery operation to eliminate the scar. Jimmy refused. He wore it with pride—but not of the sort others imagined. To him it was proof of triumph over heavy odds—and forever an assuring reminder that he could think better and faster than anyone else.

12

Neil Harkness put the typed pages aside and scanned the dark, open sea. It was calm, empty. Not a light showed anywhere within his vision range. He checked the radar. Nothing. The *Deirdre* apparently had a huge segment of the Mediterranean to herself.

Rubbing at nearly a day's growth of wiry beard stubble, Neil turned to Kenneth Dixon, who now sat in the other captain's chair on the bridge. "This guy Mitchell," he said. "I take it he's the ex-chauffeur who claimed that Wendell used J.P. as his pratboy."

Dixon nodded affirmatively. Neil grimaced. "Then it's evident he lied out of spite. So obvious that I can't figure why you bothered bringing it up at all."

"Because some other people made the same charge," Ken said. "You'll run across references later."

"Later is right." Harkness made no effort to suppress a gigantic yawn. "I'm beat. You in any condition to stand watch while I grab a nap?"

"Sure." Dixon, vitalized by their conversation, memories and ideas tumbling through his brain, was very much awake and alert. "Take as long as you want."

Neil slid out of his chair, went below. Ken took his place, punched up a computer recording-log reading. The vessel was more than a hundred nautical miles out from Cabo Verde. He glanced at the digital clock mounted on the instrument panel just as the figures changed from 03:59:59 to 04:00:00. Four o'clock and all's well, Dixon said silently. But nothing is, he thought. Nothing has been for a hell of a long time—and maybe never will be again. He gazed out at the white-froth V the *Deirdre*'s bow was cutting in the water. He began brooding, as he so often did. He felt very much alone. He wished that he dared break the promise to Harkness and have a drink. He wished that he had not made the dangerous mistakes that made a few days' absence from Spain imperative. He wished that, imperatives or not, he had stayed home. He did not think of his wife at all.

But Vivian Dixon was thinking about her husband. Or rather, sleeping fitfully in her bedroom, she was having the explicit, recurrent nightmares in which Ken Dixon and Jim Courtney were central figures—and she and numbers of other people were supporting characters. Vivian twisted and turned on her bed, and occasionally she would whimper softly and cup her hands protectively over her breasts.

A few miles away, Sybil Pearson slept too, but she had no nightmares or dreams of any sort. Her sleep was leaden, drugged, REM-less. Tense and upset after speaking to Neil Harkness on the telephone, she had first tried to unwind and make herself drowsy with a large glass of Fundador, then gone to bed. The brandy had given her a steel-band headache, and then she had taken two aspirin and a Seconal.

The vast chamber—modeled after the Hall of the Ambassadors in the Alhambra—that was James Courtney's Montemar bedroom blazed with light. Although Courtney lay on the great couch—circular and nine feet in diameter—which served as his bed, he was awake and giving no thought to sleep.

Kristin Verkerk had given herself the second injection and, in an erotic frenzy, spread her legs wide to begin playing the game with the gold coins Courtney was spreading out on the bedsheet. There were twenty of them.

"You can start," Courtney said, eyes hungry and penis distended again. The fourth time that night, he mused. How many other men stayed as virile after reaching sixty?

Kristin was spreading her legs further, easing herself down onto the couch in a split. "What's the record?" she asked.

"Someone once managed to pick up and hold nine."

She laughed. "I've got one already." He held the speculum out to her. She shook her head vigorously, causing her breasts to bob. "I don't want to look until I have more. Who was it that got the nine?"

"Never mind." Courtney had reasons for not wanting to be further reminded of Eileen Marsh.

Four A.M. Spanish time is only ten P.M. of the previous evening in New York City—and still an early evening hour by the standards of many New Yorkers, Eileen Marsh among them.

Eileen Marsh's day had been long and trying, because Evan Gerlach insisted that she make the initial approaches to James Courtney's Manhattan attorneys by herself, on her own.

"They'll think it's all your idea and no one is in it with you," Gerlach had argued. "Whatever reactions you get will give us leads on how to proceed with the next step."

The argument was convincing, and she had gone alone. The attorneys had been noncommittal—but they did appear worried under their suave veneers, Eileen thought—and had said they would have to consult with their client.

"We'll hold a telephone conference with Mr. Courtney in Spain and get back to you in a day—or two at the most, Miss Marsh."

Eileen relayed the information to Evan Gerlach at his apartment.

He said he had some things to take care of but would pick her up at her St. Regis Hotel suite . . .

". . . around nine, nine-thirty. We'll have dinner. I'll reserve a table at Grenouille."

Eileen was dressed and ready by nine. She spent the next half-hour drinking half a bottle of Taittinger. Then, piqued, she telephoned Gerlach's residence. She assumed he was on the way to the hotel, finished the bottle of champagne. At ten, she wondered if he meant for her to meet him at Grenouille and telephoned the restaurant—and was informed that no reservation had been made in his name.

Bitch-anger rising, Eileen paced the sitting-room floor, furiously smoking one Nat Sherman king-size after another. Until the door buzzer sounded. She strode angrily to the door, flung it open.

"Goddammit!" she began, then stopped. It wasn't Gerlach. She had never seen the man before.

"Good evening, Miss Marsh." He smiled pleasantly and was inside the sitting room and closing the door before she could speak. The smile stayed as he whipped something out of his jacket pocket.

"Who . . . ?" Eileen Marsh was about to ask the predictable questions, but she felt something—like a pinprick, but where, she thought, mind already fogging, knees giving out.

She slumped to the carpet, asleep. Forever.

The man stepped around her body, began searching the suite and doing a meticulous job of it. Whatever he touched and moved, he replaced exactly as it had been. At 12:15 A.M. he found what he sought, took it, made a last inspection to make certain that he had left no traces and, at 12:25 A.M., left the suite.

Neil Harkness had a built-in alarm mechanism. Having told Ken Dixon he would sleep only two hours or so, he awoke at 0600, shaved, took a superfast shower. Throwing on clothes—the inevitable khaki slacks and T-shirt—he went to the superbly equipped galley. By 0635 he came on the bridge carrying a tray with plates of scrambled eggs, toast, mugs, and a two-liter pot of coffee.

Since the *Deirdre* was headed almost directly east, the newly risen sun was blazing its rays straight into the bridge—and into Ken Dixon's eyes, which were red-rimmed and drooping. Neil set the tray down, said, " 'Morning, you dumb jerk," and reached past Ken to a switch on the instrument panel. The glare of sunlight became muted as glare-proof glass rolled up into place. "I brought us our *desayuno*—you can eat and then bunk down yourself."

Harkness carried his food and filled coffee mug to the helm, took the captain's chair as Dixon vacated it, and moved off to take his own breakfast from the tray. Neil took a large swallow of coffee, made an inspection of his instruments and electronic devices. All were in order and functioning perfectly. The radar screen showed a medium-freighter-sized blip moving south about ten miles off the port side, one or two smaller blips closer, but heading northwest. The sky was clear save for much scattered white cumulus.

Neil increased speed to twenty-five knots, reset computer and autopilot, reached for toast with one hand, forked scrambled eggs with the other.

"When do you expect to make Venice?" Ken asked through a mouthful of food.

"Sometime tomorrow—depends on how hard I want to push," Neil replied. "Fact is, I'm beginning to think I should slip in there in the middle of the night."

"Suits me . . . but any particular reason?"

"Only that my daylight experiences with my friend Fischer haven't been too pleasant." Harkness grinned. "Hunch tells me that it's safer to operate in darkness, since I'm already operating in the dark."

"You really don't know what you're supposed to do in Venice?"

"Except to meet Fischer, I haven't a clue. Say you were using this for a novel—like you started the other night—what would you have me do there?"

"Simple. Backtrack a minute. You got Fischer through to Tangier. But there were hassles. The Chris-Craft, the guys supposed to be customs agents. So our friend God gets nervous. He tells Fischer to sneak into Venice, promises to send you to take him someplace else. Of course, God tells Fischer where someplace is, and Fischer tells you."

"And then we'll travel happily together forever after."

"Like the Flying Dutchman." Dixon nodded.

Neil lit his third cigarette of the morning. He'd smoked two while preparing breakfast.

"Cheerful thought," he growled through a haze of cigarette smoke. He filled his lungs again. "Be housemaid, huh? Leave the coffee and my mug and take the rest below—and sack out."

"I will in a minute. Not yet." Ken poured himself more coffee. "You intend reading any more of that material?" He pointed to the stapled sheets folded down their middle lengthwise and propped against the marine radiotelephone near Neil's left elbow.

"Figured I'd skim through it while you're sleeping." Harkness nodded. "Your encyclopedic outline—God, but that was some book title you had in there."

"You mean the Manly P. Hall book? That's legit."

"You've got to be kidding."

"Sailor, that *Encyclopedic Outline of et cetera et cetera Philosophy* sold for a hundred bucks a copy in the 1930's, and went through several printings before the end of the forties."

"Be damned. Who bought it?"

"You'll be surprised. New York Public Library, William Randolph Hearst, Eleanor Roosevelt—and from them right on down to lunatic-fringe kooks. Not to forget James P. Last time I was in his study—late in 1970—he had a copy there."

"Probably the one Wendell had."

"Nope. His own. Actually, if you go through his library, you'll see he has practically every book ever printed in English that mentions the cabala."

"That's funny. J.P. a student of Jewish mysticism and occultism?"

"Jewish everything—Talmud, Torah, the works. Has a thousand, maybe more, books on Judaism, Jewish customs and traditions."

"Think he might have wanted to convert?" Neil asked.

"No. Being the kind of character he is, if Courtney wants to do anything, he does it."

"Well, he did do a lot for Jews after the war, I guess. Ever see that gold medal on his desk?"

"The one encased in Lucite? Often." Dixon rubbed at his burning eyes. "He once made a big thing out of showing it to me—B'nai B'rith gave it to him. He worked his ass off for Jewish refugees, helping them get out of DP camps and over to the States."

Harkness scowled, held out his empty mug. Ken filled it with more coffee from the pot. Neil was pensive as he drank.

"Hard to picture J.P. as an altruist," he muttered.

"Almost impossible," Dixon agreed, "only in this instance it's a matter of record that he was. Newspaper and magazine articles, statements by public figures."

"Maybe he had an attack of remorse," Neil suggested.

"Not so anyone noticed."

"Try this for size. There's a war. He goes in the Army and is scared shitless of being killed. Like a few million other guys, he makes a deal with God. You keep me alive and I'll do this and that."

"I don't buy that, either."

"You must've formed some theory."

"Yes . . . and no." Ken started gathering up dishes and flatware and putting them on the tray. "I'm going below to grab some sleep. Talk to you later."

Harkness fired up a Celta, reached for the papers tucked next to the radiotelephone, picked up reading where he had left off.

13

Wendell Courtney knew there had been twenty-five thousand dollars in his safe and that less than three had been recovered from Harold Mitchell. He did not dare say anything to the police about the missing twenty-two thousand. All apparent evidence of his "nephew's" bravery notwithstanding, he had vague, unformed suspicions that the money had somehow found its way into the boy's hands. He knew the youngster was remarkably intelligent, and had already seen evidence of a hard, cynical, and avaricious streak in his makeup. Wendell doubted that the boy would break and reveal anything under direct questioning, so he took a roundabout approach.

"You acted like a brave man. From now on, you're Jim and I'm Wendell—drop the 'Uncle.' When I'm not home, you're the man in charge."

He continued to lavish praise on Jim—without effect. The boy said nothing that might support his suspicions. Wendell changed tack. The boy had broken once in a sexual situation, probably would again.

"I feel I owe you a reward, a debt of gratitude, Jim. Would you like to have a woman—not the same as before, of course. I'm sure it's been a very long time for you."

Jim Courtney was fully aware of the reason behind Wendell's archaeological expeditions into his mind. He had expected an invitation of the sort and was prepared. Lupe, the Mexican girl, was expendable.

"Not so long, Uncle—I mean Wendell. You see, Mitch and I got to be pretty good friends—or that's what I thought . . ."

The Reverend Courtney snapped alert. Now, he mused triumphantly, now it's coming out.

". . . and he took me a few times. He knew a woman near Olvera Street—but I'd like to again."

Wendell's thinking processes shifted direction. Just as Jim intended. The reverend seized on the notion that perhaps the boy was innocent of any wrongdoing and Mitchell had left the money with the woman. "Not the same woman—Olvera Street, she must be a Mexican—God only knows what you might get from a greaser whore." Wendell cleared his throat. "Think I'll do my civic duty and have County Health check her for V.D. Do you remember the woman's name and address?"

Jim said he knew her only as "Lupe," could not recall the address, but did describe her house and the side street on which it was located.

Wendell made no effort to notify the County Health Service, but retained private investigators.

Lupe was Mexican. Los Angeles law always followed the tenets set by such men as Police Chief James E. Davies and District Attorney Buron Fitts. The private investigators had no compunction about breaking a few of Lupe's teeth and tearing her home apart. They found $157.41.

"She must've sent the dough down to Mexico, Reverend," they reported. "It's what all the fucking greasers do."

Wendell Courtney acknowledged defeat, but vestiges of doubt about Jim would linger for the rest of his days. Even so, he kept his promise, took the boy to a bordello, and was much relieved when he created no problems. The next day, Jim exploited what he saw as his advantage, asked that his allowance be raised to five dollars weekly.

Wendell was incensed. The amount was too great, he said. There was still a depression. Grown men were still working for fourteen dollars a week. A man with eight dependents received only ninety-two dollars a month working for the WPA—and was glad to get it. Furthermore, his own financial situation was not such as to permit the increase.

Jim was prepared for this, too. "But then I wouldn't have to ask you for money for extras—like books. Or women." He intended to cautiously augment the allowance from his hoard cached under his closet floor—and Wendell would think the five dollars covered all expenditures. Wendell repeated that it was more than he could afford, and Jim fired his decisive weapon. Pale blue eyes wide—but not too wide—with innocence, he asked, "Gee, Wendell, was it the robbery? I mean, did Mitch get more than the three thousand?"

Wendell glared at him. The blue eyes remained even, innocent.

"Very well, five dollars," the reverend said—and while he paid the allowance every Monday morning, he barely spoke to Jim again for weeks.

Not that Jim Courtney minded. He came and went as he pleased. Movie-theater admissions were as low as twenty cents, bus and streetcar fares as little as five. With his new allowance, he could claim to be seeing a different film every night if anyone asked where he went after dark—but no one did.

Simple arithmetic told him that if he took twenty dollars a week from his loot for five years—the maximum he then planned to stay with Wendell—he would still have nearly seventeen thousand dollars left. He held himself to the limit of twenty dollars, then found himself spending considerably less each week—for, as he would later boast to a college classmate:

"I discovered I could get as much ass free as by paying for it."

Free, perhaps, but not without considerable difficulty. The era of the no-age-questions-asked hotel and motel had not dawned, and decades were to pass before the permissive parent emerged and allowed sex on the living-room sofa. In those days, Southern California youth usually had their sex in automobiles or on beaches or hillsides accessible only by automobile.

Passing his sixteenth birthday, the legal age for a driver's license, Jim approached Wendell during one of the periods when he was being reasonably tolerant and friendly.

"I'd like to buy a car," Jim announced. "A used car—nothing fancy." Before Wendell could protest, he added: "I found one for a hundred and twenty-five dollars. I have the money—saved it from my allowance." The good minister had little choice but to accede, and, because Jim was a minor, sign the necessary papers as his guardian.

The car was eight years old, a 1930 Nash convertible. Its fenders were crumpled, the body needed paint, but Jim had learned enough about cars from Harold Mitchell to know it was in excellent mechanical condition. He had the bodywork repaired, paying the cost from his secret hoard. He told Wendell he had done the work himself, at night and over weekends, in a garage owned by the father of one of his friends. Of this string of lies, the last was most blatant. Jim Courtney had no male friends. None.

* * *

There could be no more home tutoring for Jim. New rules required that he attend regular classes. Equivalency examinations indicated he had reached the educational level of a twelfth-grade student, but for some unexplained reason, Wendell Courtney balked at this. Jim Courtney was enrolled as a tenth-grade student in Hollywood High School. He began attending classes in September 1938. That was the month when, halfway around the world, Britain and France signed the Munich Pact that sanctioned Nazi Germany's dismemberment of Czechoslovakia.

Publicly, in the pulpit of his Soul-Search Center, the Reverend Wendell Courtney piously led prayers of gratitude that world peace had been maintained. At home, he gleefully exulted over Hitler's triumph, which, he told Jim, was:

"Another big step toward putting Yids in their place."

The youth countered that he could not see the connection. The Czechs were overwhelmingly Christian.

"Don't let that fool you. It's Hitler on one side. The Jews are behind everything that's on the other." Wendell sneered his distaste. "They're slime, the kikes. If I told you all the stories my Hollywood people tell me about Jews, you'd be sick to your stomach."

Anyone who had grown up even on the most remote fringes of the motion-picture industry—and Jim had—knew that cinema people could be divided into three groups. There were those who were Jewish. Then there were non-Jews who had few if any religious prejudices. Finally, there were those who, although they licked the boots of the Goldwyns, Mayers, Cohns, and the rest, were rabid anti-Semites.

"I don't have any feelings about them one way or another," Jim said. At that time, he didn't.

Young Courtney was ahead of his classmates, made superior marks without having to study. He thus had the time—to say nothing of the money and the car—to enjoy himself when most of his fellow students pored over homework. He had many girls. He drove them up Mulholland Drive to the Hollywood Dam or to Malibu Beach or Griffith Park—and was careful. He used condoms, and, sharing the belief of the time that 7-Up was a surefire supersafe contraceptive douche, carried bottles of the soft drink in the Nash.

Seeing a girl give herself a 7-Up douche always fascinated and excited him. She would uncap the bottle, then hold her thumb over the top, shake the bottle vigorously, squat on hillside or sand, ease the bottle neck into her vagina, taking her thumb off the top at the precise right instant. The contents would foam and gush up inside her.

Early in 1939, Jim had a number of dates with Marianne Fields. She was sixteen, blond, pretty, an eleventh-grader who lived on LaBrae but always met him in a drugstore two blocks from her family's home. They were, she said, strict about her going out with boys (she gave girlfriends' names as alibis), and she was very highly sexed, and while insisting that he wear a condom, disdained the 7-Up douche. "It's too messy," she declared.

Eventually Jim tired of Marianne, found other girls—and then one day she stopped him outside the school cafeteria. Ashen, trembling, Marianne said she was pregnant.

"You've been the only one for months. You have to do something."

Jim was at a total loss, went about in a state of dazed terror for a few days until the girl told him she had found a solution.

"I . . . I told a married woman I know. She knows where I can have it taken care of, but"—her voice broke—"it'll cost more money than—"

"Money?" Jim was a man being rescued from drowning. He imagined that she meant a few hundred dollars, instantly recovered his swagger. "Money's easy—how much?"

"Twenty-five hundred dollars, but he's a real doctor."

Swagger was replaced by disbelief and rage. That was one hundred and twenty-five times the twenty dollars he had been allowing himself. A fortune. And how could he admit having that much money?

"Maybe your uncle will help us," Marianne went on. Then, seeing from his expression that he rejected that possibility, her eyes narrowed. They were crafty, cunning he thought as he heard her say, "He's a minister and has that church the stars go to. He'd give you the money so there wouldn't be a scandal."

Jim Courtney gave her the money two days later. His own money—in a fury and with an awful hatred. She thrust an envelope into his hand. "Please mail this if anything happens to me during the operation."

He looked at the envelope. The names Saul and Miriam Feldman were written on it, then an address. On LaBrae. He read the names aloud, demanded: "Who the hell are these people?"

"My . . . my father and mother."

"Your name isn't Feldman."

"No. They let me change it when I started high school because . . . well, because it's so Jewish."

The thought that Wendell was right flared through Jim's mind. Jews were connivers, cheats, lying scum. Marianne had lied about her name. Probably about the price of the abortion. Perhaps even about being pregnant by him. Possibly even about being pregnant at all. He could have killed her but merely flung the envelope in her face and screamed "Kike whore!" and fled.

War began in Europe on September 1 of that same year, 1939. A week later, President Franklin Roosevelt declared a state of limited national emergency. The United States split into two camps. One (then a minority, but growing) was sympathetic to the Allies and argued that sooner or later America would have to enter the conflict. The other—larger and stridently vociferous—demanded that the United States stay out at all costs, isolate itself from Europe and its wars. Many in the latter category were admirers of Hitler and Nazism and hoped that Germany would win.

It is a matter of historical record that Southern California was among the hottest of the hotbeds of pro-Nazi sympathy. There were open Bund meetings, marches, and rallies. Organizations with such innocuous names as "The Young Patriots" and "Our Flag Only" proliferated, passed out anti-Semitic tracts, pro-Nazi propaganda, denounced Jews and *the* Jew, Franklin Roosevelt, spread hate, often incited riots. For whatever reason—and this, too, is a matter of historical record—a wholly disproportionate number of Southern California's cult leaders and their churches swung immediately to the pro-Nazi side. The Reverend Wendell Courtney and his Soul-Search Center were among them. Of course, they offered neat, pat rationalizations. England and France were decadent, corrupt. Germany was clean, the protector of Christian morality and Western civilization. And, naturally, the rationalizations were wrapped in red-white-and-blue, all the more so because the pro-Nazi elements were faced with a dilemma.

Germany and the Soviet Union had signed a pact. Hitler and Stalin were allies. American Communist-front organizations were also intent on keeping the nation neutral. To set themselves apart from the Reds, pro-Nazis spiced their propaganda with raucous patriotism. America First. Rearm to defend our shores and fight our enemies within. But send not one American boy abroad. Amen.

Under these developing conditions, the Reverend Wendell Courtney needed to protect himself from charges that he was an un-American peace-at-any-price pacifist, a coward. Especially since the charges might find substance if anyone looked up his World War One record—which would show that he had been a shirker, a draft dodger. Being past fifty, there was little Wendell could do personally. But as he led the "Articulate Meditations for Neutrality" in the Soul-Search Center, an idea formed.

"America must stay out of war, but also must stay militarily strong," he preached—and at home repeated the thesis to Jim as a preamble. "These are musts, my boy, musts," he declared, patting Jim's shoulder.

"My boy"? Shoulder-pattings? Jim Courtney was mystified. He had never been called "my boy" or had his shoulder patted by Wendell before. He wondered what the hell it was all about—what the reverend had in store for him. It seemed the reverend wished to deliver something akin to a sermon—another first, as far as Jim was concerned.

"My boy," Wendell repeated, cleared his throat. "Those who want peace when there are wars and rumors of wars are often labeled cowards or worse. Even as I speak up for isolationism, we must show that we love our country and are patriots."

The mid-sentence switch from first-person singular to plural was not lost on Jim. It confirmed that there was a catch coming.

"At my age, there isn't much I can do to give tangible proof of my patriotism," Wendell continued to orate. "But you, my . . . ah . . . nephew and sole relative, are young, a perfect physical specimen . . ."

Jim Courtney racked his brains but could not imagine where Wendell was leading, braced himself for unknown worsts, and nearly fragmented with laughter at the anticlimactic revelation.

". . . and I want you to join the ROTC at school."

For a moment Jim feared that his uncle had lost his mind. High-school Reserve Officers Training Corps units were bad jokes. Only two kinds of boys signed up for ROTC. Those who wanted to avoid regular physical education and sports (for which it was an elective substitute). And those so poor that they needed the uniforms the government provided to wear in place of ordinary clothing. At Hollywood High, the ROTC was a particularly rancid joke. By tradition, the ROTC cadets served as ushers and collection-takers at many film-industry-sponsored or -supported charity events and benefits. The boys skimmed from the collection plates. It was all organized, a sort of teenage uniformed Mafia led by whoever happened to be the "cadet battalion commander," who received fifty percent of the total, the res being split evenly among the others. Jim knew personally o ROTC boys who took collections at the Hollywood Bowl Easte sunrise services and netted fifty dollars during the night, a hug sum by their standards, laughably small—the risks considered—b his own.

"Me, in a stupid uniform?" Jim spluttered, unable to contair his laughter. "You can't be serious!"

"I am. It's a gesture. On some Sundays, you'll come to the Center in uniform and join the prayers. No, you'll *lead* them." Wendell was warming to fever pitch over his idea. "You—a youth already showing your willingness to defend your country, with my approval and blessing, of course, I'll make that clear— will lead the prayers. You'll pray that you and others like you will never have to take up arms and be slaughtered in foreign wars. I'll see that Marion Davies is in the congregation the first time—we'll get fantastic coverage in the Hearst papers."

"Not on a bet!" Jim sneered. "I wouldn't—"

"Not even for a new car?" Wendell asked quickly. "A . . . a new Ford V-8 convertible?"

Never had Wendell wanted anything from him so badly, Jim realized—and made the most of the unique opportunity.

"Not for a Ford, but I'll do business with you," he said. "Make it a Buick convertible and . . . oh, say, fifteen a week allowance, and you have a deal. I'll even play the fife and drum."

Wendell fumed, argued, but Jim was adamant and had his way.

Jim Courtney signed up for the ROTC training. Oddly enough, once he put on the uniform and had it tailored to fit perfectly, he rather liked it. And while he loathed having others bellow orders at him, Jim discovered that, sex and money aside, he loved nothing more than to snap out orders and see them obeyed. A hundred-dollar bribe bought him almost instant promotion to "cadet second lieutenant," which permitted him to wear a Sam Browne belt. He thought it made him look quite dashing. So did the girls who eagerly accepted rides to the Hollywood Dam, Malibu Beach, Griffith Park, or wherever in his magnificent new Buick convertible.

Jim kept his part of the bargain with Wendell. He did go to the Soul-Search Center in his uniform on numerous Sundays and led the prayers Wendell composed for him. They were ugly, hate-filled, the hate directed against Jews.

". . . We beseech Divine protection from the conspiracies of a mongrel race that would have us waste our lives in a cause not ours . . ."

". . . Save those who believe in Your Son, Jesus Christ. Smite those who killed him once and would kill Him again through our mortal bodies . . ."

The Reverend Wendell Courtney prospered mightily from the free-will offerings of his flock. These earnings were augmented by cash payments that flowed to the Center—and like cults—from the German consular offices of Nazi Captain Fritz Weidemann in San Francisco.

By early 1940 the lunatic fringes had grown too loud to be ignored by California law-enforcement agencies. The Los Angeles district attorney's office organized a small "Countersubversive Squad." Laws guaranteeing freedom of speech and religion being what they were, it could only gather information, take no action. The DA's new unit was headed by Al Meyers and Robert Singer, who—despite their names—were not Jewish. The squad began quiet investigations of both pro-Nazi and pro-Communist groups, pursuing them with equal vigor.

Singer stumbled across the money connection between the German consulate and Wendell Courtney. He confronted Courtney with the information. Although Wendell was aware that he could not be prosecuted, he feared public disclosure and ensuing scandal, severed all ties with the Germans, presented himself to the district attorney.

"It was all a terrible mistake—a misunderstanding on my part," he declared. He was a man of some influence, and the DA was content to believe him. Wendell went on to condemn all foreign isms, then said: "Really, you should expand, do more."

"Afraid we can't. There are no more public funds available."

Wendell fired the first shot in what he intended as a campaign to protect himself no matter what happened in the future, said: "Perhaps unpaid volunteers could be utilized."

"Nobody's volunteered, Reverend. The operation isn't liked by either left or right, and people in the middle don't give a damn."

"What if individuals did offer their services?"

"Decisions on that would have to come from upstairs."

Wendell paid a visit to Louis B. Mayer, who knew of his appeal to many in the film colony, knew little or nothing more about him. An archetypal movie mogul, Mayer was paranoid, saw subversives of one kind or other lurking behind every bush and tree. He wielded enormous political power in California, made and broke governors and mayors, engaged in many bizarre activities that had nothing to do with motion pictures.

"I propose to finance an experiment, provide the district attorney with volunteer undercover operatives," Wendell said. "Like the seditionists in our midst, these will be young patriotic men who will bore from within—inside un-American organizations. My nephew has agreed to be the first."

Mayer thought it an excellent idea, but asked, "Why bring it to me, Reverend?"

"Because a single word from you to the right persons can set the machinery in motion immediately."

Mayer smiled and nodded. He liked to have his omnipotence acknowledged.

Some days later, the district attorney served notice on Al Meyers and Bob Singer that they were about to be saddled with the first of what might become many volunteer undercover informants.

"Monday, a kid named Courtney, nephew of the Reverend—"

"That fake preacher is a fucking Nazi!" Singer protested.

"You'll have to live with it. The recommendation came from Louis B. Mayer. Nobody argues with him, Bob."

Wendell made his new bargain with Jim. He was to leave school, join lunatic-fringe organizations and cults, report on them to the DA's office. For this, Wendell would pay him seventy-five dollars a week.

"What're you getting out of it, Wendell?"

"An insurance policy."

Jim was overjoyed at the thought of being allowed to leave school. There was a streak of intrigue in him, and he looked forward to being . . . well, almost like a spy. Reporting to the Hall of Justice on a Monday morning, his enthusiasm was somewhat dampened by the cool manner in which he was greeted by Meyers and Singer. They assigned him a tiny battered wooden desk with a broken chair and gave him an enormous pile of booklets, tracts, and pamphlets to read over.

"So you can get a line on some of these damned outfits," Singer told him.

It was not the kind of reception or the kind of work Jim expected, but staring at the mass of printed matter, he discovered a new dimension in himself—a peculiar and particular form of charm that appealed to men older than himself. He excused himself, went out and bought several items in a hardware store, and without another word repaired the broken chair. Then he sat down and started through the material given him. As he read—and he read with amazing speed—he made notes on a legal-sized pad.

Meyers and Singer watched him with growing interest.

Just before lunchtime, Jim held up the lined pad, asked:

"Care to see what I've been doing now—or wait till later?"

"Just tell us in twenty-five words or less," Meyers growled.

"Finding similarities and overlaps."

Singer looked interested. "Where's that get you?"

"Many of these groups are interlocked, get their instructions and their horseshit clauses from the same sources."

"Smart," Meyers said, gave Jim his first grin. He glanced at Singer. His look said: Maybe this kid can cut it, after all. Singer nodded. Meyers said, "Bob and I're going to grab a bite over on Olvera Street—care to join?"

Jim hesitated for an instant about the Olvera Street, then broke into a wide smile. "Sure . . . and thanks." He had nothing to fear on Olvera Street. Even if by some one-in-a-thousand chance he did meet Lupe, she probably wouldn't recognize him. And if she did . . . well, the two men with whom he would be lunching had badges. And guns.

After another week, Meyers felt that Jim was ready to go into the field. He was to join pro-Nazi youth clubs and groups, obtain names of leaders and members, observe.

"Don't make notes, don't take any risks—some of these bastards play rough. Report in here once or twice a week."

Jim joined the Young Patriots of America, the Turnverein Germania, the Youth Against War Society. He glibly parroted their philosophies and slogans, was "issued" a "kike-killer"—a razor-sharp broad-bladed knife with a steel-studded knuckle guard—by the Young Patriots. At the Turnverein he was given a uniform patterned after the ones worn by the SA in Nazi Germany. At Youth Against War meetings he received rigorous training in the use of weapons, and detailed instructions on how to handle explosives and blast telephone exchanges, waterworks, and police stations. On occasion, he and other members of one or another group went on "hebe hunts." They roamed the Los Angeles and Hollywood streets late at night. Sometimes they merely painted swastikas and anti-Semitic slogans on the walls of synagogues and kosher delicatessens. When they felt it was safe, they would break windows or beat up lone pedestrians—who may or may not have been Jewish. On other nights, they attended special meetings at which such American Nazi folk heroes as Fritz Kuhn raved, ranted, and prophesied that *Der Tag*—when Jewish blood would flow in rivers—was near.

Although Jim did not know his true parentage, he was not Wendell Courtney's son for nothing. He amassed a great deal of information and turned most of it over to Meyers and Singer. Most, but not all. There were many sons of extremely wealthy Southern California families in the pro-Nazi organizations. Their parents were important businessmen, civic leaders, socialites. In short, they were people who stood to lose much—face, status, prestige, public acceptance—if it became known that their sons swaggered around with kike-killers in their belts or went rampaging on hebe hunts.

Jim kept the names of these youths—and detailed records of their activities—to himself. He sensed that the material would prove useful—and profitable—someday, somehow, even though he could not then have guessed exactly how. He hid the material with his loot in the closet.

His reports to Meyers and Singer were clear, terse, and seemed complete. The two veteran professional investigators were impressed, and told the district attorney as much. Meyers said:

"The kid is good. We're getting inside dope we never could have hoped to get before. I only wish we could give him some sort of official recognition."

"Uh-huh." Singer nodded. "He should be taken into the office, even given a badge. Just in case he runs into trouble—and he's gutsy as hell, liable to do just that."

The DA hemmed, hawed, dithered—and telephoned upstairs. The net result was that James Philip Courtney, not yet eighteen, was officially named a "special auxiliary district attorney's investigator" and even given a shield—the only one of its kind—with the number SA-1.

Wendell Courtney observed the developments and congratulated himself on his foresight. Public sentiment was shifting rapidly in the United States. Sympathy for Nazi Germany dwindled markedly when Denmark, Norway, the Low Countries, and France fell to the Germans in 1940. By September the United States government was sending huge amounts of war matériel to Britain, and on September 14 the first peacetime draft law in U.S. history was passed.

By then, of course, Reverend Courtney had watered his fulminations against the Jews down to a vanishing point. He preached unvarnished belief in a "just-and-righteous God" who, in His infinite wisdom, had seen fit to "create America strong, free, the last bastion of liberty" and urged his followers to support their country and their President, "whatever may come." His followers took his fast-footwork changes of direction in their stride—and continued to be most generous in their free-will offerings.

Yet Wendell was apprehensive that, were the United States to enter the war, his past activities might become known. He was justified in being concerned, because war brings its own hysterias and witch-burnings. His nephew's work, which he subsidized entirely, was, as Wendell had said, his insurance policy, but he wanted to be doubly certain and spoke to Jim.

"Do you have access to the central files on what are called subversives, fellow travelers, and the like?"

"Sure."

"Did you ever look to see what there was on me and the Center?"

Jim looked a little suprised and shook his head. "No. Don't ask me why, I couldn't tell you, but I never thought of it." He was telling the truth. He hadn't before, but now that the subject had come up, he was ahead of Wendell. "I'll dig around the next time I'm in the office, though."

"And tell me?"

"Of course."

The entire Countersubversive Squad had been allotted a single—and superannuated—typist-clerk. The files were consequently poorly maintained. Jim stayed in while everyone else went to lunch—on the pretext he wanted to update some of his notes—and made a search. He found two reasonably thick and comprehensive dossiers—one on his uncle, the other on the Soul-Search Center. He took them, put them in his briefcase, knew they would never be missed.

"Good news," he told Wendell that evening. "Only thing they had on file was a half-page memo Bob Singer wrote after he came to see you about the German-consulate business."

"And?"

"What did you think I'd do? I burned it."

That night, Jim crammed the two dossiers into his hiding place under the floorboards of his closet. Just in case, he told himself. Just in case.

War, it seemed, was inevitable in mid-1941. The draft-extension act passed—albeit by only a single vote in Congress. Pro-Nazi groups muted their operations or disbanded entirely, leaders and members melting away, attempting to be anonymous. By then, the Nazis had broken their pact with the USSR and invaded Russia. American pro-Communists no longer sought to hamper and sabotage U.S. defense efforts. On the contrary, they were among those clamoring loudest for the United States to declare war on Germany. This had the side effect of freeing investigative agencies to concentrate on pro-Nazis, and because of developments in the Far East, on suspected Japanese agents.

In Los Angeles County, the apparent approach of war brought expansion to the district attorney's Countersubversive Squad. Two dozen regular investigators were added to the staff, clerical help was hired, appropriations were increased. This expansion worked against Jim Courtney. He was no longer needed or wanted.

"The big wheels want only pros," Al Meyer told Jim sadly, then smiled a little and suggested: "Look, if you'd like to apply for a regular job, I might be able to do something."

"Not for me." James Courtney had no desire to surrender the freedom and autonomy he enjoyed as an unpaid volunteer. Besides, there were practical considerations. Wendell was giving him seventy-five dollars a week. A district attorney's investigator received only three thousand dollars a year—less than sixty dollars a week—in salary, and were he to go on salary, Wendell would certainly cut off the subsidy.

"I think there's a way you can keep me on as a volunteer," Jim said. "Have you been reading about Wyler College, Al?"

Wyler was a large privately endowed college located in Pasadena. Its student body traditionally consisted of wealthy young men and women of prominent families who were, or thought themselves to be, intellectuals. During 1939 and 1940 there had been innumerable—and sometimes violent—Red- or Nazi-inspired "peace demonstrations" on Los Angeles area campuses, such as L.A. Junior College, UCLA, and most notably of all, Wyler College. There, firemen had used high-pressure hoses to quell student riots, and several policemen had been severely injured.

Al Meyer shrugged. "The *Examiner*'s been running that series about the Moral Rearmament and conscientious-objector groups at Wyler. Isn't much anybody can do about it, though. Too many Old Money people on the board and among the alumni. Too many leading citizens' kids in the student body. The political roof'd fall in if we started any sort of investigation there."

"No problems if I just enrolled there."

"Jesus! Let's go talk to the DA."

"Hold on, Al. It's not all that simple. I'd have to get some kind of draft deferment." Which, of course, was what James Courtney was after.

"We can fix that. Plenty of doctors work with us, Jim. I'll

have the DA arrange to get you out on a physical—4-F. You'll be a hell of a lot more valuable in Wyler than in some training camp."

The Japanese attacked Pearl Harbor on December 7, 1941. By then the X rays of a deceased L.A. County Hospital patient were substituted for those of "COURTNEY, JAMES PHILIP" in his selective-service-board file. Also in the file were solemn declarations from three physicians saying that Jim suffered from tuberculosis (arrested—but for how long, no one could foretell) and some other disabilities, any one of which was sufficient cause for deferment.

Wendell's influence was sufficient to make Wyler College accept equivalency-test results in place of a high-school diploma, and Wendell's money paid for a year's tuition. In February 1942 Jim Courtney entered Wyler College as a freshman.

14

At 0945 hours Neil Harkness was doing a five-finger exercise on the VHF radio keyboard, scanning weather channels. Kenneth Dixon, minimal sleep ration consumed, wearing a fresh safari suit, appeared on the bridge. All weather advisories being good, Neil twisted the volume knob to Off, glanced out at the sea. A medium-sized Spanish container ship, doubtless bound for Alicante, plowed west a mile off the *Deirdre*'s port bow. Some fishing trawlers wallowed far away on the starboard side. Otherwise the Mediterranean appeared empty and flat calm under the already blazing sun. Harkness turned, acknowledged his friend's presence. Dixon nodded toward the sheaf of papers once more tucked next to the ship-to-shore.

"How far did you get?" he asked.

"Junior was about to become a campus snoop," Neil replied, and, mind sidetracking, rubbed his jaw thoughtfully. "All that investigation and research must have cost you a fortune."

"Close to seventy-five thousand bucks. I wanted an in-depth picture of the man. Would've been a good investment if I'd ever written the novel based on him."

"But you never did? Why not?"

"Christ, I've told you a dozen times."

"Uh-huh, and the more I read, the less convincing your reasons sound. A fantastic amount of preliminary work—then nothing."

"It happens." Dixon's sardonic features closed in on themselves. "Hemingway simmered a project on a back burner for seventeen years before he junked it. When Bob Ruark was still alive and living in Spain, he told me he'd collected three tons of research material for a novel based on General Franco and one day decided the hell with it. He had everything destroyed—burned."

"That's the difference. You've hung on to it all. How come?"

"Grilling me, counselor?"

"Merely pondering what seem to be imponderables."

"Don't. Take things at face value—for the present."

"Face value is that you hate J.P.—for reasons never fully explained. Face value is that last night you suddenly decided to come along on this J.P.-sponsored mystery junket, again for reasons unclear."

"I wanted to get away from Cabo Verde for a while."

"Why not by plane or train, in comfort? And why without Vivi? I've never known you to leave her for more than a day or two at most."

"I wanted to be by myself for a change," Ken said, much too quickly, "and Vivi had work piled up. She had to stay home."

Neil remembered glimpsing bruises on Vivian's breasts, dark circles under her eyes. He frowned, combed fingers through his sandy hair, said: "Look. If you and Vivi are in some kind of jam—"

"We're not!" Dixon snapped, turned abruptly, and made for the ladder that led below. "I'll make coffee and then take over from you."

Ken's manner denies the denial, Harkness mused, lighting a Celta. It was fairly obvious that the Dixons were in trouble of one sort or another. But then, aren't we all? Seems to go with being a part of the James Philip Courtney universe. A mental image formed. An infinite number of saw-toothed wheels within saw-toothed wheels whirred in menacing orbits around all those who made up the Montemar-centered planetary system.

At Montemar, James Courtney was making modifications in the ordering of his universe. Kristin Verkerk's performance had been superior. He believed it could be refined to superb, toyed with the idea of installing her as resident mistress, as successor to Eileen Marsh. Courtney wanted an objective, impartial opinion about the girl. Grenville could give it. He asked the butler-confidant before going into his study that morning. Grenville rendered judgment coldly.

"A witless peasant, sir. I'm afraid you'd find her a greater liability than Miss Marsh was."

"You may be right. Get her dressed and out of my bedroom. Tell her she'll keep the CVI-annex job and be on call. Warn her . . ."

"About talking?" Grenville's eyes gleamed. "Of course."

"Oh . . . did everything go smoothly with Harkness last night?"

"He left on schedule," Grenville said, and asked his own question. "About the gold coins. Shall I make the usual exchange?"

Courtney nodded and then laughed. "It was an expensive evening. She has a fantastic set of muscles—managed to pick up and hold three Mexican fifty-peso pieces, an Austrian hundred-crown and two Krugerrands. Around twenty-six hundred dollars, U.S. Figure it exactly and give her the equivalent in pesetas."

"She'll ask if you use the coins every night—they all do."

"Tell her the usual—that it's only on the first night, but she can expect other surprises. You might drop a hint about the *cuevas*. She may be a witless peasant, but she's totally depraved. Thinking about the *cuevas* should keep her on the thin edge of orgasm."

Courtney went off to his *estudio*. As he often did, he entered by a side door that eliminated the need of going through the outer office. He settled himself behind the Bureau Plat, flicked on the closed-circuit-television set that provided U.S. stock and commodity reports for the previous day. He switched to the channel that gave New York Stock Exchange closings, manipulated a lever until he had the Chrysler Corporation readout on the screen. The stock had closed down a full point. A good sign, an omen, he thought, and made a snap decision. The diversionary buying campaign could begin earlier than planned, begin that very day. He made a mental note to telephone Heinrich Kloster in Zurich before noon, switched off the set, and called for Sybil Pearson over the intercom.

Sybil felt but did not show the after effects of her bad night's sleep and entered with her customary smile and cheerful "Good morning," and then said: "Two calls already this morning. They're from—"

He cut her short with a grunt, activated the replay mechanism.

". . . Wilhelm Fischer. Please inform Mr. Courtney that I am where he instructed me to be and will wait there."

That was all, but for Courtney enough—and gratifying. He

smiled. There was a silence, then clickings followed by Sybil's voice answering, then another terse message:

"Thibault. I would like to notify Mr. Courtney it was imperative we complete the New York transaction without delay, and we closed with both parties before midnight. Would you read that back to me, please? . . ."

Courtney silenced the replay. His smile deepened; his pale blue eyes glowed. He could now think of Eileen Marsh, the man—Courtney was unable to recall his name—and their threats in the past tense. In the past-altogether-perfect tense, he mused. The good signs and omens were piling up—in themselves demands that he move everything further, faster.

Sybil saw that the angularity of her employer's features were softened, made almost cherubic, by his smile and the glow that suffused his face. Whatever the New York transaction had been, it must have been a major coup, she thought, and said:

"You look like someone who's just won the pools, Mr. Courtney." She derived vicarious pleasure, felt a sense of participation in his swift, slashing entrepreneurial strokes and successes. He played to win, and won so that he could play again, parlay, and pyramid. She had observed the process for three years and more. Being part—even a very small part—of it thrilled, exhilarated her.

"Haven't won this particular pool yet, but I'm close," he responded, elation and impatience equally evident. "Get Kloster at the Bauerkreditbank. Right away."

Sybil hurried out of the study, placed the call to Zurich.

Courtney's conversation with the Swiss banker was short, largely one-sided, and would have far-reaching consequences.

"Your scrambler compatible yet, Heinrich? No? In that case, ask no questions. Just listen. You're to do exactly as I say. One, start the shopping the moment the New York market opens. Two, see that word of it reaches the odd quantity . . ."

Courtney paused, listened a few seconds, then rasped:

"Yes, dammit. Today. Use the most reliable channels, but be quick. Third and last, the drama we've discussed must be played out within seventy-two hours. Sooner if possible. What? No, cost is no object, pay whatever is asked. Calm yourself, Heinrich, stop spluttering. We're not changing plans. We're simply speeding up the machinery. Think of yourself as an expediter. I'll be waiting for your reports. Good-bye."

Finished, James Courtney replaced the handset, leaned back in his chair. He stroked the old scar on his cheek. He contemplated the certainty that his enemies would now begin to emerge in force, attack from all sides and without restraint or mercy. His nostrils flared at the prospect of the forthcoming battles.

La cosa está que arde, he said silently to the Hals portrait. Things are coming to a head. He winked at the chess player—and could have sworn that the chess player gave him a conspiratorial smile and winked back.

In her office adjoining the study, Sybil Pearson shuffled through telexes, letters, reports, and other documents and puzzled over events of the previous evening and night. She could not understand why Neil had broken their date and gone to visit Kenneth and Vivian Dixon at Broadmoor without telling her. Nor could she understand why he had been adamant that she remain home and not go to the *puerto* and see him off. There was no Courtney-ordained secrecy about the trip—in fact, he had telephoned her to find Neil and tell him to be at the marina an hour earlier than planned. Even Grenville knew about it; he had indicated as much in a chat they had when she came to work that morning.

Only Ken and Vivi would be able to furnish explanations—if, indeed, there were any to furnish, Sybil mused. Her paper-shufflings brought her to a copy of the CVI agreement with Globe-Aarco Metals that Tom Eberhardt had sent over from the annex. She merely glanced at the identifying cover sheet, placed the agreement into the "For Mr. Courtney" tray, bit thoughtfully at her thumbnail. She decided to forgo the always excellent lunch Grenville brought to her in the office daily, drive into the Cabo Verde *pueblo* on her free hour, stop off at Galerías Vivi. The gallery did not close for the siesta period until one-thirty. She would talk to Vivian personally and try to find out more.

Vivian Dixon also felt the effects of a restless, nightmare-ridden night, and her morning had been hectic. It began with a nine-thirty visit to Galerías Vivi by a flawlessly tailored, impeccably mannered Spanish representative of the main regional government tourist office in Málaga. His charm was enormous, his request perennial. Would Señora Dixon be willing to hold some kind of very special exhibition during the height of the July-August season? This would be greatly appreciated. The show would attract many tourists, benefit the economy, and, needless to say, also benefit Galerías Vivi. There would be much publicity and promotion. . . .

Vivian agreed without hesitation, as she did every year, but the conversation did not end there. It went on for over an hour—through three cups of café solo—while preliminary concepts were discussed. At last the official left. Not ten minutes before a tourist bus from Torremolinos brought some three dozen reduced-rate package vacationers to the gallery. They were Americans—from somewhere in the darker reaches of the Middle West, Vivian realized as they boiled through the showrooms, the women's voices loud and raucous, their men silent, sullen, all too obviously bored.

The women were more interested in Vivian than they were in contemporary Spanish paintings. They had read or heard of her—as the gorgeous, glamorous wife of *the* Kenneth Dixon, and clustered around her asking inane—and infuriating—questions.

"I've read your husband's books. Is he here?"

"Why do you and he live in Spain and not back home in the States?"

"Are you still an American citizen?"

"How can you stand it here? Some of these Spaniards we've seen look like cutthroats."

Vivian fixed a counterfeit smile on her face, gave answers, gradually broke the large group into several small ones, which she turned over to Carlos Lozano, her assistant manager, and other employees. In the end, three pictures were sold. They were credit-card purchases. Vivian left Carlos to take care of the paperwork and went into her office. Minutes later Gloria Meese telephoned. In her capacity as chairperson of the Marbella American-Spanish Friendship Society, she announced, and loosed a verbal torrent.

"Vivi, darling! I tried to reach dear Ken at Broadmoor and some servant told me he was away for *unos cuantos días*—whatever that's supposed to mean—and I'm frantic."

Vivian groaned. Gloria, like so many rich Costa expatriates, was deep into cocaine. It was her custom to awaken at eleven A.M. and, she boasted openly, do her first two lines of the day right after taking her morning bath. It was 11:35. That meant she was soaring high.

"And I woke up feeling so glorious! I had my swimming instructor for the night—the one everybody calls El Toro."

Gloria must have done more than two lines, Vivian thought, and broke into the detailed description. "He sounds magnificent, but you were calling about Ken."

"Oh. Yes. Well, there's been so much advance publicity about his new book, all our club members are dying to hear more—from him. I've scheduled Ken as our speaker for next Tuesday."

"He won't be back by then," Vivian said quickly, hoping that would be the end of it. The hope was futile.

"He has to be!" Stated as a command, then, with a note of triumph: "I've invited the press."

By and large, foreign residents viewed Spanish press and journalists with a condescension bordering on contempt, as they did much else that was indigenous—"native." For their part, Spanish newspapers and magazines published along the Costa del Sol ignored the clubs and societies organized by *extranjeros*, seldom if ever published items about their meetings, which were usually dull and of no interest to their readers. But if Kenneth Dixon was going to talk about his forthcoming blockbuster, they would send reporters and photographers. Vivian knew the project had to be killed off, and she grabbed at the easiest lie.

"Sorry, Ken had to rush off and see his English publishers. He'll be gone a week, perhaps longer, and he'll be very busy when he returns." Gloria had a short interest span. If forced to postpone, she would forget. "I'm afraid you'll have to put it off for a month or so."

Mind-blowing alkaloids sharpened Gloria's perceptions, made her malicious. "Very odd," she said, edging her tone with sugared acid. "Ken's never been away from you for long. Couldn't be that he's on something more"—a pause—"or less than a business trip, Vivian dear?"

Vivian felt a sharp cramp that signaled the onset of her always difficult menstrual period. She winced, spoke without thinking: "God, but you're a repulsive sow!" She regretted the words instantly and realized how much damage had been done when Gloria slammed down her telephone. The woman would talk, embroider, invent. The talk would spread, and there was no telling where it might lead.

Sybil Pearson dropped in unexpectedly, and Carlos Lozano, knowing she and Vivian were close friends, told her to go on up to Vivian's office. Sybil found the door closed, knocked, identified herself, was told to come in. Vivian was propped on a chaise. Sybil saw that she was pale, her gray eyes puffy, recognized the signs and asked:

"Can I get you anything—aspirin, Demerol, a drink?"

"No. The first half-hour's passed. It'll ease off now." Some color had returned to her face. She sat up on the chaise, brushed her long red hair back with both hands. "There. Almost normal. I never got around to saying hello or that it's a nice surprise to see you."

Sybil stared at the floor. "I came over because I wanted to talk to you about Neil."

"Um. Problems?"

"Puzzles. Maybe you have the answers. Neil and I had a date last night. He broke it, didn't tell me he was going to see you and Ken."

"Neil wanted a private talk with Ken," Vivian said warily and omitted direct mention of her own participation in what was to have been a long three-way conversation. "He thought Ken might rummage in his writer's imagination and find some plausible explanations."

Sybil frowned. "For what?"

"The things that happened on his jaunt to Tangier, of course." Vivian assumed that Sybil knew the story, saw from her baffled expression that she did not and was in her turn puzzled.

"I really haven't seen much of Neil since May Day afternoon," Sybil said. "A few minutes at your party, and then at Montemar, and naturally we couldn't talk there. What did happen to Neil?"

Harkness had told others, and certainly Jim Courtney knew, Vivian reflected. There was no harm in telling Sybil. Indeed, she was entitled to know, even at second hand. Vivian skimmed over the highlights as she had heard them from Neil and her husband.

Sybil's hazel eyes grew large, then narrowed. "The police found a derelict boat the next morning," she recalled aloud.

"Neil thinks it must be the same one." Vivian nodded.

"He left again last night," Sybil said, her voice a little shaky. "It was sudden and rather mysterious. He didn't tell me where he was going, either."

"Oh?" Vivian felt it better to pretend ignorance. "So that's why he rushed away after your call."

"I'm suddenly worried for him, Vivi."

"You shouldn't be. Your sailor can take care of himself if anyone can. Besides, I'm sure his trip is just routine."

"No, I'm sure it isn't." Sybil remembered James Courtney's late-night telephone call and his demand that she locate Neil and deliver a message to him.

She looked troubled, the frown deepened. "May I use your telephone, Vivi?"

"Help yourself. Checking in with Montemar?"

"No. I'd like to call your house and speak with Ken," Sybil said, reaching for the instrument on the desk behind her. "He may be able to add more to what you've told me." She lifted the receiver.

Vivian was nonplussed for a moment. On the one hand,

Sybil's worry would lessen if she knew that Ken was aboard the *Deirdre* with Harkness. On the other, no one—not even Sybil—could be allowed to know where he was. She decided it best to keep her lies consistent, stay with the version she had given Gloria Meese.

"Uh . . . you won't reach him," she said. Sybil had started dialing, stopped, held the receiver in midair. "Ken isn't home. He left for London on the morning flight from Málaga."

"Vivi." The hazel eyes narrowed again. "There isn't any morning flight to London. Won't be until the fifteenth."

Vivian thought fast, trying to remember the prevailing flight schedules from Málaga airport, succeeded. "I meant he took the early Iberia plane to Barcelona and caught a connecting BEA flight from there."

Sybil replaced the telephone slowly, eyes still narrow. Something didn't ring true, she thought. Vivian read her mind easily, recited the tale she had concocted earlier: "His English publishers insisted on having a conference with him immediately."

"You mean they called him late last night?"

Caught off guard, Vivian blurted, "Yes, right after Neil left."

Sybil was certain that no English publisher would ever telephone an author—or anyone else—after regular business hours to ask him to a conference. And English time was only one hour earlier than Spanish. Even if, impossible as it was, there had been such a telephone call, she could not imagine Kenneth Dixon, of all people, responding immediately to the summons. He would never get up before dawn to make the 7:55 Málaga–Barcelona flight—which Sybil, of necessity conversant with local airline schedulings, knew was the only one in the morning. Dixon would have dawdled until noon or so while servants packed, eaten lunch at home, taken the 2:40 direct flight to London.

"He'll be there a week or longer," Vivian added, hoping to be more convincing but only compounding her initial error and multiplying Sybil's doubts and suspicions.

"Then you'll be going to join him," Sybil said, throwing out bait. Vivian always accompanied her husband on trips lasting more than a day or two because Ken could not bear being away from her and after a short separation went on a marathon binge.

"No," Vivian responded, taking the bait; then, realizing that she had, she tried to correct herself. "I mean, not today or tomorrow"—she faltered—"or even the next. I'm . . . I'm expecting a large consignment of pictures. I have to be here."

"Oh." Sybil sensed it wasn't true, that much of what Vivian

had told her wasn't true, and felt that she had reason to wonder if anything she had said was. Sybil studied her friend for a moment from under lowered lashes. Obviously she would not obtain reliable information from Vivian.

"I'm afraid I must go," Sybil said, miming a smile. "Mr. C. might start wondering where I am."

She was in a hurry to go back to Montemar and speak to James Courtney. He knew where Neil was, what he was doing, and when he would return. She would ask Courtney, and she felt certain he would tell her.

15

It cost upwards of one thousand dollars a week to charter the *Deirdre* and her captain and crew. People who paid that kind of money expected the vessel to be well-equipped, and it was. The galley, designed to provide meals for as many as six passengers and crew, boasted a deep-freeze and microwave oven. It was a simple matter for Neil Harkness to prepare a sirloin-steak-and-trimmings lunch for Kenneth Dixon and himself. The two men ate on the bridge, continued to talk about the subject that obsessed them: James Philip Courtney. Then it was Dixon's turn to go below again and sleep while Neil stood watch at the controls.

Settling into his captain's chair, Harkness checked course and instruments, jotted notations in his log, and resumed reading what he had come to think of as Kenneth Dixon's "Courtney papers." The portion dealing with Courtney's scholastic record at Wyler College held little interest beyond establishing that he received high marks and had been considered a "brilliant" student. Accounts of his activities as a campus informer were another matter. Neil, who had not been born until after World War Two ended, grimaced distaste as he read them, gaining insight into the Roosevelt administration's suspensions of civil liberties and human rights during the war years.

After entering Wyler, 4-F Jim Courtney stopped reporting to the Los Angeles County district attorney's office. He "cooperated" with various federal agencies. They had been formed after Pearl Harbor, given acronym designations and overlapping functions. Although dismantled when the war ended, their files were turned over to other, permanent agencies. As time passed, security classifications were steadily downgraded until almost anyone had free access to the records.

Ken Dixon's researchers had needed to send only one of their number to Washington. The roster of some 2,500 wartime campus operatives had been declassified in 1961. It revealed James Courtney's interagency code name ("John Capper") and where his reports were filed.

During the war, intelligence operations within the U.S. were supposedly focused mainly on ferreting out Nazi agents and Nazi sympathizers. But some agencies like the FBI also concentrated on Communists, Communist sympathizers, "Reds," and "radicals." And some pandered to the paranoid fear of the Japanese that gripped the West Coast.

Jim Courtney handily found culprits—or sacrificial lambs—in all three categories.

A Wyler College philosophy professor praised Niezsche and Hegel, argued that Germans had made numerous important contributions to civilization. Courtney reported him—with embellishments. The professor was summarily dismissed. Some students organized an "Aid Russia" rally. He denounced them as Communists. The males in the group were ordered to appear for immediate induction into the Army; the females were expelled. Another campus group protested the forcible detention of 110,000 Japanese-Americans and the seizure of their homes, businesses, and farms. Again, a "John Capper" report—then, within weeks, induction or expulsion for those who had been involved.

The rest of the section related more of the same, with Courtney expanding his activities beyond Wyler College to scholastic conferences and conventions, off-campus clubs and societies.

The son of a bitch was like the miraculous fucking machine, served every sex and even played "God Save the Queen," Neil mused. He turned a page, fired up a Celta, went on reading.

James Courtney had a good life in 1942. He was a handsome, virile youth. He had money, an almost-new Buick convertible, and a C-card for gasoline rationing (the last a fringe benefit of being an informant). Wartime man shortages and sexual hysteria gave him free choice of women. And things were fine at home, too. His "uncle," Wendell Courtney, now treated him as friend and equal. With reason. There was much the youth could do for Wendell and his Soul-Search Center.

"Ah, Jim. A woman recently deeded some property to the Center as a love offering. Her brother is being troublesome—

claims she's not mentally competent and that I . . . ah . . . exerted undue influence."

"Which way does he lean, Wendell?"

"A bit left. He campaigned for Norman Thomas in 1932."

"That should do for starters. What's his name?"

"Clement Pryor. A dry-goods merchant. Lives in Van Nuys."

Jim passed it along as a "reliable tip," asked that—as a personal favor—the "case" be given special handling. Clement Pryor, suddenly beset by Red-hunting federal investigators, raised no further objections about his sister's "love offering."

Months later, a Los Angeles *Daily News* reporter attended a Soul-Search Center "prayer marathon" and wrote a mildly satirical account of it. Wendell, enraged, employed a private detective to check on the journalist and, findings in hand, again called on his nephew for help.

"The bastard attended the Berlin Olympics in 1936, doesn't like FDR, and thinks we should concentrate on beating the Japs."

Jim Courtney again informed, again requested special handling. SASA—Subversive Activities Surveillance Agency—went to *Daily News* publisher Manchester Boddy, said they had evidence that the reporter was a Nazi sympathizer. They cowed the American Newspaper Guild with the same assertion. The journalist was fired—and blacklisted.

On November 8, 1942, U.S. and British forces invaded North Africa, and severe fighting followed—but by the end of that month, James Courtney was affected by a different kind of invasion. Wendell Courtney had never before taken a permanent mistress. He had always preferred transient affairs, usually with women from his Soul-Search Center flock, many of whom had been film starlets, some full-fledged and famous stars. Now the reverend moved a young woman into his home and bedroom.

Stephanie Trent—the name she had adopted while trying to break into motion pictures—was in her mid-twenties, blond, with an attractive if somewhat vacant face and a statuesque body. Wendell was obviously infatuated with her. Jim neither liked nor disliked her, but knowing she was some thirty years younger than his uncle, relished the thought that sooner or later he would have a chance to bed Stephanie or, as both his uncle and he called her, "Steffie." At the same time, he was dubious about how Wendell's followers might react to their spiritual adviser openly living in sin. Wendell was unworried.

"I don't give a damn," he declared. "I've made mine. If

there's too much of a stink, I'll close the Center and sell the building and land."

"Be a shame," Jim said. "It's a good racket. I'd hate to see it go down the drain."

"No wonder. It's kept you in style all your life," Wendell said in a tone intended to make Jim feel small, beholden.

Jim said nothing. He still had fifteen thousand dollars of the money taken from Wendell's safe years before. It remained hidden beneath the floorboards of his clothes closet—a reserve that guaranteed he could, and would, be independent, no matter what Wendell chose to do. It quickly became apparent that whatever else he did, Wendell chose to spend large amounts of money on Stephanie, buying her clothes, furs, jewelry, and an unused 1942-model Cadillac, which he purchased for an astronomical sum on the black market.

Wendell spent an inordinate amount of time in bed with his mistress, began to experience occasional chest pains, but disregarded them. On a night in January 1943, in the midst of energetic lovemaking, Wendell suffered a heart attack. He was rushed to Hollywood Hospital. The attack was mild, but attending physicians were aware of his reputation as a womanizer. They warned him to refrain from sex for three months after returning home. He protested violently. They urged that he at least restrict himself to being the passive partner and use only passive positions. He agreed; Stephanie promised to cooperate.

The reverend's library of translated Hindu erotica was extensive, went far beyond the prosaic *Kama Sutra*, *Koka Shastra*, and *Ananga Ranga*. Among rarer works, the *Dehra* was devoted to "the art of giving pleasure to princes and others of great rank who are crippled or have been made helpless by wounds." After Stephanie had studied the book, Wendell obtained such prescribed esoteric devices as pipettes, surcingles, rouleaux, and resonating cones. She gave virtuoso performances; he discovered new dimensions of sexual pleasure in total passivity.

Wendell neglected the Soul-Search Center, and the congregation gradually dwindled, then melted away. He also neglected Steffie to the extent of completely ignoring her always very considerable sexual needs, claiming that the slightest exertion might endanger his health. Inevitably she went to Jim.

"The things I do take hours, and he comes two or three times—but for me, nothing," she told him. "I get hot, red-hot, and then it's climb walls or play with myself after he's asleep."

"He doesn't even use his hands?"

"No. God, I wish I knew what to do."

"I know," Jim said, by then his penis erect, straining against the fabric of his trousers. "Let's fuck." He took her hand, pressed it against the massive bulge.

"We . . . we can't," she stammered, and then, clutching him, groaned, "Not here—not in his house."

"That's easy," Jim said. "I know a hotel in Santa Monica. Tell Wendell you're going shopping this afternoon. Take your car, I'll take mine. No problem for me. He's used to me being out most of the time—never pays any attention."

They spent that afternoon and many others together over the next few months, and it was during one of their hotel-room trysts that Stephanie first asked Jim about Wendell's wealth and his will.

"He has plenty, but I don't know how much or if he's ever made out a will," Jim told her with an indifferent shrug.

"Aren't you interested?"

"Why should I be? He's always made it clear he'd help support me until I finished school and went to work. Period. I won't get a dime afterward."

"Didn't he adopt you?"

"Only sort of. When I was sixteen his lawyer explained that I wouldn't be Wendell's heir—that I'd receive nothing from his estate."

"Then there must be a will naming somebody as his beneficiary."

"Could be. Now turn over on your stomach and pull your knees up."

In mid-May Wendell suffered another heart attack. Again he survived, but doctors issued stringent warnings that he obtain much bedrest and avoid physical exertion for ninety days, perhaps longer. They prescribed drugs that would act as anaphrodisiacs, diminish his sexual desire. He refused to take them, but being afraid of death, determined to restrict himself.

"Only once a week, Steffie. So move into the next bedroom and do not come into mine at night unless I ask you."

Stephanie feared she could become expendable or that Wendell might suffer a fatal heart attack and leave her penniless. The fears multiplied as he underwent a personality change, became stingy, tyrannical, venomously bad-tempered and suspicious. He fired two servants, ordered her to help those that remained with the housework. He gave her no money, forbade her afternoon-long shopping trips. If she left the house for only a short period, he cross-examined her about where she had gone, what she had done, whom she had seen, and her answers never satisfied him.

Jim readily accepted that Steffie was no longer available to him, cared little. Good as she was in bed, there were many other women on and off the Wyler College campus, some of whom were even more proficient. For a time he could even accept the marked changes in his uncle. Only for a time—until Wendell declared he was stopping Jim's $75-a-week allowance, the amount he had agreed to provide as a subsidy for his nephew's work as a campus informant.

"Don't be a damned fool, Wendell," Jim warned him. "Cut me off, and I'll blow your Soul-Search Center wide open."

Instead of being angered by the threat, Wendell placidly said, "Go ahead. There's nothing much left of the Center. I'm already negotiating to sell the building and the land it's on. Your money stops."

James Courtney left his uncle's bedroom, returned a few minutes later carrying several copies of a pamphlet. It was *The Hyena Breed*, a tract the Reverend Wendell Courtney had once written and privately published for distribution to his followers. It was a savage attack on Jews, Judaism, and "the Zionist conspiracy." One chapter, "A Dazzling Ray of Hope," praised Adolf Hitler, the Nazis, and their anti-Semitic policies.

"A forgotten masterpiece," Jim said, holding up the booklets. "It happens I saved a few copies. The FBI should find them fascinating."

"FBI? My God! I'm ill . . . have a heart condition!"

"True. The strain of being questioned might even kill you."

Wendell turned ashen. "All right," he whispered. Jim had won.

Stephanie knew nothing of this. However, on the next night that Wendell wanted sex, she came to his bedroom determined to settle the money question in her own way.

The blond girl outdid herself stroking, caressing, titillating Wendell to erection. Then she gently inserted the resonating cone, made the gut string vibrate very slowly, sending sensations through his body for several minutes. Removing the cone, she eased a pipette up in its place, used her mouth to lightly warm-water-massage his prostate, then prolonged his orgasm by alternately tightening and loosening the penile and scrotal surcingles. When he was drained, ecstatic, she asked, "Did you enjoy it?"

He nodded, smiling.

"It could be the last for a long time, Wendell."

The smile faded. "What the hell are you talking about?"

"Only that you'd have trouble finding anyone who did it as well—and she wouldn't do it for room and board."

"I've given you—"

"You did. Past tense. Now I'm just one of the chambermaids, and you've even closed out my charge accounts."

"Whore!"

"Good-bye, Wendell. I'm going to take a bath, pack, and leave." She gathered up the implements. The sight of them excited him.

"Wait . . . we'll work something out. Once more."

"Won't that be dangerous?" Stephanie asked, but she stood, let the resonating cone dangle free. He stared at it. "For your heart, I mean."

"That's my worry."

"My worry is money, Wendell." She brushed the cone against his thighs. His penis, erect again, grew harder, and he trembled.

"What do you want, for Christ's sake?"

"Same as I had before. Not any more, not any less." She dropped the cone to the floor, produced the rubber nipple-tipped sheath, brought it to her lips. Her tongue flicked at the protruding nipple. "You love it when I use this, don't you?" she taunted, well aware that he did. He sat up, tried to grab her. She stepped back, laughed. "You love this more than anything."

He was panting, barely coherent. "You . . . Steffie. Please. Yes. The same as you had before. I promise."

Stephanie realized that he meant it—temporarily. He would keep the promise for a matter of weeks, possibly even two or three months, but no more. By then he would have found someone to replace her—regardless of what he might have to pay. However, she could use the time to think, plan, do something.

"I'll use both your favorite goodies this time," she said.

His orgasm was seismic—and then he seemed to collapse, gasping for breath, both hands clutching at his chest. The apparent seizure was brief, lasting only seconds before he returned to normal, but it was long enough for Stephanie to recognize what she could do—and very easily—if worse came to worst. Or to best, she reflected.

James Courtney also had doubts about his uncle and the future. Playing the loving nephew, he went to see Wendell's attorney. He said he was deeply concerned about his uncle's health and—

"You're curious about his will," the lawyer broke in coldly, anticipating the rest. "Reverend Courtney thought you and Miss Weinberg might be after his second attack. He specifically authorized me to tell you that neither you nor Miss Weinberg is mentioned in it. That is all I can say. Good day."

"Wait a minute. Who in the name of God is Miss Weinberg? I never heard of her."

"She is your uncle's . . . ah . . . companion."

"Something's wrong. You mean Stephanie Trent?"

"The same person, young man. Stephanie Trent is—or was—her theatrical name. She was born Shirley Weinberg."

"You must be joking. That sounds Jewish."

The lawyer sniffed as though smelling something bad in the air around him. "It is Jewish. I don't mind saying that I can't imagine what possessed your uncle to keep her with him after he learned the truth."

"He didn't know at the beginning?"

"No. It only came out two months ago."

"That explains a lot," Jim said, more to himself than to the lawyer. "Thank you for the information." He held out his hand. The attorney refused to take it. Jim shrugged, left the office. "Shirley Weinberg," he said aloud as he did—and laughed uproariously.

He did not laugh later when he told Stephanie of the meeting.

"How did Wendell find out your real name?" he asked.

"He had somebody check my birth certificate."

"You haven't a hope of getting anything from him when he dies. He hates Jews."

"So do I."

Jim did a double-take. "That's insane. You're—"

"Half. On my father's side, and in name only. He played around on my mother, so she played around on him—and got caught. With me. He walked out, but they didn't get a divorce until after I was born. I haven't any idea who my actual father was."

"Something we have in common. Neither do I."

"We have more than that in common, Jim. We're both living on Wendell's handouts, and when he goes, we'll be out in the cold. I've been there before. It scares me."

If it wasn't for the money hidden in his closet, the prospect would scare him too, Jim thought, and said: "Since we're both bastards, maybe we can put our heads together and figure some way to give him the shaft he deserves." He spoke more to lift her spirits than because he thought it possible. However, a seed had been planted in both their minds. A series of wholly unpredictable events would enable it to take deep root, sprout, and finally explode into the incident that ended one life, caused violent upheaval in others.

Wendell had been stunned to learn that Jim had saved copies

of *The Hyena Breed,* enraged that he had been blackmailed. He was afraid Jim might have kept other incriminating material from the past. There was only one way to find out if there was anything more concealed in the house. The house—and the garages and servants' quarters above them—would have to be searched, secretly. Wendell devised an elaborate scenario. Termites were a familiar scourge in Southern California. He retained private investigators, two of whom came to the house in the guise of building inspectors and submitted a written report of termite infestation. That night at dinner, Wendell complained bitterly to Stephanie that he would have to pay exterminators "a fortune" and that they would be working in the house "for days." She believed the story, and since Jim was out that evening, mentioned it to him casually the next morning. He gave it little thought but decided to stay away from home while the work was in progress.

About two weeks later he made a routine check of the cache under his closet floorboards. It was empty. What remained of the money he had taken from Wendell's safe years before was gone. He naturally blamed the exterminators, was appalled by his loss—and nearly went out of his mind with frustration. The money had been stolen in the first place. He could not report the loss, dared mention it to no one, least of all Wendell.

Then he became aware of new loathing and contempt in his uncle's attitude toward him, and the pieces fell into place. He debated telling Steffie everything, decided against it, determined to bide his time watchfully. The watchful waiting paid off. Wendell went on one of his periodic chauffeured drives to Griffith Park, where he was accustomed to stroll an hour or so for exercise that was supposed to strengthen his heart. The day was hot; he walked somewhat more than usual and was stricken by chest pains. The chauffeur helped him back into the car, took him home. His regular physician and a cardiologist were called. No, they declared, it hadn't been an attack, only a slight cardiac deficiency—probably caused by heat and overexertion.

"All the same, you'll have to be very careful, take it very easy, Reverend Courtney."

Wendell's terror of death intensified, spawned other terrors. He remained in bed, refused to eat meat or drink water that had not been boiled, ceased all sexual activity. Stephanie momentarily expected him to cut off her allowance and charge accounts again, but he seemed to have forgotten about them. His attention was focused elsewhere. He was obsessed with trying to sell the Soul-Search Center property and other real estate he owned—

quickly, immediately, and for cash—and spent hours on the telephone trying to make the deals.

Jim heard of this from Stephanie.

"You're sure he's insisting on cash?" Jim asked.

"Yes. I think he's going soft in the head. One minute he's sure we're going to lose the war—and then the banks will go under. The next, he rants that we'll win—and then the Jews will take everybody's money. Especially his. He thinks the Jews are after him."

"Does he include you?"

"No. I think he's forgotten."

"Let's hope so. You should stay close to him."

"Why? Any reason in particular?"

"Steffie, if he does collect a lot of cash, he'll have to keep it someplace, and—"

"He'll put it in a safe-deposit box."

"Uh-uh. You've just said he's worried about banks. I have a hunch he'll keep it close—maybe even in his safe. Probably in his safe, because he's a pattern person at heart."

"What's that got to do with my staying close to him?"

"So we'll know exactly when he gets any cash—and where he puts it."

"No, Jim, I won't—"

"You will. You said it yourself. Being left out in the cold scares you." James Courtney's face was hard. "Believe me, you will."

Wendell completed the property sales. Men came with documents and money. He met with them privately downstairs in his den. Jim guessed that he put the cash in his safe and, at first opportunity, tried the door. It was securely locked. Wendell suspected that his nephew had checked, and laughed at him.

"Any thief will have to blow the safe open—this time."

Now Jim was certain that Wendell knew the truth about the long-ago robbery and that it was he who had recovered what was left of the loot in its closet hiding place. Worse followed. Having collected large sums of cash, Wendell suddenly felt invulnerable.

"I'm stopping your allowance—no, don't threaten. I'm not afraid of you any longer. I'll let you live here until you finish college, but, by God, you'll get a job and pay for your room and board."

Jim realized it was useless to protest. Wendell meant what he said and would not change his mind.

Stephanie fared even worse.

"Sex is out for me—and so are you, Jew bitch. There's no

reason for me to give you another cent. You can stay another two weeks. If you don't leave then, I'll have the police throw you out."

"You were right," Stephanie told Jim. "I've changed my mind. We have to do something—but what?"

"The safe combination must be written down someplace. Find it."

"He doesn't let me be around him much, but I'll try."

"Look under his books—he may have kept an old habit."

Stephanie found what they sought with remarkable speed—by playing a hunch. She had noticed that Wendell had hidden the *Dehra* sex manual in a cabinet drawer that contained his huge assortment of medicines. She guessed that the convoluted processes of the money/sex/death-fear worm-can that was his mind would impel him to hide it under—or inside—the *Dehra*. While Wendell bathed the next morning, she went into his bedroom. A slip of paper was taped to the flyleaf. She copied down the combination—7, 19, 3, 27—took it to Jim, then had second thoughts.

"We can't, Jim. He'll find out—know we did it—and call the police. We'd be arrested immediately."

"Steffie . . . Wendell is going to kill himself."

"That's insane. All he thinks about is staying alive."

"He'd like to fuck, though."

"You're not talking sense. He'd like to, sure. Only he won't. He wants to live so desperately, he's forced himself to give up even that, because it might kill him."

"Still, if he did fuck himself to death, it would be suicide."

"I . . . I suppose so. But he has fantastic self-control. He'd never—"

"You're going to be in for a surprise. So will he."

James Courtney was a meticulous planner, even then, at the age of twenty-one. He went to his earliest haunt, the Olvera Street Mexican quarter. It was long before anyone ever dreamed of drug culture and nationwide narcotics problems, but the raunchier bars did a brisk side trade in ready-rolled marijuana cigarettes—and in cantharis. Although the powdered Spanish-fly-beetle was dangerous, it did have a powerful (often violent) effect as a sexual stimulant. Always readily available in Southern California, both supply and demand had increased enormously since the war began.

Jim bought a quantity so large that the bartender who sold it to him was moved to ask:

"What're you going to do—stage an orgy?"

"Sort of," Jim replied.

En route home, he stopped at a drugstore, bought a bottle of milk of magnesia. That was on Thursday, May 27, 1943. Wendell's eviction notice to Stephanie made speed essential. Jim set a one-week schedule, the denouement to come on the following Thursday, June 3, when the servants would be off for the night.

The next day he arranged to meet with Stephanie in Griffith Park—a touch that tickled his sense of the sardonic. He spoke to her earnestly until she was convinced and agreed, then gave her specific instructions.

"Pretend you're trying to get back in Wendell's good graces. Help in the kitchen—wash and dry dishes, mop the floors, do anything so you're around when his meals are being prepared. Insist on taking his trays upstairs to him. On Monday, tell the cook you want to make his dinner desserts—the tapioca and rice puddings he likes will hide the milk-of-magnesia taste."

Stephanie did as told. The servants enjoyed letting their employer's mistress perform unpleasant kitchen chores and take his trays up to his bedroom. If she wanted to prepare his desserts—well, who cared? Wendell took cynical delight in having Stephanie fuss over him anew. He guessed she was fighting to stay, knew he would not permit it. On Monday evening he ate dinner; the dessert was tapioca pudding. When he awoke, he had what he thought was an attack of diarrhea. He ate that day as usual. The diarrhea was worse on Wednesday. He was worried, called his physician, asked him to make a thorough examination.

"Nothing to worry about, Reverend." The doctor gave as his verdict: "It's a minor digestive upset. Otherwise, you are in surprisingly good condition. My only recommendation is that you eat bland food for a day or two."

Wendell protested that he had been eating bland foods. Stephanie, who had insinuated herself into the bedroom on the excuse that she was concerned over his lack of appetite, suggested custards, then beef broth in the evenings when he was ready to go to sleep.

"Perfect, Miss Trent," the doctor said, nodding at Wendell.

Wendell suffered his worst assault of diarrhea Thursday morning. It subsided by midafternoon, but left him weak, debilitated, and without appetite. At five-thirty the servants departed for their evening off. At eight, Stephanie announced that she was tired and would undress and lie down in her bedroom, which adjoined Wendell's. She told him to call out to her if he wanted anything or became hungry. Half an hour later, he clamored for food. She put on a robe, went into his room.

"You heard the doctor," she said. "I'll bring you some good strong beef broth and crackers."

James Courtney was waiting in the kitchen. He wore only a pair of slacks. His chest and feet were bare. Stephanie took the saucepan of thick beef soup she had made previously from the refrigerator, heated it on the stove. Jim gripped her arm reassuringly, grinned, poured cantharis into the broth, stirred it with a wooden spoon.

"Aren't you giving him too much?" Stephanie asked, seeing the quantity of finely crushed powdered beetle he put into the saucepan.

"Who cares? We want a maximum effect, Steffie, or it's no good." He patted her shoulder. "See you in a few minutes." He left the kitchen, went upstairs silently, let himself into her bedroom. She had closed the door connecting it with Wendell's. He stripped off his slacks and, naked, lay down on Stephanie's turned-down bed. He did not have to stroke or touch himself. Anticipation was sufficient to bring him erect. He lay, not moving, heard Stephanie enter Wendell's room.

"Here you are, Wendell." The sound of china clinking as a tray was set down came clearly through the closed door. "Try to get all the broth down. Want me to help you eat?"

"I can manage by myself."

"Then I'll go back to my room. Just call me if—"

"I won't want anything else tonight."

The hell you won't, Jim thought.

Stephanie entered through the connecting door, closed it behind her. She removed robe and nightgown, turned on a soft table lamp, lay down on the bed beside Jim. They did not touch or speak, lay scarcely breathing as they listened intently through minutes that seemed hours. At first they heard the faint sounds that indicated Wendell was spooning broth, breaking and chewing crackers. Then there was a gulp followed by a single clink. Wendell had picked up his soup cup, drunk down its contents, put the empty cup back on its saucer. Jim felt Stephanie tense. He reached for her hand, gave it a squeeze. The hand was icy, the palm slick with cold perspiration. She pulled it free.

More minutes passed—three or three hundred: neither of them could have judged accurately. Now there were sounds of Wendell stirring in his bed, moving this way and that—and what might have been muttered curses. The movements grew agitated.

"Jim," Stephanie whispered. She was trembling. "I . . . I can't go through with it."

"Too late," he whispered back. "It'll start soon—and be over fast." He turned his head, studied her in the soft light of the table lamp. Her eyes were closed tight, her hands clenched at the sheet. The nipples of her full breasts were flat. He brushed his palm over them. There was no response. He moved his hand, thrust it between her thighs, fingers probing, cursed to himself. He was aroused, ready, but fear had turned her frigid. She was juiceless, completely dry.

Wendell was beginning to thrash around on his bed. A glass fell or was thrown and shattered.

"Listen. I'll have to get into you fast," he whispered. Seizing one of her hands, he placed it against his rigid penis. "For God's sake, think of something—make yourself wet." She shook her head.

"Steffie!" It was Wendell's voice—hoarse, bewildered, yet demanding. "Come in here!"

"Answer him," Jim prompted her, fingers still working. She tried to move her lips and speak, failed.

"Steffie!" A bellow. "Hurry up!"

"I . . . I can't, Wendell." Stephanie spoke at last, as they had rehearsed it. "I'm busy."

"Busy? Why, you goddamned Jew bitch!"

He could be heard getting out of bed.

"Now!" Jim rasped in Stephanie's ear. He mounted her, tried to drive his penis into her as her vaginal muscles clenched. "Get your legs around my back." She obeyed. The muscles relaxed slightly. He forced through the barrier. "Move . . . act like you're loving it."

The connecting door crashed open. Wendell Courtney took one step inside the room, stopped. Massive quantities of urethral irritant had done their work. His phallus, a shaft jutting through the open fly of his pajama trousers, was so distended it appeared misshapen. His eyes were wide, wild, red—must be what a rutting elephant looks like, Jim thought, glancing over his shoulder as he pumped into Stephanie.

It was as they had expected. The sight of them coupling served to further inflame Wendell Courtney. He gave what was almost a shriek, ripped off his pajamas, and hurled himself onto the bed. "Keep doing it!" he rasped to Jim, seized Stephanie's head, twisted it to one side, forced her jaws open. "Take it—all of it!" he screeched.

To his surprise, Jim discovered that he derived pleasure from watching his uncle being fellated. He slowed his movements, stared. Wendell ejaculated almost immediately. Stephanie tried to turn her body away, but was pinioned by Jim's weight on her hips and thighs.

"Change places with me!" Wendell pushed Jim off her. His penis, still incredibly distended, caused her pain. She cried out. Jim silenced the cry and marveled how much he enjoyed using a woman together with another man, even when it was a man he hated—and who would soon be dead.

"Yid cunt. Whore." Wendell was repeating the words as though chanting, until he reached orgasm, groaned loudly, rolled off Stephanie. He knelt on the bed. His face was flushed, his body coated with sweat, and he panted, but he was still erect.

Suddenly his expression changed from one of lust to rage.

"You thieving bastard!" He grabbed Jim's shoulders, gripped them with astounding strength. "First my money . . . then cheating me—you and this kike!" His fingers dug into Jim's flesh. Stephanie tried to pull him away from Jim. He released Jim for a moment, struck her in the face. His strength seemed to increase. His hands went around Jim's neck, squeezed. "Lie on your stomach or I'll kill you!"

Jim had no choice but to obey.

"I'll teach you . . . give you a lesson you'll never forget." Wendell was raving now. Clearly something had snapped. "Your mother was a whore. Another blackmailer. Claimed you were mine"—the fingers tightened—"my bastard. Walked out on me. Gutter slime. Like you!" He suddenly released his grip. His hands moved to Jim's buttocks, clawed at them. His ravings continued, louder, but incoherent.

Jim Courtney's brain seemed to explode. Wendell Courtney was his father. He should have guessed long ago. He screamed. Not because of the pain that seared through him as Wendell drove into his body. But at the realization and what it implied. He went on screaming, heard neither Wendell's labored gasps nor the footsteps, then the voices, in the corridor somewhere outside the room.

"Reverend! What's wrong? Are you all right?"

Stephanie did hear and comprehended. Some of the servants had returned earlier than expected. She whimpered in terror, slid off the bed. Her face was bleeding. She stumbled, blindly searching for her robe.

Massive cantharis overdose and exertion and madness were having their terminal effects on Wendell Courtney's heart. Orgasm and chest pain gathered simultaneously, peaked together.

He cried out—whether in pleasure or agony, not even he knew—and slumped, knowing nothing more.

Chauffeur, cook, and a housemaid rushed in, stopped frozen, aghast. Stephanie crouched in a corner. Jim now lay on his side, in a fetal position, still impaled, motionless. Wendell had voided at the moment of death, was a limp bundle in a pool of filth.

The cook and housemaid fled, retching. "Call the cops!" the chauffeur shouted after them.

There were rigid unwritten laws in those days. Police, prosecutors, and the press swept scandals involving members of the clergy under the thickest of thick rugs—and Wendell Courtney had been an ordained minister. In any event, obvious sex offenses aside, there was little that could have been proved in a court of law.

Jim and Stephanie pulled themselves together before the police arrived and hastily concocted a story between them. She swore that Wendell had often used aphrodisiacs (no, she had no idea how he obtained them). The sex apparatus and manuals found in the bedroom and den (and gleefully confiscated by leering detectives) bore out her claim that he had always been a "weird ball" (the term was rendered as "pervert" in police reports). Jim's account of events sounded plausible.

"He was hurting Steffie. I came in and tried to stop him. He must have gone insane—tried to choke me to death and almost succeeded."

Stephanie's battered face and the bruises on his throat were ample supporting evidence. And since emergency surgery was needed to repair his ruptured sphincter, it was clear enough that an at least temporarily insane Wendell Courtney had committed forcible homosexual rape on his nephew.

"Nephew" is what James Philip Courtney remained. There was nothing—beyond Wendell's ravings—to indicate, much less prove, that Wendell had been his father. Jim thought that Wendell's safe might yield documents as well as money, but was unable to go near it, or even into the den. The den was sealed, first by police, then by Wendell's attorney, who came with court orders, a pair of burly security men—and grim news for Jim and Stephanie.

"I won't read Reverend Courtney's will to you because you are not beneficiaries, nor even mentioned. I will tell you something of its contents, though. He left varying sums to friends and servants and the rest of his estate to . . . ah . . . charity."

"Charity?" Jim snorted. "I don't believe it!"

"Perhaps I should have been more specific. To certain non-profit organizations with . . . um . . . patriotic Christian aims. I assure you, the will is entirely in order."

He let that sink in, went on. The house would be guarded around the clock, but they could stay there for a week. After that:

"You'll have to leave—taking only your clothes and personal possessions, of course."

Jim and Stephanie stared at each other. It had all been for nothing.

The press merely reported that Reverend Wendell Courtney had died of a heart attack, but details of the scandal spread over a hundred grapevines. The day after the funeral, Jim was informed by the Wyler College dean of men that although only a few days remained of the term, he would have to leave—quietly, and without any delay.

"I'm sorry, but there's been just too much talk," the dean said.

The next day, Jim was called to the Federal Building in downtown Los Angeles. The chief agent with whom he had dealt as a campus informer gave him more bad news.

"Unfortunately, you're covered with muck, Courtney. If anyone connects you with us, we'd be smeared too. From today on, we don't know you, and if anyone asks, we never did."

"Now what the hell am I supposed to do?"

"We're not ungrateful for your past services. We've pulled your phony medical records out of the draft-board files—"

"You're being grateful by having me drafted?"

"No draft. You'll enlist. We've already pulled some strings. A man with your qualifications and experience is valuable. You'll have an easy assignment and eventually get a commission."

"And report to you what I hear in the Army?"

"Not to us. You'll report to the Army about the Army. By the way, I understand you've been left out of your uncle's will and are broke."

"How in the name of Christ did you know?"

"That's what we're in business for. To know things. Anyway, the Bureau wants to give you a token for past services rendered—a farewell present. Here's a thousand bucks. Sign this receipt."

Jim took the money, glanced at the receipt. The amount shown was five thousand dollars. The agent gave him a long, hard look. He understood, said nothing, signed. Then he straightened up and, face flushing, asked:

"Can I put off enlisting until . . . until . . . ?"

He was unable to finish the question.

The agent's laugh was lewd, cruel. "Sure, we know even that. Relax. It's been taken care of. The Army's agreed to waive physical exams—a note's been made on your forms."

"In that case, when and where?"

"Tomorrow morning, nine o'clock, at Fort MacArthur. Ask for Colonel Geoghegan. He'll see to it that you're a sworn-in soldier boy before noon."

"Seems you people are in a hell of a hurry to get rid of me."

"We don't have much choice, Courtney. We found the spic bartender who sold you the fly. He identified you from a photograph. Suppose somebody else tracked him down? We're saving your neck, kid. So long. Drop by and see us after you've won the fucking war."

Stephanie had the jewelry Wendell had bought her at the beginning of their affair. She sold two pieces for almost four thousand dollars on the same day Jim went to the Federal Building. When he returned to the house, he found her packing.

"Too bad we didn't make it happen ten minutes earlier," he said, leaning against the doorframe. "We would have had—"

"Had what?" She reached for a piece of paper on her dresser. "The shyster came around today and made me go into the study while he opened the safe. This was inside. Addressed to you."

The paper was folded in half. Jim opened it, read a note that had been written by Wendell: "Once a thief, always a thief. Did you think I was fool enough to make the same mistake twice?"

Courtney crushed the paper, flung it on the floor. Wendell had never put the real-estate cash in the safe. But he had suspected Jim would think he did and try to steal it.

"There was no money," he groaned.

"There was no money," Stephanie repeated, her tone hollow, lifeless. She stared into an open suitcase. "Leave me alone, Jim. Get the hell out of here."

"We have to talk—"

"Get out!"

She had raised her voice to almost the level of a scream, and a security man hurried to the foot of the stairs, called out:

"What's going on up there?"

"Nothing. Everything's okay," Jim said. He stepped out into the corridor and went to his own room, where he too started to pack. Sometime later, he heard Stephanie carrying her bags downstairs. He did not leave his room to help her or even to say good-bye.

Jim naively loaded his things into his Buick convertible and drove to Fort MacArthur the following morning. At 11:45 A.M. he was sworn into the United States Army as Private James Philip Courtney, serial number 19046107, and given until five that afternoon to get rid of his civilian impedimenta and automobile. A military policeman was assigned to accompany him into San Pedro, where he stored the former in a warehouse and sold the latter at a ludicrously low price to a used-car dealer.

Private Courtney had little opportunity to register first impressions of Army life at Fort MacArthur. The powers that wanted him gone from Southern California had manipulated levers to set cumbersome Army bureaucracy into operation at a frenzied speed. The initial processing of a new recruit usually took a week or more. Courtney was rushed through the procedures of filling out forms, intelligence testing (he scored a remarkably high 154), uniform issue, and all the rest in less than forty-eight hours. He then received priority travel orders instructing him to "proceed without further delay" to Fort Monmouth, New Jersey, where his strange—and often equivocal—military career would begin.

16

Returning to Montemar after her lunchtime visit to Vivian Dixon's gallery, Sybil Pearson kept the promise she had made herself. Taking some letters in to James Courtney for signature, she waited until he had finished and said:

"I didn't have a chance to ask Neil where he was going. No one seems to know. Could you tell me?"

Aquiline features twitched with indecision before Courtney replied: "Harkness is making a trip under charter to me." He spoke as though that answered the question, turned to papers lying before him on the Bureau Plat.

"Do you . . . should I expect him back soon?" Sybil persisted.

The answer was another evasion, given with a trace of annoyance. "When I hear from Harkness, I'll let you know." Tone changing, Courtney issued instructions. "Tell Grenville I want to see him in an hour—I'm not to be disturbed until then. And you can leave early today if you want—at four."

"I have to catch up with some paperwork—"

"It'll wait. Quit at four." Now it was an order.

He flicked a remote-control switch turning on the stereo set. Music and a chorus of voices swelled from the speakers: "*Amour vole en tous lieux.*" Sybil, going to the door, recognized it instantly. Part three of *Carmina Burana*—"Love flies everywhere," her brain translated. She was acquainted with her employer's moods. His choice of that particular section—and in a French-language recording—indicated he was in a buoyant and randy mood, she reflected.

"*Saisi par le desir . . .*"

"And is seized by desire."

He must be, Sybil thought, going into her office and closing off the music as she closed the door. It explained why he wanted to see Grenville. The butler would speak to Kristin Verkerk and take the girl to Courtney's suite later, in the evening. But it failed to explain other things, Sybil mused, frowning. Why he was so insistent that she quit early, and above all, why he had refused to give her any information about Neil Harkness.

She sat down at her desk, reached Grenville on the house telephone, delivered Courtney's message. Hanging up, she tried to think if there was anyone she might telephone who would know something more about Neil, finally gave up, decided she would go into Cabo Verde at four and see Vivian again. Since Ken Dixon was also away—bit of a mystery there, too, Sybil thought—Vivi and she might have a drink and dinner together.

Neil Harkness was talking about Sybil.

"I'd love to show her this thing," he said, puffing on a Celta. He waved the pack of typescript at Kenneth Dixon, who leaned against the aft bulkhead of the enclosed bridge and opened a can of beer, his first of the voyage. "She'd lose her blind faith."

Dixon took a tentative swallow of beer, shook his head. "No way. Nothing you've read so far would change her opinions."

"Balls. She'd see that Courtney broke damned near every law in the statute books by the time he was twenty-one."

"You've got a lawyer's brain, Neil. Women's minds don't work like that." Ken drank more beer, grinned. "Especially not if they're Englishwomen who left Blighty to settle among romantic Latin savages."

"Is that a line from one of your novels?"

"Look. Women will forgive anything a man did when he was young—if he became rich and famous later. Especially upper-class Englishwomen. They cream over rich men with shady pasts. As for Sybil—well, she's told us all. She got to hate England, and then there was her father, the duke—"

"Viscount," Harkness corrected glumly.

"Whatever. Weak, a failure—a total washout. So she pulled up stakes. Farewell, Leicester Square . . . hello, Andalusia and all the exotic trimmings every English female freaks over. Only, Sybil did even better—hit the jackpot. She found God." Dixon scratched his back by rubbing it against the metal bulkhead, grimaced wryly. "Ever stop to think that God's sixty—only a couple of years older than her father?"

"You may have a point," Harkness said. He slammed the papers down on a shelf near his elbow, scowled out at the sea. Ken spoke again.

"Sybil has a Daddy figure she can hero-worship. Tales of his youthful pranks—damned clever murder included—won't disenchant her. Of course, as you'll see, he only got worse later, and you and I know a lot about what he's done in recent years. The sum will do the trick with Sybil when you lay it out for her."

"Not when, if," Neil said without turning his head. "I told you. He has me boxed in. All four sides, top, and bottom."

"Scared?"

"Pessimistic. The more I learn about the man, the more I become a defeatist. He started early, had himself plenty of practice, and as far as I can tell, nobody's ever beaten him."

"Not in anything big, and not until now," Dixon said, "but he has a lot of enemies. They keep trying."

"If they're like the fuck-ups aboard the Chris-Craft who wanted to stop me and come aboard, they won't get anywhere."

"I think those people would have made it except for a fluke."

"You weren't there—but go ahead. What fluke?"

"How many guys would have spotted and recognized their interceptor gear, known how to turn it back on them, and thought fast enough to do it?"

"Not many. It doesn't make any difference, though."

"Hell it doesn't, Neil. If it hadn't been for you, they would've done and got what they wanted—and it's pretty obvious that would have hurt Courtney, screwed up something important for him."

"Your logic is getting convoluted, old buddy. You've lost me."

"I'm saying that if you were able to beat people who would have beaten Courtney if it hadn't been for you, you can beat Courtney, too."

Harkness swung around in the captain's chair, laughed. "You've just nose-dived from convoluted logic to the worst English I've ever heard.'' He eased himself out of the chair. ''Climb out . . . and up into the saddle, you clown. It's your watch. I'm going to sleep.''

''Dream happy.''

''I'll probably have nightmares—about whatever our fuck-fest killer may have planned for me in Venice.''

The stereo was silent, had been for forty-five minutes, when Leslie Grenville entered the *estudio*. He found James Courtney gazing fixedly at the Frans Hals portrait of a chess player.

''You wished to see me, sir?''

Courtney's eyes seemed to be a paler, harder blue than usual as they shifted away from the painting, focused on his butler. Courtney was silent for a moment. His eyes narrowed. He had noticed something he considered odd. Grenville stood near the portrait. His normally placid, ovine face seemed to pick up some of the knowing, arrogant qualities that characterized the chess player's expression.

No, they had not been picked up, Courtney thought. They were there, had always been there, but hidden, not allowed to show themselves. He looked harder at Grenville, and the expressions faded, disappeared. This disturbed Courtney, made him slightly uneasy. He had caught Grenville in an unguarded moment, when the butler was thinking secret thoughts—*having to do with me*, intuition warned him. He made a mental note to watch Grenville more closely, probe the man for evidences of disloyalty, and finally spoke:

''I'll want the girl Kristin tonight.''

The corners of Grenville's lips twitched disapproval, but he said, ''Very well, Mr. Courtney. What special preparations?''

''Only the syringe.''

''She'll demand the coins again,'' Grenville declared firmly.

''Indeed?'' Courtney angled an eyebrow. ''Has she been talking?''

''Rather. Boasted to other women in the annex that she'll soon be rich and able to quit work—a bit of queening that hasn't been well received over there, I'm afraid.'' Grenville's tone was I-warned-you-so reproof—which Courtney found reassuring. Grenville intensely disliked Kristin Verkerk. It was reasonable to assume that his odd expression moments earlier had stemmed from nothing more sinister than a smug, superior knowledge that his opinions had been fully vindicated.

Yes, that's the answer, the explanation, Courtney thought with a sense of relief, rewarded Grenville with a grateful man-to-man smile, and said: "Bring her up tonight—but there won't be any coins." The smile broadened. "In the meantime, do me a favor or two."

"My pleasure, sir."

"It's not four yet, but tell Sybil she can go and send the guard off, too. Then telephone the appropriate friendly *funcionarios del gobierno* and inform them I want the girl's work and residence permits canceled as of tomorrow morning. Plus, to play safe, have them issue orders that she is to leave Spain within forty-eight hours."

"They'll need a reason for the record. I don't imagine you want to be involved."

"Possession of drugs. A hundred grams of marijuana, perhaps five of cocaine. Do you know where she lives?"

"I have the address."

"Good. Arrange with someone to put the evidence somewhere tonight and suggest that the police make their search early—well before dawn."

Grenville practically licked his chops. "Pity you weren't able to rid yourself of Miss Marsh as easily."

Courtney blinked; the corners of his mouth turned down. "Didn't . . . ? No. I haven't told anyone yet. I received a phone call from New York. Eileen was . . . was found dead in her hotel suite."

The butler, unmoved, asked, "Suicide?"

"No. I'm told she had been drinking and suffered some kind of embolism. The authorities have ordered an autopsy."

"I wonder what it will show?" Grenville mused aloud.

"That she died a natural death," Courtney said, voice crackling.

Clearly the subject was closed, and just as clearly, Grenville was being dismissed, sent off to perform his assigned tasks.

James Courtney was left alone. He knew that with Grenville presiding over the outer office, visitors and telephone calls would be blocked until he wished otherwise. He could indulge himself, gloat over the two telexes Sybil had brought in to him a few minutes before Grenville entered the study. They were on the tabletop. He picked them up, almost fondling them.

By coincidence, the two messages had been transmitted—and thus received—almost simultaneously. The first came from Nicosia, on Cyprus, the other from Zurich. Sent by men operating independently and unaware of each other's activities—or existence, for that matter—they dovetailed neatly. Perfectly, Courtney reflected, an ultimate of synergistic effect. Vital parts of his master plan were being implemented. They would act and react, creating a whole infinitely greater than the sum of its parts.

The telexes were in English, apparently innocuous, their texts beyond suspicion.

> From Lanarca:
> YOUR WONDERFUL GIFTS REACHED US INTACT. WE ARE WILDLY EAGER TO BEGIN USING THEM BUT MUST WAIT UNTIL ELECTRICIANS REWIRE THE HOUSE TO PERMIT GREATER CONSUMPTION OF CURRENT. THANK YOU FOR BEING SO KIND AND THOUGHTFUL. OUR VERY BEST WISHES, ALWAYS. EDGAR AND HARRIET MOSSMAN

Edgar and Harriet Mossman were actual persons, ostensibly retired American expatriates residing for the past two years in Cyprus. James Courtney had sent them gifts—a new refrigerator, electric dishwasher, other household electrical appliances. And the Mossmans did live in a villa wired for only 1.5 kilowatts—an undercapacity that required considerable increase before the appliances could be used.

It all provided a childishly simple—and foolproof—communications cover. It was far safer than telephone, for the installation of scrambler devices on perpetually troubled Cyprus would excite official curiosity, lead inevitably to serious trouble. The code—if it could be called that—reported the arrival of large quantities of arms that had been shipped as agricultural equipment by an untraceable CVI dummy company. They were being distributed—secretly, needless to say—to dissident factions in Saudi Arabia and Kuwait. When the weapons had been all transshipped, they would be put to use. The uprisings would begin. The Saud and Sabah regimes would be first shaken, then made to topple.

The second telex, from Zurich, read:

> OUR OFFER AND TERMS HAVE BEEN ACCEPTED. SUPPLIER GUARANTEES RAPID DELIVERY. KLOSTER, BAUERKREDITBANK

Courtney again congratulated himself on having coerced the banker into action. Kloster was announcing that he had concluded negotiations to have Omani Sheikh Abdul al Amari eliminated—and, the message indicated, in the manner desired. With much sound and fury in the entire-floor Olympic Towers apartment the playboy sheikh maintained. No better place than there, in New York City, Jim Courtney gloated. The event—as he thought of it—would attract maximum worldwide publicity, create maximum confusion in Arab countries throughout the Middle East. Sheikh Abdul had many friends and even more enemies there. His abrupt removal from the global petrodollar-manipulation scene would send them flying at each other's throats.

Having reread the telexes, Courtney laid them down on the table and all but purred satisfaction. The timetable was being met, even bettered, in all areas—except one, he thought, and frowned. A key part of the scheme was badly behind schedule. Bernard Rechstein should have been at his final destination the day before, and making progress on his own negotiations.

But a cog had slipped somewhere. Rechstein had almost failed before he started. Almost, not quite. It had been necessary to make an abrupt change in plans—more drastic and sweeping than Rechstein could possibly imagine, Courtney reflected. Rechstein had been told only to make a detour to Venice and wait there. He had obeyed. He was in Venice, and he would wait. That the rest of his journey would be very unlike what he expected could not be helped. Courtney could not risk other cogs slipping—and they very well might until the Abdul al Amari affair was settled and the turmoil to follow reached its peak.

Oh, Fortune, like the moon, ever changing, rising first, then declining. Courtney reflected on part of a verse from *Carmina Burana*, grunted, thought: Bernie will just have to take the cards I dealt—or rather redealt—him.

Courtney's mind switched focus to the question that had gnawed at him since May Day. Bernard Rechstein had been followed by men who knew not only that he was coming to Cabo Verde but also that he was leaving aboard Harkness's boat and going to Tangier. That meant someone at Montemar was a spy, an informer.

Who?

James Courtney had mentally gone over the roster of his employees a score, a hundred times, since. For various reasons, most were impossibles, and most of the rest highly improbables. Sybil Pearson, security personnel, and household domestic staff had been kept ignorant of Rechstein's arrival date until the last moment, told nothing about his destination or mode or transportation out. Neil Harkness? No, he had been chartered too late for him to contact anyone who would have to come to Cabo Verde.

Administrative employees in the CVI annex had been told absolutely nothing. The same was true of men like Tom Eberhardt, who were business aides several notches higher on the scale. Grenville had everything to gain by being unswervingly loyal. Eileen? Well, it was just barely possible that Eileen Marsh had eavesdropped on his conversations, Courtney thought. However, at best she would have learned fragments—which she could never have assembled. Even if she had, Eileen would not have known where to sell the information.

Courtney stroked and kneaded the scar on his cheek, abandoned the mental exercise. It didn't really matter for the present. The spy would learn nothing further of value; the chance of other cogs slipping would vanish entirely when Abdul al Amari was eliminated; in the meantime, the Velázquez and Bernard Rechstein would serve their new purpose. With Neil Harkness as unwitting catalyst in the mix.

17

The true multinational megacorporations are not the household-word ITT's, Exxons, G&W's, and others listed on stock exchanges and given exposure by mass media as well as the financial press. They are holding companies incorporated in places like Lichtenstein or the Bahamas, operate with absolute freedom and in absolute secrecy under protection of the local laws. Their stocks are tightly held, unlisted. They issue no public financial statements or corporate reports, are immune from taxes, and beyond the reach of any regulatory agencies.

These—often shadowy even though enormously rich—entities bank in countries where account balances and transactions are kept secret, Switzerland and, again, the Bahamas among them. With vast resources at their disposal, wielding immense behind-the-scenes political power on a global scale, the secrecy-shrouded behemoths are laws unto themselves. Working through entire networks of fronts and dummies, they retain anonymity as they buy, sell, rig and manipulate, make or destroy. Some tend to specialize—in precious metals, base metals, commodities, real estate, currency exchange, oil, ships, or whatever. Others carry diversification to a remarkable extent.

Courtney Ventures International, originally incorporated in Lichtenstein, was an outstanding example of the latter. It owned or controlled manufacturing plants, base-metals mines, and a host of other widely variegated enterprises in several countries on four continents. Courtney, the archetypal entrepreneur, ruled the empire in the manner of an autocrat; to all practical purposes, it was a one-man show. Being particularly secretive and having a compartmented mind, it was natural that he maintain a tightly compartmented organization. The managers of subsidiaries knew only what Courtney wished them to know about other CVI enterprises or the parent company's operations. Some were not even aware that the companies they managed belonged to CVI. They were led—and left—to believe that their firms were owned by some entirely different corporation (which, of course, was a dummy that existed solely to disguise and dissemble).

With no balance sheets or even a complete list of CVI holdings available, financial analysts could glimpse barely more than the tip of the structure. On the basis of this scanty information, they estimated CVI's assets as "being in the billions of dollars" and more confidently calculated that Courtney's personal fortune "exceeded one billion dollars, was possibly closer to two billion."

The world news media had begun to focus more and more attention on James Courtney after the spring of 1976. That was when J. Paul Getty, expatriate American oil magnate and reputedly the richest man in the world, died at Sutton Place, his palatial and much-publicized manor house in England. With Getty dead, Courtney ranked as the richest of all American expatriates anywhere—and since the public relished superlatives, the media made Courtney the new success-story folk hero. Journalists found the billionaire cooperative, willing to grant interviews, talk at length about any topic—except CVI.

Courtney's explanation that he did not want to give out information to help competitors and business adversaries was generally accepted. Generally. At times, journalists went further afield in their efforts to learn about CVI. They ran into blank walls. Of course, there were rumors. That some—perhaps many—of CVI's activities were unethical, even illegal. That wherever the company had holdings, it kept important political figures on its bribe rolls. That in some of the smaller, lesser-developed countries, it owned whole governments outright. That . . . But it was impossible to confirm the rumors, and in any event, such charges are being constantly leveled against all multinational companies.

Eventually the media tired of probing into CVI and concentrated on James Courtney as a colorful personality and success symbol. In an effort to give the public some sense of perspective, they were wont to compare him with master accumulators, past and present. Morgan, Oppenheimer, Onassis, Ludwig, Geneen, Bluhdorn were only a few among the famed tycoons offered as yardsticks against which to measure. These efforts were futile, the comparisons meaningless. The business and financial operations of the men used as examples were to considerable degree visible, identifiable, known. Too much about James Courtney and CVI was shrouded in mystery, hidden.

It never occurred to anyone to compare Courtney with Basileo Zacharia, a.k.a. Sir Basil Zaharoff. The oversight was understandable. Immediately apparent differences between the two men were far too great; the similarities could be recognized only by someone who possessed a nimble imagination and was consciously searching for parallels. Which is what Kenneth Dixon had done: used his imagination, searched—and found striking analogies.

Neil Harkness did not become aware of this until late on the second day after leaving Cabo Verde. He had been forced to stop reading Ken Dixon's material on Courtney when a series of engine and communications-gear problems developed aboard the *Deirdre*. Luckily the malfunctions had been minor and could be repaired at sea without even reducing the vessel's speed. However, the tasks proved time-consuming, and he had needed to sleep betwixt and between doing them.

Now the glitches had been eliminated. The *Deirdre* was into the Adriatic, moving up the Italian coast at a steady twenty-seven knots, only hours out from its James Courtney-ordained destination, Venice. Slightly refreshed by a short nap, Harkness had relieved Ken Dixon on the bridge, and settling into the captain's chair, resumed reading once again. He marveled at the information Dixon had somehow managed to uncover about Courtney's military career and his activities as a civilian during the first two postwar years. Without question, James Philip Courtney had been selfless, self-sacrificing, a man worthy of high praise and respect during this period. After 1949, hard data seemed increasingly difficult to obtain, and Kenneth Dixon had tried to plug many gaps with deductions, surmises, conjectures. Harkness found these reasonable, plausible. His past experience as an attorney practicing corporation law enabled him to see and grasp many implications that Ken had either misinterpreted or missed entirely.

Neil read, and patterns emerged. Taken together, they formed a picture in broad-stroke outline. Courtney Ventures International was more than a holding company shrouded in the secrecy guaranteed by the laws of Lichtenstein and Switzerland. CVI was an international business and financial apparatus designed with lapidary care to be above ordinary laws. CVI was a shadowy empire and a law unto itself.

"An empire ruled and a law administered by one man: Courtney," Ken Dixon had written. "He issues orders directly to a global network of people who may or may not be formally members of the CVI organization. An admittedly partial list of these men (compiled as of 1973) follows." Harkness studied the names, recognized none of them, read on:

"CVI has footholds in the basic industries of several countries, controlling raw materials, processing, manufacturing, distribution. There is evidence that CVI has manipulated world markets in a number of commodities and products and has financed and instigated five government coups in Latin America and Africa. Courtney has strong ties with Israel and wields influence there (as an end result of his work on behalf of Jewish refugees during and after the war, and his continued interest in Jewish and Israeli affairs). Paradoxically, he also seems to have powerful friends and business connections in the Arab countries of the Middle East."

Neil blinked at the next—a one-sentence—paragraph:

"Farfetched as the idea may be, there are reasons to wonder if James Courtney isn't a watered-down latter-day Basil Zaharoff."

Harkness surrendered to his first impulse. He laughed. Ken's imagination must have been operating on a second bottle of gin when he wrote that line, Neil thought. Any comparison between Courtney and Zaharoff was preposterous, close to an ultimate in absurdity. True that Basil Zaharoff was the first and most ruthless, amoral, *and* successful of modern conglomerators. And he did operate in such obsessive secrecy that, during the first three decades of the twentieth century, he was known as "The Mystery Man of Europe." And also as "The Hidden Ruler of Europe," Harkness mused, and laughed again. Then he remembered the "Merchant of Death" label that had remained permanently fixed to Zaharoff's name, and the urge to laugh vanished, even though that identifying label made any comparison with James Courtney more ridiculous than ever. Then, out of curiosity rather than interest, he looked at the free-form biographical notes Ken had provided on Zaharoff:

> Origins obscure. Born Basileo Zacharia, 1850 (?). Place of birth either Turkey or Greece. Believed illegitimate. At sixteen (possibly earlier) was a pimp, thief, and occasionally homosexual prostitute on Smyrna and Constantinople waterfronts. Robbed relative (protector?) of life's savings, fled to England. Changed name to Basil Zaharoff. Returned to the Balkans, took

job as salesman for Nordenfeldt machine guns. Sold to all sides and factions in the perpetual Balkan wars and revolts within individual countries.

Zaharoff prospered, soon expanded both line and territory, selling weapons of all kinds throughout Europe. Historically proven that he frequently murdered competing salesmen, often engineered the start of wars or uprisings to increase business. Quickly gained control of such old established European armaments firms as Vickers in Britain, Schneider-Creusot in France, Skoda in Austria, and others, always making his moves in secrecy, employing as many as six doubles at a given time to confuse governments, press, and public.

By the turn of the century, Zaharoff was diversifying on a scale never seen before or since. He acquired coal, iron, lead, copper mines, foundries, steel mills, and a staggering array of other properties. His vast intercontinental holdings were organized to feed each other—against the day he knew to be inevitable and helped to bring about.

During World War One, munitions factories of Zaharoff's international cartel supplied all the European armies. Arms made by his British and French companies were sent to Germany through neutral Holland—which was also the transshipment point for German-made war materials secretly sold to the Allies. Germany paid Zaharoff three shillings' royalty on every shell its armies fired against the Allies. Britain twice bestowed the Order of the Garter on him. France made him Grand Commander of the Legion d'Honneur. The British Prime Minister, French and Italian premiers were on his payrolls, received huge sums from armaments profits.

Knighted, the Merchant of Death became Sir Basil Zaharoff and a celebrated public figure. Yet it was impossible to learn much about his organization, its holdings, how and where it conducted business. Several people tried between 1914 and 1917. By regrettable coincidence, all died—in much the same way that competing arms salesmen had died earlier. Most suffered fatal accidents—while swimming, by falling from windows or down flights of stairs, in automobile crashes. Some, according to police of the countries in which their bodies were found, committed suicide or suffered heart attacks or strokes. When the war ended in 1918, it was conservatively estimated that Sir Basil Zaharoff had amassed a personal fortune of two billion dollars—in terms of 1918 dollars.

There was no other such private fortune anywhere else on the face of the earth. Most observers believed the sixty-eight-year-old onetime pimp would be satisfied. They were wrong.

Weapons and ammunition were a drug on the market after the armistice. Sir Basil concentrated on other areas—with a vengeance. Still "The Mystery Man," he hid behind fronts and dummies, acquired more mines, mills, factories, and added huge oil properties to his holdings. He was still Europe's "Hidden Ruler," and no government in Britain or the Continent hindered the furious expansion or protested his methods.

Owners and company directors were issued ultimatums—sell, and at the low price offered. Those who hesitated were ruined by frame-up scandals or threatened with death. Any who still refused? Before the 1920's ended, a dozen French and five British industrialists died in accidents or "committed suicide." Lowenstein, the Belgian mining-and-metals magnate, was hurled to his death from an airplane. The heirs of these victims knew the truth, sold their holdings. At any price.

In 1930 there was deep economic depression throughout the world. But estimates of Sir Basil Zaharoff's private wealth doubled, to over four billion dollars, and it was said that he owned or controlled thirty percent of the Eastern Hemisphere's mines and heavy industry. He was by then self-exiled in Monaco, where there were no taxes and he was constantly guarded by a small private army of ex-convicts and case-hardened cutthroats. In 1936 he died—some say he was murdered by his closest aide, a man who had belatedly learned that Zaharoff was responsible for the years-before death of his father, mother, and fiancée.

With the Merchant of Death gone, his empire disintegrated. But his personal fortune was intact. It was distributed to his heirs, who, except for a longtime mistress and the several daughters she bore him, were like Zaharoff, mysterious—indeed, as far as officials and authorities were concerned, anonymous.

Neil's craggy features were set hard, grim, when he finished. He still thought it absurd to equate James Courtney with Basil Zaharoff. The two men, born seventy-odd years apart, came from different eras, different worlds. Zaharoff had been an arms merchant on a scale that defied description, a sinister figure whose wealth came from the millions and tens of millions—soldiers, sailors, and civilians—who were slaughtered in wars and revolutions between 1875 and 1918. That he had also built a mining and industrial empire was a side issue, a by-product of dealing in death. Throughout his eighty-six years, Zaharoff had believed in nothing but himself, given sincere support to no causes but his own. Biographers were unanimous that he was totally devoid of warmth, mirth, a sense of humor, a sense of being part of the human race (which he had no compunctions about decimating).

Courtney, on the other hand, despite his many unpleasant qualities, had served, and honorably, during World War Two. True, he had not been a combat soldier, but his assignment as a military-government officer in Germany could not have been free of risk and danger. He had made the cause of Jewish refugees his own; reliable sources agreed that no individual American Christian had done more for them than he. And there were countless more glaring differences, Harkness mused. As far as anyone could ascertain, Courtney's CVI companies were engaged in peaceful pursuits. Whatever other rumors made the rounds, there were none suggesting that CVI had subsidiaries manufacturing or selling arms and munitions. It was unlikely that they would—or could—Neil thought. Contemporary armaments manufacturers operated under the aegis of national governments, were virtually in partnership with them.

Neil grew more pensive. The grim look etched itself deeper on his face. Conceding the differences, he had nonetheless noted parallels and similarities. These were, perhaps, more apparent than real, and only concidences. However, James Courtney was driven by a fierce, unrelenting urge to vanquish, win, prevail. During his lifetime, Basil Zaharoff had perfected his *système*, a formula that produced constant, continuing success, left no margin for error, and had never been equaled, much less surpassed. Following it, Zaharoff challenged the world's most powerful men and companies and cartels—and the entire world itself—and triumphed over them all.

It was possible that Courtney had recognized the ruthless efficiency of the Zaharoff formula as it applied to corporate structure and operations and adapted it for CVI. That, Harkness reflected, might in itself explain why Courtney had expatriated himself to Europe. On the Continent, anything—and everything—could be concealed through anonymous companies, secret bank accounts, corrupt (or easily corruptible) officials, politicians, parliamentarians, even princes of ruling royal houses. Were it assumed that Courtney had adopted the Zaharoff formula, the mysteries of CVI could be explained. Rather than being a multinational company, CVI was another global apparatus with hidden and, conceivably, sinister aims and purposes.

The questions now whirling through Neil's brain demanded discussion—with the man responsible for putting them there. Hitching himself forward in the captain's chair, Harkness activated the below-decks squawk box, spoke into the mike, awoke Ken Dixon, and asked him to come to the bridge. The novelist showed five minutes later, rubbing sleep from his eyes with one hand, holding a can of Aguila beer in the other, grinned knowingly when his friend, still scowling, said:

"I finished, and I'm impressed. You haven't sold me on the Zaharoff part, though."

"Intrigued, huh?" Ken drank beer.

"Curious. What made you think of him in the first place?"

"Well, I was having the research done on Courtney. Out of the blue, some publisher asked if I'd write a novel based on the arms industry. I kicked the idea around, plowed through every available book on the subject—decided too many novelists had already done it and said no, thanks. But I'd read an awful lot about Zaharoff in the process, and one day it hit me." Dixon paused to drink more beer.

"Exactly what was it that hit you?"

"The weird and wondrous similarities. Super-secrecy. Faceless people running false-front companies that deal through more of the same. All gains and profits, no setbacks or losses. People and firms knuckling under for no apparent reason. Only the one man at the top knowing what really goes on—and giving all the orders."

"Same could be said for other multinationals."

"You're rushing me. I haven't said it all—not by a long shot. Like Mystery Man Z., Courtney owns stables of political whores in every country where CVI operates, and in some where it doesn't—"

"In Spain?" Neil interrupted.

"Spain's the exception. Oh, he may have his hooks into some third- or fourth-grade *funcionarios*. Nobody at or near the top."

"Isn't that a little odd?"

"Nope. He made a deal with the Franco regime when he first came to Spain. He'd be a model guest, help the economy when and as he could, but keep his nose clear of internal politics. In return, he was promised the kind of special VIP treatment extended to super-rich foreign residents by most countries. The arrangement continued after El Caudillo died."

"Courtney made a sensible deal."

"Dog's instinct not to shit on his own doorstep. Everywhere else he bought year-round, no-limit hunting licenses. He and CVI make their own rules. Legislators who try to pass laws restricting them aren't reelected. In a pinch, they wake up in bed with ten-year-old boys, cameras clicking around them, and have to resign in disgrace. Business firms that offer too much competition go bankrupt. People who make waves and won't stop making them disappear. For good."

Ken finished his beer, dropped the empty can into a waste bin, and took the other captain's chair. His expression was at its most sardonic when he spoke again.

"That's all surface sewage, Neil. Let me dig deeper into the slime. Take two examples out of several. CVI had mining interests in Mwandi—that piss-ant country in Africa. The people down there voted themselves a new government, which announced it was going to nationalize CVI's holdings. Whereupon Ashara, another piss-ant country located next door, declares war. Before the UN gets the war stopped, a few thousand people are butchered, the new Mwandi government is replaced by a newer one—"

"And CVI's holdings aren't nationalized."

"They're increased. Properties seized from traitors et cetera are handed over to Courtney Ventures International. Much the same story in the Central American republic—I use the term loosely—of Altamira. Only there it was a revolution instead of a war. Poor dumb peons had a killfest for six months. All their crops and the capital city were burned—but neither side touched the CVI-owned factories, and the winners imposed a new tax to raise money and reimburse CVI for 'lost profits.' "

"You suggesting Courtney supplies the arms from his companies?"

"Not *from, through*. The difference in preposition marks his departure point from the Zaharoff formula. CVI doesn't own armaments factories but buys from companies that do."

"You think he's stirring more trouble somewhere?"

"It's a safe bet. He usually is."

"Any idea where?" Harkness asked.

"I'll make an educated guess. There's a hell of a big shitstorm brewing in the Middle East, ready to blow any minute, and he has all those connections in Israel . . ."

"You're logic's faulty, Ken. While he's always been a pro-Zionist and the Israelis love him, they're past the stage where they have to buy guns through middlemen. They manufacture their own—Uzi submachine guns, Kfir fighters, tanks, missiles, you name it. What they don't make, they order from Uncle Sam on long-term credits. Their weapons-shopping is straightforward, out in the open."

"Not all. Israel makes large-scale covert buys of arms that it then sells or gives to Khomeini's Iran, South Africa, Lebanese Christians, and others. That stuff does come from middlemen."

Harkness lit a cigarette. "You saying he's helping the Israelis to stoke up a new war?"

"Could be. I wouldn't put it past him." Dixon tipped his head to one side, intense eyes inquisitive. "This man you're going to meet—Fischer—is he an Israeli?"

"I told you. He's Swiss."

"Jewish?"

"He didn't say, I didn't ask . . . and who cares?"

"Maybe you should care, mariner." Ken dug into a pocket of his safari jacket, produced a small embossed silver object, asked: "Did Fischer travel to Tangier in the same cabin I'm using?" He saw Neil nod, held out the object. "A mezuzah. Must have dropped out of his pocket. I found it wedged between the mattress and bulkhead. Can you picture anyone who isn't Jewish carrying a mezuzah?"

"No." Harkness took the tiny religious talisman, studied it.

"My bet is that he's not only Jewish but an Israeli."

"Carries a Swiss passport, far as I know."

"Doesn't mean much. It's easy to get phony passports that're perfect forgeries." Ken paused, grimaced. "Especially if you're working for some Israeli outfit like Mossad or Shinbet."

Harkness laughed. "Your plot-spinning imagination's racing out of control. You don't have a thing to go on."

"Except hunch, instinct, and an educated guess about how the pieces fit together." Dixon patted his lower abdomen. "Gut feeling." He cleared his throat. "When are we due to arrive in Venice?"

"Huh?" The question surprised Neil. "Oh. Around midnight."

"What happens after we dock?"

"I'll go to see Fischer at his hotel—the Gritti."

"Correction. *We'll* go."

"No way. He's attracted trouble before and may again." Harkness was remembering the Tangier run and felt a premonitory chill along his spine. "I'm being paid to take the risks. You're not." It was gathering dusk. Neil reached for the control panel, switched on the *Deirdre*'s running lights, spoke again. "Besides, old buddy, if Courtney hears I had you along, he'd dump hard on both of us."

"Might not be the worst thing that could happen."

"My God! You've got to be kidding."

Dixon stared down at the deck. "Why do you think I came on this trip?"

"To get away from Cabo Verde for a while and dry out—or so I gathered from what you and Vivi said."

"We didn't want to tell you the truth. I'm about to be in a bad jam with Courtney."

"Why?"

"For a lot of reasons. Most go back a long way and wouldn't matter except . . . except for the new book."

"You mean your new book?"

Dixon ignored the question and, eyes still averted, licked his lips nervously. "It's had a slew of advance publicity."

"All to the good, no?"

"No." Ken's face turned grayish. "Then . . . Oh, hell, I got loaded and talked too much to the wrong people and put myself on the man's shit list. Please don't ask me for the details, because I won't give them to you. Just take it as fact that I'm going to be in deep trouble with him, and damned soon, unless I can slam at him first."

"Tagging along with me would only compound the felony—whatever it is."

"Neil. Fischer is the key to something big."

"And that's either a non sequitur or my hearing's gone."

"The two of us have a better chance of finding out what's going on than if you see Fischer alone."

"I'm not sure I want to find out. I'd rather just get the damned job down and forget about it."

"Even if you get yourself killed in the process?"

"You're being melodramatic again."

"Am I? You told me the guys on the boat that tried to intercept you had guns and took potshots at you."

Neil sneered contemptuously. "They fired across a couple hundred yards of open water. The decks of both boats were pitching. I couldn't have been safer."

"The point is, they didn't hesitate to shoot. Suppose they'd gotten aboard. Ever stop to think that they had orders to take what they were after from Fischer and then blow all of you away?''

''Maybe.'' The possibility had certainly occurred to Harkness before, but he preferred to put it out of his mind. ''Maybe not.'' He concentrated on lighting a Celta.

''Wake up!'' Ken snapped. ''Courtney's cooking up some kind of deal so very big that he's willing to risk lives—yours and Fischer's for starters. Jesus, the people he's bucking have so far tried to commit piracy, murder—who knows what else. He's pulled you into the mess—deep.''

''Only because I couldn't say no,'' Neil muttered; thought: Only because he'd ruin me, finish me off, if I didn't agree.

Dixon seemed to read his thoughts. ''Courtney has you by the balls. The same way he has me. Neither of us has a chance of ever getting loose—unless he's busted wide open.''

''You've said that before.''

''Sure. Often. It's the truth. This is probably the best chance we'll ever have. Once we find out what gives with this guy who wanders around with a metal tube in his hands and a mezuzah in his pocket, we'll have a lever, a club. I'm sure of it.''

Dixon continued to speak, hard-selling. Neil remained silent, listening, mentally digesting what his friend said, found himself gradually becoming convinced.

''Okay, Ken,'' he said at last, hoping that he was not making a grave and dangerous mistake as the chill gripped his spine again.

18

The perpetual chaos that is Italy had been whipped into one of its periodic states of total disarray. Red Brigade terrorists had assassinated the mayor of Turin. Neo-Fascists retaliated by kneecapping two leftist professors at the University of Padua. National police rounded up several hundred possible suspects in both cases, injuring some in the process. CGIL, CSIL, and UIL, the country's three great labor unions, called a seventy-two-hour general protest strike, effectively paralyzing Italy.

The port of Venice was closed to maritime traffic. Inbound

vessels rode at anchor in the roads off the Lido, waiting for tugboats, longshoremen, other port personnel, and even immigration and customs officials to resume work. Tankers, ore and grain ships, were clustered off the Porto di Malamocco channel; other craft—large and small—lay off the Porto di Lido channel, some five miles to the north.

Neil Harkness was familiar with Italian lunacies and with Venice. Informed by radio that harbor and port facilities were inoperative and that all vessels were barred from entering port, he took the news cheerfully. The situation was ideal for his purposes. He knew he could bring the *Deirdre* in somehow—and when he did, there would be no official record of the arrival.

At eleven P.M. he and Kenneth Dixon changed into clothes suitable for going ashore—slacks, sports shirts, and jackets. Then Neil opened the envelope filled with assorted currencies that Courtney had given him, extracted a sheaf of Italian banknotes, and divided them with Ken. That done, he dimmed the running lights and made for the Porto di Lido. Tricky maneuvering was needed to weave the *Deirdre* around and past the anchored freighters, cruise ships, and smaller craft clustered around the channel mouth.

The general strike was having far-reaching effects, Neil observed. Such famed Lido hotels as the garish Excelsior and more sedate Du Bains were dark, and the entire Lido commercial center was almost so. The result of power cuts, he guessed. Past the last of the parked ships and into the navigational channel, he saw that many of the marker lights were out. Smashed—by strikers or by groups or factions that sought to discredit them. However, the night was cloudless and a three-quarter moon hung low in the sky.

Through the channel and into the Venetian lagoon, Harkness turned up his running lights. Here it was better to be seen. He made for the channel, dredged through the shallows of the lagoon that led to the islands of the Giudecca, held his speed to ten knots. Within minutes a harbor-patrol vessel, its searchlight on and blinding, roared in from the starboard side. Harkness cut his throttles, gave Ken Dixon instructions, and sent him out on deck.

The patrol boat's hull bumped against that of the *Deirdre*. A blue-uniformed officer, holstered Beretta dangling from his wide leather belt, sprang aboard. He jabbered irately, windmilled his hands.

Dixon waited for the second or third angry "*Vietato!*" and produced two hundred-thousand-lira notes. The hands stopped windmilling to take them—and after that, nothing was "forbidden." The officer saluted, returned to his vessel. Neil eased the throttles forward. Normally he would have savored the experience of entering Venice. Especially at night, when the decaying splendors of the ancient city were all the more beautiful and exotic.

But tonight his mood was grim, apprehensive. He felt misgivings about the meeting with Fischer and what might ensue. Vague premonitions gnawed at him—as did regret at having agreed to let Ken Dixon come along. He ignored the moonlit domes of San Giorgio and Santa Maria della Salute and the dark, upthrusting shafts of the Venetian campaniles visible in the distance. If he noticed anything, it was the rotten-egg reek for which Venetian air is notorious and the masses of putrefying garbage that floated on the water. Then he became aware that no *motoscafi* or *vaporetti*—public-transportation passenger boats—were in evidence. Nor, on closer look, did he see any gondolas, water taxis, or work boats. Everything was strikebound. Good, he thought.

Another patrol craft materialized, came alongside. Neil stopped his engines. An officer—his uniform a light gray—boarded the *Deirdre*. Harkness spoke some Italian, went out on deck, but at first the officer did all the talking. Since immigration and customs personnel were on strike, it was impossible to allow vessels to dock or anyone to land. Hence the order to turn back and anchor offshore.

The officer was of higher rank than the one before. Neil radiated charm, and raising the bribe to what he thought an appropriate level, handed over 300,000 lire—about $250. It was enough to send the officer and patrol boat on their way.

"That should be the last until we dock," Harkness told Ken as he returned to the bridge.

"Dock? Where?" Dixon grumbled. "We won't be allowed—"

"We will—take it from me. Over there." Neil jabbed a finger toward a point just short of the Piazza San Marco, steered for it. "San Zaccharia—that's a stop for the public-transportation boats."

"Then it's probably being guarded by police."

"I'm counting on pickets."

"If we get away with it, I'll buy you a drink in Harry's Bar."

"Cheap offer. Harry's always closes at midnight—except on holidays like Christmas or New Year's—and now the whole town's closed. Take a good look, friend. Almost no lights anywhere."

There were pickets on the San Zaccahria landing stage. Three of them. Tough labor militants wearing rough clothes with red armbands on their left sleeves and carrying lengths of lead pipe in their fists. They crowded forward as Neil brought the *Deirdre* up snug against the rubber-tire fenders. The men seemed bent on violence.

Harkness clenched his own right fist, raised it as though in salute, slid a glass panel open with his left hand. "*Hola! Camaradas!*" He greeted them in Spanish, leaned out, pointed at the Spanish flag on its pole at the stern, switched to his fair brand of Italian. "*Per favore, aiutatemi,*" he began asking them to help moor the boat. It was, he said, an emergency, and went for the Achilles' heels possessed by all Italian males.

His passenger had a mistress, whom he wished to marry—quickly, because she was already three months pregnant. But he also had a wife—she was a *strega,* a *putana* who refused to give him a divorce. She was in Venice, at the Gritti Palace Hotel. With another man. If they could be found there together, a divorce could be obtained, marriage to the mistress could follow, and the expected child would be born legitimate.

The burliest of the three strike pickets—obviously in charge—thawed, gave Neil a huge gold-toothed smile, spoke to his companions. They grabbed the lines, began to make them fast.

"Act grateful—and give them each five thousand lire," Harkness whispered to Ken, who stared at him.

"Money—after the yarn you fed them? They'd be insulted!"

"There's no way in the world you can insult an Italian with money. Get moving."

The pickets accepted their tips gladly, agreed to keep an eye on the boat and pass the word to the comrades who were to relieve them at six A.M.

The short walk to the Gritti Palace seemed long. The candy-box-cover city of Venice was silent, deserted. There were no other pedestrians in evidence. The multistoried buildings that walled the San Marco canal were dark. Their windows were sealed by steel roller blinds on bottom floors, closed wooden shutters on upper stories. Here and there huge rats explored among uncollected bags of garbage, some of which had split open and spilled their contents.

"Eerie—people must be scared shitless," Dixon commented.

"Italians've been scared for years," Neil said in a tone that was a shrug. "Waiting for the whole country to blow wide open—probably afraid that this general strike might do it."

The windows of the Gritti Palace Hotel were also shuttered.

The great, ornate outer doors were closed and locked from the inside. Hard to believe, Neil thought, feeling very depressed. The Gritti was a famous luxury hotel. Closed up as it was now, it reminded him of a derelict warehouse. There was little light; power cuts had evidently affected the entire city of Venice. He stared at the double doors. The night porter's call button and its mounting fixture—both made of heavy brass—had been polished, and recently. It made him feel better—a sign of life. He pressed the button.

A bell could be heard ringing inside the building. A full minute passed before one of the doors opened—and then only slightly. There was some kind of safety-chain attachment. Luxury-category hotels did not need such precautions unless things were bad, very bad, Neil mused unhappily. Eyes peered out at him.

"Mind if we come in?" Ken Dixon said in English before Neil could speak. "We have an appointment with one of your guests."

"The name of the guest, please?"

The man spoke English remarkably well for a night porter, Harkness thought. But then, luxury hotels like the Gritti did have multilingual staffs. "A Swiss gentleman. Wilhelm Fischer."

"Ah, yes. He is one who has stayed with us and said he was expecting a visitor who could arrive at any time today or tomorrow." The safety chain was removed, the door opened wide. "Please."

Neil went first, Dixon followed. The man who held the door was no night porter. He introduced himself as Arnalfo Balducci, an assistant manager, and made profuse apologies. All hotel employees were on strike. The majority of hotel guests had been moved to the Royal Danieli, where some services were still being provided. Only three people—including Wilhelm Fischer—had insisted on remaining at the Gritti. When Neil sledgehammered in a question about the double-locked doors and safety chain, Balducci said that he and a private guard were the only people on duty and . . .

"There is talk there will be riots." He led the way into the opulent lobby, which looked dreary and dismal. It was illuminated by a few dim yellowish lights; no attempt had been made to straighten furniture or clean up. However, fluorescent bulbs glared over the reception desk. A uniformed—and armed—guard stood in the shadows, eyeing them nervously. Arnalfo Balducci went behind the desk.

"Signor Fischer is in his room. Number one hundred twenty-four," he said.

"Can you put me through to him on the house telephone?" Neil asked. The assistant manager shook his head.

"Mi dispiace—I am sorry. Our workers—they sabotaged the telephone system. *And* the *ascensores*—elevators. The guard and I must not leave the lobby. You must walk up the stairs."

The two Americans glanced at each other, shrugged, and strode off to the imposing staircase, started to climb.

"He didn't even bother asking our names," Ken said.

"Understandable," Neil said. "A general strike, the hotel's been vandalized, there's talk of riots. He's probably a nervous wreck."

Corridor lights barely glowed as a result of the power cuts. Harkness had to use his Ronson to check room numbers, finally found 124 and knocked on the door. There was no response.

"Try again," Dixon urged. "He may be a heavy sleeper."

"Let's hope that's all it is," Harkness blurted without knowing why he did or what he really meant, and rapped again, louder. There was no sound from inside the room. Neil had a sense of foreboding, bit at his lower lip, pounded on the wood paneling. Still nothing.

"Maybe he's in a different room," Ken suggested. "With the place practically empty, he might have decided to switch."

Harkness ignored him, said, "I'm beginning to like this deal even less." He tried the doorknob. It moved freely for half a turn, no further. "Locked," he muttered.

"Could be he went out," Ken said.

"Not without Balducci knowing, he didn't." Neil gripped the knob with both his powerful hands. "Lucky Italian hardware is junk." He gave the knob a violent, sustained twist. Metal snapped. He pushed the door open. Beyond the doorway, the room was in total darkness. "Wait," he cautioned, and following a hunch that was a fear, took a handkerchief from his jacket pocket, drapped it over his hand, and started fumbling for light switches on the wall, found one. It controlled the intricately fashioned Murano-glass ceiling chandelier. Its half-dozen small bulbs lit up—feebly. They were of low wattage to start, and the power reduction caused them to give even less light than usual, but it was enough. The room had been ransacked, the *seicento*-style *letto matrimoniale* stripped, covers and sheets flung to the floor. A man lay sprawled on his back across the mattress of the bed. He was naked, fat, balding, and must have been dead for hours. Rigor had begun to set in.

"Fischer," Neil groaned. "I think I expected it." He closed the door, shot the deadbolt home, turned to Dixon. "Take off your shoes and socks." He removed his own, pulled the socks over his hands like mittens. Ken followed suit. Moving in their bare feet, they switched on table lamps and finally the bedside lights. The marks on Fischer's throat were unmistakable. He had been strangled.

"What do we do next?" Dixon asked. "Call the cops . . . get Balducci?"

"Neither yet—maybe not at all. We look around," Neil said.

"For what?"

"Beats me. Not the tin tube, that's for sure. Whoever killed him must have been after it—and got it." Harkness went to the dresser. Its drawers were open. Some of their contents were strewn on the floor, some were still inside but disordered, pawed through.

What appeared to be booklets with various colored covers had been thrown into a corner. They caught Dixon's eye. "Passports!" he exclaimed, picking them up clumsily with his sock-sheathed hands. "French, British, Swiss, U.S., West German, and—I'll be damned!—Israeli." He opened the last, let the others cascade back down to the floor. "Made out to Reuven Dromi. I'll lay odds it's the only legitimate one. Like I told you when I found the mezuzah. The guy was Jewish."

"He was trying to pass," Neil said dryly. He exhibited a black skullcap and a fringed shawl he had taken from a drawer. "Yarmulke and tallith."

"Trying to pass? That proves it. He was Jewish—and religious."

"Come here." Neil returned to the bed. "Look at his cock."

Ken peered, shrugged. "A medium-sized prick. Nothing special."

"The foreskin's intact. Whatever his real nationality, Fischer was European, age about sixty. Ever hear of a European Jewish male in that age group who wasn't circumcised? Like one in every hundred thousand—if that. Now look at the inside of his left arm." Rigor had caused the arm to rise stiffly. "There. Traces of old plastic surgery."

"He probably survived a Nazi death camp and had the tattooed camp number removed after the war."

"No chance. Those numbers were tattooed on the outside of the left forearm. SS men had their blood types tattooed on the inside portion of the arm. They were a means of identification in war-criminal screenings. When the war was over, most SS men cut or burned them out and later had repair work done on the scar tissue."

Dixon grew sullen. His novelist's imagination, enamored of

the Fischer-was-a-Jew theory, was reluctant to accept a new one—Fischer-was-a-Nazi. It did not fit in with the elaborations he had created in his mind. "What makes you the expert all of a sudden?"

Neil saw no reason to mention that, while attending Columbia, he had researched and written a thesis on the apprehensions and trials of Nazi war criminals. "I saw a lot of movies and TV shows before I left the States," he said instead. He started back toward the dresser, stopped. Brow furrowing, he stared down at the oriental rug that covered much of the bedroom floor. For a moment he seemed to be shuffling his bare feet. Then, pulling the socks off his hands, he knelt and probed at the carpet surface with his fingertips.

"Something under here," he said, stood up. "Give me a hand rolling this carpet back."

They rolled the carpet back partially and a strip of canvas became visible. There were nail holes and some smudges of oil paint along its edge. The two men looked at each other. A painting that had been taken from its frame? They tugged at the strip without avail.

"Bed leg's holding," Neil said, rose to his feet, put the socks back on his hand, and stepping carefully, went to the foot of the bed and lifted the near corner a few inches. Dixon strained and managed to pull the canvas free. It was a painting—about four feet by six—and instantly curled up on itself. Obviously it had been tightly rolled for a considerable period. Harkness lowered the bed, helped Ken unroll the picture and hold it flat. The painting, glowing with color and magnificently executed, was of a mid-seventeenth-century Spanish nobleman astride a caparisoned stallion.

"Holy Christ—looks like a Velázquez," Dixon said.

"It is." Neil nodded. "I think—I *know*—I've seen it at Montemar. A prize piece in Courtney's collection. It used to hang in the main reception room." His eyes, dark green now, reflected puzzlement. "*Horse and Rider*—worth a fortune. Millions. And it's what was in the tube. Fischer removed and hid it, put something else in its place."

"Somebody has a big surprise coming."

Neil ignored the remark. "Doesn't make sense," he mused aloud. "Why in hell would Courtney want this smuggled out of Spain to somewhere else?"

"Off the top of my head, I'd guess he wanted fast cash from a secret private sale. Vivi tells me a lot of famous collectors do that when they're caught in a cash bind."

"Courtney'd never sell a picture from his collection. He has easier ways of raising a few million if he needs it—which I doubt."

But Ken was distracted. "Shit. Lot of damage . . . needs restoration." He pointed a sock-mittened hand at places where the unusually thick pigment layers had been chipped or flaked off. "Rolling must've cracked the paint, and sliding it around under carpets didn't help. Here—on the horse's belly—a piece missing the size of a matchbook cover." He leaned close to the picture. "Velázquez painted over an old canvas. There's another picture under this."

"I understand that's fairly common."

"Uh . . . yeah. Vivi says it is. Funny, just a single color here—a light gray—in squiggles that look like numbers. I can make out a two, a five . . ."

"We have to go, friend." Neil started rolling up the picture. He reached for the tassled prayer shawl. It went around the roll with several inches to spare. He tied it snug with a double knot.

Ken blinked. "We're taking it?"

"What else?"

"Those jokers downstairs will scream for the police."

"Let me write this script."

They turned off all but the overhead chandelier lights. Neil unlocked the deadbolt and opened the door. They put on their socks and shoes. Dixon, carrying the Velázquez, went to the far end of the corridor, made himself invisible in a deeply shadowed corner. Harkness went downstairs to the lobby. Balducci was behind the reception desk, dejectedly shuffling papers. The guard snored in a lobby armchair.

"We finally found Mr. Fischer's room," Neil said. The assistant manager gave an absent nod. "He's dead."

"You must knock more. Many people sleep very deep—"

"His door was open—it had been broken open. He is very dead. He was murdered—early in the evening, by the way he looks."

The information registered at last. Balducci saw that Neil was serious, turned white, began to tremble. "*Communistas . . . Brigate Rosse,*" he yowled, leaping to the conclusion that the Red Terror was sweeping through the hotel. He shouted to the guard, who awakened cursing and plodded over to the desk.

"You'd better go upstairs," Neil said.

"We have orders," Balducci croaked, shaking his head. "To stay in the" —he had lost the English word, searched his spinning brain, found it—"in the lobby. Here. Not to leave."

Harkness gambled that the Gritti's outside phone lines were also inoperative. "Then call the *carabinieri* or police." He won.

"It is not possible."

"I'll come upstairs with the two of you," Neil said with a magnanimous smile. "When you see there aren't any guerrilla armies running around, I'll go out and notify the police myself."

He was swamped with shakily voiced "*Mille grazies*," led the way.

"Whoever killed him left the light on," he said when they reached the open door. "Don't touch anything when you go inside—the police will want to take fingerprints when I bring them back."

Balducci and the guard entered hesitantly, but they entered. By then Kenneth Dixon and the Velázquez were halfway down the stairs. The assistant manager and the guard had never thought to ask about Neil's companion, just as they never thought to question Neil further when he said he was leaving and would let himself out.

Harkness did not rush. The two Italians would remain, mesmerized by their fear and horror, in Fischer's room for several minutes. Then they would return to the lobby and wait there indefinitely, assuming that he was having difficulty finding police—or that the police, preoccupied with the strike, would be slow to respond.

Neil's decision to take the painting and run had been made quickly, but it had not been made lightly. Assessing the situation in light of what he knew—and his legal experience—Harkness realized that to flee was bad and dangerous, but to stay would be far worse. Any confrontation with Italian police would lead to certain arrest and no doubt conviction on an array of charges.

The police would want to know how he and Kenneth Dixon had come to be acquainted with Wilhelm Fischer, a man of many passports and aliases, and why they had come to meet him in Venice. Art experts would be called from the Accademia to examine the painting. Once identified as a Velázquez, its ownership would be immediately traced to James Philip Courtney in Spain.

Intuition told Neil that Courtney, determined to maintain the secrets of his mysterious activities, would deny giving the picture to Fischer and claim it had been stolen. Whereupon the police would assemble an airtight case from circumstantial evidence. Harkness and Dixon were Fischer's partners in crime. They had a clandestine rendezvous in Venice—after all, didn't Harkness bring his boat in stealthily, secretly? Then—as police logic was sure to have it—the three thieves had fallen out, quarreled, undoubtedly over disposal of the loot or planned division of the proceeds, which could amount to millions of dollars. The quarrel ended in Fischer's death, caused—as who would fail to believe?—by Harkness and Dixon.

Neil had calculated that he and Dixon stood a better chance by clearing out—with *Horse and Rider*. He would get in touch with Courtney, tell him what had happened, and reveal that he had the painting. As long as he did have it, he could count on Courtney using his influence, providing protection.

It'll work, Harkness told himself as he descended the last steps. It has to work.

Ken Dixon had already opened the inner set of lobby doors and stood near them, waiting nervously. He was plagued by second thoughts and fears. For years his life had been increasingly sedentary, dull, with alcohol getting him through from one day to the next. Then, driven by a sudden need to absent himself from Cabo Verde, he had joined Neil Harkness on the voyage to Venice. During the last two days, he had rediscovered the exhilaration of high adventure, revitalized his sorely debilitated masculine ego, lived like a hardy, gutsy character in one of his early best-seller action novels. Then, while he was hiding in the corridor outside Wilhelm Fischer's room, a reaction had set in. Dixon was struck by the realization that this was not a novel; he was not a fictional character; he was in trouble, over his head.

"I'll get this," Neil said, and started to unbar the outer doors.

Ken licked his lips, shifted uneasily on his feet. "We're . . . we're practically begging to be charged with murder," he faltered.

"Relax." Harkness spoke over his shoulder. "Nobody has our names. The characters upstairs are scared shitless. They won't be able to describe us. Anyway, when the police get their act together, medical exams will show that Fischer was dead hours before we arrived."

Neil wished desperately that he was as confident as he made himself sound. The words had their desired effect, though. Ken picked up the rolled painting, held it cradled in both arms, and moved to the doors that Harkness was holding open.

They were outside, walking rapidly toward the San Zaccharia boat stop. Dixon expressed concern about the pickets; they would remember the *Deirdre*—"and us."

Neil had an answer for that, too. "Fine alibi. They'll establish the time we got here. Oh. Put on a long face for their benefit."

"Why?"

"Because you didn't find your wife. She'd skipped."

"How do we explain this?" Ken indicated the rolled canvas.

Neil kept his reply to banter level. "We met a guy selling pictures. People are always peddling paintings to tourists in Venice."

"At one-something-A.M. in the middle of a general strike?"

"So he was a scab working the late shift. Make with the unhappy look. We're almost there."

The pickets had gone. The landing stage was deserted. The *Deirdre* rocked gently at her moorings.

Dixon took the Velázquez below to Neil's cabin, returned topside, and cast off the lines. Neil went to the bridge, switched on commo gear and running lights, and started the engines. When Ken joined him, he eased the boat away from the stage and out toward the middle of the San Marco canal.

"I could use a drink," Dixon said.

"Amen." Harkness lit a Celta, exhaled smoke. "Get whatever you want and a bottle of Johnnie Walker Black for me."

Dixon left, returned moments later with bottles and glasses. By then Harkness had maneuvered the *Deirdre* into the deep channel and was making for the Porto di Lido outlet to the Adriatic. Ken stopped, cocked his head, and listened intently.

"Oh, my God," he groaned, hearing sirens. Their wail came across the dark waters—from the Grand Canal, he guessed, and had visions of vessels with police and *carabinieri* aboard roaring after them in hot pursuit. Neil hastened to reassure him.

"They're fire boats," he said calmly, swung to port, and slowed the engines to an idle. "Look over there." He pointed.

Billows of smoke illuminated by red shards of flame were visible in the sky beyond the intervening bulk of the nearer main islands.

"I'd say it's somewhere near the Santa Lucia station," Neil went on. "Explains where our friends, the pickets, went—to join their buddies in a riot *con* arson." He opened the throttles, brought the *Deirdre* back on course. "Lucky for us. Every harbor patrol boat'll rush to the scene. If the riot gets real hairy and lasts long enough, everybody will completely forget about you and me."

Ken, having relaxed a little, poured liquor. "They won't forget that corpse in the Gritti, though."

Neil took the tumbler of Scotch Dixon handed him, drank half its contents. Dixon took a huge swallow of his own gin, asked:

"Mind telling me where we're going?"

"Outside the limits of Italian waters for starters. Then I'll try to communicate with God."

"I'm awed. By prayer or ESP?"

Harkness patted the radio transmitter. "Since we can't risk using Italian commo systems even if they're operating—which I doubt—I'll raise the Yugoslav shore station in Rijeka. They'll patch me in on phone lines to Spain and Montemar."

"Suppose Courtney is out—or even away on a trip?"

"That castrated shit Grenville said Courtney would stay close to home until he heard from Fischer and me."

They were running parallel to the dark shoreline of the Lido now.

"You won't be able to tell him much over open circuits," Dixon said, emptying his glass.

"I speak to God in tongues, brother." Harkness switched on a bow-mounted searchlight. "Our exit's ahead. Lemme drive this thing."

The channel leading out to the sea was clear, but beyond its mouth lay the armada of ships immobilized by the strike and unable to enter port. The vessels themselves presented little problem. However, their anchor chains, angling into the water from their bows and sterns, created an obstacle course that required zigzagging at dead-slow speed. When the last of the anchored ships were left behind, Neil switched on the search radar. The screen indicated their were no craft ahead for at least ten miles. He rammed the throttles full forward. The *Deirdre* responded instantly to the surge of power.

The chronometer showed 0304 hours. Harkness double-checked his position, reduced speed to a minimum. "Good mile inside Yugo waters," he told Dixon, who lolled in the other captain's chair and was surprisingly sober despite having drunk his way through almost a pint of gin.

"Go drop the sea anchor," Neil said, "then put together some coffee and sandwiches on your way back."

Ken slid out of the chair, stretched, gave a mock salute, went.

Neil sat, gathering his thoughts. It was past three in the morning, and Spain was in the same time zone. He would have to allow anywhere up to an hour for the Rijeka shore-station operators to bumble around and make the necessary commo connections. No matter. He did not mind the idea of disturbing James Courtney. In fact, the prospect of waking him from a sound sleep was appealing. Neil turned on the ship-to-shore transmitter, set it on the Rijeka receiving frequency, unhooked the microphone.

19

The midnight-to-eight-A.M. security man posted in the office adjoining James Courtney's *estudio* had been given orders and a paper on which two names were typed. If, by any chance, either person telephoned while he was on duty, the call was to be put through to butler Grenville's bedroom. Grenville would personally notify Don Jaime and then give instructions whether the call should be switched over to him.

At 3:45—the guard jotted the time in his log—the telephone rang. An operator said there was a transfer-charge call from Señor Neil Harkness to Señor James Courtney, that it originated via marine radio, and would Señor Courtney accept the charges. The security man recognized the name as being one of those on the paper, asked the operator to wait a moment.

Leslie Grenville valued his sleep, but the onetime mercenary soldier—like all veterans of combat—slept lightly. The extension telephone in his east-wing bedroom purred only once, and he was awake and cursing, and reached for the receiver. He listened, said the charges would be accepted, and waited for Harkness to come on the line and say he wished to speak with Courtney; it was urgent. Although aware that his employer would want to talk to Neil, Grenville took malicious pleasure in stalling.

"It's an ungodly hour, Harkness."

"I don't give a shit. Wake him up."

"Mmm. I'm not so sure he's asleep, old boy. Fact is, I believe he's entertaining—or rather being entertained by—company. He'll be highly annoyed if I disturb him."

"He'll rack your ass if you don't, buster. I guarantee it."

"Well, hang on patiently. May take a while. I'll have to go to his suite in the west wing. It's a long walk, y'know."

Kristin Verkerk continued to soar and spin through her private dimensions of time and space, giving a performance that ran a gamut of extremes. Indignant at first because there were no gold coins, she had refused to let Courtney use the syringe. Instead, the Dutch girl had swallowed several orange-colored spansules she brought with her. "My favorite turn-ons," she said, and would not tell Courtney what drugs they contained. Their effects were remarkable, initially inducing an hour-long period of curious, but highly erotic languor, followed by sexual fury that had not yet abated.

Courtney had wallowed in pleasure for hours. *Had* wallowed. Until Kristin's mood took another sharp swing. To the sado-masochistic. Now she crouched on the bed, begging that he hit her. "Please—I want it. Please . . ."

The idea of doing as she pleaded had its appeal to Courtney. Normally he would have complied eagerly, enjoyed it. But he restrained himself. Kristin Verkerk was to be fired from her CVI job; then Cabo Verde police would order her to leave Spain. She would be enraged, vengeful. If he left marks on her body, she would doubtless exhibit them to the *policia,* claim he had assaulted her.

"*Do* it, God damn you, *do* it!" Her voice rose louder, shrill.

Thus, Courtney was grateful to hear doors open and close in the antechambers of his bedroom suite, a knock on the door of the bedroom itself, and Grenville's: "Sorry, sir. Rather important." He knew the butler had come to tell him of the hoped-for telephone call from Bernard Rechstein. He smiled satisfaction inwardly. His plans, hastily revised by contingency, were in good working order once more. Rechstein would announce that Neil Harkness had arrived and ask to what new destination the Velázquez should be taken for quid-pro-quo exchange. The inner smile deepening, Courtney started to get out of the huge extravanganza that was his bed.

"Stay here, you son of a bitch!" Kristin shrieked.

He did hit her then, a powerful slap on the side of the head. She gave a loud, soughing cry—of pleasure, for the blow had brought her to orgasm—shuddered and slumped over on her side.

"Come in."

Courtney was shrugging on a silk Cardin robe when Grenville entered. Courtney stated rather than asked: "Fischer from Venice."

"No, Harkness," Grenville said, and seeing his employer's high forehead crease into a troubled frown, hurriedly told him: "On his boat, somewhere in the Adriatic. Using his marine radio and a telephone relay out of Rijeka, according to the operator."

"I'll take the call here." Courtney moved a step toward his telephone, stopped. "Get this slut and her clothes out of here first."

"Will you be wanting her again?" Grenville was already gathering Kristin's clothing, draping the items over a shoulder.

Going to the bed, he turned the girl on her back, lifted her naked body.

"No, I'm finished with her. Put her in any guest room with a security man on guard. She's to be taken home before nine."

Grenville left, carrying the girl. Courtney closed the door, went to the telephone, and told the downstairs outer-office security man to switch the call. He stood waiting. Harkness's voice came on the line.

"Be damned careful what you say, J.P., and listen between the lines when I talk."

Courtney was slow on the uptake. "Why aren't you phoning from Ven—?"

"Shut the fuck up! I've been. I've been and found your friend gone on a one-way trip. Air-valve problems—turned off manually."

Pale blue eyes widened, then narrowed, as Courtney's mind absorbed. Rechstein—Wilhelm Fischer—was dead, strangled. It followed that *Horse and Rider* was gone, taken by his killer. That blew a hole—

"Don't fragment yet, J.P. He left hidden treasure behind—unless a daub by Diego isn't the key."

"He gave it to you?" Hope rose.

"Had it tucked away. I almost tripped over it. I guessed it's what had been entubed, as it were. Am I right?"

"Yes." Rechstein was expendable, had been expended, Courtney thought, but there was no time to replace him. He would have to use—and rely on—Harkness alone. Since Harkness knew nothing of the truth, it would be necessary to manipulate him, play him like a fish. Neil anticipated him, cut into his thoughts.

"Okay, so I have the McGuffin—and that means we're not chatting, J.P. We're negotiating."

"Very well." Harkness did not realize the painting's true value, Courtney reflected, but did sense he held the upper hand. He would make demands, and they would have to be met. For the present.

"To start, I wasn't alone. There was someone with me."

"Who?" Courtney's nerves jerked taut. Another person represented an unknown and uncontrollable quantity. A potential menace.

"Never mind, just listen. Two anonymous males walked into our absent friend's hotel and walked right out again. You have Roman properties." The Italian national government had always been for sale; Neil knew that Courtney had bought his part of it long ago. "Have them ensure that nobody tries to identify or trace the visitors."

"I can have that done." It was imperative. "What else?"

"A question. Where was I to take our friend—and Diego?"

"Beirut, but it's out of the question now. He might have given some hint, some indication—"

"Or had it squeezed out of him," Neil interjected. "I don't recommend any more sea voyages, either. My boat's been sort of ubiquitous in all these to-ings and fro-ings."

"Perhaps. Unfortunately, travels by train or air—"

"Are old-fashioned *customs.*" Neil put heavy emphasis on the last word. Courtney feared that the Velázquez might run afoul of customs inspections at frontier crossings or in airports, was certain he could eliminate the risk. "I'll guarantee there won't be any problems if I fly anywhere"—a two-beat pause—"provided I go by way of Zurich."

"Zurich?" Courtney echoed, not comprehending.

"In Switzerland. Where all the banks are." There was a note of cynical amusement in Neil's tone.

Courtney read the message. Lips tight and right fist clenched against the realization that he was cornered, he snapped, "How much?" The figure Harkness named should indicate the extent of his knowledge or suspicions about the picture's true importance and value.

"A million. In cash that I can cart out of one bank and take next door to deposit in a numbered bank account in another. The figure is not—repeat not—negotiable."

"What about your boat?" James Courtney did not care in the least about the boat, but needed a few seconds to think.

Harkness guessed as much. "I'll park it in Rijeka or Split. What's the answer—yes or no?"

"Yes." Courtney abhorred being forced into a situation where he had no options. Especially when the forcing was done by someone like Neil Harkness, whom—as he had told Bernard Rechstein—he had owned for years. However, it was evident that Harkness considered the painting as nothing more than a painting. Even based on its estimated value as a Velázquez, the amount he asked was not unreasonable. Its real value? The billionaire drew a deep breath. A million dollars was only a fraction of a fraction, he reminded himself, said: "The Bauerkreditbank. Bahnhofstrasse. Herr Kloster. I'll tell him today to have the money ready whenever you arrive. He'll inform you where to go and whom to meet for the delivery. Don't try to contact me until after it's been made and you're ready to start back."

Courtney disconnected, sat down on the edge of the bed, thoughts and questions milling through his brain. He was trusting Harkness. But he held any number of Damoclean swords over Harkness's head—and would be giving him a million dollars. Those factors taken into consideration, it was reasonably safe to assume that the man could be trusted. Besides, he did have *Horse and Rider*—which left no other alternative. But who was the "someone" who had been—was perhaps still—with Harkness?

A woman? Despite his ongoing affair with Sybil Pearson, it was entirely possible that Harkness had acquired a woman companion somewhere along the line. Possible, but not so, Courtney decided, remembering that Neil had been specific where it counted, in his demand for across-the-board protection from Italian authorities. He said "two anonymous males." That message was clear enough. Harkness and the other man had gone to the Gritti together, found Rechstein and the Velázquez, and departed in haste, without giving anyone their names.

The existence of the unidentified companion troubled Courtney. By trusting Harkness, he was trusting another person, someone about whom he knew nothing, blindly. With time being of the essence, it was impossible to learn who he was, where he was vulnerable, what pressures could be applied to control him. He was a joker in the deck, perhaps a wild joker, an imponderable risk, and James Philip Courtney did not like to deal in imponderables.

However, the situation, unpalatable as it was, had to be accepted for the present. Courtney made mental notes to telephone Rome—Senatore Giambella and Justice Minister Piresi—later in the day. Then, Zurich—Heinrich Kloster. There would be no need to speak cautiously with Giambella and Piresi. The Italian politicians would sell their mothers and daughters over an open circuit, never caring if they were overheard by a thousand line-tapping eavesdroppers. The conversation with Kloster would be ticklish, but luckily the banker's new scrambler—compatible with that at Montemar—was finally installed and operating. Ticklish matters could be discussed freely, openly.

Jim Courtney should have been ready for sleep. He was not. A host of misgivings and anxieties—some vague, formless, others specific and precisely defined—churned through his brain, ate at him. Stroking the scar on his right cheek, remembering past victories won against impossible odds, failed to bring relief from building inner tensions. He cursed aloud, seized the telephone, and punched the in-house connecting button to Grenville's bedroom.

"Is the bitch asleep?" Courtney rasped.

"Very much awake and still quite randy, the last I saw of her."

"Good. Bring her back."

"Yes. sir."

Courtney replaced the handset with a vicious chopping movement, stood up, began pacing the floor of the opulent bedroom. A priceless Raphael hung on the left wall. It was a painting of Saint Sebastian crucified and bleeding from numerous arrow wounds. Raphael had depicted Saint Sebastian's face contorted with suffering, yet alight with the religious ecstasy of martyrdom.

Courtney paused in front of the picture, gazed at it. He hoped that Kristin Verkerk's mood had not undergone further alteration, that she still desired to feel pain.

Kenneth Dixon had overheard the entire conversation, for everything James Courtney said had been relayed by radio from Rijeka and come over the receiver loudspeaker on the *Deirdre*'s bridge. Ken had listened silently, drinking black coffee so strong he grimaced with each swallow. But his expression and manner showed steadily increasing disapproval of what he heard. When Neil Harkness switched off the transceiver and, smiling broadly, rubbed his large hands together, Dixon spoke at last.

"Soon as you make port, I'm dropping out." Ken's tone was cold, unfriendly.

"It's your prerogative." Neil continued to smile, turned, and bent over a nautical chart. He psyched what lay behind the announcement but wanted Ken to lay out the reasons himself. Seconds passed; then:

"Great job of peddling your ass, Neil."

"Compliment accepted." Harkness continued to study the chart. "Even with inflation, a million bucks is a lot of money, more than I ever expected to earn—least of all in a single chunk."

"Take it, and you're locked inside Courtney's trained-seal cage for the rest of your fucking life."

"Better rich in the cage than poor, old buddy."

Dixon's expression turned to one of contempt. "The Velázquez is the key to something big—something a hell of a lot bigger than a million dollars."

"Has to be. Otherwise Courtney would never have agreed to pay so much so fast."

"With the painting, we could have—"

"We still can—with infinitely greater chances of succeeding than we had before."

"Horseshit. You sold out."

Neil tired of the game, straightened up, and faced Ken squarely. "Your habit of overlooking the obvious is showing, and you're full of shit—horse or otherwise. I didn't peddle my ass. I saved a pair of them—yours and mine—from being caught in an Italian sling."

"Sure. You made it part of the deal."

"Would you rather I hadn't? Go on, tell me you'd prefer to have the Italians bloodhounding after us."

"No." Ken was faltering. "Still . . ."

"You claim to know a lot about Courtney and the way he thinks, and from what I've observed so far, you do. Can you imagine him agreeing to anything if I hadn't squeezed for money—enough money to make him think I may have learned more than I have? He would've suspected that I was going to pull a double-cross or had already sold out elsewhere. He'd send his own people to waste me—and under the circumstances, when I say 'we,' it means *you* and me, friend."

Dixon's resolve was weakening, but he had not yet changed his decision. "The million—you intend to collect?"

"Collect and keep—after dividing it with you."

"With me—why?"

"Simple. You're entitled to half," Neil said. He expected Dixon to protest, insist that, as a world-famed author, he had ample money of his own. Surprisingly, Ken did nothing of the sort. Instead, he drank half a mug of now-lukewarm coffee, set the mug down, licked his lips nervously, and asked:

"Whether or not I ride along for the rest of the trip?"

Harkness cocked an eyebrow, purposely hesitated a beat before answering: "Yes. Either way." Intuition told him that he had glimpsed a hitherto unseen side of Kenneth Dixon. It defied quick analysis, but Neil determined he would look for it to show again.

Ken averted his eyes. "You're going to follow through, go on from Zurich." It was a statement rather than a question.

"Uh-huh. Like a car rally. Press on regardless."

There was silence save for the soft throb of idling engines and the lap of water against the *Deirdre*'s hull. Dixon was deep in thought, closed in around himself. At last he grunted, threw out a question:

"What's the itinerary?"

"I'll be making for Split. Train from there to Zagreb. A JAT flight Zagreb to Vienna—or direct to Zurich, if there is one."

"The picture."

"Goes with me."

"With *us*," Dixon amended, the emphasis signaling a change of heart and mind.

Harkness read the message implicit in the inflection on the pronoun. Quick about-face, he thought, and wondered if it had been inspired by the lure of a $500,000 out-of-the-blue payoff. Very probably was, he mused. But so what? Results count; who gives a damn about means? What he was planning would not work well—if at all—as a one-man operation. The chances of success—to say nothing of survival—would be infinitely greater with Kenneth Dixon along.

"We have to find a way to hide the Velázquez," Ken was saying, thinking aloud. "Can't attract attention when we carry it. Metal tubes are out. We'll be going through airport and customs checks." He suddenly gave Neil a hard, probing stare. "Besides, the people who wanted Fischer's tube are bound to have it by now. They've found out he outsmarted them." The stare shaded to a look of alarm. "They'll go back to the Gritti—if they haven't already—and come after us."

"We have a long head start, and they don't have much to go on."

"They know about the boat from back when you took Fischer to Tangier. A lot of somebodies in Venice are liable to remember it. Police wouldn't make anything of your conversation with Courtney, but if the bad guys were monitoring your receiving frequency . . ."

"All possibilities," Neil said gravely. He felt the side of his coffee mug. It was cold. He lit a Celta instead, gazed out at the foredeck, the bow, and the surrounding sea. "Remote, maybe, but possibilities."

Dixon seemed to be wavering once more. "I don't like any of it. Unless we're able to conceal the painting . . ."

"No problem." Harkness turned, his expression smug. "Follow the bouncing ball while I clue you in. We'll be going to Zurich . . ."

"No clue there, sailor."

"Hell there isn't. What does Switzerland have to offer besides banks?"

"Cuckoo clocks. Chocolate bars."

"The correct answers are Alps and ski runs. For public consumption, we're on our way there to slalom."

"This time of year? The season's over."

"Nuts. We're not Beautiful People—just a pair of slob American tourists." Neil ground his cigarette out in an ashtray. "There's all kinds of sports equipment aboard. I carry it for charter passengers who want to go ashore and play outdoor games. There're two sets of skis and poles in a locker below . . ."

"The picture."

"I'm getting to it. We'll bundle up the skis and poles, wrap 'em first at midsection with a piece of cloth, then in the Veláquez—unpainted side of the canvas out—and finally a top layer of wrapping paper. Airport security X rays won't reveal a thing—except the skiing gear. Any customs inspector who gets curious will simply tear a hole in the paper and give the canvas a squeeze. If that. We'll be prototypal ski-happy jerks wearing Day-Glo ski jackets and caps."

Ken groaned. "You carry those aboard too?"

"No, we'll buy 'em." Harkness laughed. "Wait till you see what the Yugos turn out for ski wear. Jackets in wild red, white, and blue that have 'God Bless America—Souvenir of Yugoslavia' silk-screened across the back."

"I can't wait."

"Neither can I. Haul in the sea anchor. We'll make straight for Split." Neil checked the chronometer. It read 0511.

20

It was natural for Sheikh Abdul al Amari to make his New York home in the Olympic Tower, a soaring high-rise on Fifth Avenue and originally an Aristotle Onassis project. Abdul al Amari had been involved in many mutually profitable enterprises with the Greek shipping magnate, the most notable in 1973. A Westernized, Princeton-educated Omani, the sheikh enjoyed the confidence of Arab rulers. They gave him advance warning of the October 6 Egyptian attack on Israel and the oil boycott they would impose on much of the world. Al Amari shared the information with Onassis, and together they bought enormous quantities of oil cheaply on the spot market. Selling the oil after the boycott was under way, they had divided a clear profit of more than one billion dollars.

Amari had purchased two entire floors of the Olympic Tower, spent untold sums transforming them into what newsmagazines liked to describe as "the most luxurious duplex condo apartment on the face of the earth." And it was a pleasure dome surpassing those of legendary khans and sultans, yet equipped with all the amenities and wonders that modern technology and limitless riches could provide. Slender, falcon-faced Sheikh Abdul al Amari certainly had the latter. Still in his thirties, he had been rated a billionaire for more than a decade. Some of the wealth came from oil. Some, by no means all.

There were rumors that Amari was deeply involved in manipulations of stock, commodities and gold markets; illicit arms deals; even global drug-trafficking. It was whispered that he enjoyed close friendships with Libya's Colonel Qaddafi and Palestine Liberation Organization head Yassir Arafat. But there was no hard supporting evidence, and Abdul al Amari maintained a low—an almost invisible—business profile. His private life was something else again. The continent-hopping Omani sheikh moved in café- and high-society circles and was ubiquitous as a partygoer and host. Swarthily handsome, radiating both charm and raw animal magnetism, he was forever being seen in the company of beautiful, often famous women. Predictably, the mass media were wont to label him the "Playboy Sheikh" or "Playboy Prince."

Various considerations made it logical for Sheikh Abdul al Amari's Rolls-Royce limousines to be armored and that he be accompanied by a bodyguard wherever he went in New York City. Even when he returned to the Olympic Tower with Gail Manners, the ravishing musical-comedy star, at the (for him) early hour of eleven-thirty P.M. The Rolls drew up in front of the building entrance. A bodyguard riding front seat with the chauffeur dismounted first. He checked sidewalks and street, waited for building doormen and security men to position themselves, helped Gail Manners from the car. Abdul al Amari emerged next. He took the young woman's arm, and they entered the lobby.

Gail Manners pressed herself close to his side as they walked. They spoke to each other in low tones, laughed, and went directly to the private elevator that would take them nonstop to Amari's apartment more than forty stories above street level. It was waiting for them, the doors open. They stepped into the car.

The bodyguard started to join them. The flawlessly dinner-jacketed sheikh raised a hand.

"No need to bother." There were other guards on duty in his apartment. "You're free until tomorrow. Good night."

The doors slid shut; the car started up.

"Gorgeous piece, that dame," a building security man said.

The bodyguard glared disapproval of the remark, and being conscientious, watched the floor indicator to make certain the elevator reached its destination. Numbers flashed in rapid succession, reached 39, 40, 41, and he relaxed. Another few seconds, he thought, turning away at the exact moment that the sound of the explosion thundered down the elevator shaft.

The lobby-level elevator doors bulged and shook as expanding gases thrust against them. The men in the lobby froze in surprise and shock for a split second, thawed to shout and mill. There was an ear-splitting grating screech as the car plunged down and there were loud metallic whipcracks as sundered steel cables fell, flailing. Another moment and the lobby floor trembled when the plummeting car struck bottom with a terrible crash at a subbasement level.

There were no screams or cries. No one could have survived the drop and the crushing effect of the tons of cable that slammed down on the splintered wreckage of the car.

Doormen rushed to double-lock the entrance doors; then one grabbed a telephone to call for help. Building security men and the bodyguard sprinted for the staircase that led down to the Olympic Tower's below-ground floors. Reaching the smashed car, they found only pulped flesh and splintered bone.

The New York *Times* and the 26 Federal Plaza office of the FBI each received a telephone call within ten minutes after the blast. The caller—a male—identified himself only as a member of the "International Zionist Action League," said the organization took full responsibility for the outrage, and declared:

"Abdul al Amari was an archenemy of Israel and of Jews everywhere. The League is ready to assassinate all others like him."

David Lippmann was spending two days in New York. Since his expenses were being paid by James Philip Courtney and his own superiors had instructed him to "travel five-star class," he was staying at the Helmsley Palace Hotel on Madison Avenue. Lippmann awoke at his customary time, seven A.M., used the remote controls to turn on the television set and the Channel 2 news broadcast.

Lippmann had been an amateur middleweight boxer while attending high school in Detroit and an undergraduate at Princeton. At thirty-five he retained a hard-muscled physique, and his leap from bed carried him halfway across the bedroom. He stopped, at first only listening to the TV:

". . . shortly after eleven-thirty last night. The blast sent terrified residents of the ultrafashionable condominium apartments fleeing into the street. . . ."

David Lippmann's brown eyes had been somewhat weakened by untold thousands of hours spent poring over books and peering closely at paintings and reproductions of paintings. The eyes narrowed slightly as he focused them on the video screen. It showed film taken some hours before. A building entrance illuminated by emergency floodlights. Policemen, firefighters, milling people . . .

". . . the bomb, allegedly planted by Zionist extremists . . ."

Lippmann winced inwardly. Although proud of his Jewish heritage (but not religious), he abhorred the idea that Jews would resort to acts of terrorism. That, he believed, was amoral, cowardly—and, from a purely practical standpoint, counterproductive, a sure way to lose sympathy and support. "Damn," he muttered, rubbing fingers through a thick thatch of hair which, like his eyes, was dark brown.

" . . . the star of many smash-hit musicals, was with Sheikh al Amari and also killed . . ."

"Damn," Lippmann repeated.

Except for a nose twice broken and once improperly set, by some accident of genetics David's face bore an uncanny resemblance to that of Robert Redford. This had always been a source of amusement to him, his family, and his friends, Jewish and Gentile alike. The broken nose wrinkled, the Robert Redfordish face scowled as the anchorman wrapped up the story.

Insanity, Lippmann thought, switching off the set. Now Arab terrorists will retaliate, escalate again—crazy fucking vicious circle. He went into the bathroom to shower and shave in a hurry, for he had a full day ahead and would have to follow the counsels given him the day before by Quentin Ashburn, director of Southern California's famed Wyler College Art Museum. Ashburn was David's friend, mentor, and chief. He had been instrumental in getting Lippmann the coveted assignment of cataloging James Philip Courtney's great art collection. True that Lippmann, a full professor and highly qualified art historian at Wyler College, deserved it. But colleges and museums—and most particularly college museums—are perpetually racked by intramural political wars.

"You'll be walking on eggs with extremely delicate shells," Ashburn had said. "However, if Courtney is satisfied with your work, you'll be able to write your own ticket here at Wyler."

That last was beyond question, Lippmann mused, stripping off his pajamas and turning on the shower tap. James Courtney had once attended Wyler, but had not graduated. He had broken off his education suddenly to volunteer for the Army during World War Two. Many years passed before Wyler heard from him directly again. In 1960—and to the surprise and delight of college trustees and administrators—the not-quite alumnus, now a super-rich expatriate entrepreneur, made an unsolicited fifty-thousand-dollar contribution to the museum building fund. The next year, he donated a Chardin still-life. Over the two decades that followed, Courtney made other money contributions and gifts of art. And he dropped hints that he might will his entire collection to Wyler—a prospect that sent the trustees into raptures.

Lippmann let the needle-spray shower play over his body, stepped clear, lathered himself with soap, remembered the excitement that had been caused earlier in the year by a letter from Courtney. The billionaire wrote Wyler deploring his own failure to have his collection properly cataloged. He asked college and museum to choose the best-qualified art historian for the work and allow him to spend an entire year in Spain, at Montemar. He would pay all expenses for whoever was selected and left little doubt that if he found the work satisfactory, the collection would be left to the museum in his will. Quentin Ashburn had lobbied successfully for David—who was, of course, overjoyed. Divorced, childless, David had no family considerations to hold him in California, and a year in Spain at full-pay-plus appealed greatly. Then, when Courtney sent the Wyler Museum an inventory of his collection at Montemar, Lippmann was even more elated. The collection included numerous great works, an astounding number that were important by any standard, many more that were less so, but still fine. Any art historian's mouth would have watered at the thought of seeing and studying the paintings, and the person who cataloged the collection would make a name for himself in art and academic circles, assure the future of his career.

Museum Director Ashburn's final word of advice, given the previous day, had been shrewd, reflecting his knowledge of private art collectors and their peculiarities.

"Your itinerary gives you a stopover in New York City,

Dave. Use the time to advantage. Scurry around seeing people in the large museums and more reputable sales galleries. Chat with them."

Lippmann had been grateful—and amused. "You mean lead them into saying nice things about Courtney's collection so I have a stock of favorable comments to repeat when I arrive in Spain."

"Exactly." Ashburn had nodded. "Collectors are prima donnas everlastingly on ego trips."

Landing at Kennedy, David had checked most of his personal luggage and his trunk filled with research materials and reference books at the airport and gone to the Helmsley Palace, arriving there at six in the evening. Tired, he had dinner sent up to his room and had gone to bed early.

Now, finished with showering and shaving, a huge bath towel wrapped around his waist, he sat down at the writing table in his room and looked over the list of New York museums and sales galleries to visit during the day. Among museums, he gave top priority to the Metropolitan and Frick. He was personally acquainted with curatorial personnel at both. They would supply him with all the latest New York art-establishment gossip and could be relied on to make quotable comments about James Courtney and his collection. Among sales galleries, he picked Knoedler as a must and Wildenstein as a maybe if there was time. Thus engrossed, all thoughts about the Olympic Tower bomb blast were banished from his mind.

Sybil Pearson heard of the terrorist outrage while drinking her morning coffee and listening to the Torcal F.M. radio news broadcast. The newscaster had naturally given precedence to such earth-shaking Spanish events as the Prime Minister's latest speech on the economy, a bank robbery in Seville, and plans for a new low-cost housing project in the province of Alicante. Eventually plodding through numerous more or less similar items, he came to the roundup of foreign news. There would be NATO maneuvers in summer. The Soviet Union was protesting U.S. arms buildups. More violence was reported in Belfast. An emergency meeting was scheduled by OPEC. Tacked onto the end of the roundup was a brief item about assassination by bomb explosion in New York City. The name of only one victim was mentioned: Sheikh Abdul al Amari. It rang a faint bell in some remote quadrant of Sybil Pearson's back brain, but recognition eluded her.

Memory banks failed to operate until Sybil was driving from

her Cabo Verde apartment to Montemar. She was in the process of warily overtaking a heavily laden truck on the Carretera de Cádiz when it struck her that James Courtney had once had dealings with an Abdul al Amari. She had heard him mention the name, and there had been some transoceanic calls from him in the past. Since Courtney seldom listened to morning news broadcasts, she decided to tell him about the incident first thing when he came downstairs.

Grenville intercepted Sybil in the corridor outside her office. "Tread softly this morning," he warned in a low voice. "He's likely to be in a rather odd mood."

"Because Sheikh al Amari was blown up?" Sybil asked, the subject on her mind.

The butler seemed to lose control over his eternally bland expression for a moment. His eyebrows shot up a visible fraction of an inch, his lips tightened. "Of course not!"

The response led Sybil to an understandable conclusion. "Oh, then you heard it on the radio too."

"No—that is, yes. I did." A pause. "Mr. Courtney hasn't, though."

"Think I should tell him?"

"I think he'd like to know." Grenville started to move off. "I'll have your tea brought, miss."

Sybil, a little puzzled by his manner, nipped at her lower lip with her teeth, sighed, and went into her office. Paco was on duty as guard. She went through the customary exchange of greetings, looked at the papers on her desk, started sorting them. Tea was brought. She was just pouring a cup when Courtney came out of the *estudio*. He was already being rather odd, she thought, putting the teapot down. He had come by way of the private hallway that led to his office rather than through the house as he usually did, and he was almost half an hour ahead of schedule.

"I'd like to see you," he said. No "good morning" to her, no "*buenos días*" to Paco. She stood up, caught a glimpse of his face just before he turned around and strode back to his desk. The normally sharply defined angular features appeared blurred, and there was a largish Band-Aid taped on his upper lip. She followed him, closed the door, continued on, and stood in front of the Bureau Plat. He seated himself. She saw that there were dark circles under his eyes, and the bandage, stark white against his suntanned skin, drew her own.

"Cut myself shaving," he said abruptly, conscious of her stare.

Another oddity, Sybil thought. He used an electric razor.

"Tried my old straight razor," he said, as if reading her mind. "Must have lost the knack." The blue eyes gazing at Sybil were steady but streaked with red. They flicked away. His jaw flexed. "Listen—and carefully. You'll have people asking questions concerning Kristin Verkerk today. She's been sacked—without notice—and they'll want to know the reason."

Sybil was astonished, tried not to show it, failed.

"You're surprised? So was I when the Cabo Verde *policia* informed me that she was a drug-dealer."

"Kristin—I can't believe it!"

"Tell that to the police. They found large amounts of drugs in her apartment." Courtney gave his personal secretary a smile. "Please inform the curious regarding the circumstances of her dismissal." He leaned back in his chair. "And now you can bring in the correspondence."

"Yes, Mr. Courtney—but I think I ought to tell you. There was a news report from New York this morning that a Sheikh Abdul al Amari was assassinated by terrorists. I remembered the name—"

"Your memory is excellent, Sybil. I knew Amari slightly. Only slightly. Even so, I was sorry to learn—"

"Then you did listen to the news."

"What? No." The jaw flexed again. "Grenville told me."

Odd becoming odder and odder, Sybil thought. But then, it was possible that Grenville had forgotten mentioning Sheikh al Amari when he went to the master bedroom suite to awaken Courtney. Or was it possible? Grenville had seemed positive that Courtney did not know. She went to her office, gathered up telexes and letters. The intercom light on the line to the CVI annex reception room lit up. Juggling papers, she pressed the corresponding key.

"Sybil? This is Conchita . . ."

The secretary to Tom Eberhardt, a CVI executive whom Courtney often used as a glorified file clerk and messenger boy.

". . . Mr. Eberhardt is wondering if you have any information on Kristin."

Sybil's innate English sense of fair play made her reluctant to pass on what Courtney had told her. It was presuming the guilt of a person who had not been formally charged, much less tried and convicted. However, she had her instructions.

"It's . . . well, a police matter. Something to do with possession of contraband"—her instructions had been much more specific—"I understand there was a mention of"—a last hesitation—"of drugs."

"*Drogas?*" Shock caused Conchita to lapse into her native Spanish. "*Dios mío! Kristin no es santa de mi devoción, pero . . .*"

Kristin isn't—wasn't—a favorite of very many people, Sybil conceded silently, and said: "Yes, well . . . I'm very busy, Conchita." She neutralized the key, took the morning's urgent telexes and letters in to her employer. He went through everything with even more speed than usual. When done, he said:

"I'll be making some telephone calls. They're not to be taped. Make certain the recorders are inoperative."

Sybil's brow wrinkled. "You can bypass them by turning that red switch," she reminded Courtney. "You'll also bypass my lines and have to place the calls yourself."

"I'm well aware, and I've already cut the red switch, but I want to be double sure. Is there anything further?"

"Just two questions—one business, the other personal. Should I draft any kind of condolence message for Sheikh al Amari?"

"No. I take it that was business. What is personal?"

"Have you heard from Neil yet?"

The red-streaked eyes glared. "Harkness? Not a word." The glare faded down to an indifferent, almost blank stare. "It may be another day or two before he checks in with me, Sybil."

"I see. Thank you."

Sybil found Paco arguing in Spanish with Eberhardt's secretary, Conchita. He stopped when Sybil closed the studio door behind her with a sharp click, said "*Basta, Paco,*" in an even sharper tone, and motioned Conchita to enter. The young woman—in her early twenties, buxom, and sultry—sniffed at the guard, bustled across the office to Sybil's desk.

"What's the problem?" Sybil asked in English, inclining her head in Paco's direction to indicate that they should avoid speaking Spanish, the only language he understood.

"Kristin is being sent out of the country," Conchita said. She did not appear to be very upset about it, Sybil noted. "I have a friend in the *municipio*. He telephoned me."

"The police?" Sybil asked. Paco sat bolt upright, ears perked, antennea extended. "Police" was one word he understood in any language.

Conchita nodded. "It is what you said—big trouble for her."

And you're smiling, licking your chops, Sybil told her silently. Aloud she said: "You came over to tell me—how nice of you."

Remark and sarcasm were ignored. "Kristin used to come over, and you gave her things to do."

Sybil thought back, remembered the art-collection inventory. Courtney had wanted new Xerox copies because the art historian was due to arrive soon from California. Kristin Verkerk had come over to the mansion, picked up the original, returned it and the copies—and ended up where she wished to be. In Courtney's bed. Now Conchita was eager to take her place.

"Kristin did run some errands" was all Sybil would concede.

"I am very good at errands." Conchita's smile was openly lascivious, as though to emphasize what she really meant.

Visions of vaginally harvested gold coins were dancing through the girl's head, Sybil thought, her inner laugh a giggle, and she mentally debated whether to tell Conchita the truth. James Courtney adhered strictly to a self-imposed rule. He avoided sexual involvements with female employees who were Spanish citizens. It was a sensible precaution. If a Spanish girl complained—or even talked too much—local authorities would be forced to open the eyes they closed to his sexual adventures with foreign women on the CVI payrolls.

Sybil decided to say nothing of this. God knows how Conchita would take it, she thought with another inner laugh. Wouldn't put it past her to make a scene, scream that Don Jaime was a bigot, a racist who discriminated against native Spaniards, refused to give them equal opportunity in their employment.

She said: "Okay, I'll make a note to call for you."

"You must tell Mr. Eberhardt."

Sybil groaned silently. The girl was Tom Eberhardt's secretary. Although Eberhardt was known to have little sex drive, it did manifest itself on occasion—with Conchita the willing object of his feeble lusts. Tom Eberhardt would not like the idea that she was actively campaigning, even if it was for an extracurricular position she could not, in any event, gain. He would sulk, be jealous and resentful, and this would have a negative effect on his work.

"I don't have the authority," Sybil said. Evasion and stalling were handy weapons in the diplomacy she practiced when dealing with lower-rung intrigues at Montemar. "I promise I'll mention you to Mr. Courtney and ask *him* to tell Mr. Eberhardt. May take Mr. Courtney a while to get around to it, though. He's very busy."

"But you do promise?"

"Swear it. Cross my heart and hope to turn into Lady Falkender if I don't."

The girl departed, her smile hopeful rather than lascivious.

"Cristo, qué trabajo!" Paco grumbled. Evidently he had

grasped the gist of the conversation—very probably from Conchita's voice tones and facial expressions and from the names that were mentioned.

Sybil was unsure if Paco's "Christ, what a job!" referred to his job, hers, Conchita's, or was intended to condemn the Montemar working environment in general. Whichever, Paco had to be contained before he chewed over his disgruntlements and blabbed to his colleagues—or worse, to Cabo Verde townspeople in the bars where he drank.

Her attack was anything but subtle: "*Paco, pienso que usted está agotado. Necesita un descanso.*"

The threat of a layoff was implicit in the observation that Paco seemed overtired and needed a rest. He responded volubly that he had never felt better—not in his entire life. He was bursting with energy (leaped from his chair and then jumped in the air to prove it) and would never dream of taking special leave from such a fine and rewarding job.

Having brought Paco to heel, Sybil at last turned to her own work. Numerous pieces of incoming correspondence were set aside, marked for the attention of various people in the CVI office annex. I should've let Conchita take them over, she thought. The top item, a letter from Globe-Aarco Metals in New York, was for Tom Eberhardt to handle. All the more reason I should have.

A sudden impulse struck. Sybil's hazel eyes lit up to twinkle with mischief. The smile that formed on her pretty face was at once impish and, strangely, determined. Bugger petty-minded little men like Tom Eberhardt and Paco, she told herself. It was improbable that Conchita could beguile James Courtney into breaking his no-Spanish-women rule. However, there was always a remote possibility that she might succeed. And if that was what she wanted so desperately, well, why not give her a chance? Let Eberhardt (the jealous, possessive once-a-month lover) and Paco (the hypocritical prude) stew in their own bile.

Sybil pressed an intercom button, heard Conchita's voice:

"Mr. Eberhardt's office."

"It's Sybil. Is he there?"

An expectant gasp, quickly stifled; then: "Just a moment."

Two seconds, perhaps three: "Good morning, Sybil."

" 'Morning, Tom. I have some things here for the annex—a letter you'll have to wrestle with among them. Mind sending Conchita over to make the pickup?"

There was a protracted throat-clearing. "Uh, she *is* my secretary, Sybil. Isn't there an ordinary clerk or someone of the kind?"

Pompous, status-happy ass, Sybil thought, the impish smile turning positively fiendish as, having already taken the inch, she decided to risk the entire mile.

"The Kristin fiasco has put Mr. C. off lowly serfs," she lied shamelessly and with relish. "He wants a more experienced and reliable girl to do messenger chores between the house and the annex." She could visualize Eberhardt, eternally beset by job anxieties and fears of sexual inadequacy, gritting his teeth, going slightly pale.

"Uh, Sybil. Several men over here are junior to me and have good secretaries. Give the flunky assignment to one of them." He practically whined even as he tried to pull rank.

"It's not up to me." Sybil loaded her tone with innuendo. "Mr. C. asked for your secretary. Specifically. By name"—a one-beat pause to make the stroke of the gelding knife even more effective—"and by physical description."

A dead silence as Tom Eberhardt contemplated the face he would lose in the eyes of his colleagues in the annex.

Sybil, certain he would never dare question instructions she presented as having been given by Courtney, was sympathetic and helpful. "Tell you what, Tom. I'll switch you on to his line so you can take the matter up with him personally."

Another silence; then, the man cowed, his tone defeated: "I'll see to it that Conchita comes over right away."

A blow for every woman's inalienable right to choose the bed she strives to lie in, Sybil thought as she neutralized the intercom key. And shriveled glands to the man who first cries "whore." She chortled at her pastiche of mangled and fragmented misquotations.

Sybil Pearson was gloating. She had won a victory—trivial, perverse, farcical—but a victory nonetheless. It never occurred to her that she would have reason to regret it. Deeply and soon.

21

Vivian Dixon was in her top-floor Galerías Vivi office, seated at her desk, going over bills and invoices. Hearing footsteps in the hall outside, she looked up. Carlos Lozano, the bright, capable young Spaniard who worked as her assistant and supervised the gallery's employees and routine operations, appeared in the open doorway.

Carlos was accompanied by a girl of about twenty-two. Vivian made a first-glance guess that she was there to apply for a job, then quickly revised the appraisal. She was obviously the daughter of a well-to-do, emancipated, and rather sophisticated Spanish family. She wore wrapped knickers and matching top—Vivian recognized them as being by Ronaldus Shamansk and expensive. The outfit accentuated a slender, diet-and-exercise-conscious figure. It was a bright shade of red that provided dramatic counterpoint for luminescent dark eyes and black hair framing an intelligent face that fell short of being beautiful only because the cheekbones were a bit too widely set.

"Excuse me, Vivi, may we come in?" Carlos asked.

"Certainly, please do." Since Carlos had spoken in English, Vivian did too, but glanced at the girl, wondering if she understood.

"This is Ms.—she insists on the Ms.—Marisa Alarcón," Carlos said, answering Vivian's unasked question and confirming much of what she had surmised after taking a second look at the girl. "I've already learned that she attended school in Switzerland and England."

"Hello, Marisa—please call me Vivi. Everyone does."

But Marisa Alarcón was in a great hurry to explain why she was there. "I went to your home, Mrs. Dixon—as your husband wrote I should. The servants said he was away and I would have to speak with you."

Vivian was baffled. "Please sit down—you, too, Carlos."

"*Con permiso,* there are customers waiting," Carlos said, and left.

Marisa took a chair facing Vivian, who smiled uncertainly, asked: "Ken wrote to you?"

The girl's expression reflected even more uncertainty as she handed an envelope to Vivian across her desk. Vivian stared at the face of the envelope. It bore Marisa Alarcón's name and an address in a fashionable Madrid residential quarter. The sprawling handwriting was unmistakably that of Kenneth Dixon. Vivian's exquisitely molded features held a smile. But her gray eyes were troubled. She took letter from envelope, read the beginning:

> Dear Miss Alarcón,
>
> Thanks for the high praise of my books. I'll be glad to cooperate. Mrs. Dixon and I will be happy to put you up at our home, Broadmoor, while you interview me and gather material . . .

Vivian read no further. "Ken must have forgotten to tell me—or maybe he did, and I've forgotten. Are you a journalist?"

"I want to be one, a writer," Marisa said earnestly. "It is so hard to make a start. My father"—she blushed, embarrassed at admitting parental help—"is a . . . well, a rich businessman. He spoke to some of his friends who are publishers of Spanish magazines."

"One of them gave you an assignment?"

"No, but many said they would be interested to see an article about Kenneth Dixon written by a woman of my generation. He—your husband—is the most famous American novelist to live in Spain since Robert Ruark."

"You asked Ken for an interview."

"For many interviews, Mrs. Dix—Vivi. The article must be . . ." Marisa faltered, searching for the right words.

Vivian, all too familiar with the jargon, supplied them: "In-depth, multidimensional, incisive, et cetera." She sighed. "Unfortunately, Ken isn't even in Spain. He's away on business."

"Because of the new book that will be published soon?"

"Well, yes, and some other matters." Vivian was growing uneasy but not yet approaching panic. It would be easy to send Marisa Alarcón back to Madrid, she thought, and, radiating sympathy, said: "I know it's a terrible disappointment for you, but Ken may be gone ten days, possibly even two weeks or more."

"That is good. I will wait."

Vivian blinked. "Good? Wait?"

"Yes. I can stay in a hotel and gather information from people in Cabo Verde and on the Costa del Sol. There are many who must have colorful stories and wonderful anecdotes about Mr. Dixon."

"A waste of your time," Vivian improvised. "They've all been told in the past. You can find them in newspaper and magazine back files."

Marisa shook her head. "The material would not be fresh." She beamed a humorous and captivating smile. "And not interpreted by someone like me, a woman of the ex-post-Franco generation—the first to be totally free from *mantillas* and *dueñas*."

"Ex-post-Franco," Vivian said, amused, liking the girl. "That's very good—is it original?"

"I think so. It just popped into my mind."

You're liable to be a very good and clever writer someday, Vivian thought. Too bad that I have to try to get rid of you. "Staying in a hotel will cost more than your article could possibly bring, Marisa. Why not go home and come back later, when you're sure Ken is here."

Again the blush. "The cost is nothing. My father is very generous and very liberated. He wants to help me start my career."

"That's very nice," Vivian said inanely, no longer far from panic, her mind racing. Marisa Alarcón was bright, fiercely ambitious—and determined to wait for Ken in Cabo Verde, use the time to dig into his past and present. There was no telling what pieces of information and gossip she might obtain, how she might fit them together. The girl was potentially an instrument of disaster. Vivi's best—sole—defense was to co-opt, she realized.

"No hotels," she said. "You'll be my—and Ken's—guest at Broadmoor." Marisa started to protest; Vivian stopped her. "I'll take a little vacation—I can use it—and work with you, give you insights into Ken and his work, dig out his early notes and journals. We'll go over them together, page by page." Line by line, even word by word if necessary to keep you preoccupied. "Betwixt and between, we can swim and sunbathe. How does that sound?"

"Marvelous!" Marisa's eyes glowed. "You're marvelous." She looked at Vivian with a degree of admiration that was almost adulatory. The coppery-haired American woman was at least ten years her senior. And she was a ravishing beauty, worldly, the wife of a world-famed author and herself a noted art dealer. In short, Vivian Dixon was an embodiment of the capital-P Person that Spanish women of the ex-post-Franco generation aspired to be, Marisa thought, making a mental note to use the line when describing Kenneth Dixon's wife in her article.

Vivian read what the girl was thinking almost verbatim, wondered how she would react if made aware of the truth. The prospect of that happening gave Vivi a chill, queasy feeling in the pit of her stomach. She fought it off, reached for her telephone.

"I'm going to tell the servants to have a room ready for you, Marisa," she said, "and then I'll drive you over to Broadmoor."

"Please, it is so much trouble. I have my own car."

"In that case, I'll ride with you." Vivian did not want Marisa Alarcón and her alert, inquiring mind to be alone at Broadmoor, not even for a mintue.

In Rome, Senator Raffaello Giambelli was making certain that Justice Minister Vittorio Piresi was not alone, either. CGIL, CSIL, and UIL, the omnipotent trio of national labor unions, had suddenly and surprisingly ended their general strike at six A.M.

This had eliminated the need for doom watches in Italian government offices and enabled officials to return to their homes—or, as was the case with Vittorio Piresi, their hideaways.

Piresi had a house in Monteparioli. He shared it with an ever-changing cast of adolescent boys, plump of body and cherubic of face. But the current incumbents had been sent off to amuse themselves in the city when Senator Giambelli arrived at the house to confer with their patron. Both men had received telephone calls from James Philip Courtney earlier in the day, and these calls were the subject of their discussion.

"*Difficile, molto difficile,*" Justice Minister Piresi was saying for the dozenth time. "They are watching us—all of us."

Senator Giambelli did not believe it was "difficult—very difficult" because "they"—the labor unions—were, in wake of the general strike, watching the actions of all government officials very closely. Of course, being unofficial bagman for the Christian Democrat party and a heterosexual, he felt much more secure than Piresi, who was neither. His patience exhausted, Giambelli dispensed with formalities and even common courtesies and said:

"*Basta,* Vittorio. This is a man whose support we cannot afford to lose. You will tell Testolini"—the interior minister—"to discover that the ugly business in Venice was carried out by the Red Brigades."

"There is no evidence—the left will raise questions," Piresi objected.

"*Caro,* your head is a cunt. These days, no one in Italy—not even the left—asks for evidence against the Brigate Rosse. An accusation is sufficient. Everyone believes, no one is surprised when the police fail to find the perpetrators."

The justice minister nodded surrender. Giambelli hammered his point further home.

"Think, Vittorio—if you remember how. Hundreds of crimes are laid to the door of the Red Brigades every year. What is one more or less?"

Piresi agreed, promised to do as Giambelli suggested. It was, after all, the simplest and easiest solution. Besides, he thought, glancing at his wristwatch, the *ragazzi* would be coming back soon, and visions of their plump bodies and cherubic faces danced before his eyes.

In Zurich, Herr Heinrich Kloster, head of the powerful Bauerkreditbank, the fourth- or fifth-largest banking institution in Switzerland, depending on whose statistics one read, was entirely alone. He would not be for long, however. Kloster, like many German Swiss, looked to be a square cut Wilhelm-era Prussian with close-cropped white hair and a stern, coarse-featured face. The Prussian *offizier* stereotype called for a monocle, but the banker wore gold-rimmed eyeglasses. When alone and in a meditative mood, he was wont to remove them, polish the lenses with a handkerchief, and hum or sing in a barely audible, appallingly off-key voice, as he was doing at three in the afternoon while seated at the dark oak monstrosity that was his desk. Having hummed a few bars of the first song in Carl Orff's *Carmina Burana*, he went on to sing some words from its second verse:

"Schicksal, Ungeschlacht und eitel, Rad du rollendes . . ."

He stopped. The fragment, railing against the ever-turning wheel of a dread destiny and empty fate, sufficed as a requiem for Bernard Rechstein. Heinrich Kloster had known Rechstein well enough once, not seen him for almost thirty years, heard about his death from James Courtney earlier in the day. *Death in Venice*, Kloster mused. Written by Thomas Mann about Gustav Mahler. Now so apt, so applicable to Rechstein—who would have exploded in rage, doubtless become violent, if anyone had mentioned the names of Mann and Mahler in the same breath they used to mention his own.

Enough of Rechstein, the banker thought, wiping memories of a figure made dim and hazy by the passage of time from his mind, shifting its focus to other matters he had discussed with James Courtney. They had been able to speak freely over the line, which was made secure by compatible scramblers at each end. They had reviewed the progress of the covert Chrysler stock purchases, the Abdul al Amari assassination, other moves that had been made. Courtney's overall satisfaction had been marred, of course, by the development in Venice that demanded yet another alteration in plans. He had issued new instructions, which Heinrich Kloster had already relayed in part to appropriate employees of the Bauerkreditbank. Whenever a Mr. Neil Harkness made his appearance, he was to be shown straight to Herr Direktor's office, there to receive a million United States dollars in banded packets of hundred-dollar bills. Kloster would then tell him where to proceed from Zurich and whom to meet at his destination.

"The Venice incident was trivial—a nothing," James Courtney had assured Heinrich Kloster. "Everything is going ahead beautifully. There should be excellent news from the Middle East within hours."

Bankers are necessarily skeptics. Kloster was no exception. He had waxed properly enthusiastic over the telephone, said nothing about his sudden doubts and reservations. He mulled over these as he continued to sit and polish the eyeglass lenses. The "Venice incident" could scarcely have been "trivial—a nothing" if Courtney had to revise plans and pay out a million dollars in order to rectify the situation. True, a million was less than petty cash compared to what was at stake. On the other hand, it was obvious that James Courtney had been remiss in his calculations of risks and was caught unawares. The possibility that there might be repercussions, aftermaths, could not be ignored. However, Henrich Kloster was content merely to think, speculate, and keep an otherwise open mind until the "excellent news from the Middle East" materialized.

"Herr Kloster, Herr Schelegter," the voice of the banker's secretary came over the intercom. Arndt Schelegter managed the bank's information-gathering department—a full-scale newsroom. Wire-service teletypes, closed-circuit television, informants using special telephones, kept the Bauerkreditbank apprised of what was happening everywhere in the world. Kloster reached for a green telephone on his desk; it was permanently on in-house scrambler, for conversations with Schelegter were often highly confidential.

Lifting the receiver with one hand, Kloster put his glasses on with the other. He felt uncomfortable speaking to anyone—even over an internal telephone line—unless he wore them. " *'Abend*, Schelegter," he said—and listened.

"*Herr Direktor*, a Reuter's bulletin reports an armed uprising in Riyadh and says there is heavy street fighting . . ."

That *was* excellent news, Kloster thought, his skepticism easing off a notch. There was no better place in the Middle East for the curtain to rise. The Saudi Arabian regime was shaky. It had almost been toppled in 1975, when King Faisal was assassinated, and again in 1979, when Muslim fundamentalists seized the Grand Mosque in Mecca. The latter had been a severe blow to Saudi prestige. It had taken a huge force of troops two weeks of bloody fighting to oust the fanatics from the mosque, and enormous loss of *sharaf*—honor. Global oil glut and consequent sharp fall in Saudi revenues had caused more damage, which not even U.S. pandering to Saudi demands could help repair. One strong shove, and the entire edifice would collapse . . .

". . . but our representative in Riyadh telephoned minutes ago with an entirely different account," Kloster heard Schelegter say. "According to his version, army and paramilitary units have defeated the rebels. Mass executions of them are under way."

"Inform me of any further reports," Heinrich Kloster said, and slowly replaced the receiver. The Bauerkreditbank's agent in Riyadh was an objective, totally reliable observer—his statements infinitely more credible than those of some part-time correspondent that Reuter's maintained on a stringer basis in the Saudi Arabian capital.

Of course, failure in Riyadh did not necessarily mean failure elsewhere, Kloster reflected. Still, it might be prudent to hedge a little. A banker must be a careful man, especially when he has cause to be skeptical, Kloster mused. The skepticism that had eased off momentarily a few minutes before had now risen to a new high.

True, there was nothing yet in the situation to justify an outright shift of allegiance. The foothold on his chosen side of the valley had to be firmly maintained, for it could well prove fatal to abandon it. All he needed was a bare toehold on the other side. That would make it possible for him to straddle the *Bergschrud*, the crevasse, and leap to safety in the event of disaster.

The toehold could be obtained with a small earnest, a token to show that he was a reasonable person, one not averse to cooperating with the opposition if there was no other alternative for survival. Kloster breathed an inner sigh of relief. He had the earnest and was in a position to make a gift of it: the American, Neil Harkness, and the Velázquez.

Kloster weighed what—to him—were the moral factors involved. Their loss—or at least loss of the Velázquez—would hurt James Courtney. However, it would not in itself cripple, much less defeat, Courtney. His scheme—our scheme, Kloster corrected himself—could be carried to a successful conclusion without the painting. Provided all other things are equal, he added. If they were not . . . Well, regardless of the final results, Heinrich Kloster and the Bauerkreditbank would emerge unscathed.

Highly polished eyeglass lenses glinted as Kloster nodded, telling himself that the decision was correct and unavoidable. He reached for the direct-outside-line telephone that was connected to both scramblers, old and new, and direct-dialed a number in Bonn, West Germany.

Teresa, Vivian Dixon's personal maid, smoldered inwardly. She felt ill-used by her employer, scorned by officials of the Cabo Verde *ayuntamiento*, betrayed by the local workers' grievance committee of the Andalusian Communist party. It had all begun with the Dixon's May Day *tertulia*. Teresa had resented being asked to work late and as an ordinary domestic, like the other servants. Then there had been the caricatures of revered Communist leaders with which Vivian decorated Broadmoor. At night's end, Teresa appropriated two of them. During the days that followed, she had given vent to the proletarian outrage that filled her overample bosom.

She went first to the Cabo Verde City Hall, tried to file a formal *denuncia*, a legal complaint, against Vivian Dixon. Spanish bureaucrats possess certain qualities seldom found among their counterparts elsewhere in the world. They listen with courteous patience to complaints and have a fine (if sometimes elemental) sense of justice which is leavened by a sense of humor. Hearing that Teresa had agreed to work overtime and had received generous extra pay, the *funcionarios* and *oficiales* made a great show of consulting lawbooks and, with much rhetoric, declared she had no grounds on which to base a *denuncia*.

Teresa stormed that they were fascists, puppets of the *extranjeros* who were exploiting the Spanish working class, and swore that she would denounce them all in a petition to King Juan Carlos. Instead of the king, she next appealed to the Partido Comunista Andaluz, of which she was a member. Appearing before the workers' grievance committee, she demanded that her *camaradas* stage a demonstration and take other reprisal action and flourished the two sketches she had taken from Broadmoor. The comrades had burst into laughter.

"*Reagan y Kennedy!*" the chairman of the committee spluttered—and declared that the caricatures were sufficiently acid to qualify as *comunista* propaganda posters.

Teresa still smarted from these indignities. When Vivian telephoned and told her to prepare the best of the spare bedrooms at Broadmoor for a female guest, Teresa assumed the visitor was a rich foreigner. She obeyed, but with proletarian and xenophobic malice aforethought, and did a slipshod job. Then Vivian and Marisa Alarcón arrived. Teresa was in the entrance hall and underwent an instant and amazing transformation into the very model of a cheerful, willing personal lady's maid. Excusing herself, she rushed upstairs to rearrange the guest bedroom, make it sparkle.

Vivian glanced at Marisa with curiosity, for she had long experience in Spain. Teresa types were end products of centuries of tradition and conditioning. Democratic constitutions, secret ballots, and women's-rights legislation notwithstanding, they remained the same end products at heart. Immediately recognizing Señorita Alarcón as a Spanish woman—and, what was more, an upper-class Spanish woman—Teresa felt compelled to do her best, *tener bella facha*—cut a fine figure. Vivian was interested in what Marisa's reaction might be.

"*Nosotros los españoles somos muy urgullosos,*" Marisa said in Spanish, then switched to English. "Sometimes I think our pride makes many problems for us. It takes over and makes us do stupid things." She sighed, asked, "Is Teresa married?"

"No."

"Ah, that's her problem."

Vivian blinked. Was this the sovereign remedy for all women's problems as seen by an educated, liberated Marisa Alarcón? she wondered. "Do you mean that she'd be better off with a husband, babies, cooking pots, and floor mops?"

"Certainly a husband." A smile played over Marisa's lips.

"Well, I don't know anything about her sex life, but maybe a husband . . ."

"What does sex have to do with it? Spanish women need to have husbands for only one reason, so they'll have someone to blame for whatever happens."

"Interesting theory. Where has all the *machismo* gone?"

Marisa grinned. "We allow men to think it hasn't gone anywhere, but Spanish women have a new saying. *La mujer debe gobernar la casa y el marido*."

"The wife must manage the house—and the husband," Vivian translated mentally. The concept is hardly new to me, she thought dryly. It's what I've been doing for years. She said:

"Your bags are being taken up to your room. Would you care to see the house before you unpack?"

Marisa said she would, very much, and Vivian gave her the grand tour, playing chatterbox guide as she did. She made certain to give out the kind of information that would fascinate the aspiring article writer, yet give away nothing that might raise difficult questions.

". . . always was Ken's dream to have a house like this. He came to Spain in 1967, after *Gusher!* became a best-seller, bought this property, and had the house built. He didn't build the swimming pool and beach cabanas until 1969, when *The Midas Engram*—his roman à clef based on J. Paul Getty—was made into a film."

"Did you know him then, Vivi?"

"No, not until later. We were married in 1972."

Eventually, having seen the outside and ground floor, they went upstairs.

"This is my bedroom."

"Oh, I love it—so airy, so beautifully decorated!" Marisa exclaimed; then her dark eyes asked the question Vivian had already anticipated.

"Ken's is here—through this connecting door." She opened the door. "You see, it's austere, almost Spartan—which is how he prefers it." She gave a loving-wife-tolerant-of-her-husband's-whims look, finished off to perfection with a fond, almost maternal smile. "He also reads—or just lies awake thinking—frequently until dawn."

"That is why you have separate bedrooms?"

"Not for any other reason, I promise you."

Marisa gazed around her with an expression bordering on awe, then frowned. "He does not have a desk."

"Not here. In his den—his sanctum—down the hallway."

"Could I see it, please?"

"I wouldn't *dare* let you—or anyone else—inside when he's not here to give permission. Some creative people are like that, very jealous about their work space."

Marisa nodded solemnly. "I am like that too. At home I do not allow the servants to clean the room I use to study and work."

"Ken would never go *that* far." Vivian laughed. "He must have someone clean for him—and clean up after him." In more ways than one, she added to herself. "Well, if you're ready to start unpacking . . ."

Marisa was delighted with the large corner room that was to be hers. Teresa was there, expectantly waiting to help take clothing from luggage and put the items where they belonged. Marisa said she would bathe after the unpacking was finished and join Vivian in two hours.

Vivi left her guest, went by Ken's den to make certain it was locked, then downstairs and to the portico overlooking beach and sea. She settled into a lounger, stared at the eastern horizon, thinking.

She took it for granted that her husband had reached Venice, for Neil Harkness was a superb sailor and the *Deirdre* as safe and sturdy a vessel as any afloat. But Vivian was growing concerned at not having heard from him, all the more so because Neil had not communicated with Sybil Pearson, either. The two men had probably gone on a prolonged drunk, she thought miserably, remembering Ken's solemn promise to lay off booze, dry out while he was gone.

Vivian estimated that Ken needed to stay away from Cabo Verde for another week. By then the potential storm centers he had created in his drunken, self-destructive state would have been dispersed by the limits of human interest and attention spans. Even so, it was imperative he return with a clear mind, alert and able to reason. Otherwise he would stir the storms again, and they would be devastating. Especially with Marisa Alarcón, a new, totally unexpected danger factor on the scene.

Vivian sat up in the lounger, shook long red hair back from her face, arched her slender neck, and allowed the cool late-afternoon sea breeze to caress her for a moment. Leaning back once again, she mused that Ken Dixon was a hapless sucker for adulators, particularly if they were young and attractive women. Marisa Alarcón would have to be distracted until Ken arrived, and contained after. Her own life would have to be suspended until Marisa had gone. Vivian's acceptance was resigned and practically reflexive. She had become accustomed to putting her own wishes and desires—herself—aside in deference to others during her thirty-three years.

There had been her mother, Mrs. Alexandra Blascombe, Vivian reflected. "Lexa"—famed beauty, hypochondriac, restless and impulsive traveler. Lexa was forever changing places of residence, men, doctors. She gave only vague answers when Vivian asked who her father had been—and the source of her mother's comfortable income.

"Your father, Robert Blascombe, and I were married in Europe," Vivian could hear her mother saying. "You were born in Paris. We were divorced soon after, but I kept his name because of you, and he died two years later. My money comes from a trust fund."

Vivian had lived with her mother in many countries on the European continent—France, Italy, Switzerland, with short stays elsewhere—and England until she was thirteen. Then they returned to the United States and Lexa's native Philadelphia. Alexandra Blascombe seemed content to remain there, and Vivian had to live her life around her mother's. She attended boarding schools and spent her entire summers at camp because Lexa's social and love affairs and her visits to clinics, hospitals, and health spas left neither time nor energy to expend on her daughter.

Vivian showed a talent for painting, wanted to study art. Lexa scoffed at the idea. When Vivian was seventeen, Lexa snared an exceedingly wealthy Philadelphia Main Line lover. Having had the mother, he wanted the daughter. Vivian acceded when he (1) agreed to convince Lexa to allow her to attend the Pratt Institute in New York and (2) gave her five thousand dollars "to help with your expenses."

Vivian did attend Pratt. Instructors said her work showed considerable promise. Her mother's lover slipped away from Philadelphia only once a week "to amortize my investment," as he put it. Then Lexa died. Vivian discovered there was no trust fund. Lexa's paramour urged the girl to take her mother's place—"you'll have a generous allowance." Vivian had two thousand dollars. It was enough to let her refuse and say what, she was certain, Lexa had also wanted to say for a long, long time: "You're a lousy lay—a clumsy pig!"

It was late 1969. Mijas, on the Spanish Costa del Sol, was at its peak as an artists' colony, and one could live well in the delightful and picturesque mountainside village for the equivalent of forty dollars a week. Vivian went to Mijas and for the first time—and, as it was to turn out, the only time—in her life was able to live, love, and work as she pleased . . .

. . . Until the end of 1970. When the sixteen-month period she had managed to block from her mind began. Her 1972 marriage to Kenneth Dixon was to have been a new beginning, pure bliss . . .

And it was, Vivian thought, gray eyes misting. For a time.

"Señora." Juan, the manservant closest to being the butler in the Dixon household, appeared carrying an extension telephone, the long wire trailing behind him. He placed the instrument on a table beside her. "Señor Lozano."

"*Gracias,*" Vivian said, dismissing Juan, lifted the receiver. "Yes, Carlos?"

"There are two matters, Vivi. Ken telephoned. I told him you had gone home. He will call you in fifteen minutes. And"—Carlos paused and Vivian could hear him take a deep, fortifying breath—"Mrs. Meese has been here"

Vivian groaned. Over-rich, overbearing Gloria was an enormous pain, the personification of the very worst American expatriates. Yet she was a power in foreign-colony social circles.

"She asked for you. I told her you were very busy and could not be disturbed."

"Thank you for that, Carlos."

"She was furious because Ken cannot speak at her club."

"Tough."

"She raved that you lied to her and are hiding something."

"Never mind, Carlos. I'm not going to worry about Gloria

Meese," Vivian said, knowing that she would worry a great deal. Gloria loved to make trouble almost as much as she loved cocaine and Costa studs. "I'll speak with you tomorrow." Vivian put the receiver on its cradle and made a mental note to keep Marisa Alarcón far away from Gloria Meese.

Time passed slowly, and it was forty-five rather than fifteen minutes before the telephone rang. Vivian had been waiting impatiently for the call from Ken, but braced herself as she answered. She said only: "Hello, Ken." She wanted to hear him speak, judge whether he was sober or drunk before saying more.

"Hi, Vivi! I almost gave up hope of getting through. This Yugoslav phone system is a fucked-up mess."

His voice was buoyant, almost boyish with repressed excitement. He was high, but not on alcohol, Vivian thought, elated. She could not remember when she had last heard him sound like that.

"Yugoslav phone system?" she repeated. "I thought you and Neil were going to—"

"We've been to Venice." Ken spoke hurriedly. "Look, I have to make this fast. We're in Zagreb—at the airport. Neil's over at the ticket counter getting us tickets to Vienna—"

"I don't understand, Ken. You two left here in the *Deirdre*—"

"It's in Split. We took a train here—"

"Why to Zagreb . . . and why Vienna?"

"Can't tell you any more. Just wanted to check in."

"Has Neil called Sybil?"

"No, and for Christ's sake, don't tell her or anyone else where we are or even that you've talked to me. Okay? Uh . . . Harkness is waving to me . . . I have to run—"

"Wait. You should know there's a Spanish girl here . . ."

But Ken had gone off the line. Vivian jiggled the hook, heard only the dial tone, gave up, and replaced the receiver. Her mind whirled, trying to sort out what her husband had said and make some sense of it. She heard a sound from the doorway that led into the house, started to turn around.

"I am sorry. I was coming out and could not help but hear." It was Marisa Alarcón, freshly bathed and dressed.

Just how much did you hear? Vivian wanted to ask, remembering that she had mentioned the names of people and places, silently cursing herself because she had. She wished she could run and hide when Marisa went on blithely, answering the unasked question—with a vengeance: "It is so nice that Mr. Dix—that Ken called. I see it surprised you. Was it because he is in Zagreb? It is a horrible place—he will like Vienna, though. Vienna is lovely in May."

Vivian thought fast, said: "Marisa, can I share a secret with you—I mean, will you promise to keep it until you've seen Ken?"

"Yes . . . and yes."

"Well, it's like this," Vivi said, knowing that the lie she had so quickly concocted was consistent, plausible. "Someone—I'm not allowed to say who as yet—has bought the film rights to one of Ken's books. Ken and the man who will probably direct are going to various countries, looking for locations—places to film certain episodes and scenes. It's really very routine and ordinary, but the motion-picture business is very secretive."

Marisa was enthralled. "Is the Neil you mentioned the director?"

"No, he's . . . well, Ken's companion."

"You mean his agent?"

Vivian blurted, "Yes, his agent," in hopes that the reply would stem the flow of questions. It did not.

"And Sybil—she is an actress, the star?"

God, I can't wade any deeper into this. She might—she probably will—meet Sybil, Vivian thought, shook her head, and smiled. "I hate to disappoint you. Sybil Pearson is an English girl who lives and works right here in Cabo Verde."

"Oh." Marisa was disappointed, but had not yet exhausted her store of questions. "Is it Ken's latest book that is going to be made into a film, Vivi?"

"Let's talk about it all later—after we've had a drink. Over dinner," Vivian said. "I'll just run upstairs and clean myself around the edges."

The ragged, jagged edges, Vivi thought, feeling cold. Her intuition was working furiously. It told her that Ken had gotten himself involved in something that spelled trouble, warned that allowing Marisa Alarcón to overhear her conversation was a mistake for which she and Ken would pay dearly.

II

22

There is no census of the Arabs who now spend most of their time or reside permanently, as expatriates from their native countries, in Spain. Certainly they number in the many thousands, probably in the tens of thousands. Most arrived on Spanish soil after 1972. A goodly percentage (and the wealthiest) of them have chosen to settle in Andalusia, on the Sun Coast. Some of the immediate reasons for their choice are readily identifiable. The Sun Coast climate is similar to that found in North Africa and the Middle East. Andalusia was the part of Spain longest held by the Moors. Evidences of their influence and achievements abound—in everything from music and cuisine to architecture of ancient Moorish buildings and modern architectural styles derived from it.

There are other, less evident reasons and motivations for the Arab influx-invasion. Spain is the sole Western European nation that has not recognized the state of Israel. The lack of formal diplomatic ties between Spain and Israel gives Arabs a sense of security. Many believe their own governments are shaky and fear as inevitable a showdown war with Israel that will completely alter the anatomy—as well as complexion—of the Middle East.

It is significant that the latter-day Moorish invaders-colonizers have arrived in waves, each surge following some marked change or upheaval in the Arab world. The steep OPEC oil-price rise following the 1973 Israeli war with Egypt and Syria was one; assassinations like that of Saudi King Faisal in 1975 and the 1978 Iranian revolution—which threatened to spread, tear the Arab world apart—were others.

For the most part, the new Moors are excellent guests. They bring astronomical amounts of money with them, spend freely, are generous to Spain, their host country, and its people. (After building his palace at a reputed cost of ten-million-dollars, Prince Salim made a three-million-dollar gift to the city of Marbella for the construction of public housing.) They create no scandals. They respect Spanish laws and customs, make no effort to meddle in Spanish politics or domestic affairs; they prefer to shun politics of any kind, being content to live in splendor, enjoy their pleasures and luxuries. By and large, while they will negotiate and transact business involving tens and hundreds of billions of dollars, their business is legitimate.

By and large.

But there are exceptions, Arab expatriates who reside on great, heavily guarded estates and, while they may meet openly enough in each other's homes, what they plan and discuss together is secret. This, of course, is hardly unique to Arabs. Expatriates of all nationalities often use—or abuse—the hospitality of a host country to aid them in formulating and implementing conspiracies, plots, and counterplots. Their machinations may be and—history and headlines show—often are—intended to topple governments and political systems and may affect the fate of entire continents and even the whole world. Since many exiles, expatriates, and émigrés are necessarily masters at the art of keeping secrets and maintaining pretenses, their host countries are unaware of what they plan and do.

Rashid el Muein, a Lebanese Arab, was born in Beirut, the only son of a trader in camels, and began his own business career in 1947. Rashid was then twenty, and most of the world was in the grip of postwar economic chaos. But Rashid el Muein was precocious, with a sharp mind for commerce and a sharp eye for opportunity and profit.

People in the Levant and Middle East wanted automobiles. New cars were unavailable. The United States was then the only important producer of motor vehicles. The American auto industry, not yet fully reconverted to peacetime production, struggled to meet pent-up domestic demand and ignored export markets. As new cars came off the assembly lines, they were snapped up by U.S. buyers, most of whom traded in their decrepit prewar models. An estimated 1.5 million worn-out and worthless old automobiles languished on U.S. used-car lots, their numbers increasing daily.

This gave rise to a global swindle of awesome proportions. Crooked American middlemen bought the automobiles for what they would fetch as scrap metal. Engines and chassis were steam-cleaned, bodies given superswift one-coat applications of cheap paint, tires were recapped. The gussied-up wrecks were then sold and shipped by sea to equally crooked black-market brokers and dealers in Latin America, some parts of Western Europe, the Middle East, and elsewhere, then retailed to car-hungry dupes at insane prices.

In 1947, junkyard 1938 or 1939 Fords and Chevrolets were

bringing seven-thousand dollars in many Central and South American countries, more in parts of North Africa, the Levant, and the Middle East. The black-market prices of disintegrating Pontiacs, Oldsmobiles, Buicks, De Sotos, Mercuries—to say nothing of Packards, Lincolns, Cadillacs—and other, originally more expensive makes, were correspondingly higher. Worldwide, the monumental ripoff was swindling gullible end-use buyers out of countless millions of dollars.

Rashid el Muein had recognized opportunity, yet was acutely aware of the numerous and stringent restrictions placed on him by circumstances. Lebanon was a small country, and demand for overused American automobiles was correspondingly limited. In any event, commerce in Beirut and throughout Lebanon was controlled, virtually monopolized, by Maronite Christians, who despised their Muslim fellow countrymen. In the eyes of Lebanese Maronites, Arabs like el Muein were little more than animals, people to be given the most menial work and ruthlessly exploited at every turn. Certainly they could not be permitted to engage in the import trade, which was among the most lucrative of Maronite monopolies . . .

. . . unless, of course, he agreed to relinquish the major portion of his profits to his Christian brothers.

El Muein was agreeable, for he intended that his Lebanese operations serve merely as a base. The bulk of his business would be transacted out of the country, and the bulk of his profits would be beyond the reach of Maronite hands. Being Lebanese—Lebanon is a hodgepodge of races and ethnic strains—he spoke Arabic, French, English, and possessed an innate ability to learn more languages very quickly. Thus armed, and with the modest capital furnished by his father, Rashid went into business. Used-car jobbers in the United States were delighted to receive letters written in good English rather than in the fragmented pidgin used by most black-marketing importers abroad. Syrian, Egyptian, Iraqui, and Palestinian Arabs were delighted to deal with a man who—*min kan bisadik!*—was a Muslim like themselves and spoke Arabic and their local dialects fluently. Muslim bankers in Arab countries were delighted to stretch points and provide letters of credit for one of their own.

Rashid's business flourished. Working out of a tiny office in the Bab Edriss quarter of Beirut, he imported a few cars into Lebanon to keep up appearances, split profits with bagmen for the Maronite import-export cartel. His real—and huge—profits came from the sale of great numbers of used automobiles in neighboring countries. Such was his success that it led to his downfall in, and self-exile from, Lebanon.

American automobile manufacturers piously denied any knowledge of the roaring export trade in junk cars. But their industry—from Detroit factories to local distributors and dealers—was a small world unto itself, one in which word, good or bad, spread swiftly and far. By mid-1948, every manufacturer had heard of Rashid el Muein, who was importing hundreds of junkers into Middle Eastern countries each month. With production rising and backlogged domestic demand gradually being whittled down, sales executives were looking ahead to the day when they would need foreign markets. Some reasoned that el Muein could probably do a fantastic job of distributing new cars in Arab countries in the future. The Packard, Hudson, and Studebaker companies each eagerly sought to obtain Rashid's exclusive services as the future Middle Eastern distributing agent for their new automobiles.

Maronite importers in Beirut heard of this, investigated, and belatedly learned that el Muein had made fortunes outside Lebanon. They issued an ultimatum. He would surrender not part, but all, of his profits—or he would be killed. With much of the Arab world still embroiled in war with the new state of Israel, Rashid fled to Istanbul. He would be safer there personally; his wealth was already safe in the banks of England, France, and Switzerland.

He did not stay in Turkey long. The Arab-Israeli war ended in 1949, and by then U.S. auto makers were producing far more cars than they could sell at home. Overseas demand for the junkers had all but vanished. At the same time, it was becoming apparent that the world desperately wanted Middle Eastern oil, and Western countries were prepared to pour limitless sums into the region to find and develop new sources. ARAMCO was already expanding operations in Saudi Arabia. AMINOIL had bid sky high to obtain a Kuwaiti concession.

Rashid el Muein realized there would be need for the construction of everything from housing for workers to highways and port facilities. Contracts were already being let with little concern for cost. Many of these had been won by Emile Bustani, a Lebanese whom Rashid had known in Beirut. Although a Maronite Christian, Bustani had ingratiated himself with Muslim Arabs by taking a fanatically anti-Israeli stand and giving financial support to Arab terrorist organizations that were being formed. El Muein, familiar with Arab countries, also knew that construction-contract plums in Kuwait would be awarded to a Kuwaiti—as they were later to the firm owned by youthful Badr Mulla.

The kind of business Rashid envisioned could only be directed from a Western capital, with London the logical choice. He went there, formed Muein MidEast Trading Ltd., a company with offices in Old Broad Street. Commuting to and from the Middle East, he obtained lucrative contracts to supply various oil-producing Arab countries with trucks and construction equipment. Behind this facade, he dealt in arms. Huge stocks of World War Two surplus weapons and ammunition were still available from illicit sources on the European continent. El Muein bought, then sold to Arab countries that were trying to rebuild military strength shattered by the war with Israel. And he also sold to dissident factions, active rebels, and terrorist groups in the Middle East and North Africa.

Profits were astronomical. Rashid's wealth multiplied. He was welcomed into international financial and social circles, became an influential behind-the-scenes figure in the Arab world, and was allowed to participate directly in grand-scale oil ventures. He lived, for the most part, on an estate he purchased in Kent, was an extravagant spender. In 1960 he married an English actress. She divorced him two years later, receiving—it was reported—a fifty-million-dollar settlement which scarcely made a dent in his constantly growing fortune.

Arabs fought Israelis yet again in 1973, and Arab oil producers imposed a boycott. The boycott was followed by the first of what would be a series of sharp rises in the price of oil, ushering in the era of the oil sheikhs, whose wealth defied calculation. The sheikhs—members of royal and ruling families—aside, by the late 1970's two men were acknowledged to be the richest and most powerful Arabs. Saudi Arabian Adnan Khashoggi ranked first. Western news media described Khashoggi as a financier/industrialist/oil-magnate/arms-merchant and estimated his wealth to be upwards of three billion dollars. The originally Lebanese Rashid el Muein ranked next, his fortune pegged in the neighborhood of one and a half billion dollars.

Sharaf—which may be translated as "honor" or "prestige" or even "status" is vitally important to all Arabs. Hence, it was hardly surprising that Rashid strove to surpass Khashoggi. His rivalry culminated in what bemused gossip columnists dubbed "the great yacht battle." Adnan Khashoggi spent thirty million dollars to build the 270-foot *Nabila*—named after his daughter—which carried a crew of sixty-five and was hailed as the most luxurious yacht afloat. Whereupon Rashid el Muein spent forty-five million dollars to build a 290-foot craft that was even more richly appointed, required an even larger crew. Being childless, he named it *Houri*—which proved to be a gaffe. In Arabic, *houri* means one of the beautiful dark-eyed virgins who are allotted to men who attain the Muslim paradise. Most Arabs thought that Rashid had added much luster to his prestige, gained a large *sharaf*-step on Khashoggi by building the vessel. However, some rabid Muslim fundamentalists muttered that naming it for a nymph promised to the faithful by the Koran verged on sacrilege. The Ayatollah Ruhollah Khomeini went so far as to decree that el Muein be banned from doing business in Iran. Rashid kept the name—to change it would have meant a loss of *sharaf*—but the reaction and the ban rankled and would have far-reaching effects.

Rashid el Muein waited until 1980 to join the Arab invasion of the Spanish Costa del Sol. He came by sea, aboard the *Houri*, and deployed a large force of his aides. They were armed with instructions to make it clear he would spend freely. He intended to settle, join Arab colonists who had come before, and eclipse them all but one. He feared that outshining Saudi Arabian Crown Prince Salim might be construed as an act of lèse majesté, an affront to royal *sharaf*, a risk he dared not take. Not yet.

The site for Rashid's estate was chosen with a fine eye to protocol—near Marbella but a discreet three kilometers distant from the tract owned by Prince Salim. El Muein retained English architects, told them to design a residence that was palatial, yet slightly less splendid than that of the crown prince. He made another stipulation. Moorish themes were to be avoided. The grandest Moorish-style mansion on the Sun Coast belonged to James Philip Courtney, and Rashid worried that it might be said he was plagiarizing from the expatriate American billionaire. He had known Courtney well enough in the past, had ample cause to feel hatred toward him. Not the envious rivalry he felt toward Adnan Khashoggi. Raw hatred.

In the end, the architects did plagiarize—and shamelessly—from designs favored by Hollywood stars of the silent era. They designed a greatly aggrandized version of a mansion in the so-called "Spanish hacienda style" peculiar to Southern California. When built, it had fifty-odd rooms, a structure that seemed to stretch endlessly, and made only one statement: that huge sums had been squandered—rather than lavished—on building it. Among the curious anomalies were the roof tiles. Instead of being Spanish, they were imported from Italy, where they had been handmade; Rashid apparently took pride in the knowledge that each tile had cost the equivalent of twelve dollars. The house was completed in late 1981, decorated and furnished in what might be best described as Awesomely Expensive style, and Rashid el Muein took up residence there.

He gave a huge party to announce his arrival, one worthy of Scheherazade's *Arabian Nights* tales, and memorable even by the standards of longtime Costa residents. Almost a thousand guests attended, many flying in from distant corners of the globe, but three figurative next-door neighbors were conspicuous by their absence. Although invited, Crown Prince Salim and tycoons Adnan Khashoggi and James P. Courtney failed to attend (and, known only to the host, even failed to acknowledge the invitations). The affair nonetheless firmly established el Muein's *posición social* among Costa del Sol expatriates.

This objective achieved, he withdrew from the limelight and concentrated on others of greater moment. He was determined to outstrip—or crush—all rivals and become the number-one magnate in the Middle East, the supreme business force in the entire Arab world. For a year, he made progress, then began to encounter resistance and setbacks. A group of Bahraini investors reneged on participating in a $1.2 billion New York City real-estate venture. A supertanker owned by an el Muein company and loaded with oil bound for Japan exploded and sank; insurers seized on a technicality, refused to pay. South Africa inexplicably canceled huge contracts for el Muein-brokered heavy industrial machinery.

The incidents formed a pattern. El Muein realized that the moves against him were being orchestrated—but by whom? Investigation ruled out Khashoggi and others he thought likely suspects, finally produced an answer he could hardly, but was forced to, believe. A new player had entered the Middle Eastern game: James Courtney. And there were signs that Courtney's operations were part of a complex and far-reaching scheme.

Rashid was himself a brilliant intriguer, and no coward. He reasoned that Courtney—a non-Arab, not even a Muslim—would never be able to gain ascendancy in the Middle East. On the other hand, anyone—and it could only be an Arab—who vanquished Courtney and took over his Middle Eastern interests would be hailed as a pan-Islamic hero and be given a voice in the highest Arab councils. Furthermore, el Muein knew that with the American's holdings added to his own, he would be the very richest nonroyal Arab, far and away ahead of even Adnan Khashoggi.

These considerations made him decide to oppose James Courtney alone, without seeking allies in the Muslim countries. While there would be no others to share the risks and dangers, there would be none to share in the winnings, either. To his dismay, el Muein found that Courtney seemed to have influential—and invisible—support in the Middle East and North Africa and was steadily escalating his efforts. Rashid drew on his own considerable resources, financial and otherwise, to retaliate. His moves were thwarted, failed. Now he did scramble frantically to find allies, but was rebuffed by his fellow Muslims. They dismissed his claims of having uncovered a huge plot as the fanciful tale invented by one business titan who wanted help in battling another. They maintained that the Arab world's only real enemies were Israel, international Zionism, Muslim fundamentalist extremists, Communists; these they were fighting and would continue to fight.

El Muein was left to seek confederates elsewhere, and did. Those he found came at high price but were renowned for a degree of skill and efficiency which, so far, they had failed to show.

When in his twenties and a Lebanese importer of worthless American used cars, Rashid el Muein had been swarthy, slender of face and body. Thirty-odd years later, his face was seamed and his body was ropy-lean. Eyes deep-set in their sockets were those of a shrewd and tightly self-disciplined bedouin Arab; he had total control over what they expressed. For several minutes now he had wanted them to show what he felt: frustrated rage. They were ablaze as he berated the much older man seated opposite him in the extravagantly furnished drawing room.

". . . your supposed professionals are blunderers, fools!" El Muein was continuing his tirade. Although the man was a German, he spoke in English. It had long been the second language for them both. "They allow Rechstein to reach Tangier. They do not stop him there. When I learn that he is going to Venice, you guarantee—"

"The orders were carried out," Horst Thiele—it had been decades since he dropped the "von" from his name—interrupted. He had the arrogant calm of a Prussian-born septuagenarian who spoke only when certain of his ground, and he was doubly tired, having only just flown into Spain from Riyadh, in Saudi Arabia. The trip, plagued by airport delays, had been wearying. And he was even more weary of Rashid's complaints. "You wanted a painting Rechstein had in an aluminum tube and were not more specific. My men took what they found in his possession—"

"A daub he bought in some Venetian tourist shop!"

"They are not art experts." Thiele shrugged and inclined his head. Once it had been shaved in Prussian *offizier* style. Now it was entirely bald. The effect was the same. "Even so, if you had identified the picture as a Velázquez or described it, they would have realized their error."

Thiele's tone implied an accusation. It was intentional. Fault for the failure to recover the right picture did lie with el Muein, and reminding him of it would stop the diatribe, enable them to discuss other, more vital matters.

Rashid el Muein disdained the casual clothes favored for daytime wear by foreign residents of the Costa del Sol. He preferred Savile Row suits, even when in his home. The one he had on today was tropical weight, fawn-colored. Momentarily nonplussed by Thiele's words, he busied himself brushing imaginary lint from the razor-sharp crease of a trouser leg—an uncharacteristic gesture not lost on the German.

"We should perhaps speak about some other unfortunate occurrences," Thiele said, driving his barbs deeper. He had been an SS Sturmbannführer during the war, showing undying loyalty to party, unit (the Fifteenth Panzergrenadiers), superiors, and subordinates. There was no party now, no unit save the civilian organization he headed. Yet it was imperative he demonstrate loyalty to its members by driving home the point that they were blameless and that real problems lay in different directions. "You—we—lost a friend when Sheikh Abdul was so cruelly killed." He paused. "By Jew terrorists."

"Not quite a friend," Rashid said, "but he could have been useful." He took a *sibah*—a string of Muslim prayer beads—from a jacket pocket, fingered it moodily. Omani Sheikh Abdul al Amari might have been valuable in many ways, he thought. He was still unable to decide what to believe about the Olympic Tower explosion that had killed al Amari. The claim that the bomb had been planted by Zionist militants seemed a little too pat. Still . . .

Thiele interrupted his musings. "Then there is the information I bring from Riyadh."

El Muein continued to fondle the *sibah*, looked up. The heat was gone from his eyes. "Is there evidence?" he asked.

"Evidence? How could there be evidence?" Thiele waved a gnarled, liver-spotted hand. "A man such as Courtney does not advertise that he is supplying arms to rebels."

Rashid concealed his disappointment in a silence broken only by the barely audible click of the beads. Unlike Adnan Khashoggi, he was not on close terms with the Saudi Arabian royal family, did not enjoy entree to Crown Prince Salim, who was then in Spain on an extended visit to his Marbella estate. El Muein had hoped that Thiele would bring some kind of proof—by which he could gain audience with Prince Salim. Once again, Thiele broke into his musings:

"Neither Salim nor anyone else would listen to you even had I brought proof. The uprising failed, crushed even as it began."

"The Saudis would be grateful to learn the truth."

"*Mein lieber freund,* they believe they already know it, and Courtney is a clever fox. The weapons were of Czechoslovak manufacture and the rebels were members of an underground Communist faction. Some of them were captured alive and broke under interrogation, confessing that the arms were sent to them by agents of Moscow."

Thiele smiled his appreciation of Courtney's guile, went on.

"The explanation fits the preconceptions of the Saudi Arabian government and the American CIA operatives stationed in Riyadh. If plots are not the work of the Jews in Israel, they must be the work of Communists. They are not alone. The American and Western European press have already swallowed the version whole."

"Yes," el Muein said, conceding all that Thiele had said.

"It was a diversionary maneuver, and brilliant." Onetime tank-regiment Sturmbannführer Horst Thiele was well qualified to judge the merits and effectiveness of diversionary maneuvers. "The main effort is yet to come. Unless there is preemptive action."

His smile told Rashid that Thiele was dangling bait; he decided to take it. "You have a suggestion," he said—as a statement, not question.

"*Naturlicht*. I suggest a final solution. Through special action." Thiele's parchment face livened; the euphemisms evoked nostalgic memories of the days of the Third Reich.

El Muein scowled. Was the German so stupid as to think he had not explored that idea thoroughly? Then he spoke, with exaggerated patience, like someone explaining primer-level facts of life to a backward child.

"Don't be a damned fool. Courtney's security force at Montemar is even bigger than mine. His personal limousine is armored. Whenever he leaves the grounds, he's accompanied by bodyguards. Besides, Thiele, this is Spain—not Italy or France or the United States, where the police are lax and corrupt."

Thiele said, "Courtney also travels much in his private aircraft—as did Emile Bustani, or have you forgotten?"

Rashid remembered very clearly and with a sense of triumph. Emile Bustani had been a Lebanese tycoon with business interests throughout the Middle East. By 1963 Bustani was offering competition that el Muein found intolerable and decided to eliminate once and for all. He retained Horst Thiele and his organization. A few weeks later, Emile Bustani and some associates boarded Bustani's private airplane at Khaldeh Airport in Beirut. The pilot took off. When the plane reached seven-thousand feet, it disintegrated in midair. Everyone aboard was killed. *Naturlicht*.

"Courtney won't be flying anywhere," Rashid said. "He'll stay close to home until the issue is settled."

"You are certain of this?"

"Yes. As I've told you before, I have sources among people on his staff. What information they manage to obtain and pass on to me is always accurate." A tone change to the dry and reproving: "Just as it was about Rechstein and his movements."

Thiele ignored the last remark—his organization was blameless, and the *verdammt* Arab knew it. Indulging in more heavy-handed euphemisms—which appealed to his Teutonic sense of humor—he said: "Then my surgeons must go to Courtney's home to practice their skills."

El Muein, unamused, snapped: "How soon?"

"Within days, and I guarantee the operation will be successful. The patient will not survive." Thiele smiled at his own wit.

"What's your price?"

"High. Two million dollars."

"Payable after Courtney is dead?"

"Immediately after."

"Done," Rashid said without hesitation. His look said: Our business has been concluded for the present; it's time for you to leave.

Thiele chose to disregard the silent dismissal. There were questions that had been nagging at him. Why had el Muein wanted a painting that was owned by James Courtney and being smuggled somewhere by Bernard Rechstein? The Arab was neither art collector nor art lover. Even the unfortunately belated explanation that it was a Velázquez did not suffice. True, a Velázquez might be worth six or seven million dollars—and bring that price if sold by the legitimate owner. If offered by someone who was not its owner? A fraction of that amount, possibly nothing. But even seven million was a piddling sum compared to the stakes for which el Muein was playing. What made the painting so valuable to both Courtney and the Arab?

"I am curious," Thiele said.

Rashid merely raised an eyebrow.

"I am most curious," Thiele repeated with added emphasis, took a breath that failed to expand his old man's chest, went on. "The effort mounted in the Rechstein affair cost you more than half a million dollars for our services alone. The excuse—if you will pardon my frankness—was preposterous. Never once did I believe that it was all because of the picture, not even after you told me the swine had been carrying a masterpiece." He stopped, waiting for comment.

El Muein had expected the question to arise sooner or later and was fully prepared. Horst Thiele's mind was set in a rigid mold, which made matters simple.

"You're right, of course," Rashid said. "The painting itself is—was—unimportant. There is something written on the canvas that makes the thing priceless." El Muein told the truth, confident that Thiele would be convinced he was lying.

"*Ach*, a message in invisible ink, perhaps," the German tried to probe further. His expression was openly skeptical. In this day of supertechnology, who would rely on such primitive devices as invisible-ink messages written on large canvas surfaces? No one. Least of all men like James Courtney and Rashid el Muein.

"Surprising as it may seem, yes," Rashid said, still hewing close to the truth.

"Written by Courtney, no?" Thiele persisted. "Orders, instructions—?"

"I don't know what was written or by whom," el Muein broke in. This time, he lied—and Thiele believed him. Why else would the Arab spend a fortune, if not to learn what the message contained?

23

David Lippmann, freshly washed and shaved, returned to his seat in the first-class cabin of the Iberia Airlines DC-10. The prelanding fasten-seat-belts warning came a moment later. Lippmann latched his belt, braced for what he fervently hoped would be the final verbal gush from the two Americans—husband and wife—occupying seats across the aisle. They ("I'm Tom Bates, this is Jennifer, we're from Madison, Wisconsin") had drunk their way across the Atlantic. One or the other had replayed the same progressively more slurred refrain a dozen times. This time, it was Tom's turn again:

"Can' get over it, fella. Y' look jush like Robert Refford—only with a busted nose."

David played his own broken record. "Uh . . . thanks." He forced a ha-ha. "That's the best compliment I've had this year."

"Betcha hear it all time—"

But there was a crumping sound. The wheels were going down. Jennifer Bates gave a start, gasped. Tom Bates turned to grope for her hand. David Lippmann also turned, to look through the window next to his seat, watched the Marbella airport runway rise up to meet the plane.

Lippmann felt a twinge of regret. He had been to Europe many times before. As a student of art history and later an art-history teacher, he had come whenever he could to tour the great museums and libraries on the Continent. Then, as a professor and an assistant curator in the Wyler College art museum, there had been several occasions when he had come on museum business. Whenever in Spain, he had always made a point to visit the Prado in Madrid. That vast storehouse of art treasures held a particular fascination for David.

A stopover in Madrid and a visit to the Prado would have been a pleasant opener for this trip. But the nonstop New York–Marbella booking had been made for him by the Manhattan office of Courtney Ventures International. David assumed that James Courtney was impatient to have work begin on the cataloging of his art collection. He could not risk irking the billionaire by changing the arrangements. Courtney, a benefactor of the Wyler College Art Museum, had considerable clout. Lippmann had to think first of his career at Wyler. However, he would spend many months, possibly as much as a year, in Spain working on the extracurricular project. He consoled himself with the thought there would be many opportunities for him to visit Madrid and other parts of the country—on long weekends, if nothing else.

To his surprise, David received a VIP welcome at Marbella Airport. An Iberia official escorted him through the passport-stamping ritual, said there was no need to bother with the *aduana*. Someone would collect his luggage, shepherd it through customs, and deliver it to Montemar. And Don Jaime had sent his private secretary and a car to meet Señor Lippmann—yes, there she was.

"*Bienvenido* and all that. I'm Sybil Pearson—I do wish you'd make it Sybil—Mr. Courtney's dogsbody."

The smile was warm, genuine, the young woman attractive—extremely attractive, David thought, shaking the slender hand that shook his own firmly. Hazel eyes smiled along with the soft lips. Freckles were splashed on the uptilted nose.

The car was a gleaming black Mercedes behemoth, complete with chauffeur and shotgun-riding security man. Sybil Pearson kept up a running commentary on the Costa del Sol during the drive from the airport. She stopped when the limousine turned off the Carretera de Cádiz and paused at a guard gate. The guards saluted, the car drove through. A moment later David caught his first glimpse of Courtney's mansion. He had seen photographs of it in newspapers and magazines—but this?

"Agog?" Sybil laughed, seeing his reaction. "Most people are. I still am at times."

"It's not an *imitation* Moorish palace," David said. "It's an exact reproduction."

"Mmm. Nothing improvised, nothing fudged. Quite an accomplishment, really."

They made the final turn in the private road. David could see the full sweep and grandeur of the house, the vast reflecting pool in front of it, the great expanse of lawn and gardens. He felt a stir of excitement, of eagerness to see the inside, Courtney's works of art.

Sybil introduced the liveried butler who opened the huge double entrance doors. Lippmann had taken an instant liking to her and it was obvious that she and Grenville were on the best of terms and Grenville was correct and pleasant. But something about the butler rubbed David the wrong way—maybe the too-correct expression on the rather sheeplike face. Then he stepped into the entrance atrium and stopped thinking about Grenville. Ceilings soared, furniture even there was antique and priceless, and what paintings were visible, fabulous.

"My God!" he exclaimed, despite himself, and moved toward a corridor that opened off to the right. He was drawn to the Titian *Adoration* he could see hanging on a wall, remembering that it had been listed on the inventory Courtney had sent to Wyler.

Sybil stopped him.

"Mr. Courtney would like to see you for a minute before Grenville takes you up to your suite."

David turned. "Did I hear you say suite?"

"Yes, sir. Upstairs in the east wing," Grenville answered for her.

Literal bastard, Lippmann thought.

"Mr. Courtney said you're to have three rooms—bed, sitter, and one for work," Sybil said.

She led the way, down a corridor to the left, and David wished that she would walk more slowly. They seemed to rush past the paintings that hung in profusion on the walls, pictures that would have done credit to almost any museum, he thought. It was one thing to read about them in an inventory, but to actually see them . . .

They turned a corner.

"This is my office—don't pay much attention to Paco. If you'll wait a second, I'll pop in and tell Mr. Courtney you're here."

It was only a matter of seconds before Sybil emerged from what David thought of already as the tycoon's inner sanctum. She ushered him inside, made the introductions, and left.

Lippmann was struck by the size and tasteful opulence of the study and amused to see the Bureau Plat du Roi about which there had been so much comment in the press. The Royal Writing Table was, indeed, its owner's work desk—and standing up very nicely under its load of electronic gadgetry.

"Delighted that you've arrived safely," Courtney said. He had come around from behind the desk and shook David's hand warmly. "Take a chair—we'll have a short chat."

James Philip Courtney made a surprisingly good first impression, Lippmann thought, canceling out the ideas he'd had of a powerhouse-martinet type. Casual in dress, outgoing in manner, Courtney had a good face, sharp-featured and angular, yet likable. An old scar on the right cheek added dash. So much for press photographs that made him look cold, aloof, sardonic, Lippmann mused. Courtney's smile was spontaneous, genuine, as he once more seated himself at the Bureau Plat and, finger poised over a call-button console, asked:

"Care for a drink, David—is it okay if I call you Dave?"

"No, thanks, on the drink, and Dave is fine, Mr. Courtney." David wondered if Courtney would reciprocate, tell him to drop the "Mr." and address him less formally. Nothing of the sort was forthcoming. "Mr. Courtney" it would have to be until further notice.

Courtney had much else to say, though, and he did it rapidly. He had fond memories of his alma mater, Wyler College, he declared, and Wyler obviously had a very high opinion of David Lippmann.

". . . I wanted the best art historian for the job, and the people at Wyler informed me that you were the man. . . ."

He explained why he had not had his collection cataloged before.

". . . wanted to wait until I felt the collection was complete, but I kept on acquiring more pieces."

"You're not alone, Mr. Courtney," David said. "Many of the great collectors—past and present—have done the same." It was true.

"You mean fall into the same trap?" The billionaire's smile was almost boyish. "It's easy to do. I can't tell you how many times I decided this was it—no more. Then something would come on the market, and my good intentions would vanish. I'd buy."

"That shows in your inventory," Lippmann said with a broad grin. "The acquisition dates—"

"Oh, yes. The inventory."

Courtney's eyes, a faint blue, seemed to pale even more.

"The inventory," he repeated. "You've familiarized yourself with it?"

"I've practically memorized it," David said, not exaggerating.

"Then you remember the Diego Velázquez *Horse and Rider*."

"God, yes—and I'm looking forward to seeing it."

"That, I'm afraid, is impossible. I began to have doubts about its authenticity. Had it examined by experts from the Prado." The billionaire shook his head sadly, but his eyes remained fixed on David. "They gave me a unanimous verdict. A late-nineteenth-century forgery . . ."

Lippmann felt a surge of sympathy for Courtney. Such things happened all too often, but they were always a hard blow to a serious collector, regardless of how much money he had.

". . . and so I had it destroyed."

Bravo-plus, David thought, his opinion of James Courtney soaring. More than a few collectors—again regardless of their wealth—would not have demonstrated equal integrity. Discovering that a picture they owned and thought a masterpiece was a fake, they would tell no one. Instead of being destroyed, the forgery would be foisted off on some small museum (with attendant tax deduction for the supposed value) or sold as real to some unsophisticated buyer through a less-than-ethical sales gallery.

Courtney had been studying Lippmann's face to read his reaction. Evidently satisfied by what he saw, he leaned back, abruptly switched to another topic.

"I want you to be comfortable and at ease here, Dave," he began. Again speaking rapidly, he ticked off the points he wished to make. Lippmann would be free to work—and come and go—as he pleased. An automobile—would a medium-size Peugeot sedan be satisfactory?—would be his to use. If he needed secretarial or clerical help . . .

"Just ask Sybil. She'll get someone for you from the annex."

As for most other needs . . .

"The servants have orders to consider you one of the household, Dave. You can have meals served in your suite or take them with me . . . or explore the Costa offerings when the mood moves. There are some superb restaurants, incidentally."

"Sounds great—fantastic, Mr. Courtney." It did.

"Oh. One more thing. You may have noticed that we're security-conscious here."

Lippmann had noticed the guards, uniformed and plainclothes, but did not think it unusual. Wealthy people everywhere felt the need to be guarded, protected—and, David had to concede, with ever-increasing justification. It followed that the super-rich be even more careful.

"It figures," he said, smiling. "I saw pictures worth a total of millions walking from the front door here to your off . . . er, study."

"Goes beyond the question of theft," Courtney said. "The world is filled with homicidal maniacs. Couple of years ago, one got as far as the hallway outside Sybil's office."

David didn't know quite what kind of response was called for, compromised on: "May I ask what happened?"

"My butler, Grenville, blew his head off."

I'll be damned, Lippmann thought. If it wasn't completely absurd, I'd take that as some kind of warning. He made it sound like one. No, it can't be. I'm imagining it.

"Well, I imagine you'd like to settle in, Dave."

The cue unmistakable, Lippmann stood up, recited the appropriate exit lines, turned to leave. He had been sitting with his back to the Frans Hals portrait of a chess player and noticed it for the first time. Eyes widening in surprised admiration, he stepped closer to the picture and exclaimed:

"Magnificent—in a class with *Laughing Cavalier!*"

That brought Courtney across the room to stand at his side.

"A recent acquisition?" David asked.

"Hardly. I bought it soon after the war."

"Funny." Lippmann was studying the vibrant colors laid on with an unhesitating brush. "I can't remember an inventory listing."

"That's because there isn't any."

"Oh?"

"No. I don't consider this a part of my collection—or even as a picture." Courtney's gaze was fixed on the portrait, and he seemed to be speaking to it rather than to David. "We're old, dear friends—partners, in a sense."

Lippmann, perplexed—not by what the billionaire actually said, but by the near-reverent tones in which he spoke—glanced at Courtney, and perplexity turned to astonishment. The faces of Hals's chess player and James Philip Courtney not only resembled each other but also had expressions that were, at the moment, identical.

A complex character, David thought. He's destroyed a fake Velázquez, losing millions. He makes a point of telling me that his butler—no wonder that guy's vibes are wrong—is a dead shot who blows off heads. Then he shows a mystical attachment to a Hals chess player. Why? Because the portrait looks like him? Or because he's like a man who grows to look like his dog—in this case, painting?

Surfacing abruptly from what had become an almost trancelike state, Courtney said: "If you decide to stay in this evening, I'd like to have you join me for dinner."

The invitation was voiced as a command.

Grenville waited in the outer office.

"May I show you to your suite now, sir?" he asked when Lippmann emerged from the *estudio*.

There's either something wrong with my hearing or I'm getting paranoid, David thought. The butler's inquiry had also sounded like a command.

•

Gleaming-clean tram cars—usually coupled in twos or threes—run primly along their tracks in the middle of Zurich's Bahnhofstrasse. The street, itself ever spotless, is lined with somber buildings that resemble nothing more than fortresses, and in a sense they are. It is in these bastions that leading Swiss banks have their headquarters, and where they transact much business—some open, some secret.

The Bauerkreditbank is one of the largest financial institutions in Switzerland, and hence, among the most powerful in all Europe. Its five-story building on the Bahnhofstrasse is fittingly impressive on the outside. Inside, on the main floor, the atmosphere is more that of cathedral than fortress. Ceilings are high, vaulted. Walls are paneled with ancient dark oak that gleams softly in the light admitted by tall, narrow windows. Bank employees and the minor executives who work on the ground floor are perpetually bent, as if in prayer, over their desks and counters. They seem to be poring over sacred manuscripts rather than ledger sheets, and a hushed silence prevails.

Large numbers of people intrude on the calm each working day. They are of all ages, nationalities, races. They come in varying states of dress. Americans are likely to appear in casual garb. Even in rumpled slacks, garish ski jackets, and caps. Like the two men who had just entered. One was of medium height and suntanned; the other, much taller—a giant—had skin burned a much darker shade by sun and wind.

The shorter man lagged behind as his companion went to the nearest teller. The teller assumed he wanted to change money or cash traveler's checks, instead heard:

"My name is Neil Harkness. Herr Kloster is expecting me—more or less."

An eyebrow rose a fraction of an inch. There was only one Herr Kloster in the bank, Herr Henrich, and he was its head. "You will wait, please. I must telephone."

"Sure." Neil turned to Kenneth Dixon. "Plant yourself in one of those antiques." He pointed to a row of monstrous turn-of-the-century but beautifully preserved leather armchairs. He had to see Kloster alone. "If I'm not back in half an hour, notify the Chase Manhattan," he added, grinning broadly.

"Asshole. You haven't even got the okay to see him yet."

A bank official appeared, announced that he would escort Mr. Harkness to see Mr.—he dispensed with the "Herr"—Kloster.

Heinrich Kloster proved to be very much what Neil had expected: an uptight Swiss German—or German Swiss, he couldn't be sure which, but he knew from experience that there *were* differences. German Swiss, he decided after Kloster, eyes remote and wary behind the gold-rimmed eyeglasses, opened the conversation. He wasn't quite as unctuous as a Swiss German.

"Please, your passport, Mr. Harkness. For identification."

Neil produced the document, flipped it across the banker's desk. "A little silly, isn't it? J.P. must have given you my description."

Kloster thumbed through the passport, gave it back, asked: "You have the object Mr. Courtney wishes to have delivered?"

"That's none of your business." The Velázquez was in a Zurich airport checkroom, wrapped around two pairs of skis. "You're supposed to give me a name, an address, and money. Period."

Heinrich Kloster's expression turned vinegar-sour. "Go to Paris, the Hotel Lutetia-Concorde. It is on the Left Bank—"

"I know it."

"A man using the name Carl Orff will visit you there and further identify himself by giving you a Deutsche Grammophon record album of *Carmina Burana*. You are to give him the . . . object."

"Silly . . . childish," Neil said. "Third-rate cloak-and-dagger—"

"Those are the instructions. And there is one more. You are not to telephone Mr. Courtney until after you have delivered the"—Kloster paused again before adding—"object."

It was a shade too obvious. Neil sensed that the banker knew exactly what the "object" was, and for some reason felt constrained to indicate that he did not.

"Okay," Harkness said. "We're all set. Except for my engraved paper. The money," he said, in case Kloster had failed to understand, but the banker was already pressing a call button on his desk. A man, a square-cut thirtyish Swiss-banker type, entered carrying a canvas money bag that appeared to be of proper weight and bulk. He put it on Kloster's desk.

"If you will count, please."

"I won't bother." Harkness rose from his chair, unfolding his six-three frame, and took the bag. "If you've shorted me, the deal's off, and I tell J.P. why. *Auf Wiedersehen.*"

Kloster glared. The younger banker looked horrified. Never in his banking career had he ever seen anyone accept a quantity of cash without counting it.

Ken Dixon was sprawled in the leather armchair where Neil had left him, sprang to his feet.

"The bank's been robbed—you carry the loot." Harkness handed him the money bag. "You're more accustomed to handling big dough."

Dixon's novels and the films made from them were said to have earned him several million dollars. Neil Harkness had never had more than fifty-thousand-dollars of his own.

"Where next?" Ken held the bag in one hand, patted it with the other, and his eyes gleamed.

"Across the street."

There was, of course, another bank on the other side of the Bahnhofstrasse. Like all Swiss banks, it asked no questions when anyone came to deposit cash, and a lower-rung officer opened two secret numbered accounts in less time than it took tellers to count the money and divide it into two five-hundred-thousand-dollar piles.

Harkness waited until he and Ken were in a taxi going to the airport before passing on what Kloster had told him.

Ken barely listened. He was gloating over his share in the windfall—a shade excessively for someone accustomed to earning millions, Neil thought, but only in passing.

Dixon's only comment on the instructions received from Kloster was: "Sounds like it should be quick and easy in Paris."

"Sounds like and should be," Harkness repeated, lit a cigarette, and blasted smoke through his nostrils. "That's probably what Willy Fischer or whatever his real name was thought about Venice."

"Jesus Christ! I almost forgot about him."

"Yeah, I figured you did," Neil said, and lapsed into a moody silence.

Heinrich Kloster would have never used the American expression "Cover your ass," but it was precisely what he did, telephoning James Courtney in Spain. With the Vocoder scramblers activated at both ends of the line, he could speak freely, use names, announce:

"Your man Harkness was here. He made no mention of Rechstein—"

"No, he's cautious," Courtney broke in. "You gave him the money?"

"Yes. He is going on to Paris."

"Good. Listen, Heinrich, I was going to call you anyway. Put a hold on buying more Chrysler stock."

"What? You are stopping?" Kloster spluttered in consternation. "J.P., we have been working through brokers in a dozen different countries. They will wonder, ask questions—"

"Why should that bother you?" Ice was forming on Courtney's tone. "Or have you been making side bets, Heinrich?"

"Of course not!" Kloster snapped. Of course he had been. He had bought shares through dummies for his own account. He intended selling them to Courtney when his buying caused their price to rise several points. Never mind, the banker consoled himself. He would recoup losses a thousand times over through his private grand design. His *Ding an sich*—the reality that lay behind the facades he had created. "I shall do as you wish, J.P. If there is nothing further . . ."

"But there is. I want all stock already acquired to be sold—dumped—immediately."

"You must be joking," Kloster protested. "The price will plummet."

"Thereby sowing confusion, Heinrich. Everyone believes that Arab money has been trying to take over Chrysler to obtain control of its tank and armored-vehicle factories. Now they'll believe the Arabs have suddenly abandoned the attempt and wonder why. Then I'll have a rumor spread that they've made a deal with the Russians for tanks and have no need to produce their own. The story will be swallowed whole in every Western capital."

Courtney had never mentioned that fillip before, Kloster thought, and ventured to ask: "You have altered strategy, then?"

"My strategy is always flexible—haven't you noticed?" Scramblers distort human voices slightly, but a faintly mocking note was evident. "I alter it to meet changes in situations. When Harkness has delivered what he's carrying"—the mockery was stronger—"all shall be revealed to you, Heinrich. Rest assured."

Courtney's own *Ding an sich* is hidden beneath countless surface layers, Kloster mused, unperturbed. He was in a unique position. He alone was in touch with all the realities. Regardless of what might transpire, he would gain, perhaps the most of anyone.

24

Marisa Alarcón listened with rapt attention as Vivian Dixon spoke.

". . . you see, Ken had many different jobs before he actually started to write."

The two women lolled on canvas recliners under a candy-striped unbrella on the beach at Broadmoor, the Dixons' Cabo Verde home. Vivian knew it was necessary to keep the Spanish girl's mind occupied, hold her interest, over the days until Ken returned. She could not allow the aspiring *periodista* to roam free on the Costa, asking questions about her husband.

". . . it's his greatest strength as a novelist. The broad range of personal experience is reflected in his novels . . ."

Vivian had been dragging everything out, going into endless detail. The previous evening, she had taken the original manuscript of Kenneth Dixon's first best-seller—*Gusher!*—from the files and given it to Marisa. The girl had taken the yellowing pages of typescript as though they were holy relics and stayed awake most of the night going over them. In the morning, she expressed eagerness to discuss the book and hear all that Vivi could tell her about Ken's early life and career. Vivian gained hours by stalling until after lunch, when she suggested going down to the beach. It was midafternoon, and they were still there; Vivian was still imparting information (some of it improvised or invented) and Marisa was still fascinated.

". . . Ken himself admits that his books are more faction than fiction. You can use that in your article on him—although I don't know how well it might come across in Spanish."

"I will find some way of saying it," Marisa said, scribbling in the notebook she had brought to the beach.

Vivian wore mirrored sunglasses, could safely study the girl from behind them, and smiled wryly to herself. Marisa Alarcón, stunning in a white bikini, very much together at most levels, had starry-eyed illusions about writing, writers—and especially *grande novelista* Kenneth Dixon. Someday, the illusions would be pulverized, Vivi mused. But certainly not by her.

Marisa wanted to hear more about how Ken came to write *Gusher!* and asked: "He really worked in the oil fields?"

"As a driller." Vivian nodded, perpetuating a myth created more than a decade before she had even met Ken. Actually, he had been a Skelly Oil Company clerk in Tulsa, and only for a few weeks. "Then he struck out on his own as a wildcatter, prospecting for oil." Or so the publishers had claimed in their press releases. "He didn't stand a chance, though." Vivi added the long-ago embroidery of a press agent that had become part of the Ken Dixon legend: "He was forced out of business by the majors."

"The majors?"

"Giant oil companies—the Seven Sisters."

"I understand now. The *monopolio* of Standard Oil, Texaco, and the rest." Marisa made more notes. "He was very brave to fight them. I must . . . stress? . . . yes, stress that."

Vivian raised her sunglasses, winked a gray eye. "Biblical allusions go over big in any language. You can say that Ken was a David lost because he was battling too many Goliaths."

"Wonderful!" Marisa scribbled furiously, finished. Closing the cover of the notebook, she turned deeply pensive and gave Vivian a searching, yet embarrassed look. Vivi let her sunglasses drop back into protective place. She sensed that Marisa was about to go off on a tangent and grew wary.

"There is much explicit sex in your husband's books."

"Mmm." Vivian pretended to think. "Yes, I suppose there is."

Marisa hesitated, her tanned olive skin reddening.

She's actually blushing! Vivian chuckled to herself. Liberated Spanish women can burn all their bras, but they really should have hung on to their fans for another generation.

The girl finally worked up sufficient courage to ask: "What he writes in the sex scenes is also from experience?"

How to play this one without losing points? Vivi mused, chose a nonanswer: "What do you think?"

The blush deepened. "I think yes."

"Well, then?"

"I am not a virgin, Vivi. I have had affairs."

"Wow! That's the non sequitur of the month."

"It was to tell you that I am not a prude."

"There must be more."

"Yes. When you read what your husband has written from his experiences with other women—"

"The first lesson any author's wife has to learn is never be jealous of a printed page," Vivian interrupted, hoping to wrap up the subject and bury it.

"But people all over the world also read the books," Marisa persisted. "They share your husband's sexual life—no, I said that wrong. He shares it with them—with everyone."

"Ken is my husband, Marisa," Vivian said firmly, guessing that the show of possessive loyalty would do the trick, adding an I'm-the-luckiest-woman-in-the-world smile for insurance. It worked. Marisa's expression changed; she radiated complete understanding, sighed and said:

"I am envious of you."

Vivian turned away, stared at the gentle Mediterranean surf washing against the beach, thought: Oh, Christ! but said: "Oh?"

"What woman wouldn't be envious of you?" Marisa effused. "Your career, your husband—both marvelous. It is . . . You have . . . everything, a perfect life."

Vivian continued to gaze at the surf. "Perfect?" she began in a harsh voice, caught herself, edited her tone and words, said: " 'Perfect' is a very big word, Marisa. Much too big, I'm afraid."

"It is," Marisa said solemnly, as though chastised. "I meant that your life is full and you are very happy. That is right, isn't it?"

Vivian Dixon pretended not to hear, stood up from her sling chair. "The sun is getting low," she said. "Let's go back to the house."

* * *

Carlos Lozano loved, rather than merely liked, being the manager of Galerías Vivi. Because he was in love with Vivian Dixon. It was the kind of adoring, unspoken passion that only sensitive, proud Spaniards still seem capable of feeling for a woman. Carlos was acutely, often bitterly aware of the factors that were insuperable obstacles. *Ni pensar en ello!* It was out of the question to think of himself ever telling Vivian how he felt.

She was married. In itself, their age difference—Carlos was twenty-seven, Vivian thirty-three—meant nothing. But she was much more sophisticated, possessed a degree of cool emotional maturity that made Carlos think he must seem callow by comparison. And Vivian owned the gallery, paid his salary, was his employer. Thus, all things considered, she was unattainable. Carlos worshiped secretly and, figuratively speaking, from afar.

Unrequited love and its classic torments, *sí*.

Lack of sexual outlet, *no—nunca*.

Sex is never a problem for male natives of Mediterranean resort areas and tourist centers, where vacationing foreign women swarm in avid search. Those who visit the libido-fixated Costa del Sol tend to be the most purposeful and least inhibited, and Andalusian men knowingly rate them on an availability scale by national origin. Scandinavians, Americans, and Dutch lead. Germans, English, French, and Swiss follow in that order. Andalusian women understandably have their own views. To them, the foreign women are *putas*, perpetually in heat, their *ardor sexual de la hembra* insatiable.

Carlos Lozano, being attractive, virile, and intelligent, could afford to be selective in his choice of bedmates. His choices were governed by more than the customary physical-beauty elements that lead to such value judgments. Unlike countless other Spaniards, he bore no resentment against foreigners as a whole for their disdainful use of the country and frequent abuse of its hospitality. He understood that tens of thousands of resident expatriates and tens of millions of annual tourists brought foreign currency to Spain. Without it, the hard-pressed Spanish economy would be in dire straits.

On the other hand, there were the *extranjeros* who went too far, making it clear that they considered Spain a sort of third-rate comic-opera kingdom, Spaniards as an inferior (and subject) people. They were arrogant and contemptuous, with—by and large—Americans, Britons, and Germans being the worst and most frequent offenders. Carlos always made certain that any foreign girl he met socially was at minimum congenial, warm, *simpática*, before deepening acquaintance, much less bedding her.

Naturally, he could not exercise an equal degree of discrimination at work. Galerías Vivi was open to the public. Its customers were mainly foreigners: permanent-resident expatriates, limited-stay holidaymakers, or passing-through tourists. Good business sense—to say nothing of fierce, secret-lover's loyalty to Vivian Dixon—demanded that Carlos treat them courteously. There were occasions when he had to swallow pride along with angry responses that sprang to his mind, elicited by ugly remarks and outright personal insults.

". . . just another tourist trap. This stuff is shit."

". . . I've been told the owner is American. I want to see her, not a Spanish employee."

". . . look, spic. I said cut the price in half or forget it."

". . . bloody Spaniard . . ."

Although such incidents were rare, they happened, and memories of them ate like acid. However, the continuing arrogance and insolently patronizing attitude of some regular gallery customers were even worse, but had to be tolerated. And with smiles and polite murmurs. Gloria Meese—whom Galerías employees called "the American sow" behind her back—was one example out of several. Since she bought many paintings, subsidized gigolo-artists, and queened it over a segment of American expatriate society, the millionairess considered it her right to be thoroughly obnoxious. She took particular delight in harassing Carlos Lozano. She had once offered him twenty thousand pesetas to spend a night with her.

". . . if you're a good fuck, you can move in with me for a while."

Carlos, forcing a polite smile around gritted teeth, refused.

That was in 1981. Gloria Meese had hated Carlos since and had shown it whenever she saw him, which was fairly often, for she came to Galerías Vivi frequently. The most recent visit—when she demanded to see Vivian and be told where Ken Dixon was—had ended badly. Stoned—not on her favorite cocaine but some other drug, Carlos guessed—Gloria had stalked, cursing, out of the gallery. When last seen, she was lurching across the Plaza José Antonio, presumably toward wherever her chauffeured Rolls waited.

Carlos had not expected her to return soon—if ever—and blinked astonishment when one of the sales assistants hurried to the rear of the second-floor gallery where he was talking to a customer and, in a whisper, warned him:

"The American sow is downstairs."

Lozano excused himself, turning the customer over to a sales assistant. He took the stairs leading down to the main floor two at a time, but felt that he could for once dispense with the smile and politeness.

Gloria Meese, braless, heavy breasts waggling beneath haute-couture silk, stood immediately inside the sheet-glass entrance doors. Evidently she—or her chauffeur—did not want to take chances this evening, Carlos thought, hurrying across the carpeted floor. The Rolls, in defiance of strict no-parking rules on the plaza streets, stood directly in front of the gallery.

Gloria's eyes were usually tinged with red streaks. Today they were redder than ever. Not for ten million pesetas, Carlos thought, remembering her offer, and—still not cracking a smile—said:

"*Buenas tardes, Señora Meese.*" She was one of the innumerable foreigners who lived in Spain, knew only a few words of Spanish, insisted that anyone speaking to her do so in English. "*Cómo está Usted?*"

Even that much Berlitz-phrase-book-level Spanish annoyed her.

"I didn't come here to talk with a flunky. I want to see Vivi."

Carlos switched to English: "Sorry, she's not here."

The bloodshot eyes glared suspicion. "Vivian never stays away from work for days at a time. What the hell is going on?"

Carlos was slender, at five-feet-ten taller than the average Spanish man, and he earned enough to buy well-cut ready-made business suits. The overall effect gave him a confident, dapper appearance—which made his careless shrug all the more disdainful. It goaded the sow the way a deeply thrust *bandillera* goads a bull, Carlos thought, cheerfully mixing animal species, sexes, and metaphors in his mind. She'll explode like a bomb—if she doesn't drown in her own bile first.

Gloria Meese did a little of both, spluttering: "Get on the telephone. Call her. At once!"

Carlos wondered why she had not telephoned from her home and saved the drive from Marbella to Cabo Verde, gave another shrug, said: "I don't have the time, Mrs. Meese. A customer is waiting for me".

"*Cabrón!*" Gloria Meese spat. It was one of the few Spanish words she knew. She turned, straight-armed a glass door open, went to the illegally parked Rolls. The chauffeur stood beside the car. Carlos could hear her give him a shrill-voiced order to drive her to Broadmoor.

* * *

Vivian and Marisa were having predinner drinks—pale, aged Jerez for them both—on the portico. Vivian was in the midst of explaining why Ken had chosen to call the house he built in Spain "Broadmoor."

". . . for sentimental reasons, and for luck. It was the name of the apartment house he lived in when he wrote *Gusher!*, and money from the book made it all possible."

Marisa laughed. "I thought it might have been a joke, because there is a famous Broadmoor prison . . ."

She stopped speaking, having noticed that Vivian had a puzzled look and was listening attentively to the crunch of automobile tires on the graveled drive. "Can't imagine who that is," Vivi said, then relaxed in her lounger. "I'll let the servants find out."

"Maybe it's Ken," Marisa said.

"No chance. He would have let me know."

The car stopped. A moment later door chimes ringing inside the house were audible out on the portico. More moments, then the sounds of the front door opening and voices—Juan, the Dixons' number-one manservant, and a woman—rising in volume.

"Damn, I'd better go see," Vivian said, and stood up, started toward the doors that led from portico to house. But Gloria Meese, with Juan at her heels making futile protests, emerged. She was in a vile mood—hung-over or in a nerve-shattered trough after a drug high and belligerent, Vivian thought, and was furious. She wanted no unexpected visitors while Marisa Alarcón was staying at Broadmoor—least of all Gloria Meese—and had considered herself safe enough. It was a gross breach of Costa foreign-colony etiquette to barge in on anyone's home without invitation or prior notice. Even so, she had taken the extra precaution of telling the servants to say she was not home. Which Juan had obviously tried to tell Gloria, whose temper had been further aroused by the lie.

"Get that lying son of a bitch off my back!"

Vivian bridled, then made an effort to maintain her composure. She gave Juan an apologetic look, waved at him to leave.

"You're all goddamned liars—you, your greasy stooge Carlos, Ken, especially you." Gloria pushed her way past Vivian, advanced on Marisa. "Who the fuck are you?"

Marisa got to her feet, her expression startled, shocked.

"A friend," Vivi answered for her. "Marisa Alarcón. Marisa, this is Gloria Meese—who won't be staying long."

"Won't I?" The woman planted herself in a garden chair, glaring defiance. "I'll stay until I have some answers." Her gaze shifted from Marisa to Vivian and back, and she sneered. "Turned lesbian, Vivi? The two of you hiding away together while Ken's gone? Or is that why he went?"

"You're in bad shape, Gloria, better go home," Vivian said, knowing it was hopeless. Gloria would not move unless carried—or thrown—out bodily, not in her condition and mental state.

"If . . . if you will excuse me . . ." Marisa was trying to escape.

"Scared?" Gloria jeered.

"Might as well stay, Marisa," Vivian said bleakly. "I don't know what this is about, but—"

"More lies—nothing but lies." Gloria rasped her breaths. "Ken promises to speak at my club—"

"The American-Spanish Friendship Society—if you can believe it," Vivian said to Marisa. She crossed her arms, stood, pretending to be calm. "Made up of"—a telling pause—"of *ladies* like Gloria."

Gloria ignored her. "Then he disappears from Spain . . ."

Vivian saw Marisa grow alert.

Gloria continued to rant: "You've been feeding me crap ever since."

"Shut up and go home, Gloria." Vivian feigned boredom but felt an apprehensive chill, hugged her folded arms closer to her body.

"Not yet, I won't." Gloria was pure malice. "Not until I'm finished. I've been wondering about a lot of things since your big party. I have friends in London and New York . . ."

Maybe not friends, but being an extremely wealthy woman, she did have connections, Vivi thought and, chill intensifying, braced.

". . . I found out that there isn't any movie offer for Ken's new book."

"There's been no public announcement." Vivian improvised. "The publishers—"

"Hilarious! I asked people to check Ken's publishers in New York and London. Both said they hadn't heard from Kenneth Dixon in more than a year!"

"Ken stays at arm's length, deals with them through his agent," Vivian parried swiftly. "Now, please leave."

"Sure, his agent." Gloria sneered, rose unsteadily to her feet, evidently willing to go—at last. But not before a final thrust. "Turns out to be a man named Barrett Folsom. Fifth-rate, works out of his Greenwich Village apartment, doesn't even have a Dun and Bradstreet rating. In fact, my brokers learned he's considered a terrible credit risk." Gloria's look was evil. "Not what you'd expect of someone who represents the great Ken Dixon, is it, Vivi?"

Vivian glanced at Marisa Alarcón. The girl had drunk in every word, grasped all the implications. Her face was clouded, troubled.

"Good-bye, Vivi . . . and you," Gloria said.

"*Adiós*. Do me a favor. Run, don't walk, to the nearest exit."

Vivian stood aside, made an all-out effort to appear nonchalant as the woman crossed the portico and vanished into the house. Then, manufacturing a smile, she turned her attention to Marisa, who was wide-eyed.

"*Basura*," Vivi said in a manner clearly intended to characterize both Gloria Meese and what she had said as garbage, and very foul garbage at that. "Since we can't fumigate the air, I'll settle for another sherry to wash the bad taste out of my mouth. You?"

"Yes, please." Marisa nodded, but her eyes remained wide, and although obviously embarrassed, she was determined to ask questions about what she had just heard. "Who . . . *what* is Mrs. Meese?" she inquired as Vivian filled their glasses.

"Our local blight." Vivi grinned. "American. Much-divorced. A troublemaking bitch. Loves to invent vicious gossip."

"She doesn't love Spaniards."

"Wrong," Vivian said airily. "She has a passion for Spaniards, provided they're male and built like stallions."

"Oh, one of those." Marisa's nose wrinkled in disgust. The pride Spanish women had in their men made them loathe the thought that male Spaniards would rent themselves to foreign women as studs.

Vivi raised her glass: "*Salud, amor, y pesetas*."

Marisa smiled, wanly, Vivian thought, murmured something, took a swallow of sherry, gathered courage, blurted:

"She said horrible things."

"Not said, tried to imply"—Vivian was elaborately casual—"hoping that I'd snap back and give her an excuse to throw a little mud." A bit weak, make it stronger, more plausible, she thought, went on: "Seems Ken and I've suddenly become her favorite hate-and-smear objects—because of what she imagined was a slight."

Marisa was silent, but her expression asked for details. Vivian obliged, with fact and plausible fancy. Gloria Meese had been among the guests at the May Day party she and Ken gave. There was much talk about Ken's forthcoming new book.

". . . advance press notices had appeared—teaser items . . ."

"I read some of them," Marisa said. "They were very vague."

"Mmm, that's where the trouble started. Gloria begged Ken to speak at her next club meeting, talk about the book and its plot. He'd had a few drinks and agreed. Then he had to rush off and didn't have time to call her and apologize. She's been building a Supreme Court case out of it since."

Vivian hoped the matter would drop there. The hope was in vain.

"Why would people say what she claimed? That there aren't any film negotiations?"

"It's called playing close to the vest." Vivi's laugh sounded spontaneous.

"Do publishers claim they have not spoken with him for the same reason?"

"Marisa, you're assuming that someone actually did talk to Ken's publishers. Our Witch of Endor probably invented that on the spot—tossed it off the top of her stoned head while she sat here." How many more answers do I have to toss off the top of my pounding head while I sit here?

"But you believed her."

"I *did?*"

"You only said that Ken works with them through his agent, Mr. Barrett Folsom."

You have a great memory for names, and this is getting to be a cross-examination, Vivian thought, and holding her sherry glass with both hands to conceal that they were trembling, said: "It would have been stupid to argue and give her reasons to stay longer."

Marisa persevered. "She made terrible accusations against Mr. Folsom. What if they are true and he is a bad agent and so poor?"

"Hah!" Vivi was ready with a response that would convince anyone anywhere in the Western world. "Taxes, Marisa. Income, capital gains, property—and on and on. The smartest people in America are the ones who talk poor, act poor, and keep their income and assets hidden."

Marisa nodded that she understood. She had met many Americans who lived abroad. They complained incessantly about the murderous taxes levied by the United States government and were forever boasting how they avoided or evaded paying them.

But Vivian nervously sensed that the girl's doubts aroused by Gloria Meese had not been stilled, much less dissipated. She would ask more—and yet more—questions. Tonight, tomorrow, over the days that followed. Inevitably her sharp and inquiring mind would lead into areas Vivi desperately wanted to avoid. God only knew what she might uncover, guess, deduce, Vivian thought, forlornly sizing up the situation and reviewing her options.

Marisa's father was a prominent and influential *madrileño*. He—and by extension, his daughter—had excellent connections with leading Spanish magazines and newspapers. Were Marisa to present editors with sensational revelations about Kenneth Dixon, *el grande novelista norteamericano*, they would publish them. Publications around the world would pick up the exposé, fill in gaps, build it bigger and bigger . . .

Marisa spoke, breaking into the thoughts and giving cause for immediate fear. "I'd love to see some of the new book, Vivi. You must have a copy of the manuscript or the *prueba*—proofs."

Vivian flinched inwardly. She had to shunt the girl's inquiring mind off in other directions quickly and keep it sidetracked until she forgot about Gloria. The surest way was to overwhelm her with personal revelations, a course Vivian dreaded taking, but there seemed to be no alternative, and she led into it by saying:

"I couldn't show them to you before publication. It would be . . . well, like being unfaithful to Ken. Even worse than if I went to bed with another man." Vivian's smile was faraway, loving. "I'd never hurt him by doing either."

The ploy worked. Marisa was wide-eyed again. With astonishment. The Dixons were Americans. They moved in circles where marital fidelity was an obsolete and derided concept. Especially for people who had been married more than a decade.

Vivian prodded the girl toward the tangent. "Have I said something wrong? You look . . . mmm, the word 'thunderstruck' fits."

Marisa blushed furiously. "I was surprised you do not . . ." She was stammering. "I mean, not going to bed . . ."

"Hey, I'm Ken's *wife*."

The stammering went, the blush stayed. "I apologize. I have much to learn. I thought . . ."

"That Ken and I are wild swingers." Vivian smiled, set her empty glass on the table beside her lounger. "Let me tell you something about my life—no, you'd be bored."

"Please. I want to hear. Please tell me." Marisa sat bolt upright, then leaned forward. Her younger-woman's interest had been aroused, the desire to hear about Vivian Dixon's views on sex and marriage, about her life, suddenly paramount.

Vivian sighed. "Just between the two of us? Off the record?"

"Yes, I swear it."

Vivian was not wearing a watch but guessed it to be around seven-fifteen, forty-five minutes before dinner would be served. It gave ample time to start the story she had never before told anyone—and which would grab Marisa's attention, become *the* topic she would want to discuss for days.

"Where to begin?" Another sigh. "With a quick-skim review of my sex life, I suppose. My virginity went when I was seventeen, and that led to a complicated and messy affair." She could leave details of the relationship with her mother's lover for later; they would keep Marisa fascinated for hours. "And there were other men while I was still in the States—I did my share of sleeping around."

"The men were good?"

"Standard batting average. Some good, some mediocre, some god-awful. Hasn't it been the same for you?"

"More bad than good," Marisa said quietly.

That explains a lot, Vivian thought, said: "Well, anyway. I came to Spain in 1969. I wanted to paint and went to live in Mijas. I had two thousand dollars or so—a lot of money then . . ."

It was, Vivi remembered. Houses in the delightful hillside town—in 1969 still a village and an artists' colony—rented for the equivalent of forty dollars a month. One was able to live well—and she had—on thirty dollars a week.

". . . and I splashed paint and had fun. I also had more affairs. Most of them were fun, too."

"You were very lucky, no?"

"I was nineteen and on my own, free to do exactly as I wanted to do. That's what made life fun for a long while."

Vivian remembered the joy and exhilaration. White houses, their latticed windows overflowing with flowers. Streets that were narrow, steep, and twisting or not streets at all but long flights of stone, of concrete steps. Painting or not painting, depending on her mood. All-night sessions with other young artists, drinking wine or *sangría*, smoking pot, arguing about any and every conceivable subject. Entire days in bed, making love.

"Did you and Ken meet while you were in Mijas?" Marisa asked, snapping Vivian back into the here and now.

"No, it was much later, after a great many things happened. First there was the point where I decided to give up on my painting."

"Why? I think you must be talented."

"Talent doesn't count much if you're female. Women can't

break the sex barrier in art. The maximum allowance is one Rosa Bonheur or Mary Cassatt or Georgia O'Keeffe per generation."

Vivian grimaced dourly, went on.

"Anyway, my money was running low, and I found myself reverting to all-American type. Consumeritis set in. Instead of looking at my easel, I drooled over advertisements and store windows, wanting at least one of everything I saw."

"That is why you gave up and left Mijas?"

The point of no return is just ahead, Vivian thought, an inner chill spreading through her body, and she said:

"It's why I let myself be talked out of leaving. By a man I'm sure you've heard about. James Courtney."

"I think everyone in Spain has heard of him—the American Midas who owns the great *finca* here," Marisa said, and thinking that she was a step ahead of Vivian, added: "I understand what you mean—you went to work for him."

"Close . . . in a sense," Vivian said, staring at empty air. "I lived with him for almost a year"—a pause—"as his mistress."

Marisa gasped. Whether in shock or surprise or delight or a little of each was hard to judge, Vivian thought, but it was obvious that the girl was firmly on the hook. Which was the object of the exercise and the lesser—and less deadly—of two evils.

Vivian believed that Gloria Meese, having created an ugly scene and spent her rancor, would forget Ken and find some new target for her venom. But Gloria had raised questions and created doubts in Marisa Alarcón's mind. Unless Marisa was distracted, she might ponder the discrepancies and hit on the truth. That Kenneth Dixon had run dry in 1971, not written a word since.

Dixon had been at the peak of success when he suffered a block. His publishers believed it would be only temporary, but wanted to capitalize on his reputation and track record. They proposed that a ghost write a novel under Kenneth Dixon's name.

"It's as much to your advantage as ours," they argued. "You'll have the credit for turning out another best-seller—and we'll pay you half the usual royalties."

Dixon had agreed. What the hell, he rationalized, it was a one-time arrangement. The writer's block would disappear soon, and he would return to writing his own novels.

But the block persisted. A ghost writer continued to produce a novel supposedly authored by Kenneth Dixon each year, and the publishers steadily reduced his share. In 1980 they announced there would be no more royalties, only an annual flat fee.

"Fifty thousand a year—for use of your name, provided you follow the rules."

The rules permitted Ken Dixon to pose and posture as a successful author. They were far less lenient about what he was allowed to say in public.

"You're not to say a single damned word about any Dixon novels until after they're published—then you can talk all you want."

The forthcoming Kenneth Dixon novel had been a hush-hush project from its inception. Dixon himself was allowed to know nothing about what the ghost writer had written. Then the advance promotion campaign began. Titillating items appeared in the international press, the Dixons gave a May Day party, and Ken had drunk too much, made wild statements and even wilder promises. He had left Spain to avoid the consequences and could return safely in another week, perhaps less, when the book was actually published.

Marisa once again broke into Vivian's thoughts. "Don't be angry with me, but I'm dying to hear about your relationship with"—her eyes glowed, she was already enthralled—"the richest man in the world."

"I'll tell you," Vivian said. I'll use up days telling you. "Not this evening, though. We'll go down to the beach again tomorrow." She stood up. "It must be almost eight—time for dinner." She led the way into the house.

25

The silver candelabrum in the center of the table was Lamerie, an exquisite piece—worth upwards of one hundred thousand dollars, David Lippmann estimated. Grenville and a footman, both liveried, moved noiselessly, serving mousse de foies canard and a superb Château Cloq—the accent tonight is French rather than Spanish, Lippmann thought, amused.

He was dining with James Courtney. Not in the vast Montemar banqueting hall. In a small, intimate dining room more suited for the talk they would have over dinner—about Courtney's art collection, David had assumed. Wrongly, as it turned out. His host set the course of their conversation by raising his wineglass and saying:

"L'chaim."

The Hebrew toast to life seemed oddly out of place, but David had responded in kind, and from then on Courtney had talked about his work with Jewish displaced persons in Germany after the end of World War Two. Although familiar with the story—a much-chronicled part of the James Philip Courtney legend—Lippmann listened with interest only partially feigned, hoping to learn why his host had chosen to hold forth on the subject.

Courtney had begun by telling of his experiences as a first lieutenant assigned to a U.S. Army military-government team. It had been his job to inspect the displaced-persons camps housing the survivors of the Nazi holocaust.

". . . conditions were a disgrace, intolerable, at their worst in camps with large Jewish populations. It was due to intentional selective neglect—the term I used in my reports to higher headquarters. The reports were shelved—simply ignored. People in the upper echelons were closet anti-Semites and didn't *want* to do anything for the Jews."

Whereupon he had gone to the very top. With copies of his reports and photographs he had taken inside the camps. The situation improved somewhat. Not enough. He redoubled his efforts and made a little more progress. Still not enough. Bureaucrats were making it extremely difficult for Jewish DP's to leave Germany and enter the United States. Courtney elected to be separated from service in Germany and remain there as a civilian, without any official standing or authority, but determined to help . . .

". . . unclog the bottleneck. I nagged—harassed, is more like it—press correspondents and the junketeering congressmen and senators who swarmed all over Europe in those days." A pause, a chuckle, and Courtney digressed for a moment. "You weren't even alive then, were you, Dave?" Eyes steel blue in the candlelight fixed on Lippmann, who said:

"Just barely, I guess. I was born in 1947."

"Yes," Courtney said absently, but his eyes continued to hold.

By then, they were on coffee and cognac. The billionaire smoked what he said was his one cigar of the day, a Monte Cruz panatela, and he picked up the thread of his monologue.

"Well. Where was I?" He blew a lazy smoke ring. "Oh, yes. I finally went further upstairs to apply pressure. Right to the Truman-administration cabinet, and established connections with

John Snyder, the treasury secretary, and Julius Krug, who ran the Department of the Interior. That''—another chuckle—''gave me clout and I managed to get quite a few Jews out of the camps and across to the States.''

''According to what I've read, several hundred,'' David said, and, sensing that further comment was expected, thought to give the Wyler College president a plug. ''George Dockweiler wrote a pamphlet about famous Wyler alumni. *He* puts the figure at over a thousand.''

Courtney shook his head. ''Much too high—unless he was guess-estimating the number I may have helped indirectly. I can take personal credit for bringing only about two hundred to the States.''

''They're the ones who formed the society and have kept in touch with each other—and with you?''

''Seventy-two of them did. That was the original membership—if you can call it that, because it was and is all very informal.''

Courtney waited for Grenville to pour him more coffee and then began a discourse. Jews in German DP camps, deeply grateful for what he did for them, called him *''Pflegebrüder''* —foster brother. The honorific stuck. A group of men—seventy-two, Courtney repeated, of those for whom he won entry into the United States—formed an organization, the Pflegebrüders. They said they felt as though they were all Courtney's—and each other's—foster brothers.

''. . . some have died since, of course,'' the billionaire went on, ''but we all maintain contact.''

''The cover story *Time* did on you a few years back said it went further than that.''

''It does,'' Courtney said, smiling. ''After I went into business and achieved a little success, I naturally thought of sharing it with friends—and who were better friends than those men who considered themselves my foster brothers?''

He had aided some Pflegebrüders financially so they could start business enterprises of their own. Courtney Ventures International companies dealt with these firms whenever possible—and a dozen former DP's still held positions within the CVI organization itself.

''. . . My critics sneer that I'm an accumulator, Dave, and they're right. I've always enjoyed acquiring and owning—companies, this house, fine art, other things that I've wanted. Yet my most treasured possession is a medal B'nai B'rith gave me for the work I did in aiding Jews.''

Courtney paused. Taking his bow, waiting for the ovation, Lippmann thought, and said: "No question you earned it, Mr. Courtney." Oh, hell, lay it on thicker. "I can't think of anyone who's ever deserved that kind of medal more."

Courtney was silent, studying the base of the Lamerie candelabrum. David glanced at Grenville, who hovered behind Courtney's chair, blinked, and did a double-take. Grenville's face—bland and impassive whenever David had seen it before during the day—bore an expression that was an equal-parts mixture of high amusement and low contempt. The butler became aware that Lippmann was looking at him. The expression vanished instantly.

What or who amused that character, what or whom does he feel so damned superior toward? Lippmann wondered, puzzled but not really caring. He fidgeted mentally, because lack of sleep, too much food and drink, and boredom had taken their toll. He longed for the canopied bed he had found—and for a few minutes that afternoon tested—in the princely east-wing suite that had been assigned to him. Courtney was either having similar thoughts or had a fine-tuned ESP for his eyes snapped up abruptly and he said:

"Thank you for joining me this evening."

Dinner and conversation—such as it had been—were declared at an end. Grenville stepped forward to hold his employer's chair. David stood up—his chair held by the footman—much perplexed. There had been no mention of the cataloging project, no indication of how he should proceed with it.

"Shall I come to your study in the morning, Mr. Courtney?" he asked.

"I'll be tied up this week and next, but, yes, talk to Sybil. She'll help you get started."

The reply turned perplexity into bewilderment, which Lippmann eased by telling himself that the ultrarich were a species notorious for their whims and inconsistencies. He took his leave politely and, after only some twelve hours at Montemar, found it unremarkable that a security man accompanied him through the house and upstairs to the door of his suite.

Sybil Pearson had turned down an invitation to have dinner with friends at El Gaucho in Puerto Banus. It was unusual for her to refuse. She doted on the restaurant's elaborate English-style mixed grill. But she had still not heard from Neil Harkness. Neither had James Courtney—she had asked him. She was growing concerned.

Sybil threw a meal together in the kitchen of her Cabo Verde flat, overcooking a trio of *chuletas de cordero*, quartering a tomato, and not tasting what she ate. Neil did not live with her in the apartment but had spent enough nights there for his continued absence to create a sense of emptiness. A full bottle of Torres *rosado* drunk with the lamp chops failed to raise her spirits, and she telephoned Vivian Dixon, seeking moral support.

"I wish I had a cat," she said, a little tipsy and trying to be comical. "Trouble is, I don't know whether I'd stroke it or kick it." The try fell flat. Vivian may or may not have "Mmm'd," but nothing more. "I'm feeling low, Vivi. Like the French lieutenant's woman pacing the sea wall."

That brought a response: "He hasn't called you?"

Sybil realized that Vivian had said "he" rather than using Neil's name, and that her tone was off, guarded. "No—and I take it you have guests."

"Singular, not plural. But keep talking—if you don't mind my going monosyllabic on you every now and then."

"Grunts that comfort are better than no comfort at all. Any news from your own wandering boy?"

"Zero."

"Men are right bastards, all of them. Let's go somewhere for dinner tomorrow night—have a hag party and cry on each other's shoulders."

"Much as I'd like to, I can't."

Sybil and Vivian had long since established a close friendship and rapport. Sybil had no compunctions about inviting herself over to Broadmoor. "Then I'll drop by for a few minutes in the evening."

"Please don't."

No explanation, just "please don't," Sybil thought. It was totally unlike Vivian.

"How about the following day," Sybil tested, "assuming that neither of our absent *caballeros* is back by then?"

"Afraid not."

Sybil frowned. "Vivi, are you in some kind of . . . well, trouble?"

"What a ridiculous idea!" Vivian's voice exclaimed emphatically.

A shade too emphatically, Sybil thought and, baffled, made a few nothing remarks and ended the conversation. Going into the kitchen, she opened the fridge, reached for another bottle of chilled *rosado*, stopped, closed the door. A stiff brandy was more to the point, she decided. It would induce the kind of sleep in which there was no awareness that one side of the bed was empty.

The Hotel Lutetia, a hulking stone monolith on the Boulevard Raspail, was always a favorite of reasonably well-to-do middle-class French and Continental Europeans. The rooms were spacious and comfortingly old-fashioned, the service excellent. Two restaurants and an oyster bar, although unstarred by Michelin, offered some of the best food in Paris. The Lutetia underwent extensive interior refurbishing in the late 1970's, but the clientele remained much the same: mainly French and European, some British, Latin Americans and Japanese. U.S. tourists were a very small minority. Their arrivals elicited ripples of interest in the otherwise insouciant staff. Especially when, reservation having been made for one male American, two arrived, both dressed in hideous ski jackets and shapeless trousers with only airline bags and some clumsily wrapped skis as luggage.

Gallic eyebrows at the reception desk had risen to their apogees, lowering gradually as the huge American, skin the hue of a Moroccan—the Monsieur Harkness in whose name a reservation was held—explained. He and his friend Monsieur Dixon had been skiing in Switzerland. M'sieu Dixon decided at the last moment to come with him to Paris. Swiss Air had lost the rest of their luggage. Under these circumstances, he believed it best to allay any doubts and make a substantial advance deposit against their bill—and could they have a large room with twin beds?

But of course. It so happened that Room 412 was available. The gentlemen should find it entirely satisfactory. If they did not, a change could be made, but only the following day, for the hotel was otherwise fully occupied. No, there was no M'sieu Carl Orff registered, and there were no waiting messages of any kind for M'sieu Harkness.

Neil quietly told Dixon to go up to the room alone, keep an eye on the skis, an ear open for the telephone—and the door locked—and left the hotel. He was gone more than two hours.

Guns are not as easy to buy in Paris as in, say New York City or Milan or even Marseilles. However, if one knows the narrower streets of Pigalle, it is possible to find merchants who deal in handguns that have been stolen from NATO depots in other Western European countries and smuggled into France. The weapons are expensive. The price of a nine-millimeter Browning automatic with detachable silencer and three loaded clips is nine thousand francs, close to fifteen hundred dollars, five times its legitimate retail value. Harkness paid without hesitation. The money came from the envelope of assorted currencies that James Courtney had supplied before Neil took the *Deirdre* out of Cabo Verde, bound for Venice.

Ken Dixon had been napping on one of the twin beds in Room 412. The skis with their Velázquez wrapper were propped in a corner. The telephone had not rung, Ken said, and looked on sourly while Neil sat in an armchair, examined—and loaded—his purchase.

"What the fuck are you going to do with that thing?" he demanded.

"Nothing except stick it under my pillow—I hope."

"The melodrama is getting thicker by the minute."

"Maybe." Harkness checked that the silencer was properly attached. "Just remember our private Pearl Harbor—fat guy named Fischer, plus aliases." He put the gun aside, lit a Gauloise, the closest approximation of Celtas available in French *tabacs*, grinned. "Quit bitching, author. We've banked half a mil apiece. Think of how much more you're going to make."

"More? How?"

Neil looked at Dixon with amusement. "When you write a novel based on all this, what else?"

"Oh, that." Ken's sardonic face appeared to pale beneath its tan. "Sure." He cracked the knuckles of his right hand, said: "I'm hungry. Let's order up some dinner."

There was a handsome room-service menu on the writing desk. Neil reached for it; the choices listed inside were no less attractive than the cover. He flipped across to Dixon.

"I'm starting with a couple dozen *huitres* on the half—and then I'll go on from there," Harkness said. He stood up, went to his bed carrying the Browning, slipped it under the pillow, returned to the small refrigerated-drinks dispenser, which he unlocked. "I'm having Scotch. Gin for you?"

Ken was studying the menu, looked up. "Jesus Christ! I forgot all about that gadget."

"Or you would've had a few while I was gone?"

"Hell, yes."

"Then it's a good thing you forgot, buddy." Neil began taking out miniature bottles of liquor.

"I'll have gin," Ken muttered. "Straight. No goddamned ice."

They ate dinner. Dixon augmented the limited dispenser stock of gin by ordering up a bottle of Tanqueray, drank his way through half while they stared at the brain-numbing tedium of

French television. At midnight they turned in. Ken began snoring the moment he lay down. Harkness remained awake for a while, thinking, then fell into a light sleep. He was alert for the ring of the telephone—or sounds that might give him reason to reach for the Browning under his pillow.

Kuwait has an area of less than eight thousand square miles, but its 1.4 million population enjoys a per-capita income of thirteen thousand dollars, considerably higher than the figure for the United States, more than double that for the United Kingdom.

The wealth derives from oil.

An emirate, the country is ruled by the Sabah dynasty, which has been magnanimous in sharing the riches with its subjects. The Sabahs have created a welfare state without equal anywhere. Medical services, education through university level, even telephone service are free, and for all. Housing is subsidized to a degree where only token rents are charged. Liberal grants of money are given to any who wish to start business enterprises. Poverty and unemployment are unknown: there is one millionaire for every 230 citizens.

But only some thirty percent of the work force is native Kuwaiti. The majority of the others employed are Palestinian Arabs, Saudis, Egyptians, Iraqis, Pakistanis, and they are entitled to share in the womb-to-tomb welfare benefits and earn infinitely higher wages and salaries than prevail in their own countries. Nonetheless, many of them secretly belong to political or fundamentalist Muslim factions that seek to destroy the Sabah dynasty. These dissidents plot eternally, pose serious threat to what is an economic paradise at the northwestern end of the Persian Gulf.

The center of paradise is the capital, Kuwait City, a futuristic oasis in the midst of a desert where 125-degree temperatures are commonplace. It is forested with ultramodern high-rise buildings, which are mainly white—blinding white in the sun. There are three air-conditioning units for each of the city's 190,000 people. There are magnificent highways. All roads are wide, kept smoothly paved despite a volume of automotive traffic proportionately heavier than in any Western capital. Stores and shops and banks and even stockbrokers' offices are perpetually thronged; money that is so readily available is freely spent.

Danger from dissident elements—a matter of deep concern at government levels—is ignored by merchants and ordinary people. Or it was. Until midnight on May 10, when a series of violent explosions ripped through the ports of Mina-al-Ahmadi and

Shuaibah. The blasts destroyed dockside cranes, warehouses, oil-storage tanks—which burst into flame, spreading uncontrollable fires. Then unmarked jeeps and Land Rovers materialized from nowhere. Filled with heavily armed men, they roared along the magnificent highways and the wide, smooth-surfaced roads. The men threw grenades and fired machine guns, blowing up people along the storefronts, and before the tiny Kuwaiti army could respond, the vehicles vanished.

"Jews . . . Israelis!" was the first stunned—and enraged—reaction.

It seemed the sole explanation. The Israelis had staged another of their slashing raids—like those they had made at Entebbe and so often into southern Lebanon. Then the theory had to be discarded. The raiders had come by neither air nor sea. That meant they had to be based in either Iraq or Saudi Arabia, the only two countries sharing land boundaries with Kuwait. Or, the unthinkable . . .

At three-thirty A.M., Western correspondents in Kuwait were reporting the outbreak of revolt.

". . . heavy casualties and property damage . . ."

". . . there is panic in Kuwait City . . ."

". . . no official word from government sources, and old hands here are divided in their opinions of who may be behind the rebellion. Some believe it is the PLO. Others think Iraqi Ba'athists are responsible. Yet others point fingers at the Soviet Union . . ."

William Moore was an American. He had been a middle-rung purchasing executive for ARAMCO in Riyadh, Saudi Arabia. Until it was discovered that he had taken kickbacks for issuing purchase orders to a company owned by Rashid el Muein, when he had been summarily fired. Since then he had worked for el Muein. At reasonable pay, but as a glorified fetch-and-carry factotum. A middle-aged bachelor, Bill Moore lived in a tiny house on el Muein's estate outside Marbella. Among his duties, he was required to arise at six each morning, go to the main house, and listen to early-morning news broadcasts. If anything of consequence had occurred overnight, he was to inform Rashid.

The bulletins Moore heard were of very great consequence. He jotted notes and hurried to awaken el Muein. He knocked on the bed-chamber door, entered without waiting for an invitation. It did not disturb him in the least that he found a boy of about eleven in bed with Rashid. He knew el Muein enjoyed young boys—and this one was the son of an Arab couple who were employed as servants in the house. Besides, Moore himself was gay, and if he felt anything, it was a twinge of jealousy.

"*Yalla*—go!" Rashid ordered the youngster, slapping his plump buttocks. The boy leaped from the bed, ran naked into an adjoining room. Bill Moore said:

"All hell's broken loose in Kuwait."

That brought Rashid leaping from the bed faster than the boy. He scooped his *sibah* from a bureautop and, fingers fretting at the prayer beads, paced the richly carpeted floor while Moore repeated what he had heard on the radio.

". . . and the latest report says there have been more attacks," he concluded.

El Muein stopped, barked, "*Yalla!*"—the same curt Arabic order to go, get out—that he had used with the boy.

"Yes, sir."

When the door closed behind Moore, Rashid, the *sibah* looped around one hand, sprang to his bedside telephone. He punched out the number of the Meliá Don Pepe, where Horst Thiele was staying. The hotel operator put him through, ringing Thiele's room. Several times. Thiele's voice came on at last, gruff, annoyed at having been awakened, stayed so even after el Muein identified himself.

"What in the name of your Allah could be important enough to talk about when it is not even seven o'clock?"

Rashid told him. The tone changed.

"This could be his main effort," Thiele said. "I predicted that he would make one."

"You'll have to move faster, Thiele."

"I promised you, within days."

"Kuwait will fall apart fast, very fast, and everything else will follow. Bring your"—Rashid searched for the euphemisms Thiele had used, remembered—"surgeons in today."

"They are already in Spain."

"Then have them operate today."

"Today is impossible," Thiele purred, knowing he held the upper hand and could dictate the terms. "They must make their preparations. Tomorrow is not so impossible—if there is a premium."

"How much?"

"Double what we agreed."

"On the same basis?"

"*Naturlicht*. The fee is payable after the surgeons have completed the operation. Successfully."

"Yes, double," Rashid el Muein said, and replaced his receiver. Even four million dollars was a cheap price to have Courtney finished off.

Habitually an early riser, James Courtney heard the news himself while breakfasting in the parlor of his bedroom suite. He finished eating quickly and was in his study at 7:45, more than an hour earlier than usual.

He informed the outer-office security man that he was not to be disturbed by anyone for any reason. Then, locking the *estudio* door, he sat behind the Bureau Plat, manipulated remote controls that turned on his stereo set. He played an eight-track tape of the *Carmina Burana* through, listened immobile in his chair with an expression as intense as that of a man experiencing orgasm.

The tape ended. He switched off the stereo, called for Grenville, and unlocked the door to let him in, relocking it after he entered.

"Sit down, Grenville. I'd like to have a talk with you."

The butler took one of the Barcelona chairs. Courtney sat in his own, stroked his old scar, said: "Neil Harkness should be coming back to Cabo Verde within twenty-four hours or so."

Grenville's lips twitched. Courtney drew his own taut in what might have been a smile.

"He'll return to make a report. Probably fly in from Paris."

"And his boat?"

"He left it somewhere and will want to leave again and go after it."

"Yes, sir," Grenville said, there being nothing else to say.

"You don't like Harkness, do you?"

"He's not quite my favorite person, no."

"Drop the British understatements. You hate his guts." Courtney did not have to ask why. The personalities of Grenville and Neil Harkness would have clashed, and violently, under any circumstances. The fact that Leslie Grenville had been emasculated, sexually neutered by a shell burst, only intensified his hatred. Harkness, aggressively masculine, was a reminder to Grenville of what he had been, a painfully taunting symbol of all he had lost.

"I've formed a dislike for him myself," Courtney said, tipped his head to one side, waited for the butler to speak.

"Indeed?" He was surprised. "I'd always thought you rather liked the man."

"He was useful and malleable. His usefulness is close to being over—and he has stopped being malleable."

"Oh?"

"Harkness has developed symptoms of megalomania. He squeezed a large sum of money out of me."

"Very stupid of him."

Courtney shifted position. "You might even say suicidal."

"I take it you've decided that it was, sir."

"I've decided that it should prove to be. On the same day he returns. Before he can leave to recover his boat."

"My pleasure, sir. An accident?"

"Natural causes." Courtney pressed hard on a segment of his desktop. A small secret compartment, originally built into the Bureau Plat du Roi for Louis XV, opened. Courtney took out what looked like a straight-stemmed briar pipe, closed the compartment, laid the pipe on the far edge of the table for Grenville to take. "A full turn to the right for priming, full turn left to use."

In 1975, a blue-ribbon investigating panel headed by Vice-President Nelson A. Rockefeller disclosed that the U.S. Central Intelligence Agency had developed a bizarre arsenal of weapons for use in assassinations. There was, for example, the "M-1," described by the CIA as "a device capable of introducing materials through light clothes subcutaneously without pain." A silent "gun," the M-1 could be concealed in "all sorts of objects"—umbrellas, miniature cameras, even lipsticks and fountain pens. It "fired" poisoned darts so tiny that powerful magnifying glasses were needed to detect where they penetrated clothing fabric and human skin. Some of the CIA-formulated poisons induced apparently natural death—seeming heart attacks or brain hemorrhages—and could be timed to have delayed-action effects, leaving absolutely no trace.

Design details of the M-1 were highly publicized, but the poison formulas remained closely guarded secrets. Then the Carter administration took office and appointed its share of mindless political hacks to key posts in the United States intelligence establishment. Over the ensuing years, the poison formulas were released to three different privately owned companies under provisions of the controversial Freedom of Information Act. The companies were engaged in the manufacture of pharmaceuticals and claimed they needed the information for research purposes. One of them was Ohio-based Omicron-CV Laboratories, Inc., a wholly owned subsidiary of Courtney Ventures International.

Leslie Grenville examined the pipe with a professional eye. He had seen somewhat similar disguised weapons before—like single-shot small-caliber pistols concealed in the casing of what appeared to be a ball-point pen. They were dangerous to use, though, for they made noise when fired, and their bullets did not necessarily kill or inflict fatal wounds. This one was operated by a gas compressed under enormous pressure in a tiny metal canister, made no sound, and the dart discharged from the stem end caused certain death. The thing had been crafted with meticulous attention to detail. The bowl was charred, caked, the stem bore tooth marks. To all outward appearances, a much-smoked briar, and since Grenville was known to smoke pipes occasionally, the camouflage was perfect.

"Time element?" he asked.

"The substance has its effect one hour after the dart penetrates. Then instant massive coronary." James Courtney ran fingers through his gray-streaked auburn hair. "Identical pathology."

Grenville permitted himself a smile. "Didn't Miss Marsh die suddenly of natural causes in New York City?"

Courtney nodded slowly. "An autopsy showed that Eileen suffered a fatal myocardial infarction in her hotel suite. As, by bizarre coincidence, did a certain Evan Gerlach, whom she knew well and who was stricken a few hours earlier in his own apartment."

"I see."

"Only the obvious so far." Courtney's expression said: Let what I'm going to tell you be a lesson—and a warning. "Eileen and Gerlach were also attempting to squeeze me." He took a deep breath, exhaled. "It was my fault. I knew Eileen was a bitch, but I thought she was an empty-headed bitch and grew careless. Then I . . . um, repatriated her to New York and discovered that she had an uncanny faculty for retaining and piecing together what she heard and observed."

Angular features grew sharper and darkened as Courtney remembered incidents that had seemed trivial when they happened. Eileen had pushed past an outer-office security guard and barged into the study while he was closeted—door incautiously left unlocked—with Oliver Ashton-Plummer, the British financier and a limited but informed partner in the grand scheme. She had overheard a fragment of what Ashton-Plummer was saying when she entered.

". . . mind boggles at the irony. Buying *jihad* with a Velázquez . . ."

That was all, and it should have been incomprehensible to Eileen Marsh—and probably was, at the time.

Then there had been the dinner à trois—Heinrich Kloster had flown in from Zurich, and when they were finished talking business, Courtney saw no reason to bar Eileen from joining them at dinner in the banqueting hall. But Kloster, awed by the grandeur of Montemar and assuming Eileen Marsh was confidante as well as mistress, had been carried away. Raising his wineglass—after peering at the breasts three-quarters exposed by Eileen's low-cut bodice—he had, in a burst of lumpish Swiss gallantry, offered a toast:

"To you, exquisite young lady." Then, with a sly wink at Courtney. "Soon, queen of a new oil empire." Another wink. "You must promise not to hide such beauty behind a veil, J.P."

There had been other slips. The Gershon letter, absentmindedly slipped into a pocket and then tossed on a table in the bedroom. Some unguarded, musing-out-loud phrases. The two urgent telephone calls taken in the bedroom during early-morning hours, the conversations short, in themselves revealing nothing. The probability that Eileen had tried to eavesdrop on other occasions—and the slender yet still possible chance that, despite security measures, she had succeeded.

Whatever, however, she had assembled the fragments, Courtney reflected. The picture puzzle had been far from complete, but even with the gaps, it gave her the power to ruin him.

Courtney returned himself to the present. "Eileen was my fault, my mistake," he told Grenville, reiterating his admission of carelessness in having underestimated her. "It's not a mistake I'm going to make again"—a two-beat pause—"with anyone."

His gaze bored into and through Grenville, who held it steadily. Courtney was the first to break it, glancing at the red light that blinked once from the intercom box, signaling that Sybil Pearson had arrived for work and was in the outer office. Grenville guessed that was what had drawn his employer's eyes away and, face more lamblike than sheep in its blandness, he said:

"The girl is close to Harkness." He toyed with the briar pipe, then eased it into a side pocket of his morning coat. "They"—his features slipped, betraying emotion, recovered—"sleep together. Haven't a clue how he feels, but she's in love with him. Might cause post-Harkness complications. As your secretary, she knows—"

"Only what I've wanted her to know . . . and she is the daughter of a viscount."

"Sir?"

"No offense, Grenville. British aristocrats have singular qualities. They transmit them to their children." Courtney was grinning. "Sybil has them. Blind loyalty to constituted authority—which, being her employer, I am. A good mind, but rigid, unimaginative. The king can do no wrong." He shrugged. "However, if there are signs—post-Harkness—to the contrary, she'll leave as her predecessor did."

"Miss Denby was before my time. I've heard only vague stories."

"Bettina—not Betty, Bettina—Denby quit without notice. Not a word. She left here on a Friday afternoon and apparently spent the entire weekend packing feverishly. She failed to appear Monday. Some of the people in the CVI annex tried calling her. The telephone had been disconnected. They went to her apartment in . . . wait, yes, I remember . . . outside Fuengirola, and found it empty. She had taken everything she owned—and vanished." The grin returned. "I was in South America and returned to find myself without a secretary."

"I understand, Mr. Courtney." Grenville sensed that the talk was now ended and stood up. He patted the coat pocket containing the briar pipe, stopped, looked as though he had just thought of something. "What you've told me about Miss Marsh. Could she have been the one who gave out information about Mr. Fischer and his going to Tangier with Harkness?"

"No. It must have been someone else," Courtney replied, and let it hang there. He picked up a manila folder that lay on the table surface, opened it, began reading the contents.

Sybil Pearson's night had ended badly—with a third stiff brandy—and she had awakened with a hangover, partly from alcohol, mainly from emotional strain. She was almost glad to find Luis, the perpetually gloomy security man, on duty when she arrived at her office. Luis was even gloomier than usual, matching her own mood, but for different reasons. Had she heard the *noticias*? he asked. Not having bothered to listen to a news broadcast, Sybil said no, and Luis, his knowledge of geography faulty, told her there was a war in Kuwait, which he believed was in Southeast Asia instead of the Middle East. An ardent neo-Falangist, he naturally placed the blame on *comunistas* and *soviéticos*—on whom the *norteamericanos* should shower nuclear weapons without further delay.

Luis finally ran down, and Sybil began her morning routine. Telex traffic was heavier than usual. She sorted the messages that had backed up overnight. Several required James Courtney's personal attention. Grenville emerged from the study.

"How's the weather?" she asked, a reference to Courtney's mood.

"Calm at present, might be subject to change. I'll have your tea sent in directly."

Courtney did not call for her. She tackled the mail.

David Lippmann arrived before the tea. He, at least, appeared to have slept well and to be filled with energy. His smile and cheery greeting were an aid to Sybil's morale, and she perked up.

"Hello, Robert," she needled. She had remarked his resemblance to Redford the previous afternoon, and he had told her how often it happened—and how tired he was of having it happen.

He groaned, then smiled and took a chair Sybil offered with the wave of a hand, crossed his legs. "Boss man told me to see you this morning. You are—and I quote—to help me get started."

A servant brought the tea tray.

"Care for a cup?" Sybil asked.

"No," David said. He had been served a trencherman's breakfast in his suite, and: "I do want to 'get started,' honest."

"Commendable spirit. How can I help?"

"I have only one copy of the inventory . . ."

"Mr. C. had new copies made." Sybil was reminded of Kristin Verkerk and frowned.

Lippmann noticed the frown. "Problems?"

"No. I just thought of a girl I know. Poor dumb thing was . . . well, I suppose deported. Never mind."

"I'm curious. Who deported her and why?"

"The Spanish authorities. Because they found drugs in her flat."

"Is that how the Spaniards do it?"

"Sometimes, with foreigners. Saves the trouble of having a trial and all that." Sybil poured tea through the strainer.

"Makes sense—I guess."

"Oh, it does." Sybil set the teapot down on the tray. "I feel sorry for her, though." Kristin was like most women, wanting something, almost getting part of what she wanted, then losing everything. "Sorry. Back to you, David."

"Boss man calls me Dave."

"Then back to you, *Dave*. I'll have the new inventory sets sent up to your suite. Next item."

"Well, eventually I'll have to start plowing through the documentation." There would have to be masses of documents supporting authenticity and tracing the provenance of the pictures.

"All those papers are kept over in the annex."

"Filed in any sort of order?" Lippmann asked, mentally

crossing his fingers. Many collectors were sloppy about record-keeping; this forced an art historian to waste endless time bringing order out of chaos before he could start his real work.

"You'll be amazed at the method and order." Sybil grinned. "Everything pertaining to a given picture arranged in a separate folder, according to date, and with cross-references."

"Amazed? I'm exuberant. And grateful. You—"

"Not me. The system was set up by"—Sybil almost said "Vivian Dixon," but remembered the taboo about mentioning her name at Montemar—"by someone else. She knew quite a bit about art and lived here—"

"She? The girl who was deported?"

"Oh, no. She was here years and years ago, long before I started to work for Mr. C." Sybil concentrated on drinking tea and wished that David would switch to some other subject.

He did. Like most art historians, he was intrigued by successful art forgeries, curious to learn how any fake of a painting by a master could have been fobbed off as genuine for decades, even centuries.

"Is the documentation for the Velázquez *Horse and Rider* still in the files?"

"I suppose so. No reason it shouldn't be."

"Great. I thought that because the picture was destroyed—"

"Destroyed?" Sybil blinked, put down her teacup. "It hangs in one of the rooms in Mr. C.'s bedroom suite. I never go up there, but I would have heard."

"He said experts from the Prado declared it a fake."

Sybil frowned. "I don't remember anything of the sort. You must have heard wrong or misunderstood." She got up from her desk, went to a file cabinet, took a copy of the most recent inventory from a drawer, riffled through the pages, her frown deepening. "How strange. Can't seem to find the listing."

She took another Xerox copy from the drawer, opened it to the V section, turned pages: "Vanderlyn. Vandyke. Velázquez should be next—there's only the one—but the next heading's Vermeer." She put the inventory copy back in the drawer, more puzzled than ever. "The *Horse and Rider* page seems to be missing." Surely she would have known about the Prado experts, their verdict, and destruction of the painting. Courtney would have been in the vilest of vile moods for weeks. Then she had a second thought. Perhaps he had forced himself to say nothing out of embarrassment at having been duped. It was a possibility, one that made it inadvisable to ask him any questions. She closed the file drawer.

The intercom came alive: "I'd like to see you now, Sybil."

She hurried to her desk, told the box: "In a moment, Mr. Courtney." Gathering up telexes and correspondence, she glanced at Lippmann, said: "Sorry, Dave. Rush hour's started." She moved to the door of the *estudio*. "Should be a lull by eleven."

"I'll be back then." Lippmann stood up, gave the sour-faced guard a nod, and went out into the corridor. His mind was on the Velázquez, the missing inventory page, Sybil's mystification. It didn't add right, he thought, and determined to find out how and why.

26

They were on the beach by nine A.M.

Vivian Dixon, again wearing a halter-necklined one-piece suit that hid bruises not yet entirely faded, curled into a sling chair. Marisa Alarcón sat cross-legged on a beach mat beside it. Like a bikinied acolyte at the feet of a master—in this case, at the feet of a self-confessing mistress, Vivian thought bleakly.

Marisa's look pleaded: Please begin.

"I was living in Mijas," Vivi said. "My money was low, and my morale was even lower. One night I went to Torremolinos with some friends. It was Spain's Haight-Ashbury then, the City of the Stoned." Torremolinos was overrun with foreign drug-culture dropouts in the late 1960's and 1970's. Unwashed, underfed, because whatever money they had or panhandled was spent on drugs ranging from the light to the superheavy, they wandered the streets and slept in alleys or on the sand along the *playa*. Since they had entered the country legally as tourists, the Franco government dared not expel them for fear of creating international incidents. Torremolinos police could only jail a few worst offenders, and it had been estimated that there was an average of one o.d. a day.

"I'd often gone to Torremolinos before, but this time was an eye-opener," Vivian went on. "It hit me that night. If I didn't do something with my life fast, I'd end up in that scene. Terrified me."

"You could have gone home to the United States."

"That's not my scene either."

"Wouldn't your family have helped?"

"The only family I have had was my mother"—and the "uncles" who were her lovers—"and she died before I came to Spain."

"Oh, I am so sorry."

"Please don't be, it's all right." Vivian's lips smiled; her eyes were invisible behind her mirrored shades. "So." The smile held. "From then on, instead of going to Torremolinos, I'd dress up and go into Marbella. From Mijas via *autobús*, in my party clothes."

Marisa laughed, amused. The picture of Vivian, ravishing in "party clothes" and riding a jammed Spanish bus that careened down the winding mountain road from Mijas, struck her as extremely funny.

"I went to places like the Marbella Club to see how the Beautiful People lived—and to let them see me. Simple as that. I wanted to meet a man who had money, and on my third try, I hit the jackpot."

"Jackpot?" Marisa frowned, then grinned. "Yes. I understand. James Courtney. You went to bed with him?"

"Not that night. He came on like Prince Charming and sent me home in a limousine. The car came to Mijas for me the next afternoon. He showed me through Montemar—his bedroom the last stop. Into bed, and it was good, and he made me an offer I refused to refuse: move in and share the wealth. Eleven months later, I moved out. We haven't spoken since. That's it. *El final.* End of story."

Marisa's reaction was what Vivian had known it would be, disappointment bordering on indignation. She wanted to hear everything in detail. Vivian had promised to tell her.

"Look," Vivi said with a deep sigh, "I've never talked about those months to anyone but Ken—and not even to him for years and years. If I start now, I'm liable to go on forever." She shook her head. "I don't even know *where* to start!"

"With him," Marisa suggested. "What was he like—with you?"

"A *Cosmo* girl's dream—at first. Considerate, protective, supportive, generous, and no male chauvinist, not Jim. He refused to consider me a sex object, he said. I was a person with an identity of my own. He encouraged me to keep on painting and even had a room at Montemar converted into a studio for me. Except when we traveled together, I worked there, and he worked in his study."

Jump-cut recollections whipped through Vivian's mind, outpacing her narrative. After a month, Courtney arranging to have two dozen of her paintings displayed by a Barcelona gallery. The lethal reviews given them by the critics: "hackneyed," "trite," "inept." Her ego devastated. Jim comforting, consoling. She becoming submissive, dependent. All according to plan—his plan. Only much later did she learn that he had bribed the critics to write what he told them.

"He insisted that I would be successful," Vivian said, continuing her story. "Do you know the Moreno Gallery in Barcelona?"

"It is one of the best." Marisa nodded and squiggled forward on the beach mat. Even though Vivian seemed to be digressing, she wanted to hear every word.

Room-service breakfast had been eaten, the wheeled serving table pushed out into the corridor. Neil Harkness, a Gauloise between his lips, sprawled in an armchair, skimming through the newspapers he had ordered sent up to Room 412. There was another armchair. It was occupied by Kenneth Dixon, who stared morosely at the half-empty bottle of Tanqueray on the nearby table.

"I'm going stir-crazy," Ken said.

"Want to read the *Herald Trib*?"

"Anything in it?"

"The usual. Pope made a speech, claims we have to pray more—or maybe that was Falwell, he made a speech too. Some East Berlin woman athlete pole-vaulted over the wall into West Berlin. Arabs are shooting at each other—in Kuwait this time around. *Peanuts* is funny, though."

"Forget it. I'll have a hair." Dixon retrieved the bottle and a glass, poured a drink. "Wonder when our guy's going to turn up?"

"It's only nine-fifteen. Figure that part of what he banked is for waiting time. If you're getting claustrophobia, open the windows and let the Paris traffic noise in. You won't be able to hear yourself think and . . . Hey, there's an article on new shipboard radar sets in the London *Telegraph*. Let me read it."

Ken drank and, out of desperation, took the *Herald Trib*. The two men were silent, reading, turning newspaper pages, reading again, for almost a quarter of an hour, when the telephone rang.

Neil leaped up and went to the nightstand between the two twin beds. He grabbed the receiver, answered by giving his name, heard:

"Carl Orff, Mr. Harkness." The male voice was high-pitched.

"Will twelve or twelve-fifteen do?" The English was good, unaccented.

"Noon is fine. Meet you in the lobby?"

"I'll come directly to your room. I have the number."

The line went dead. Neil replaced the receiver and, telling Dixon what "Orff" had said, crossed the room to the door. He made certain the DO NOT DISTURB sign hung on the outside knob, and after closing the door, secured the inside safety lock.

"Give me a hand," he said, going to the corner where the skis were propped, and laid the awkward bundle across the twin beds. He untied the twine from an outer layer of brown paper. "I want Velázquez out of sight when Orff first walks in—under a bed, maybe." He removed the paper. The rolled canvas was still tied with Wilhelm Fischer's tallith—a reminder that a man had already died because of the painting. Ken was silent as he helped undo the knot in the prayer shawl and then lean the skis back against the wall.

He and Neil flattened the picture on the beds.

Harkness groaned, Ken cursed. They had noted some damage previously, in Venice. Spots where the impasto had flaked or fallen off. More—ruinous—damage had occured in transit. Velázquez's regally garbed rider had only half a face. The barren spot in the belly of his caparisoned stallion had grown to a size of a salad plate.

"Holy Christ!" Dixon exclaimed for the nth time. He was aghast.

Neil was bending over the picture, brushing at the bare patch in the horse's belly with his fingertips. "Son of a bitch," he muttered, glanced up. "You said there were numbers here."

"Huh? I thought so—in Venice."

"They're here. Numbers and lines." Harkness bent low, tapped at the canvas. The numbers were written in gaps in the lines—which appeared to be concentric, but were uneven and wandered. "Contour lines, the numbers indicate elevations."

Neil straightened. "Velázquez never painted this. It's a fake to cover up a terrain map."

Women like Gloria Meese thought that Kenneth Dixon's eyes had a "compelling" intensity. They were intense now—with disbelief. Then he laughed. "Courtney will fly up his own asshole when he hears that his Old Master's a phony."

"He must've known it all along, Ken. The painting never meant a damned thing. It was the map."

"That doesn't make any sense."

"None," Neil agreed. The paint could have been stripped at

Montemar and what lay beneath it copied by hand or camera, the copy then reduced photographically to the size of a postcard or even a pinhead.

"Funny, I was right," Dixon said. "Remember when you came back from Tangier and told me about the hassles you had? You couldn't figure out what Fischer had in his tin tube and guessed it might be blueprints. I said there were only two possibilities. One, that it was something that couldn't be copied—the object itself had to be delivered. Two, if it was blueprints, they were only for camouflage. Turns out to be down the middle, a little of each."

"Still leaves us with a question. Why can't a terrain map be copied?" Neil said absently, hearing alarm bells ring in his back brain. Seeing the areas of bared canvas, Carl Orff—whoever he might really be—would assume that Harkness had seen them too, and would have to assume that what lay under the impasto had been recognized as a map. What then? The secret had already cost one life.

He shook off gathering apprehensions, said. "Hold that end," and he and Ken rerolled the blighted painting, tied it once more with the tallith and pushed the roll under one of the unmade beds.

Neil lit a Gauloise, eyed Dixon steadily through a curtain of smoke. "I can handle Orff. Why not take a walk before he shows—only a couple of blocks to Brasserie Lipp or Deux Magots. You can drink literary atmosphere along with your gin." He was thinking that Ken was a married man, and as such should not be taking more risks than he already had.

"I'm staying." Dixon's tone was determined.

"Still want to be the author who lived every scene in the book?"

"I want to earn my advance."

Neil grinned, gratefully, and to lighten both their moods said: "Half a mil tax-free isn't bad."

Ken was staring at the carpet. "It's a pardon and a new passport," he said in a low, detached tone.

Neil, certain he had heard incorrectly, did a double-take. "Huh?"

"Nothing," Ken said hastily. "A dumb private joke."

Harkness let it slide, and moving toward the door, spoke over his shoulder: "Be back in five minutes."

"From where?"

"Checking out the floor plan."

"What for?"

"In case we have to get out of here in a hurry."

Marisa had an insatiable appetite for details, large and small. Vivian was glad of her questions. They slowed the progress of her narrative further. After an hour and a half, she had not gotten past her first days at Montemar. There were too many answers to be given:

". . . he was close to fifty then—forty-eight, I think, and I wasn't quite twenty."

". . . no, I didn't think in terms of marriage. Neither did he. Men like Jim Courtney—very rich men—either marry often or not at all. He never mentioned the subject."

". . . use? Oh, a diaphragm."

". . . yes, I was his hostess. He made no secret of our relationship."

It was at that point, at ten-thirty, that Carlos Lozano arrived. Since Vivian was not going in to Galerías Vivi, Carlos brought correspondence and bills for her to see, letters and checks to sign. Vivian welcomed the break and was amused by Carlos and Marisa.

Carlos, recognizing Marisa as being of the upper class and uncertain exactly where she stood on Vivian Dixon's scale, was careful to observe proprieties. He sat almost primly on a canvas chair, open attaché case on his lap. Vivi was amused by the looks Carlos and Marisa gave each other: his was best described as demure, hers under-the-lashes appraising. Their small talk was more amusing yet: formal and banal.

"*Qué día tan bueno!*"

To which Marisa replied, yes, it was a *very* lovely day, adding that, of course, the Costa del Sol did have the most wonderful climate in Spain. Which took them off on the subject of comparative prevailing climatic conditions. Majorca, the Canaries, the French Riviera.

Vivian finished, Carlos departed, still the model of politeness. Marisa watched him mount the stairs that led from beach to house. An odd smile played over her lips.

"Carlos isn't usually that formal," Vivian said. "I think you turned him on and he was ultraproper in defense."

"It was not because of me," Marisa said, still smiling. "You are to blame."

"Me?" Vivi raised the sunglasses, gray eyes registering surprise.

The girl asked: "He has worked for you long?"

"Why, yes. About six years, and he's a very good manager."

"And you do not realize he is in love with you?"

"That. Is. Preposterous." Vivian spaced the words. She shook her head. "Carlos plays the tourist field. He has swarms of women—"

Marisa laughed throatily. "I do not doubt it. He is very attractive. He could have me in a moment, and I am not even a tourist. I am Spanish, and I can see. He does not wear his heart on his sleeve. It is said better in Spanish. *Lleva el corazón en el mano*. The heart is in his hand. He holds it out to you."

"If you're right—my God, poor Carlos."

Marisa laughed again. "Do not feel sorry for him. He is Spanish. It is a normal condition for a Spanish man to suffer because of love for a woman he cannot have, and a very good thing for women like the tourists."

"Oh?"

"You have been to *corridas*?"

"A few. I'm anything but an *aficionado*."

"But you have observed how pain arouses furious power in the bull?"

"Yes."

"It is much the same with our men. The pain of . . . wait, yes, unrequited love for one woman turns them into *toros* with others."

"I see what you're driving at, Marisa," Vivian said, glad to spin out their digression. "Your analogy is bad, thought. The bull always loses."

"So do our men."

"Some do, I suppose."

"Most, and sooner or later Carlos will be like them, with one wife, several children, and many complaints of the liver."

"Now I really must say 'poor Carlos.' " Vivian grinned. "Where will the tourist women fit in?"

"*Como coños por consuelo*," Marisa said with a shrug.

Vivian chuckled appreciatively. Although the girl had played a bit loose with Spanish grammar for the alliterative effect, the line was clever and barbed, translating into "As cunts for consolation." And "*consuelo*" could also be translated as "comfort" or "relief" or "cheer." All suited her sense of meaning and conjured hilarious images of middle-aged and liverish Spanish husbands frantically seeking coital solace for their plight with grateful foreign women.

"You opinion of marriage isn't very high, is it?" Vivi asked.

"I would not like it for me. I want my career."

"*Nothing* else?"

"Oh, I want to have affairs!"

Vivian fine-tuned into Marisa's woman-to-woman wavelength and said: "And there's one affair in particular you'd like to have. With Carlos Lozano."

The girl blushed. "No!" She looked at Vivian, whose smile was understanding, sympathetic, blushed more deeply, faltered: "Yes . . . I . . . I would like to see him again and . . ."

"Make it with him."

Marisa nodded. "You are not interested in him—I believe that. Would you mind if I tried?"

"Mind?" Vivi beamed. "I'll find an excuse to insist that he come here for dinner this evening." Carlos could tell Marisa nothing she should not hear—not even across a pillow—and even a brief involvement would distract the girl. "After dinner, I'll send the two of you off—you can go to a disco, maybe—and if you're not in bed together before the night's over, it'll be your fault."

Vivian realized that she had been raising her voice gradually over the last few seconds, and became aware why. A light two-place—and extremely noisy—helicopter was approaching from seaward. The craft flew at less than two hundred feet altitude and angled in to cross the shoreline directly over the Dixons' private beach.

The craft had a bulbous-nosed stubby fuselage and a metal skeleton frame extended aft, a lattice with the tail rotor at its end. Vivian glanced up as the racketing chopper came overhead. The man beside the pilot held a motion-picture camera. Hardly unusual. The Costa del Sol was constantly being photographed from the air by makers of travel or promotional films.

The helicopter swung left, receded toward the southwest on a course that would carry it directly over Montemar.

James Courtney's study was soundproofed to seal out all noise. He did not hear the chopper hovering over the house until Sybil Pearson opened the outer-office door and entered with a just-arrived telex.

"What the hell is that?" he demanded.

"A helicopter. It's been clattering around for a few minutes."

"Can't be mine." The CVI copter was undergoing maintenance and servicing in Málaga.

"I checked with security men on the grounds. It's another of those aerial film crews."

"I haven't given anyone permission to overfly this property in months.'' Courtney pressed buttons on his control console. Paco hurried in from the outer office, hurried out even faster when told to have the craft waved off. Grenville appeared seconds later.

''Get the chopper's ID numbers,'' Courtney told the butler, then turned to Sybil. ''Make formal complaints about trespass and intrusion to the Guardia Civil and to the *gobierno militar* in Málaga as soon as Grenville has the information.''

Sybil went out. She closed the door, shutting out the noise. Jim Courtney left his Bureau Plat and went to the immense picture window. Numbers of grounds-security men were staring up into the sky, waving arms and shaking fists. He caught a flash of the copter flying by at an altitude of less than a hundred feet.

Grenville entered without knocking. Courtney spun around on his heel to face him: ''Well?''

''Pair of fools out to make a little money from films of wealth and glamour, I imagine. An ancient two-place Bell, with a pilot and motion-picture cameraman. I have the registration number, and 'Agencia Higuera' is painted on the fuselage. It's turned tail, should be well beyond the property boundaries by now.''

''Give Sybil the data.''

Grenville hesitated. ''Is it worth making an official complaint, sir? This Agencia Higuera might have connections with the press. Might stir nasty comments or ridicule about a fortress mentality, and this is hardly the time to attract attention.''

Courtney mulled, then nodded. ''You have a point. We'll forget the matter. Thanks, Grenville.''

The butler took a step, paused. ''Can you spare me for an hour or so this morning? I should go into Cabo Verde and do some personal shopping. Since my car is down with gearbox ailments . . .''

''Use a limo and driver.''

''Thank you. Incidentally, sir, our Maimonides with the broken nose is roaming the house with an inquisitive look. Shall I ask him along for the drive and probe a bit?''

''Do that, and let him see you smoking a pipe.''

''I intended to. One of my own, needless to say.''

Grenville found David Lippmann in the library, scanning the books that lined wall-to-ceiling shelves. An entire section was devoted to volumes on Judaism and Jewish history, another to works on World War Two, its background and aftermath, with heaviest emphasis on Germany, Hitler, the Nazis. A third section was devoted to books on art, painters, and painting. Many of them were very old and very rare. All were exquisitely bound in tooled leather.

"I'm going to run into the village, Mr. Lippmann," the butler said. "Mr. Courtney suggested you might like to come along and orientate yourself to the surroundings."

David had hoped for such an invitation from Sybil Pearson, but he accepted gladly. Perhaps the butler—and, apparently, Courtney's confidant—might be familiar with the story of the Velázquez and able to reconcile the inconsistencies.

The Mercedes was black and air-conditioned. Grenville, who addressed the driver as "Ignacio," did not bother raising the glass that separated rear and front compartments. During the drive through the grounds, he gave a running commentary:

"You can't actually see the annex from the road. It's behind the house, screened by those rows of pines, and beyond them, an orange grove. Ah! Directly to the right. Lovely little chapel, a baroque gem, built for Mr. Courtney's Spanish employees. They seldom use it. It's not like it was when Mr. Smith was alive."

"Mr. Smith?"

"It was the name we Brits used for Franco when Spaniards like Ignacio were listening. Made it safer to say things about him. Now . . . to the left, in the middle distance. Ten acres of olive trees . . ."

When they were through the gates and on a highway David remembered from his arrival to be the Carretera de Cádiz, Grenville produced a pipe and tobacco pouch, asked:

"Do you mind, sir?"

"Not at all—please." Lippmann watched Grenville scoop tobacco, pack it into the bowl, thought he would fish. "Fabulous place, Montemar."

"It is, indeed."

"Filled with fabulous things."

"Yes."

"Too bad about the *Horse and Rider*."

Grenville had been doing a meticulous job of pipe-filling. But now his hands twitched. Tobacco spilled onto his trouser legs and the car seat. "The Velázquez. . . ." was all he said, and brushed at the tobacco crumbs.

"Mr. Courtney told me he had it destroyed. It must've been painful for him."

"He took it quite well, actually—Ignacio, watch those bloody *camiones*—sorry, Mr. Lippmann, he always pulls up to within inches of their rears before veering out to pass."

Grenville finished readying his pipe, lit it.

"What you're seeing directly ahead is a terrible pity. Acres of orange trees were torn out to make way for a new *urbanización*. There'll be five, six hundred apartments in the complex. Financed by Arab money. See, bulldozers gouging at raw earth. Much the same a kilometer farther on. Bastards are building the biggest *ipermercado* in Spain. Like one of your American shopping centers in the suburbs."

The turnoff and overpass to Cabo Verde.

"Possible to glimpse the Puerto from here. I have to stop at a *farmacia*—need anything? No. Then we'll make a quick run down there before going back—has to be quick, I don't have much time."

"Don't let me screw up your schedule. I can do my sightseeing some other day."

"Wouldn't hear of it, sir. I promised Mr. Courtney to show you the Puerto."

The pharmacy was on the Calle San Gabriele, Cabo Verde's main shopping street, located some blocks from the Plaza José Antonio. The Mercedes eased to a stop at the end of a column of other cars already double-parked. Grenville went inside alone. David studied the Andalusian street scene and was impressed at how well developers of the town had managed to make old and new architectural styles complement each other harmoniously. The harmony did not extend to motorists on the traffic-snarled street. Their horns blared and they cursed in a babel of languages. A woman pushed a baby stroller past the front bumper of the Mercedes, glowered at Ignacio. A boy went by on a bicycle, slapped his hand against a fender. Ignacio flung his door open, bellowed "*Cabrón!*" and closed the door.

Grenville did not wait for Ignacio to open the passenger-compartment door, but climbed in. He carried a typical pharmacy plastic sack, well filled with an assortment of items, and said it was later than he thought. They would have to hurry.

Ignacio apparently knew where to go next. Grenville settled back, relit his pipe. "Can't very well do this when I'm on duty in the house," he said, puffing contentedly. David's visit to Puerto Cabo Verde was a whip-through tour. Although Ignacio drove along the quays at the slow, posted twenty-kilometer-per-hour speed, Lippmann obtained only blurred impressions of moored pleasure vessels, open-air bars and cafés, hordes of people—all with the look of the rich—sitting in them or merely walking about, forming knots, speaking to each other, then moving on. Some were Arabs.

"Doesn't Rashid something-or-other who has the world's biggest yacht keep it here?" David asked as they were driving out of the marina.

Grenville took the pipe from his mouth, gave Lippmann a sharp look. "Rashid el Muein, the *Houri*. No, he moors it the same place Adnan Khashoggi moors his yacht, *Nabila*, in Puerto José Banus. Any particular reason why you ask, sir?"

"Dumb curiosity. You seem to be an authority on local Arabs and what they do with their money—figured you might know."

They were out of Cabo Verde and had just turned onto the Carretera de Cádiz when Grenville reached down to shift the sack of pharmacy purchases on the floor. He paused, opened the mouth of the plastic bag wide, rummaged through the contents.

"Bloody hell!" He straightened up. "Damned fool forgot to put in my prescription."

"Let's turn around and go back," David suggested.

"Can't. Haven't time. Mr. Courtney will be furious if I'm much later. I'll telephone the bugger from up ahead. He can be at Montemar with it almost as soon as we are." Grenville leaned forward, tapped Ignacio's shoulder. Until the late 1970's, public telephone booths were almost impossible to find in Spain. Then came the deluge. Booths were installed by the uncounted thousands. The telephones in them work more often than not, and they can be found in improbable places. Like on a weed-covered hump of ground alongside a main highway.

Ignacio pulled off onto the shoulder of the road. Grenville said he would be only a moment, leaped out, and walked back about five yards to the booth, entered it. That he closed the articulted door carefully was understandable. He would swelter, but the din of high-speed traffic would be muted.

The entire purpose behind Leslie Grenville's excursion had been to get away from Montemar and then establish an excuse for using an isolated pay telephone that could not possibly be tapped. The call had to be made quickly. He positioned a twenty-five-peseta piece—he had none smaller—on the inclined track, dialed. There was a reply. He released the coin into the slot.

"Mr. William Moore. His good friend calling." He smiled, the "good friend" tickling his sense of the sardonic. The relationship between the two men was anything but friendly. Like most once-virile males who have lost their genital organs to wounds or surgery, Grenville loathed and despised homosexual men. And Moore feared Grenville.

"Bill Moore."

"Is he there?"

"I'll have to ask."

"Tell him he has to talk."

Moments passed, then Grenville heard Rashid el Muein's voice:

"Are you on a secure line?"

"No, I'm shouting from a housetop."

"Very clever. Well?"

"The helicopter. You sent it."

Grenville's first glance at the chopper had told him something was very wrong. The craft was too aged, too dilapidated—the intended effect lost by being overdone. Yet it was being flown with the skill and precision only a top-notch and highly paid pilot could achieve, and the camera being used by his passenger was of a kind only a major motion-picture or television firm could afford. Then, when the copter dipped down to less than fifty feet and hovered, he had seen the pilot's face.

"What I do is my business. You're paid to perform certain services."

"I'm entitled to know what's going to happen around me."

"There is nothing for you to know."

"Hell there isn't. You're escalating. I recognized the pilot. Kyle Dunne. We were together in Angola."

"I fail to see the significance."

"Ex-mercenaries have a grapevine of their own. Dunne has been with Horst Thiele's organization for years." Grenville glanced out at the Mercedes. Both its occupants remained inside. "You were using Gruppe Thiele." Some of its members had pursued Harkness at sea. Others were rushed to Tangier. Still others to Venice. Grenville had furnished the information on which they acted.

"This conversation has lasted long enough." El Muein's tone, never warm, dropped to near-freezing. "It's leading nowhere."

"Now it is. I expect more—"

"Stop expecting *anything*, eunuch. Your services are terminated." A serrated laugh. "Say a word to C., and he will terminate you. I suggest you find a place to hide."

El Muein cut the connection. Grenville paled. He *is* escalating—and fast, he thought, replacing the handset. And he was right. Any attempt to warn Courtney would be tantamout to a confession. The .357 Magnum would be of little help against Courtney's army of security personnel. On the other hand, that same army protected Montemar, Grenville thought, blood seeping back into his face. The estate and house were impregnable. The safest place for him—and James Courtney—to be was there.

"Sorry, Mr. Lippmann, there was a balls-up at the *farmacia*. My prescription won't be delivered until late afternoon."

"Be glad to run in for it myself."

"Wouldn't dream of it, sir." Then, in a transition that broke all existing records for being abrupt: "You were asking me earlier about Mr. Courtney's *Horse and Rider*."

The limousine was edging off the shoulder and into the traffic stream. Dave Lippmann blinked mentally, stammered:

"Uh . . . well, yes." Having received encouragement at last, he fired off questions. Grenville answered them—fully, it seemed to Lippmann, but it also seemed that inconsistencies and contradictions increased rather than lessened.

When they returned to Montemar, Grenville excused himself, took his purchases upstairs. David went directly to Sybil's office.

There was a lull, and more than an hour to go before lunch, she said. What would he like to do with the time?

"Possible to have a quick look at the documentation files?"

"I'll take you over to the annex. You can rummage on your own."

Grenville entered from the corridor, stopped.

"Thanks," Lippmann was saying to Sybil. "I only want to find the file on the Velázquez."

Grenville went on into the *estudio*, shut the door firmly behind him. Courtney, seated behind the Bureau Plat, said:

"You look as thought there's something wrong."

"There may be. It's the Jew."

"Lippmann?" Courtney's right eyebrow climbed. "What's he done?"

"It's what he might do, sir. He's developed an obsessive interest in the Velázquez. Suppose he stumbles across something?"

"Then we'll rid ourselves of the damned kike."

27

They had brainstormed possible scenarios, Ken Dixon allowing his imagination to run free. At one point he telephoned the concierge, inquired when the floor maids went off duty for their lunch break.

"Noon to twelve-forty-five," he told Neil Harkness. "Orff wants to show when they're gone, to cut his chances of being seen on our floor."

That led to a discussion of the worst possible scenario, moves and countermoves—and then rehearsals.

The knock came at 12:15.

There were two men instead of one—no great surprise, for all the scenarios had anticipated that Orff would not be alone. Both wore conservative business suits and quiet neckties. The shorter of the pair—in his mid-forties—spoke in a high-pitched voice and said he was Carl Orff. His companion was twenty years younger, an inch under Neil's six-three. Powerful muscles—and a shoulder holster—bulged under his buttoned coat. Orff introduced him simply as "my associate, Paul." Paul carried an oversized satchel. It appeared to be empty and was, Harkness guessed, large enough to hold *Horse and Rider* if the picture was folded rather than rolled.

"I was informed you'd be alone," Orff said when he and Paul stepped into the room and saw Kenneth Dixon.

"*My* associate, Ken," Neil said. The corridor had been softly lit, but the room was bright with sunlight. He could better assay the men. He did not like the results. Both wore wigs—superb in workmanship and perfectly fitted, but wigs nonetheless: Orff's dark brown, Paul's lighter, ostentatiously wavy.

Harkness had not offered to shake hands with either of them before. Now he held a hand out to Orff, who took it indifferently. It was as he feared. Orff's fingers were coated with a barely detectable pliant colloidal substance. He would leave no fingerprints. He shook hands with Paul. The same.

"Anyone care for a drink?" Neil followed what he and Dixon had called the "ultimate script."

Ken slumped into an armchair, patted the almost empty gin-bottle on the floor beside it. "I've got mine here."

Orff and his companion ignored Neil's invitation for the drink and to sit down. "I'd like to get our business done," Orff said. He took a tape cassette from his coat pocket, gave it to Harkness. "*Carmina Burana* by Carl Orff"—no smile, no change of facial expression at that—"a Deutsche Grammophon recording."

Neil pretended to examine the plastic case and the cassette inside it.

"Satisfied?" Orff stared fixedly at Harkness, but the younger man, Paul, was glancing around the room. He had an ugly face, Neil decided, lumpy, while Orff's was well-put-together. He could have been a clean-shaven Harvard Business School–graduate corporation executive. Could well be, too, Neil mused, saying:

"It's what Kloster said you'd give me."

"The painting."

"Don't rush me." Neil shot Dixon a look. "It's safe."

"I want it."

"Have to get it out of storage," Harkness said, testing.

"You were supposed to have it with you." The corporation-executive face also turned ugly.

"Relax, for Christ's sake." Neil had to be sure. "I'm going to order myself some coffee. Care to join me?" He stepped to the nightstand between the beds, reached for the telephone. Paul's karate chop would have broken his wrist, but he was alert for something of the kind, moved his arm with the impact, and groaned much louder than the actual pain justified.

"You crazy son of a bitch!" Neil held the wrist with his left hand, grimaced as though in agony. He staggered away from the beds, halted halfway across the room.

"Where is it?" Orff's voice had risen to the shrill. He stepped close to Neil, who put out his hand to ward him off. Orff knocked it aside, but not before it touched his coat front.

No shoulder holster, Harkness thought. Orff lets Paul carry the arsenal. Jesus! Wrong! Several inches of steel blade appeared from under Orff's coat sleeve. The point went to Neil's throat.

"For God's sake, tell him!" Ken yelped, cowering in his chair.

Paul spoke. "Has to be in the room . . . uh, Carl." He opened the closet door. Finding the closet empty, he went into the bedroom, emerged later, hammy fist gripping a silencer-tipped Beretta.

Neil's mind raced, adding up. Wigs, colloidal coatings. A knife and a silenced gun. As Ken had argued, there was no safer place to kill than a crowded, busy hotel—if the killing was done swiftly, quietly. In and out. No wonder that less than ten percent of all homicides committed in large hotels were ever solved. Harkness arrived at a total that equaled the sum of their ultimate scenario. He and Dixon would be finished off, whether the picture was delivered or not.

"Can I have a drink?" Ken pleaded. He reached for the Tanqueray bottle.

Neither Orff nor Paul paid attention to him.

"I want that painting!" Orff pressed the knife point against Neil's jugular.

"Under that bed," Harkness said, gambling that Orff would look, then drag the canvas out and examine it. The gamble paid off. The knife vanished up Orff's sleeve.

"Watch them," he said to Paul, going to the bed. He groped under it, got down on his knees, pulled the rolled canvas out and onto the carpet. The knife flashed into view again. He used it to cut through the tallith, retracted the blade, and started to unroll the painting.

"That it?" Paul asked, Beretta muzzle traversing back and forth between Neil and Dixon, who was clutching the bottle to his chest.

"Step on this edge," Orff said. "Hold it down."

Paul took a step, planted a foot on the painting. Orff bent low, peering. Then he snapped upright and leaped to his feet.

"The motherfuckers know," he said.

"Who cares?" Paul's eyes did not waver from Harkness and Ken, and he blurted final confirmation. "We were going to waste 'em anyhow." The lumpy face was smug. He was ready to shoot.

"Not yet." Orff's voice was a soprano quaver. The knife was out. He advanced to Ken, obviously the weaker of the pair. Paul trained his automatic on Harkness, finger easing off the trigger slightly. "Did you tell anyone?" Orff demanded. "Who else knows?"

"The moment of truth," Neil said. That was the cue. The next lines were improvisations to fit the particular circumstances. "May take Ken a while to remember the list." He sneered at Paul. "You can fuck yourself with that gun until he does." He hoped for a reaction. The hopes were realized. Paul closed, kicked, driving his foot into Neil's groin.

Harkness rolled with the kick, but doubled over and lurched back to fall on his bed. His karate-chopped hand flailed wildly, went under the pillow.

Orff spun around at the commotion.

Ken Dixon sprang from his chair, the Tanqueray bottle swinging.

Neil's hand came out from under the pillow. It held the Browning. The finger-snap sound of the silenced nine-millimeter and the hollow thud of the bottle slamming against Orff's skull came simultaneously.

Paul folded, gut-shot, the Beretta dropping. He fell to the carpet in a fetal position, both hands clutching at his belly, and moaned.

Carl Orff had slumped to the floor like a grain sack and lay silent and motionless, facedown. He would be unconscious for hours.

Neil crouched beside Paul.

"Alive?" Dixon asked, his voice a whisper, face ashen.

"Not for long." Neil examined the wound. Luckily it welled rather than poured blood. Moving quickly, he opened the man's shirt, gathered up the pieces of slashed tallith, thrust them inside.

"Why?" Ken wanted to know. "Soak up blood."

"Uh-huh—and add confusion." Holding the Beretta gingerly to avoid leaving fingerprints, he replaced it in Paul's shoulder holster. "These aren't the kind of guys who go around with Jewish prayer shawls." He rose to his feet.

"Think you can hold together, Ken?"

"Do I have a choice?"

"Check the corridor and fire stairs."

This part of the ultimate script had been dry-run-rehearsed.

Dixon went out, returned. "Clear. Nobody."

"Hold the doors." Neil strained, hefting Paul up in his arms. Dragging him would leave marks on the carpets. Out of the room, three yards to the left, through the emergency-exit door held open by Ken, down the fire stairs to the next-floor landing, where he dumped Paul. He sprinted back upstairs. Dixon followed.

Harkness had wiped the Browning clean of his fingerprints. He wrapped the weapon in a handerchief and stuffed it into a trouser pocket. Orff was lighter, easier to manage. Only moments were needed to carry him down, put him beside Orff, and press the Browning into his unconscious hand. Dixon scampered down with the satchel—it contained nothing. Neil cracked the third-floor fire door open an inch, wedged a corner of the satchel into the opening. It might hasten discovery of the two men. The sooner that happened, the sooner he and Dixon would be questioned by police—and free to go.

"Lock up," Neil said when he and Dixon were once more inside Room 412. Ken had a handkerchief out and was wiping at surfaces that might have been touched by Orff and his companion. "Never mind, the bastards did us a favor," Harkness said, and explained the colloidal coatings. He lit a cigarette and frowned deeply. "It'll work," he declared after seconds. "Police find two guys. Both obviously trying to disguise themselves with wigs, their fingertips protected. Thugs, thieves, or political assassins—God knows Paris is full of those. Both armed. One shoots the other."

"There's a hole a mile wide. How did Orff get hit, and with what?"

"Empty suitcase. Third guy slugged Orff, took off with the contents."

"You should've been a criminal lawyer."

"Instead of an *ex*-lawyer criminal?" He took a final drag on his Gauloise, crushed it in an ashtray. "Let's get to work."

They inspected the room for any signs that there had been visitors. There were none. The carpet where Paul had fallen was free of bloodstains.

"We have to go out the way we came," Neil had said.

They rolled the painting around the skis, wrapped the roll in the old brown paper. Dixon retrieved the twine that had been tossed in a bureau drawer. It was sufficient to hold the ungainly parcel even without the *tallith*.

The bundle was propped where it had been, in a corner.

"You sure about the rest of this?" Dixon sounded dubious and reluctant.

"Never underestimate the powers of surprise and applied psychology when you're dealing with dirty minds. Yes, I'm sure."

They remade the bed Ken had slept in—neatly. So neatly it looked as though it had been unused. Neil rumpled his even further. Dixon ducked into the bathroom, emerged with the bottle of Spanish hair conditioner that his servant, Juan, always put inside his toilet kit. It was white, viscous stuff. He opened the bottle, turned it upside down, and shook it, splattering conditioner here and there on the bedsheets. "Enough?" He looked at Harkness.

"Plenty for now. Put the bottle in the nightstand drawer, so we can"—Neil laughed—"freshen up later."

Harkness removed his clothes, hung outer garments neatly in the closet, dropped shoes, socks, and shirts in a pile beside the bed. Naked, he walked to an armchair, folded himself into it. "Get with it, lover."

Ken stripped. Neil's eyebrows rose and he whistled. "Hey, you've got two-thirds of a hard-on."

"Had the other third-plus while I was hitting Orff and you were taking out the other guy. Normal fear reaction, or don't you read the shrinks?"

"Funny. When I'm scared, mine shrivels. Must be abnormal."

"Nope. The experts say there're two kinds of normal fear response. Like elevators. Up or down. Has to do with the fight-or-flight impulse. Hard cock means you want to fight. Soft means you want to run." Dixon managed to chuckle. "Theory's full of shit. I wanted to run."

"Only half-full. I did, too. Take a drink and pass me the bottle."

"You? Gin?"

"We need to reek. Gargle before swallowing."

They finished the last of the Tanqueray between them.

"From here on, we keep quiet." Neil reminded his friend, "and listen for the offstage noises."

Some thirty minutes—they seemed as many hours—passed before they heard muffled voices and distant footsteps hurrying up stairs. Ken started to lever himself from his chair.

"Not yet." Harkness waved him back. "Be a while before they get around to us."

The volume and variety of noise increased gradually. Voices grew louder. The number of moving feet multiplied to herdlike proportions. There were door knockings and openings in the outside corridor, conversations that grew excited.

"Okay," Neil said.

They went to his bed. The hair-conditioner splotches on the sheets had dried, leaving stains. Dixon fished the bottle from the drawer, held it in one hand as he and Harkness lay down. The twin was narrow, cramped. They lay on their backs, naked bodies pressed close. But it was imperative that they achieve convincing effects.

"Do me a favor." Harkness grinned and spoke in a near-whisper. "If you get another of your normal fear reactions, point it away from me."

"No chance. You turn me off."

"Hold it." Neil raised his head. "They're next door." He glanced at Dixon beside him. "Shit." He scrubbed Ken's hair into a disheveled tangle with one hand, his own with the other.

A knock. A voice, male, through the door: "*Pardon, messieurs.*" The voice said more, but neither man listened. Ken uncapped the bottle, splashed globules of conditioner on his thighs, then on Neil's pubic hairs. Neil sprang from the bed, sprinted to the door. Dixon remained where he was.

"Hey, can't you read the sign?" Harkness babbled through the door. From this point on, he would be an all-American who neither spoke nor understood French. "Come back later—in a couple of hours."

"We are the police." A Frenchman with basic English. "I must say to open."

"Wait a minute . . ."

"Now, please."

Neil unlocked and opened the door a crack, saw a plainclothes *flic*, behind him a uniformed gendarme.

"I want to get dressed."

"No." The detective gave the door a hard push. The guest-register printout he carried showed there were two men in Room 412, Americans. What difference did it make if one or both were naked? *Merde*. He was impatient, annoyed, frustrated—as police almost always are when investigating a crime committed in a large hotel.

There is usually little they can do except interview staff members and go from room to room asking the routine "Did you see or hear anything?" questions. Worse still, none of the hundreds of transient guests could be detained for further interrogation without probable cause. In any event, the detective and his colleagues swarming through the Lutetia were already inclined to believe that the two victims—one dead, the other with a fractured skull—were either politicals or involved in the narcotics trade.

Harkness backed into the room, the policemen following. The detective noticed splatters of whitish fluid on Neil's pubic hairs. Ken was scrambling out of bed, making for the bathroom. The gendarme grabbed him, saw the sticky wetness on his thighs, pushed him away roughly, glanced with loathing at the stained bedsheets.

"Your passports," the detective said, his face registering disgust. The passports were produced, inspected. The gendarme jotted information from them in a notebook, and instead of returning the documents, flung them on a table.

"What the hell is this all about?" Neil took his shorts from the floor, climbed into them. "We're consenting adults—"

"You are filthy swine."

"If this is an arrest, I want to call the American consulate."

The detective sneered, said that, much to his sorrow, it was not an arrest—and he would ask questions and the filthy swine would answer them or it might become an arrest, after all. Where had the filthy swine spent the day?

"Here, in the room."

Yes, that was revoltingly evident. Had they heard any strange noises?

"A few minutes ago . . ."

"Before then."

Neil thought. Dixon, sitting on the edge of the bed with a segment of sheet drawn over his midsection, thought. They both said no. But the windows were open, Harkness added, gesturing toward them. The traffic sounds were very loud.

"As you can hear, Inspector."

"What happened?" Ken piped up.

"There has been an incident in the hotel." Let the American *cochons* ask someone else, the detective thought. "*Bon jour*." He and the uniformed gendarme found their own way out.

"Dress and pack—we have about fifteen minutes," Neil said.

They had less than ten. The telephone rang. Neil answered it. The call was from an assistant manager of the hotel, who was polite but firm. "I am sorry. The police have informed us—"

"I understand."

"We must ask you and Mr. Dixon to leave."

"When?"

"Immediately. A porter is on his way to your room."

Neil hung up, grinned. "Off we go, lover."

"Where? Kloster in Zurich or Split and pick up the *Deirdre*?"

"Neither. Home. I want to see Courtney."

Dixon's face closed down. "I shouldn't go back to Spain yet."

Neil thought he knew why. He remembered the night they left Cabo Verde. He had glimpsed bruises on Vivian Dixon's breasts and felt the tension between drunken husband and troubled wife. He assumed there had been an ugly marital battle and that Ken went with him as much to allow time for rancors to cool as to dry himself out. Dixon had said nothing to confirm the assumption since, but he seemed to have now.

"Look, give Vivi a chunk of the half-mil as a surprise," Neil suggested. "Give it all to her—what do you care?"

"Funny, I forgot the money." Ken took a deep breath, went to one of the open windows, stared down at the Boulevard Raspail below. He turned, faced Harkness. "I'm going. Fuck everybody—"

The door banged open. The porter had not bothered to knock, but used his passkey and barged in. "*Mesdames*." He spat the word and stood glaring his contempt. Neil pointed to the overnight bags, took the skis from the corner, and carried them himself.

They took a taxi to Orly. The last nonstop Paris–Málaga flight had departed at 1300 hours, they were told. There was an Air France flight to Madrid at 1605, easily connecting with the 2010 Iberia flight from Madrid to Málaga. Harkness bought tickets. They checked overnight bags along with the skis, which could not be taken into the cabin in any event, and went to eat abominable food at insane prices in a concourse snack bar.

"Want to phone Vivi?" Neil asked when they were through. "She can bake you a cake or have a hot paella waiting."

"No, I'll make it a surprise. You ought to call Sybil, though."

"At work? The phones at Montemar are bugged. Anyway, if she doesn't know I'm coming, neither does James P. Him, I really want to surprise."

They ambled past duty-free-shop counters and display cases. Ken halted beside a display of radios, tape recorders, and cassette players. "Where's the tape Orff gave you?"

"In my bag."

"Shit. I wonder what's on it."

"*Carmina Burana,* what else?" The sole purpose of the tape was to confirm Orff's identification. Neil intended turning it over to Courtney, along with the painting.

"We've got a Velázquez that's a map," Dixon said. "The tape just might be something else too."

"I doubt it."

"Be worth a listen, though."

"Can't argue." Neil scanned the countertop, selected a portable Sony cassette player, and motioned to a salesclerk. "I'll dig out the tape when we go through customs in Madrid. We can play it while we're waiting for the Málaga plane."

28

Heinrich Kloster was growing increasingly apprehensive. The Paris transaction—as he thought of it—should have been completed by one o'clock at the latest. That would allow ample time to have the painting X-rayed and then turned over to the people James Courtney had designated. It was now almost four. Kloster had still not received any word. Tired of alternately polishing his eyeglasses and drumming fingers on his desktop, Kloster telephoned his contacts in Bonn.

"Nothing yet, Herr Kloster."

He hung up, debated, decided, and telephoned the Lutetia in Paris. Yes, Monsieur Harkness had been there, but he had checked out.

The banker resumed his eyeglass polishing, fingers trembling slightly, a starter film of perspiration forming on his forehead. Trembling and perspiration increased minutes later when James Courtney telephoned. Kloster went on scrambler.

"Has Harkness delivered or hasn't he?"

"I have heard nothing to the contrary," Kloster dodged the question clumsily. "I will attempt to find out—"

"Do that, Heinrich—*schnell*!"

Courtney chopped himself off the line. Kloster's sweat glands pumped, and he had to make two tries before he managed to seat the receiver in its cradle.

David Lippmann was thoroughly mystified. He had found a thick file of documents on the Velázquez. They provided *Horse and Rider* with impeccable credentials. Its provenance was traced, owner by owner, from the mid-seventeenth century down to 1947, when it had been acquired by Regnier Frères, one of the most prestigious sales galleries in Paris. The following year, it had been sold to James Philip Courtney for $275,000—a not unreasonably low price for the time. There were numerous certificates of authentication—all from recognized experts on Velázquez and his works. But there was nothing in the file to suggest that Courtney had come to doubt the picture, much less copies of correspondence with the Prado. And there would have had to be letters back and forth before Prado experts came to Montemar, written statements of their findings and opinions after they had examined the painting.

The papers had to be filed elsewhere, Lippmann thought, and in midafternoon stopped by Sybil's office.

"I don't know of any other file," she told him. " 'Course, it's a possibility that Mr. C. might have it."

"Could you ask him for me?"

"Perish forbid." Sybil lowered her voice, and there was an amused glint in her hazel eyes. "Shouldn't think it prudent for you to do, either. He doesn't"—voice lowered more—"much like being reminded of his mistakes. I'd advise you to forget it." Loyalty to Courtney moved her to add: "It was his picture, after all. He could do whatever he wanted with it."

"Seems he did." David grinned. The short morning outing with Grenville had whetted his desire to go off the estate and see more of Cabo Verde. As far as he knew, Sybil Pearson was unattached. "It's forgotten. Next question. Are you doing anything for dinner tonight?"

"No," Sybil replied glumly and without thinking. "I'm not."

"If you pick the restaurant and show me where it is, I'd like—"

"I'd like, too—but you can't. It almost slipped my mind. Mr. C. said you're invited to have dinner with him again this evening."

"Tell him, or I will, that I'm sorry."

"Un-possible. I know his moods. It's a command performance."

Horst Thiele's confidence was infectious. Rashid el Muein felt he could afford to loll on the reception-chamber couch and allow the *sibah* to dangle loosely from his fingers.

Thiele had been the model Sturmbannführer briefing a superior on what would take place the next day and had convinced el Muein that his men could not possibly fail.

". . . excellent films," he was saying once again. "My surgeons"—to Rashid's annoyance, he persisted in using the euphemism—"have viewed them over and over this afternoon, memorizing every detail—"

"The pilot was a man named Dunne," Rashid interposed to jolt Thiele and lead in to a point he had been waiting to make. "He flew low and was recognized."

"By Courtney?" The German's gaunt face remained impassive.

"By the eunuch, Grenville."

"What matter? He is in your pay."

"Not any longer."

Thiele's nostrils twitched. He scented an even higher fee. "You wish to have the eunuch undergo surgery also." A flat statement rather than a question.

Rashid smiled placidly; the Levantine Arab bazaar haggler was emerging. "*I* haven't any wishes one way or another, Horst. It was *your* man who was recognized."

Thiele sighed, acknowledging the elemental justice of the argument. Leslie Grenville would have to be taken out. At no extra charge.

The Spaniard is half-idealist, half-realist. The halves are in eternal conflict, and in order to survive and function, Spaniards force some sort of balance between them. Ideals are preserved—as ideals. Day-to-day living is governed by reason and intellect. At least with Spaniards like Carlos Lozano.

Although Carlos adored Vivian Dixon, he was able to face reality. The telephoned invitation to dinner at Broadmoor pleased but did not mislead him. He knew that he had been asked because of—"for" was more accurate—Marisa Alarcón.

Carlos had assessed Marisa that morning on the beach. He recognized her as the pampered and willful daughter of a wealthy family—the kind that prided itself on being modern, liberated. Marisa was intent on proving herself no less emancipated than English, American, French, German women. Instincts honed sharp by much experience told him that he aroused her sexually. And at that level, the attraction had been mutual. She was beautiful, intelligent, and, doubtless, good in bed. Very well, Carlos thought. He would enjoy the dinner, and then enjoy an adventure with Marisa. *Por qué no*?

He interrupted his musings and went into the main sales gallery. Rosa, a sales assistant, was having problems with a pair of expensively dressed thirtyish American women. One had taken an eighteen-inch-high terra-cotta sculpture from a display shelf and was holding it carelessly.

". . . please, it is most fragile," Rosa was pleading.

"You mean junky. Who made it?"

"Excuse me." Carlos introduced himself as the manager, took the sculpture from the woman's hands. "The artist is Jacinto Belles Ortiz."

"How much?"

"Thirty thousand pesetas."

The women were familiar types. Attractive, vacationing without their husbands, the instantly available fringe benefits of dealing with the tourist trade on the Sun Coast.

"What's that in real money?" the second woman, eyes interested in Carlos and not the price, asked.

"Two hundred and seventy-nine dollars."

"Can you pack the statue so it won't break and bring it to our hotel?" the first, blond hair shoulder-length, asked. Her look added: Bring it personally.

The second said: "We could have a drink together."

"I'm afraid it isn't possible today," Carlos said, thinking of Marisa. However, their adventure might last only a single night, and bored American wives vacationing in pairs were magnificent performers in threesomes. "Will you still be at your hotel tomorrow evening?"

"We'll be there another week," the blond woman nodded, moistening her lips.

"Tomorrow night will be fine," the other said hastily, and then asked the inevitable American question: "Do you take credit cards?"

Carlos was visualizing positions and combinations as he recited: "Yes, we do. Visa, MasterCard, Carte Blanche, American Express."

In Spanish, *la baraja* means a pack or deck of cards. The plural form of the noun is *las barajas*. The related verb *barajar* means to jumble together, to wrangle, to scuffle. Many have observed that Madrid's Aeropuerto Las Barajas is aptly named. Once inside the sprawling terminal whose extensions jut in all directions, passengers are jumbled together with what seems a vengeance. They wrangle in scores of languages over reservations, the tardiness of flights, precedence in endless ticket-counter lines, and the time of day. The wrangling often leads to scuffles, which are quickly defused by alert airport police and tricorn-hatted Civil Guards. They also rush to the aid of unwatched children who race around, bump into baggage carts, passengers, or each other and trip, fall on the stone floor. These incidents trigger more wrangling as parents jabber in polyglot tongues to accuse the officers of having assaulted their offspring while the children add ear-splitting counterpoint with their shrieks.

There was just such a scene in the Barajas customs hall when Neil Harkness and Kenneth Dixon made their way to the counter. A pair of policemen had helped a brat with skinned knees to his feet. The parents were screaming in Dutch, the youngster merely screaming. Customs officials were scowling at the din, giving luggage only cursory glances. One passed the skis and handbags, raising no objection when Neil opened his and took the tape cassette from it, and the baggage was shifted to a conveyor for transfer to the Málaga flight.

The tables in the main terminal snack bars were filled. Neil and Dixon settled for stand-up beers, and although they had more than an hour to wait, checked in at the Iberia counter in the *nacional* section of the terminal, found adjoining plastic-covered armchairs in a crowded waiting room.

Neil checked the tape, inserted it into the Sony, and keeping the volume low, pushed the Play key. He and Dixon listened intently. German composer Carl Orff had composed *Carmina Burana* in the 1930s. It is based on medieval songs, the manuscripts of which had been discovered in 1803, in the Benediktbeuren monastery in Upper Bavaria. The songs were those of young minstrels and students who railed at fate, celebrated the joys of nature, love, and drinking, raged at the bitter ironies and misfortunes of life. Brilliantly orchestrated for a huge chorus, *Carmina Burana* was first performed in Frankfurt in 1937. It immediately received wide acclaim, especially in Germany, where the Hitlerian regime was seeking to make Germans acutely aware of their early historical beginnings. Such lines as "Ablaze inside/ my rage boiling" reflected the Nazi spirit toward Germany's enemies, as did "May our critics be routed/ never counted among the just"—and there were many hundreds of lines in the twenty-five songs.

Neil played through the ten songs on the first side of the tape.

"It's what it says so far," he said, flipping the cassette. "Good version. Better than what I have at home."

"Play the rest," Ken urged. "Passes time." He noticed the occupant of the chair on the other side of Harkness, realized the man had been sitting there throughout. Dixon grinned inwardly. The man was unmistakably a Brit of about sixty-five. Florid face, neatly clipped white mustache, fine-checked sports jacket, and regimental tie all spelled retired British Army or Navy officer. The face seemed slightly familiar, but there were many like it on the Costa del Sol—where he, too, was presumably headed.

The Brit leaned forward as though to speak, then sat back as Neil started the Sony playing again. The second side played through. Harkness switched off the machine. "Just chorus and orchestra," he said. The man next to him cleared his throat.

"Ahmmm. I'm Peter Osgood. Live near Estepona—I've seen you both before, haven't I? You're . . . Wait, yes, Harkness.

You have the charter boat in Cabo Verde. And aren't you Kenneth Dixon, the writer?"

Acknowledgments were followed by handshakes, and Osgood offered to buy a round of drinks at the waiting-room snack bar. Ken and Neil accepted gladly. Having finished with the tape and found it to contain nothing unusual, they still had time to wait.

They squeezed a path to the bar, ordered—Scotch for Neil and Osgood, *ginebra* for Ken.

"Couldn't help hearing the music," Osgood said.

"Hope it didn't bother you," Neil apologized.

"Not at all." Peter Osgood stroked his mustache. "Brought back memories." The drinks were served. "Cheers!" He downed the whiskey. "Y'see, I'm not much for music as a rule. Can't tell one tune from another. Wife says I'm tone deaf."

Ken sighed, ordered another round.

"Never forget *Carmina Burana*, though." Osgood pronounced it "Car-*mine*-ah Boo-*rain*-ah." "From right after the war."

"Oh?" Neil oh'd politely, prepared for interminable tales of battles fought by the Slopstep Light Infantry or HMS *Flounderer*.

"No harm talking about it, I s'pose." Osgood cleared his throat again. "When we took over our occupation zone in Germany, I was posted from the Royal Kents to a field intelligence unit that was tracking down Nazi war criminals. Had to listen to that record until I'd memorized every note and the German words—hellish job, that."

Neil and Dixon exchanged bored glances. Harkness raised his refilled glass. "*Salud*—not to forget *amor y pesetas*."

Osgood joined in drinking, went on doggedly with his tale.

"Bloody Nazi fugitives used *Carmina Burana* as their theme song. Then they used bits of the music or some of the verses for identification and recognition signals, finally started making up codes out of it."

The glances Neil and Dixon exchanged were puzzled but no longer bored.

"Bastards had an underground organization—"

"You mean Odessa?" Ken interrupted.

Osgood gave the Americans the kind of condescending look World War Two veterans are wont to give men too young to have served in it. "Odessa was formed later. This was early on, in the first year after the Nazis surrendered. The bastards called it Gemeinschaft Orff." Osgood snorted. " 'Association based on kinship' named after a silly music composer! We ran inter-Allied checks on him, of course, but he wasn't involved."

Neil told a barman to bring more drinks. "Did you round up many of the members?"

"Damned few. Most slipped over into the American and French zones."

"What happened to them there?"

"Haven't a clue. We passed our information on to the Frenchies and you Yanks—became their problem from then on. Had enough left of our own." Osgood reached for his freshly filled glass, chuckled. "Won't forget that damned music until the day I die."

The p.a. system began a trilingual announcement that Iberia Airlines Flight 009 for Málaga was ready to board. The three men finished their drinks.

"You never heard anything more about the Gemeinschaft?" Neil asked as they joined the typical Barajas stampede to the boarding gate.

"Not a whisper." Osgood spotted another acquaintance in the Málaga-bound crowd, shook hands, excused himself, pressed forward, calling out, "Arthur, I say, Arthur!" and waving an arm.

Harkness and Dixon were silent until they were seated aboard the old DC-9 that Iberia still used on the evening Madrid–Málaga run. Then, stowing the Sony under his seat, Neil said, "I'll be damned." He latched the seat belt, frowned deeply. "Colonel Blimp wasn't handing us a line," he said.

"Nope," Ken agreed. "His kind of Brit might polish a war story up a little, but he won't lie. Which is leading your devious legal brain where?"

"Around in circles. Let's go back to Fischer. He had a concentration-camp number tattooed on his arm and a Jewish prayer shawl in a drawer, but he wasn't circumcised. You didn't meet Kloster in Zurich, but I'll swear he's Kraut, not Swiss. Next item, our contact in Paris goes by the alias Carl Orff and identifies himself with a tape of *Carmina Burana* . . ."

"Could be crazy coincidences."

"Wait for the capper. Sybil tells me that J.P. has a favorite piece of music and plays it often on the stereo in his study."

"You telegraphed the punch line. *Carmina Burana*."

Harkness was silent, then shook his head. "There can't be any connection. Courtney has a clean record in that regard. Hell, you had his whole life history investigated. He hated the Nazis once he got overseas, and worked his butt off to help Jewish DP's."

Dixon switched his memory to the reports that had been compiled on James Courtney for him. "Yeah, that's true. He sent a lot of the DP's over to the States. They even formed a Courtney admiration society—the Pflegebrüders, if I'm pronouncing it right. Means foster brothers. I think my researchers said he started shipping them over in February of forty-six. . . ."

29

The war in Europe ended on May 7, 1945. Defeated Germany was divided into occupation zones, each administered by one of the victorious Allied powers. The largest single segment—in the east—was controlled by the Soviet Union. There were three zones in Western Germany—United States, British, French—and forms of military government were established in each sector.

Occupation forces faced problems that were myriad and seemed insuperable, among them the hunt for Nazi war criminals and the need to care for those of their victims who had survived. The numbers of both were staggering. There were hundreds of thousands of wanted Nazis on the loose, in hiding, and there were several *million* survivors of concentration, slave-labor, and death camps.

The search for the fugitive war criminals went on as best it could, hampered by manpower shortages in the occupation forces, lack of cooperation from the German people, and the general chaos that prevailed. The survivors—Jews and non-Jews and of every European nationality—were officially designated "displaced persons," often abbreviated to "DP's." They were housed in new camps under Allied jurisdiction, fed and clothed, provided with medical care, against the day when they could be returned to their homelands and homes.

The task was monumental, even though religious and other private relief organizations sent personnel and supplies to help military governments care for and relocate the DP's. Many had neither homes nor homelands, as they had known them, to which they could return, and their families had been wiped out. Many others were in no physical condition to be moved anywhere until they had rebuilt their health and strength. In any event, transportation facilities were in shambles, making large-scale movements of people impossible.

After having spent a comfortable overseas duty tour on a U.S.

Army planning staff in London, First Lieutenant James P. Courtney was transferred to Germany, assigned to military government. He was assigned to the AMGOT subheadquarters in Munich, and although promoted to the rank of captain, was still a very junior officer in the military-government hierarchy. Or would have been, had it not been for the tiny "PI-I" stamp on his personnel records. This signified that he had political influence by virtue of having rendered services to U.S. intelligence agencies before he entered the Army. It was the long-arm reward for his activities as an informant while attending Wyler College in Southern California.

Even full colonels and brigadier generals deferred to low-ranking officers marked with the "PI-I" label. There was always a possibility that young Captain Courtney still maintained his contacts—and might, if his toes were trod on, forward derogatory reports on whoever had trod on them.

Courtney's job was to conduct periodic inspections of displaced-persons camps in the area surrounding Munich. Officially, it was his duty to determine if and how conditions might be improved for the DP's and to expedite their relocation. Unofficially—and this came from the headquarters G-2, the intelligence officer:

"Keep an eye and ear open for Communist agitation—there's a lot of that going on in the camps, and if you can pick up any information on Nazis, we'd like to hear about it."

"Might be war criminals hiding right in the camps, sir," Captain Courtney suggested.

The intelligence officer, a major general, laughed.

"Nonsense, Captain. The kind of Nazis we're after made a religion of racial purity. They consider those people subhumans and would never hide among them. Even if they did, the DP's would recognize them for what they are sooner or later and save us the trouble of hanging the bastards. Just listen for stories of atrocities we might be able to use for evidence."

The major general was not alone. Many other highly placed officers in the United States, British, and French occupying forces held similar beliefs. They could not conceive of Nazis, long arrogant in their pride of being pure Aryans and despising all who were not, seeking refuge among the *untermenschen*—to their minds, the mongrel human garbage—in the displaced-persons camps.

Courtney went about his assigned duties efficiently, following instructions to the letter. He inspected camps, saw to it that food rations were increased here, more coal supplied there, clothing distributed more rapidly in a third place. His official reports were clearly and concisely written. His informal reports were delivered orally, to the major general.

"We have a big Communist cell developing in B Camp at Ulm, General. Hungarians, mainly."

"Jews?"

"About half and half. I have the names."

"Find an excuse to transfer them over to the French zone."

"I've already prepared the papers. 'Reason to believe that the displaced persons listed have claim to French nationality.' We'll truck them over the zone boundary and dump them and the papers on the Frogs."

"Good. Good work. Anything else?"

"More atrocity reports. They're being typed as depositions. Care to see them when they're finished and signed?"

"I've seen enough. Just buck them over to the war-crimes section."

Courtney had charm, showed genuine concern for DP's, and was beginning to learn languages. He won the DPs' confidence, always had time to listen to their complaints, and was often able to do something about them. He appeared particularly sympathetic to the plight of Jews in the displaced-person camps. Few wished to return to their own countries, where they had been savagely persecuted and where they no longer had relatives or friends. Many wished to go to Palestine, but Britain, which controlled Palestine, refused to permit Jewish immigration. Other Jews hoped they might leave Europe and enter the United States, which was slow and reluctant to accept them. There were numerous American and international Jewish organizations working to break the bottlenecks, but only with limited success. Jews continued to languish in the camps. Courtney frequently heard them tell the representatives of refugee organizations:

"I have relatives in America. They will pay my fare, send the money. It will not cost your organization or the government a penny."

The unvarying reply: "It is not a question of money."

The hell it isn't, Captain Courtney thought after a time, and if there are so many Jews who can get their hands on money, something might be done. He studied the rules and regulations and the bureaucratic procedures involved in obtaining admission into the United States for Jewish DP's. There were, as he anticipated, loopholes and angles—and where there weren't, he could create them easily in the confusion that prevailed.

Munich was still a wasteland of rubble in February 1946, and all Europe was experiencing the worst winter weather in decades.

Captain James P. Courtney lived in superheated officers' billets, with additional warmth being provided nightly by *schatzes* pathetically grateful for a meal and two packets of PX cigarettes they could sell on the black market. His office was a snug Quonset hut on a bombed-out site near the Rathaus on the Adalbertstrasse, and the first Jew came there—with ten thousand dollars sent him by relatives in Baltimore, Maryland, USA.

"How long?" the Jew asked.

"Fifteen days," was Courtney's promise. He kept it.

He dug the Jewish DP's papers out from among thousands, filled out complicated forms, added rubber stamps, and scrawled illegible signatures. He hand-carried the documents through the labyrinths of military-government and civil-affairs bureaucracies. If there were doubts, no one cared to voice them. What the hell, everyone in the occupation force had a private racket going. Captain James Courtney was by no means the only officer who expedited the processing of papers with illegible signatures by walking them through one office after another.

The Jew left, pathetically grateful.

"Write to me," Courtney told him. "We'll keep track of each other."

There are always grapevines.

Courtney was inspecting DP Camp Jefferson south of Munich. A male DP brushed past him, thrust a scrap of paper in his hand. He looked at it five minutes later, read: "Rechstein, Bernard. Barracks 3. $50,000."

He checked the camp records. Bernard Rechstein was registered as a German Jew who had survived four years in Auschwitz. His home was Dresden, in the Soviet zone. He had no documents and no living relatives anywhere.

Courtney had a private talk with Rechstein, began it by saying, "Let me see your left arm." Rechstein hesitated. Courtney drew his service .45. The sleeve was rolled up. No tattoo on the forearm. In itself, this proved nothing. There were a few Jewish death-camp survivors who had not been tattooed with identity numbers by their SS guards.

"Unbutton your trousers," Courtney ordered. "Show me your *putz*."

Rechstein turned to run. Courtney grabbed him, rammed the .45 muzzle into his well-padded belly—another suspicious sign.

"You're what—Gestapo, SS, SD?" Courtney asked calmly, nudged the belly. "*Machts nichts* to me, but the price goes up."

Myopic eyes stared. "How much?"

"A hundred thousand—do you have it?"

"I can obtain it." The English was good.

"From where and how soon?"

"There is a group. In days."

Bernard Rechstein was still in his twenties, but he had been an ardent Nazi and risen high in the SS for his age, heading a "Special Action" unit in the SS Dirlewanger Brigade, later carried out mass executions in Czechoslovakia and Austria. He was wanted, under another name, as an important war criminal by all the occupying powers. Since he, like so many other Nazis involved in the extermination of the Jews, had learned to speak Yiddish and familiarized himself with Jewish history and customs, he managed to pass as a Jew.

"But I have to be careful and piss alone." He was not circumcised.

Courtney collected the first fifty thousand dollars, signed Rechstein out of camp, and found him lodgings in a half-destroyed Munich rooming house.

"Get yourself a number and have it aged," Courtney said.

A small but thriving industry had sprung up in German cities. Tattoo artists, professional ex-SS-semi-pros and enterprising amateurs, were tattooing concentration-camp numbers on the arms of Nazi fugitives. The forearm tattoo was accepted at a glance as proof of incarceration, and anyone who had been held in a concentration camp was accepted as being above suspicion. Untold thousands of Nazis slipped through Allied war-criminal nets merely by baring their arms when stopped for questioning. Mengele was among them, and he tattooed himself. But the needle marks and ink could not appear new, fresh. It had to seem that the tattoo had been applied years before. The appearance of age was achieved first by using a diluted ink. Then the subject's entire upper body was alternately doused with heavily salted brine and exposed to violet-ray sunlamps. The skin was roughened, burned dark—just as it would have been if the individual had labored for years in the open, stripped to the waist. The process took three weeks—the same length of time it required for James Courtney to prepare and clear necessary papers for the poor homeless Jew Bernard Rechstein.

"There are others of us," Rechstein said, paying the other half of the agreed amount. "What more can you do?"

"It's expensive to manufacture Jews," Courtney told him.

"We have an organization—and money."

"Tell me."

"Someone else will."

Someone else did, a week after Bernard Rechstein left Munich bound for the United States.

It was Artur Hinze, a former *gauleiter* notorious for hi savageries, who told Courtney about Gemeinschaft Orff. Hinze enjoyed a remarkable degree of safety. His face had been horri bly maimed by a bomb splinter during an air raid on Nürnberg and was unrecognizable. He had a soldier's book and othe papers identifying him as a lowly Wehrmacht private—a creature of no interest to Nazi-hunters.

Hinze had briefly attended Oxford University before the war but whatever language he spoke was distorted as he forced each word past lips that had been sewn hastily by surgeons and were twisted like the rest of what remained of his face.

"We. Have. Funds. American. Currency. Gold. Bearer bonds Many. Other. Valuables."

"Loot." Courtney shrugged.

"Spoils. Of. War."

"Loot," Courtney repeated.

Hinze represented himself as the leader of Gemeinschaft Orff—and, it turned out, he was. There were over two hundred men in the organization. Each would pay one hundred thousand dollars.

"No set price—it'll vary," Courtney told him. "And two hundred is out of the question. Some, yes, and I'll have to work them in with legitimate Jews."

Artur Hinze protested.

"There have to be real Jews—and after we manufacture Jews out of your people, they'll have to stay Jews the rest of their lives."

"They. Will. Refuse."

"Then they can forget any idea of ever reaching the States and staying there. If their acts ever slip, they'll be finished. People are going to hate Nazis for decades and keep on trying to chase down any German who's been labeled a war criminal. Think about it. See what your people have to say. If they agree, come back to me—say, in a month. With money."

Courtney was certain that Hinze would return, and hurried to lay the groundwork. He picked six Jews at random and expedited their passage to the United States, charging them nothing. He became a hero to all Jewish DP's in the camps. Jewish organizations working in occupied Germany took notice of him. He was lauded. Before the month was out, a group of junketeering U.S. congressmen insisted on meeting the young captain and praised him to his superiors.

The last was a remarkable stroke of luck. The entire U.S.

Army command was convinced that he had very powerful political influence indeed. Courtney no longer needed to forge illegible signatures. Those DP's he designated as worthy of expedited, bend-the-rules treatment received it.

Hinze brought two hundred thousand dollars in U.S. currency and said that the members of Gemeinschaft Orff had seen the light. Much as the prospect sickened them, they realized that what Courtney had said was true. They would pretend to be Jews—until they died, if necessary. Some, the former *gauleiter* added, had already undergone operations for removal of their foreskins—extremely painful for men in their adult years.

That was another booming German industry, Courtney knew. Surgeons were circumcising males right and left. German men had gotten the idea that if they showed circumcised penises to Allied military authorities and claimed to be Jews, they would receive housing, extra food rations, jobs.

During the months that followed, James Courtney aided twenty Jews to reach the United States—shrewdly taking no payment so they would sing his praises. In the same period, he cleared the way for thirty of Hinze's manufactured Jews, from whom he collected a total of more than three million dollars.

Captain James P. Courtney was becoming secretly rich—and publicly famous.

An Associated Press feature article printed in hundreds of U.S. newspapers declared him "a single-handed battler for justice and humanity against the stupidity of bureaucracy."

Life did a picture spread showing Courtney—natty in his uniform—inspecting camps, chatting with DP's, wearing a yarmulke while attending services in a makeshift synagogue. *Life*'s deep captions noted:

"The young captain, whose blue eyes express deep emotion when he speaks of the plight of Jewish DP's, is not himself Jewish. Courtney was brought up by his uncle, the Reverend Wendell Courtney, a Baptist minister."

Elsewhere Courtney was quoted as saying: "My uncle was deeply religious, but he had no prejudices about religion. I remember how early he began to condemn the Nazis for their persecution of the Jewish people. They were, he said, God's people. I grew up feeling the same way. I want Jewish people to think of me as their foster brother."

Courtney was finally too rich secretly and too famous publicly to stay in the Army. He qualified for release and chose to be separated from the service in Germany. He remained there and continued what some media elements were rhapsodizing as his "mission."

He discovered that he could accomplish more as a civilian than he had as an Army officer. The military and civilian officials were intimidated by his reputation and his connections in high places. Why, he had been guest of honor at a dinner given by General Lucius Clay, was visited by senators who came abroad, corresponded directly with members of the Truman cabinet.

Jews sponsored for entry into the United States by Courtney were rushed through the processing mill. No one wanted to risk receiving "IMMEDIATELY ADVISE REASON FOR DELAY IN DISPOSITION" cables from Washington.

It was Artur Hinze who presented the idea to Courtney. By then, almost fifty members of Gemeinschaft Orff were in the United States, where they joined synagogues, told of their sufferings under the Nazis, and took jobs or began small businesses. Hinze himself had decided to remain in Germany. His ruined face protected him. Later, plastic surgeons might be able to refashion it, but not in original and recognizable form. Then, eventually, there would be a place for him—and his unremitting Nazi political philosophies—in whatever Germany emerged from the defeat.

"You. Have. Been. Paid. By. Us. Almost. Six. Million. Dollars."

Courtney admitted the figure was accurate enough and said he expected it would be higher—much higher—before they were finished.

Hinze gave the wet gurgle that was his laugh. The relationship between members of the Gemeinschaft and Courtney should change from that of buyers and seller to one of associates, partners, he said. A partnership over which Courtney held control, he added as hastily as his impaired speech permitted.

The Gemeinschaft Orff had over seventy-five million dollars in cash and instantly negotiable assets. Including thirty-five million dollars in bearer bonds of industrial corporations in France, Belgium, and Holland. Industry was reviving in those countries. Bearer bonds were what their name implied. They belonged to whoever had them. Ownership of the bonds enabled one to exercise certain—often decisive—pressures on the companies that had issued them.

Why not use the resources to establish a business empire? The ersatz Jews would work for and with Courtney. Passing for Jews, they would be enormous assets, working from within what

Artur Hinze still believed was a Jewish monopoly of commerce, industry, and finance in the Western world.

"How many more do you want to get across to the States?" Courtney asked.

"Perhaps. Forty." The rest had already taken their shares of the spoils, severed connections with Gemeinschaft Orff, and found their ways to South America or the Arab countries of the Middle East. "They. Will. Associate. With. You. Also."

Courtney remembered the *Life*-magazine interview, snapped his fingers. "Window dressing!" he chortled. "We need it. We have it. A loose, informal group like a social or friendship society. The Yids—the ersatz Yids—are so grateful, they organize the Pflegebrüders. They're my foster brothers. I'm theirs. We can seem to operate in the open—a band of friends, always ready to help each other. Who'd ever stop to wonder what goes on behind such beautiful sentiment?"

"Pflegebrüders." Hinze laughed his wet gurgle. "Yes. Good. Very. Good."

Part of the arrangements were settled then and there. James Courtney was to be the head and final arbiter—and, of course, the front man. A full half of all profits ever earned would be his. The other half would be divided among his "foster-brother" associates. They would follow whatever orders or instructions he gave.

Courtney sent a dozen real Jews; then, in groups of five and six, the thirty-nine more that Hinze sent to him. Then he and Hinze met again.

James Courtney was in high spirits. The Gemeinschaft Orff Nazis already transmuted into Jews and sent to the United States had formed the "Society of the Foster Brothers" in a moving ceremony widely publicized in the American press. Jewish organizations throughout the world were loud in praising him. B'nai B'rith, most influential of them in the United States, had struck a special medal honoring his work on behalf of Jewish displaced persons; a leading rabbi would come to Germany and present it.

Courtney wanted to show the clippings and the letters from B'nai B'rith to Hinze, who brushed them aside. He had infinitely more important and pressing matters to discuss. There had been a leak, the security of Gemeinschaft Orff compromised. The source had been identified—and liquidated. However, this posed new and immediate dangers, demanded that their "program" be accelerated. The first steps had been taken. Gemeinschaft Orff's remaining assets had been taken to Switzerland, placed on deposit or in safe-deposit boxes at the Bauerkreditbank in Zurich.

There they would be at Courtney's disposal, subject only to Hinze's overall supervision. The bank was headed by Heinrich Kloster.

"He. Is. One. Of. Us."

Farsighted Nazi-party and SS chieftains had begun sending loyal, reliable men out of Germany as early as 1939. They were planted in key positions abroad to serve as conduits for illicit transactions and serve as safety hedges in the event Hitler was overthrown or Germany lost the war.

"Kloster. Will. Take. His. Orders. From. You."

Then Hinze issued a warning.

"There. Must. Be. Complete. Mutual. Trust."

Courtney understood. He had understood all along. The Pflegebrüders would be totally, blindly loyal to each other, instantly liquidating any of their number who faltered. And they would serve under and obey him in like, SS-style fashion—on the same basis. A wrong step, and he would be killed, without delay, for they would always know exactly where to find him.

There was one item of Gemeinschaft property that had not been transferred to Zurich, Hinze continued. Its potential value was beyond calculation. He would show—and give—it to Courtney:

"After. You. Have. Gone. To. Paris. And. Done. What. Is. Necessary."

The Regnier Frères Gallery in Paris had a painting for sale. *Horse and Rider*, a masterpiece by Diego Velázquez, priced in the neighborhood of a quarter of a million dollars. Courtney was to buy the picture with Gemeinschaft Orff money, but in his own name, and obtain all documents Regnier Frères had pertaining to the work. These latter he was to bring back to Munich.

"And the painting?"

"Take. It. Where. You. Cannot. Be. Seen. And. Burn. It."

Courtney sensed there was icy reasoning behind the apparent madness and went to Paris. The final price was $275,000. He paid in American currency and requested that the picture be detached from its frame and rolled up. It was unusual, but not the most unusual of requests. M'sieu Courtney was obviously an eccentric American millionaire—*grâce à Dieu*, they were beginning to reappear in Paris, gallery employees told each other as he took the picture away in a rented Citroën which he drove himself.

Courtney drove several miles into the country in the direction of Rouen. He found an abandoned farm, its fields overgrown with weeds. He poured gasoline over the painting, tossed a lighted match, watched $275,000 go up in smoke. When the ashes cooled, he trampled them into dust and into the earth. He left Paris the same night.

Artur Hinze lived on the western outskirts of Munich in a small house that had escaped bomb damage and was located a considerable distance apart from its neighbors. Courtney found that Hinze had a weedy, unkempt man of about sixty-five with him:

"Professor. Franz. Josef. Eichenbach. A. Very. Learned. Man. In. Many. Disciplines."

Professor Eichenbach clicked badly worn heels, gave a bobbing bow, shook hands, and spoke the flawless English of an academic who has studied and been a visiting professor in the United States.

"Ivy League—like Putzi Hanfstaengl." He smiled.

They went down into the cellar. Hinze switched on a bare-bulb overhead light. Courtney gaped. The painting he had burned in Paris hung against the far unplastered brick wall. There were several wooden crates on the floor. Hinze eased himself down on one, motioned Courtney to another. "We. Must. Hear. A. Long. Lecture."

Eichenbach sat on a third crate, keeping both his audience and the picture in his direct vision line, breathed deeply.

"It was my honor to be director of Meisterwerken—the Masterworks Project. Reichsführer SS Himmler himself appointed me to the post." The professor glanced at Courtney. "You have heard of it?"

Courtney nodded. Everyone in AMGOT had heard of the awesome and long-successful Masterworks Project. The SS had rounded up every forger and counterfeiter in Europe—hundreds of them. They were put to work in a maximum-security compound attached to the Gröss Rosen concentration camp, given generous food rations, allowed wine and liquor and women. They counterfeited engraving plates to print Allied currencies, passports, official forms, forged every conceivable kind of document—and, as Courtney was just learning, evidently works of art as well.

". . . Kirschwasser, the painter"—Eichenbach waved a hand at the picture—"was a genius. A Jew, of course, and that endows a particular irony."

The professor paused.

For what? Dramatic effect? Courtney wondered. To relate how Kirschwasser had been killed? No. No irony there. Every last one of the Gröss Rosen forgers and counterfeiters—Jew and non-Jew alike—had been exterminated in December 1944.

Eichenbach's pause had been to reorganize his thoughts.

"What do you know of the Muslim religion?" he asked Courtney.

"Only a little."

"You understand the nature of the Koran?"

"It's the Bible, the sacred book, of the Muslims."

"It contains Allah's revelations to the Prophet Muhammad, according to believers. But Muhammad was illiterate. According to Muslim tradition, he committed the revelations to memory. Later he repeated them to one of his lieutenants, Zayid ibn Thabit. Again by tradition, Zayid wrote down what he was told on scraps of parchment, smooth stones, and dried palm leaves. The Koran was not actually codified until after Muhammad's death—twenty-five years after. The version was not accurate."

"Rather difficult to judge whether it is or not, I'd say," Courtney remarked. He was unable to imagine where the lecture was leading—and why.

"Patience. Muhammad and his armies fought against the Jews in the Hejaz. During the opening years of the seventh century, he overwhelmed many Jewish settlements. There were learned scribes among the Jews taken prisoner, versed in Arabic as well as their own tongue. It was to them that Muhammad dictated the True Koran, and they wrote it in letters of gold on the finest parchment."

"More tradition?"

"Fact." Franz Josef Eichenbach gave a pedant's smirk. "After it was completed, the True Koran was stolen by a Jew who escaped. He took it to Medina. The Jews intended to hold it hostage for the release of other prisoners held by Muhammad. Their messengers failed to reach the Prophet. The captives were buried alive in the desert. The Jews kept the True Koran, the holiest of all Muslim writings. Muhammad dared not admit its loss to his followers."

"You're sure this isn't a variation on the Holy Grail legend?"

"Absolutely certain." Eichenbach winked at Hinze. "The parchments were passed on by generations of Jews and finally hidden in Jerusalem at the end of the nineteenth century. Then, in 1939, a rabbi in Berlin was given a routine interrogation by the Gestapo. When the questioning grew strenuous, he broke apart and began to rave and babble. Fortunately, his ravings were transcribed and later read by experts in the Jewish Affairs Section. Much was senseless, but the late—oh, yes, by then he was dead—rabbi gave away the secret of the True Koran."

The professor clapped his hands.

"Imagine, if you can, what this meant! Whoever recovered

the original Koran—pure, free of the errors and changes that had been made in the other early versions—and returned it to its rightful owners would gain undying gratitude and loyalty from the Muslim world."

"Himmler. Sent. Agents. To. Jerusalem," Artur Hinze interjected.

"They searched for the True Koran and found it concealed in the wall of a synagogue at the end of 1943—too late," Eichenback said and, lapsing into German, dolefully recited lines from *Carmina Burana*: *"O Fortuna, wie der Mond, so veränderlich, wächst du immer oder schwindest."* Fortune, ever-changing like the moon, rises and declines. "Germany was no longer everywhere triumphant. British control over Palestine was absolute. Our agents were betrayed by Arabs they had trusted. One of them, disguised as a bedouin, went into the desertland of the Sinai. He hid the parchments in a cave on a hillside and returned to Jerusalem."

"Then the True Koran is lost again?"

"Only hidden. Our agent made a very good map. But all papers leaving Palestine by whatever means, even if carried in a man's pocket, were being examined microscopically by the British, and he did not have photographic equipment. He hit on the idea of having the map copied on a large canvas, then painted over with a picture. The British were unlikely to suspect that anything so large and obvious could be other than what it appeared."

"That Velázquez hides the map," Courtney said.

"Wait. The map was copied on canvas. A select group of *mujtahidun*—religious spokesmen for the fundamentalist Shi'ite sect—who had remained loyal friends of the Third Reich pressed their inked thumbprints on the canvas. This was so the map would be recognized as authentic in the future, when a new search for the True Koran could be made. The original map was, of course, destroyed. Then an American artist daubed a landscape over the canvas. Our agent, using a Turkish passport, eventually made his way back to Germany with the picture."

No landscape that, Courtney mused, staring at the painting.

"The picture came to me at Gröss Rosen in September 1944. By then most of us knew Germany could not win. However, there would be another time—and there will be. The map had to be preserved for then, to be used when the German people had risen from defeat and would not repeat the mistakes that caused them to lose. The picture had to be transformed into one so valuable its owner could have it guarded constantly without arousing questions."

The professor stood up, went close to the Velázquez.

"My Masterworks Project experts removed the landscape, leaving what lay below intact. The canvas exactly matched the dimensions of *Horse and Rider*, which was in the possession of Baron Maximillian von Ostertag. It was purchased—von Ostertag was convinced that he should sell. Then the Jew, Kirschwasser, duplicating Velázquez's pigments, style, brushwork, everything, painted this flawless reproduction."

"What did I buy—and burn—in Paris?"

"The genuine von Ostertag. It was taken to the Regnier gallery last month by the person whose name appeared on von Ostertag's bill of sale. The person had all the baron's documents relating to the picture and pleaded poverty because of losses suffered in the defeat. He asked only fifty thousand dollars, and that the gallery wait thirty days before selling it, to give him an opportunity to obtain money and buy it back. The day before you arrived in Paris, he telephoned Regnier and said he would be unable to redeem *Horse and Rider*."

"Complicated but damned clever." Courtney laughed. "From now on, that's the genuine Velázquez, supported by reams of documents, and can travel anywhere as such. With me, I suppose. I'm the buyer of record."

"Exactly," Hinze said.

Courtney looked dubious. "Some of this doesn't add. You must have had the finest photo equipment at Gröss Rosen, Professor. Even a Leica shot would have produced a perfect copy and saved everyone a hell of a lot of trouble."

"You fail to understand. *Any* copy would be worthless. Arabs have literal minds. Literal and narrow. The map *on canvas* is already a legend among the Shi'ites. They speak of it as an almost sacred object that has been lost and will one day be recovered and lead the faithful to the True Koran. They must see it and the original thumbprints of their *mujtahidun* or they will not give aid in the search."

"Who needs them? We have the map."

Eichenbach made clucking sounds, launched out on an explanation. The German agent who hid the parchments had believed the fortunes of war might reverse and the Nazis would again take the offensive on all fronts. Then someone would be sent from Germany to retrieve the True Koran. It was to be given to the Nazi-lining Grand Mufti of Jerusalem, who would call all Muslims to wage Holy War against the Allies in the Middle East. In the meantime, the Holiest of Holy Books would require an added measure of protection. He kept the precise site of the cave secret from the Shi'ites, but told them of the general five-hundred-square-mile area in which it was located.

"Tribesmen of the region have sworn blood oaths to kill any strangers who intrude unless they have the very map their *mujtahidun* saw drawn in Jerusalem."

"Okay, it does add," Courtney conceded. "In an irrational way."

"The Muslim is like the Jew. He lives by his religion. When has religion ever been rational?"

"Never." Courtney chuckled, remembering Reverend Wendell Courtney's lunatic "Soul-Search Center" and the fools who made up its congregation. The chuckle expanded into a laugh. At Wendell, the pretended uncle who was his father and grew rich by mulcting his gullible followers. Wendell had cheated him of his inheritance. That he was already many times wealthier than Wendell had seemed a most satisfying form of revenge. The laughter subsided, stopped entirely. "Go on—there must be more."

"There is." Eichenbach nodded. "The map and True Koran have no practical value at present. The Allies are strong. The Muslim countries are weak, divided among themselves—they will pass through another *ayyam al-'Arab*, a long period of internecine struggles. We must wait until the time is ripe for them to unite and wage *jihad*."

It was early 1948. The first of the Dead Sea Scrolls had been discovered near Qumran in Jordan some months before. They contained Hebrew religious writings that predated accepted versions of the Old Testament and were, Jim Courtney reminded the two men, creating a furor among Christian and Jewish theologians alike. If the Dead Sea Scrolls could cause so much controversy, the True Koran would inflame Muslim fanatics whether they were ready to make war or not.

". . . we could create turmoil . . ."

"No more than wind from Arab *arschloehers*," Eichenbach dismissed the argument. "And for what purpose? To blow up clouds of sand? Later, when the times and world conditions are right, the word of the Prophet, written in gold, will inspire Holy War against all infidels throughout the Middle East and North Africa and much of Asia. And those who restored the Holy Book to its rightful owners will reign as the *kafir*—infidel—kings over the Muslim rulers who emerge victorious."

"May have a damned long wait," Courtney said.

"Worth. It," Hinze declared. "Control. Over. The. Arabs. Means. Control. Over. Their. Oil."

"Yes, it's worth it," Courtney agreed. He stood up, stretched. "In the meantime, I'm left with the picture. How do I explain suddenly deciding to buy a masterpiece?"

"You. Like. Fine. Art?"

"Of course, always did, but never had occasion to buy any before."

"You must become a collector," Eichenbach chimed in enthusiastically. "There is much art for sale in Europe now, and very cheap. The value will multiply. You will make large profits on investments in art."

And pole vault myself up into cultured-rich circles, Courtney mused. What could possibly add more polish to my image? He stroked the scar on his cheek, said: "I'll have to start living in style somewhere." He had been giving the matter considerable thought for months. Return to the United States was out. If he were there, people might probe, pry, dig back into his history. Besides, he would be dealing in huge sums of money; the Internal Revenue Service would want to know their source. He had decided to remain on the Continent as an expatriate, but, as he was saying: "Not here in Germany, not in England or France either. Switzerland is a maybe." Numerous Americans were finding haven there, actor Charlie Chaplin for one . . .

"Spain," Hinze said. "We. Have. Friends. There."

"Could be," Courtney said.

It was.

James Philip Courtney established residence in Spain. At first in a stately Madrid town house (the Cabo Verde estate would come later). The Velázquez *Horse and Rider* hung in his bedroom, greatly admired and envied by all who saw it. As were the other excellent paintings he began acquiring rapidly. A Tintoretto, a Giotto, two Vandykes, the Frans Hals *Portrait of a Chess Player*.

Courtney Ventures International was organized, initially incorporated in Liechtenstein. Observers in European financial capitals were astounded by the scope of its operations and its success. CVI entered the marketplace to buy entire companies rather than goods and products. Purchases were made outright, with cash—and, in some instances, with bearer bonds presented as cash and, because they had matured and become payable during the war years, accepted as such. Then there were whispers of CVI subsidiaries buying stockpiles of surplus arms, other subsidiaries selling them to newly independent African and Asian countries, to rebels and revolutionaries.

Although there was no evidence to support the rumors, some characterized James Courtney as a mystery man—possibly, they said, even a latter-day Basil Zaharoff, arms dealer and merchant of death. The theories were short-lived, made to look ridiculous as CVI branched out into entirely legitimate and visible fields—mining, manufacture, property development, import-export.

A new theory emerged to explain the successes of James Courtney and CVI. Although Hitler was dead and, with him, the Third Reich, anti-Semitism continued to flourish in Europe and the United States. There were those who recalled Courtney's record in aiding Jewish displaced persons, the press ballyhoo of the Jewish DP's who had formed the association of the Pflegebrüders, and the B'nai B'rith award.

Courtney, his jealous detractors claimed, had sucked up to the Jews and won support and backing from the international Jewish industrial-commerical-banking cabals. As his fame and reputed wealth grew, there was a period—until the writers tired of their efforts—when he received considerable quantities of hate-mail . . .

30

". . . not only letters," Jim Courtney was telling David Lippmann over dinner. "Soon after I started building Montemar in 1951, some *anti-semiten*"—he used the Yiddish expression—"rag in Louisiana devoted an entire issue to me. 'Courtney the Kike-Sucker' was one of the more delicate descriptive phrases . . ."

Lippmann squirmed. Another dinner, another monologue on Courtney's friendship for Jews and its consequences, good and bad, had gone on for over an hour. Through tempting food courses—among them crisply roasted duck, normally David's great weakness—at which he only picked. Out of boredom, embarrassment, and puzzlement, in equal measure. Lippmann was proud of being Jewish, period. He was neither religious nor obsessed with being Jewish, as Courtney appeared to believe he was. He could not comprehend why the billionaire persisted in delivering the harangues. And despite Sybil Pearson's warnings to the contrary, he wished that the conversation would somehow veer to the subject of the catalog of the Courtney collection, so he could nudge it toward a discussion of the Velázquez.

". . . my attorneys urged me to sue. I refused. Can you guess why?"

Grenville stepped beside Lippmann's chair to pour fresh coffee. Grenville had been wearing the half-amused, half-contemptuous smile permanently etched all evening, David thought, and replied:

"Lawsuits only generate more bad publicity."

"That wasn't the reason, Dave. A libel and defamation action would have dignified—confirmed—the filth. It would have said that I *did* feel libeled and defamed because a hate sheet said I was a friend of the Jewish people. Do you follow?"

"Yes." Lippmann raised his coffee cup, pretended it was slipping from his fingers, and made a show of securing it to avoid saying anything more.

"Oh. I'm told you're taking a great deal of interest in *Horse and Rider*."

That came out of the blue, and the cup really did almost slip from David's fingers. Who had told? he thought. Not Sybil. Grenville had moved outside the circle of light given by the candelabrum, stood . . . Smirking? Naturally, it had been Grenville. What the hell. It makes no difference. At least we're off Jews and onto what I want to talk about. "Frankly, I'm fascinated by the whole mystery."

"Mystery?"

"The documentation was textbook perfect. Not one picture in a thousand is as thoroughly authenticated. Yet . . ."

"Yet it was a forgery. Declared so by the final authorities on Velázquez."

"That's my point, Mr. Courtney. They must have found glaring proof to negate what experts said about the picture for centuries. I'm fascinated to know what—I'd love to see their reports."

"Must remember to let you read them one day soon." Courtney's mildly quizzical expression hardened. His eyes turned colorless, skewered David. "By the way, I went over your résumé again this afternoon—idle curiosity—and noticed that you've been to Israel."

Back on his one-track Jewish monologue. Lippmann groaned inwardly, said: "Twice. A week on a package tour in 1978. The next year I received a grant to make a quick-skim study of ancient art there and stayed four months."

"The grant was from the Israeli government?"

"There was an exchange program going. Wyler College made a reciprocal grant to an Israeli art instructor."

"But *your* expenses were paid by the Israelis?"

"By their Ministry of Education."

And there, conversation suddenly sank without trace. "Sorry I have to cut this so short, Dave," Courtney said. It was only 9:20; they had been at the table barely an hour. "I still have some work to do this evening."

Lippmann took his leave. Courtney remained alone with Grenville in the small dining room. He stared, frowning, at the chair David had vacated. "You have a good nose, Grenville," he said. "No normal Jew can show so little reaction to talk about Jews and anti-Semitism. It's not in their nature unless they've been trained, and he has been. Familiar pattern. American Yid makes a short trip to Israel and he's contacted and recruited. He returns for a longer period on some seemingly legitimate pretext and is taken in hand by Mossad or Shinbet. Mossad, most likely. Its Section Aleph often operates its agent training behind a Ministry of Education cover."

Courtney flung his napkin on the table.

"They planted Lippmann on me! God, what incredible planning and maneuvering it must have taken." Courtney was musing aloud, assembling thoughts in order. "Understandable, though. Once the Shi'ites have the map, *jihad* wipes Israel off the face of the earth."

He looked sideways at Grenville, who stood at his right.

"Mossad or Shinbet must have learned about the painting long before Lippmann first went to Israel—how they did is a moot question for the present. My ties with Wyler College are widely known. They pinpointed and recruited a Jew-boy on its staff, ran him through indoctrination and training courses. They told him to remain ready. Eventually a means would be found to insinuate him into Montemar. I unwittingly provided the means by asking Wyler to send me someone to catalog my collection." He paused, scowling. Grenville asked:

"Wasn't he chosen by the faculty and board of Wyler?"

"On the face of it. I can imagine the Jew manipulations that went on behind the scenes. Cohens or Rappaports offering endowments if their favorite candidate won the assignment."

Grenville smirked. "How long will he be staying on with us, sir?"

"In a day or so, I'll ask him to drive into Málaga on an errand for me. The fatal accident rate on the Carretera de Cádiz is appalling. Hold my chair, please, Grenville."

Instead of going upstairs to his bedroom suite, James Courtney went to his study, locked himself in, and sat down at the Bureau

Plat. He had concealed his nervousness and apprehension at dinner, even from Grenville. Now he could let them show.

His repeated telephone calls to Heinrich Kloster had been fruitless. Kloster, who was remaining in his office, claimed to be moving heaven and earth to obtain information, but had failed utterly. He had promised to phone at 9:30, but—it was 9:35—had failed to do even that.

Courtney lifted his telephone, stabbed at keys. Kloster answered on the second ring. Fear approaching terror was evident in his tone; not even the Vocoder could mask it.

"I . . . I have wanted to call, but—"

"You didn't have the guts. Talk!"

Kloster, voice quavering, stammered out what he had finally managed to learn. There was no trace of Neil Harkness, and he had not been in touch with Kloster. There was a bizarre coincidence. One man had been shot to death, another critically injured at the Lutetia Hotel in Paris.

"Jews? Agents of Mossad?" Courtney demanded, part of his mind still on David Lippmann.

"Perhaps." The banker's voice sounded almost relieved. Why? Courtney wondered, listened further. "It would explain why the Paris police refuse to identify them even to my representatives there."

"What of the people who were to take delivery?"

Kloster seemed to be regaining his composure. "They arrived at the hotel to find it filled with police," he said evenly. "They decided it was wiser to leave, but not without informing Harkness, and used the house telephone to call his room. They were told he and his friend had paid their bill and left."

"Friend? You didn't mention any friend before!"

"He was alone when I saw him here in Zurich."

"Then the son of a bitch must have picked up a woman."

"No, no. He registered with a man. My people obtained his name. An American. A Kenneth Dixon." Kloster cleared his throat. "Could he be the novelist who also lives near you in Spain?"

Courtney gaped, momentarily speechless, heard Heinrich Kloster laugh lewdly.

"They were made to leave," Kloster chortled. "It was the scandal of the hotel staff. The police found them in one bed together and soaking with each other's semen!" The chortle became a titter. "This Dixon I do not know, but I have seen Harkness. Who would believe that such a great bull of a man is a *fegeleh*?"

Courtney found his voice, but only just. "Stay there. I'll want to talk later." He disconnected, slumped back in his chair, brain in a state verging on chaos. Events were taking place beyond his control, and defied understanding. Although they were not in themselves critical threats—his apparatus was constructed to be flexible, to absorb many heavy shocks—they were occurring at great speed, one on the heels of another, yet forming no discernible pattern.

Where were Harkness and the painting, and what was Kenneth Dixon doing with him? Courtney took that as the first of the puzzles to try to solve. He knew the two men were friends, but that they had a homosexual relationship? He attacked that aspect mentally, for he thought it might provide a key—and leads to their whereabouts.

No, he would not have suspected it of Neil Harkness.

Courtney sat upright, uncapped his pen, drew a lined memo pad toward him, started to draw geometric figures, as he always did when wishing to achieve total, analytical concentration. The first figure he drew was a circle, a zero—it represented Ken Dixon, a nothing.

Courtney remembered discovering that Dixon was a has-been. A permanently psychologically blocked writer who lived on past glories and whatever publishers would pay for use of his previously established name so that facile hacks might continue to churn out what the public believed were more Kenneth Dixon blockbuster novels. Amused, he had further investigations made quietly. They revealed that Dixon, like many other writers who lose their creative abilities, had also become sexually impotent.

Courtney kept the sum of his knowledge to himself, certain it would someday be useful, have a practical value, as such knowledge always does.

He drew a narrow oval. Not a zero. A shorthand female sex symbol, the representation of a vagina. Vivian. Vivian Blascombe, when he met her. Fingers that trembled slightly raised pen from paper. He had wanted her, taken her, shaped and molded her, Courtney reflected. She grew more beautiful, more desirable, and more submissive as the weeks and months passed, a source of limitless pleasure. Then she had told him she was pregnant and intended to have the baby. The fingers holding the pen trembled more noticeably. He could hear her voice saying across the years:

"I want to have the baby, Jim. I'm not asking you to marry me—in fact, I'd say no if you did."

He offered to fly her to Switzerland, anywhere she wished, for an abortion. She refused the offer. She also refused him:

". . . no, Jim, I'm in my sixth month—only plain and gentle sex. I won't mind at all if you have the way-out kinds with somebody else."

It had been rejection. Quarrels started, grew more violent. She offered to leave. He acted repentant, begged her to stay. She had been in her seventh month when, frustration peaking, he used the syringe, thrusting the needle into her arm while she slept. Then he woke Vivian. She was drugged, wild, insatiable. The next day there were spasms. The fully formed fetus was expelled before a doctor could arrive. It was dead.

The doctor advised a two-week wait before Don Jaime resumed having . . . ah, conjugal relations with the . . . ah, *señora*. Courtney flew off alone on a trip to the Far East, stayed away three weeks. Vivian submitted . . .

". . . like a goddamned clothing-store dummy!" he had raged.

"There's no feeling, no sensation left, Jim. Nothing."

Days and nights of bitter quarrel followed. The last was a horror—for both of them. Vivian, emotionally drained, realizing she could not stay with Courtney longer, went to the room that she had for a time used as her studio. It was where she kept the things she had brought with her when she first came to Montemar. She started to sort through them. Courtney stormed into the room.

"Where the hell . . . ?" he began, stopped. Vivian had some photographs in her hand. They were of her mother. Courtney had never seen them before. He tore the photos away from her.

"Where did you get these?" he demanded.

"They're mine." She reached out. He leaped backward.

"The fuck you say. You stole them from me!"

"You must be insane, Jim. That's my mother. Alexandra Blascombe."

"Lexa, yes—Lexa Shields." Courtney's face went gray. "She pulled the same stunt on me. I paid her to get out and have—"

Vivian screamed. The mysteries surrounding her mother's life, the supposedly dead husband—and her own parentage—were no longer mysteries. Lexa Blascombe had called herself Lexa Shields when she had an affair with James Courtney and became pregnant by him. James Courtney was Vivian's father—and she would have borne his, her own father's, child.

No wonder there was such a powerful attraction between us from the start, Courtney mused. His fingers trembled violently.

Even though she was a whore like her mother. In his mind, he had been victimized by both women.

Courtney's fingers steadied, and he laughed out loud. The rest had been simple. He had not wanted the sexually frigid emotional wreckage of Vivian near him. On the other hand, he dared not let her go too far away. She knew too much about him. Kenneth Dixon was the answer, he had realized.

Threat of exposure made Dixon willing to do whatever he was told. Vivian had been like the walking dead, going in whatever directions she was prodded. They were married. Courtney gave Vivian—he never thought of her as his daughter—two hundred thousand dollars; it was with part of this money that she later started Galerías Vivi. Courtney had been unable to resist a vicious thrust at the couple:

"You're a perfect match—impotent and frigid. Should make for quiet nights."

Dixon had wanted to hit him then, but was restrained by Vivian.

"Stay away from us, Jim," she had said.

That had been slightly more difficult to accomplish, Courtney mused. The area of the Costa del Sol is finite. Expatriate colonies tend to be socially incestuous—and sometimes sexually so. He grinned to himself. There are only so many places where people go and gather. However, they had managed to avoid each other, and Costa hosts and hostesses knew better than to invite Courtney and the Dixons to the same affairs.

Vivian frigid, Courtney thought, and inked in the oval, symbolically sealing her vagina. An unbidden erection formed as he did it. Need a woman, get one tomorrow. He refocused attention on the Ken Dixon zero. Impotent. Or is he? Was he ever? Could it be that he was a closet fag all along? Instead of subsiding, the erection increased. Courtney unconsciously dropped left hand into lap and massaged his hard penis through his trousers. He drew an isosceles triangle, its apex touching the bottom of the zero. Harkness often took Dixon along on fishing trips aboard the *Deirdre*, he mused, and extended the tip of the apex until it thrust up into the circle of the zero. The hand in his lap continued its massaging motions, but he was oblivious of them. But Harkness was having an affair with Sybil Pearson. So? He could be bisexual.

"That's it," Courtney said, left hand moving of its own will back to the tabletop, erection ebbing. They had both decided to come out of the closet—together—but neither of them had enough money to pull up stakes and leave Spain. They could now, with the million dollars Harkness had squeezed. They had undoubtedly planned it like that—and Courtney cursed. Then another thought struck him, and he cursed even more—and loudly. No wonder they had disappeared from the hotel with the picture. They believed it genuine, would try to sell it, and probably succeed. The forgery was so good that some unscrupulous dealer accustomed to handling stolen artworks would buy, give them several hundred thousand dollars, and ask no questions.

Courtney was already putting himself through to Heinrich Kloster.

"I have nothing further, J.P.—"

"Shut up. Listen. You must immediately begin calling the Zurich, Paris, Swiss, and French national police to report a major theft. Damn you, stop spluttering. I consigned a painting to your care last month, the Velázquez *Horse and Rider*—yes, it is what I am saying and what you will say. To your horror, you have just discovered it stolen, but you know the thieves. Neil Harkness and Kenneth Dixon. They are traveling under their own passports—you have the data from Neil's, the Lutetia has a record of Dixon's. Demand an immediate Interpol alarm—they're dangerous—and that watch be kept for them at all airports, railroad stations, and seaports on the Continent."

"They should be under arrest before the night is over."

"Hope that they are, Heinrich."

Courtney returned to his memo pad, drew two juxtaposed equilateral triangles, forming a six-pointed star, the Jewish Mogen David. He was ready to address the problem of Mossad and Shinbet, the Israeli intelligence organizations—with which, he was now certain, it would be necessary to cope. But the previously drawn figures attracted his eye, and then his pen. He went over the filled-in oval with the point, darkening it further, and blood pumped, engorging his penis. He shifted the pen to the circle pierced by the triangle apex, drove the peak up higher into the circle with short vicious strokes, and then hurled the pen across the room. His erection was an agony.

He tore open the central drawer, fumbled, found the hidden photograph that had been taken of Ken and Vivian Dixon years before. He laid it flat on the tabletop. He took a fine lawn handkerchief from a pocket with his left hand, opened his trouser fly with the other, and levered out his rigid penis. Holding the handkerchief wadded over himself, he stared at the photograph. Ejaculation was instantaneous. Courtney was panting as he swiveled his chair and ran the sodden handkerchief through the same documents shredder into which he had once fed the *Horse and Rider* inventory sheet.

31

Vivian, an experienced hostess, knew the fine and subtle art of speeding the pace at which meals are eaten without guests being aware that they are being hurried. It was even easier than usual, for Carlos Lozano and Marisa Alarcón were showing signs that they were more interested in each other than in food or even the Cordoniu NPU Reserva that Juan served with a flourish.

"Carlos wants to go to the Marbella Club. Please come with us, Vivi," Marisa said, not really meaning a word of the invitation.

Carlos added appropriate invitation-and-urging phrases—in English and Spanish—and did not really mean any of them either.

They left, in Carlos' Seat rather than Marisa's Porsche, a major defeat of her earlier headstrong declaration that they would take her car and she would drive.

Vivian stood on the portico and waved an arm as the Seat pulled away from the front of the house. She felt a slight sadness—very slight, but then, how can one feel more over what's been unknown and unfelt for more than eleven years? she asked herself. She went back into the house. Juan and a maid had cleared the table. The dishes were already being washed in the kitchen.

Vivian was relieved to have the evening free. The strain of holding Marisa's attention hour after hour was beginning to tell. She wandered aimlessly through the house, seeing and not seeing, said good night to the servants, and went upstairs and made certain, as she did several times a day, that her husband's den was locked. She noticed that Marisa had left the door to her room wide open, went to close it, paused in the doorway.

Marisa had asked for copies of Ken Dixon's books in American and Spanish editions; she wished to compare the Spanish translations with the English-language originals. Vivian had given her the twenty-odd novels in each edition, more than forty books in all. Marisa had stacked them haphazardly on a bureau top. Vivian entered the room and moved to the bureau to tidy the piles. The English version of *Gusher!*, Ken's first best-seller, lay atop one. The dust jacket had been shellacked. The colors of the jacket illustration—an oil well that had blown out and geysered blazing oil—remained bright, crisp. She picked up the book, turned it over. The photograph of a man she barely recognized was on the back of the jacket. A Kenneth Dixon in his early twenties, the face that had turned saturnine even before she met and married him, wryly amused at the world and at himself.

Vivian had seen the photograph thousands of times, but tonight it struck a chord. Poor Ken. Her eyes misted. She replaced the book, reached for another, *The Golden-Hearted*, which had been published only last year. The illustration on the front of the dust jacket conveyed that the novel dealt with money, power, sex. She turned the book over. No photograph of Ken. Hard-sell blurbs and excerpts from favorable reviews. Although his name was featured prominently, the lack of a photo made it seem as though the man himself had ceased to exist. And he had, in more than one sense, Vivi thought sadly. There was nothing of Kenneth Dixon in the pages of the book, or in more than a dozen of "his" books. The words on them had been written—by whom? The publishers had consistently refused to tell Ken the names of the hacks they hired to ghost-write his later novels and imitate his style, which critics had praised as being brilliant, electrifying, scorching.

Instead of replacing *The Golden-Hearted*, Vivian yielded to an impulse, reached for *Gusher!* again, and took both books to her own bedroom. She closed the door, eased off the sandals she was wearing, and, otherwise fully clothed, lay down on her bed, snugged the books close to her side, stared up at the ceiling.

"We can help each other," Ken had said a millennium ago, and they had both tried. The first year of their enforced—there was no other word for it—marriage had been one of honest and constant effort, each seeking to heal, to resurrect the other mentally and emotionally. Sexual interest would develop naturally later, they both thought—and hoped, for mutual dependence rapidly produced a form of love which gained depth and dimension even without the sex factor.

Vivian began to recover first, taking keen interest in the house and in Ken's life and comforts.

"You're young—no wonder you bounce back fast," he had said, happy for her.

She knew he was living—and maintaining appearances—on money left from earlier years (it was dwindling) and what publishers paid for use of his name (the amounts diminished each year). She believed that an easing of the financial bind would loosen his writer's block, enable him to begin working again.

She gave him half of the two hundred thousand dollars received from Jim Courtney.

"Your share of the bribe," she said. By then they had reached a point where they could joke about it.

She used the other half to buy the town house on Pueblo Cabo Verde's centrally located Plaza José Antonio and convert it into Galerías Vivi. She realized her mistake too late. The gallery's immediate success was a hard blow to her husband's eroded pride and ego. He drank more than before, became subject to wild mood swings, between which he would be reasonable, affectionate, kind, loving. But still their relationship was platonic. Until the day in 1974 when, announcing he would take "another stab" at writing, Ken locked himself into the den. The clatter of the electric typewriter, frequently interrupted by periods of dead silence, could be heard hour after hour.

Vivian had waited up, as though holding a vigil, in the second-floor sitting room. He had burst in on her shortly before dawn, sheets of crumpled typescript clutched in one hand, tears streaming down his haggard face. He was very drunk. She stood up, stepped toward him.

"It's shit . . . I still can't . . ." He was stammering.

"Ken, let me read—"

"No." He flung the papers on the floor and hurled himself at Vivian. She lost her balance. They fell on the carpet together. Ken was on top of her, his hands tearing at her robe. She struggled, terrified. Terror changed to dismay a moment later as she felt a hard pressure against her thigh. Something had, by some miracle, broken through the barrier of his impotence. There was no response within her.

"Please, Ken . . . anything . . . of course, darling, but not like this."

He did not hear. The robe was open. His hands were crushing, mauling her breasts and shoulders. Vivian whimpered in pain. The pain exploded into agony as a thumb and forefinger clamped on her left nipple, twisted viciously. She screamed. His free hand struck the side of her head, then seized her right breast, fingers gouging at the flesh.

He mumbled incoherently. Then his muscles corded and his back arched. He gave a loud soughing cry, gasped for air, and collapsed limp on top of Vivian. She wept, stroked his hair, tried to kiss his face. He rolled away into a fetal position on the carpet and sobbed. Vivian pulled herself to her feet, stood weakly and badly shaken—and then realized that she, too, had experienced a form of release.

It was the beginning, and the pattern soon established itself. Ken's moments of arousal were infrequent, always brought on by extremes of emotional stress, and Vivian submitted—and responded. As she had the afternoon of the May Day party. There had been much publicity about a forthcoming Kenneth Dixon novel—which Ken hadn't even seen yet. He went on a protracted drunk. Friends and acquaintances among Costa expatriates besieged him with questions about the book, and he improvised wildly. Drunk, torn by guilt and anxieties, he had been especially violent that afternoon, but instead of being tranquilized by release, continued drinking during the party and made even wilder statements and rash promises to the guests.

Even promising Gloria Meese to discuss the book at her next club meeting, Vivian remembered. If he had, or simply babbled more to people in the expatriate colonies, he would have finished his reputation and himself. When the novel finally came out, the discrepancies between what he had improvised about the novel and what it actually contained would be apparent to all.

Thank God Neil had to make a trip and was willing to take Ken along, Vivian told herself. Neil Harkness was the one person able to handle Ken, drunk or sober, and keep him out of trouble. There had been only a single call from Ken since they left, Vivi mused—from Yugoslavia, of all improbable places. He had hurriedly said something about going on to Vienna and Zurich and warned her to say nothing to Sybil. Odd, peculiar, Vivi thought. She wondered where Ken might be, what he was doing, and when he would return—but since he was with Neil Harkness, she did not worry.

Vivian picked up the copy of *Gusher!* she had brought from Marisa's room. She decided to read it again. It would bring her closer to a young and furiously creative Kenneth Dixon she had never known.

Horst Thiele was in his five-star Hotel Melià Don Pepe room, also lying shoeless but clothed atop his bed and reading. His book was a copy of the Koran, in Arabic.

Thiele was an atheist. Although he had spent most of his postwar years in Muslim countries, he had not converted to the religion of Islam on the entirely valid grounds that his hosts would have construed it as a hollow gesture. It was far more advantageous to remain formally an unbeliever, yet demonstrate utmost respect and reverence for the tenets of Islam. For years he had been going through the laborious process of memorizing the entire Koran, which has 114 chapters, some of which consist of two hundred or more verses. The chapters are called *surahs* in Arabic. Any who commit them all to memory are given the honorific title of *hafiz* and are highly regarded. Almost no infidels have ever managed the task, but Thiele had made much headway. His ability to quote whole *surahs* from memory was a great asset when dealing with devout Muslims (but only bored such renegades as Rashid el Muein).

Thiele was reading the eleventh *surah*, smiling in amusement at the savagery to be found in all holy books. "Perish the hands of Abu Lahab and perish he!" Thiele skipped a line, went to: "Burned in blazing fire he shall be, and his wife . . ."

He yawned, put the book aside, and was more amused still—at himself. He was wasting time and effort memorizing the accepted version. Soon it would be discarded—burned in blazing fire like Abu Lahab and his wife, no doubt, he thought. And the True Koran will ignite the greatest of all conflagrations and holocausts. With Courtney and el Muein the first to be immolated—figuratively speaking, Thiele corrected himself. They would be expunged, but not by burning.

The fools!

Thiele had bought a copy of the *Frankfurter Zeitung* earlier at a Marbella newsstand. The paper lay on his bedside table. He glanced again at the headlines. They announced that the revolt in Kuwait had grown into full-scale revolution. The Kuwaiti government was crumbling. The ruling Sabah family was poised to flee the country.

Yes, fools!

Thiele was deprecating Courtney and el Muein, not the Kuwaitis and Sabahs. Courtney had planned well, and his plans were bearing fruit, but he had failed to offer Horst Thiele a share in the spoils. Rashid was equally stupid; deciding to oppose Courtney, he had taken Thiele on as a retainer rather than taking him in as a partner. They would be played off against each other. Both would lose because of their incredible stupidity, Thiele mused smugly, savoring the situation that had been created—and served up to him to exploit.

Courtney had placed reliance on Arab Shi'ites, and el Muein had countered accordingly. Horst Thiele had broader vision. He had concluded what was nothing less than a pact of alliance with Iran's Ayatollah Ruhollah Khomeini himself. Khomeini was revered by tens of millions of fanatical and ultrareactionary Muslim fundamentalists. The Ayatollah would announce that he had received the True Koran by divine intervention, and they would believe. When he declared it a sign from Allah to begin *jihad*, they would believe that, too, and rise as one and be joined by all other Muslims to sweep through the entire Middle East and North Africa. All Iranian and Arab oil would become the property of Islam, not of individual countries—with Horst Thiele, rather than James Courtney or Rashid el Muein, in control of oil sales and allocations to non-Muslim countries.

In that position, Thiele—and the men he expected to gather around him—could influence the course of history. He had already influenced it, the former Sturmbannführer gloated. He had elicited a solemn oath that Israel was to be the first attacked, overrun, left a bloody hole in the pages of history. Thus, his own oath, given in 1939 to the Führer himself, would be fulfilled.

Thiele looked at his wristwatch, grimaced impatience. Almost ten, and still no word from Bonn. Heinrich Kloster, the banker who faced both ways, had guaranteed that the arrangements had been made with military precision and there could be no mistakes. Kloster had been in touch with Thiele's agents in Bonn, given them orders. They were to do away with the man who brought the picture to Paris and work swiftly. The painting was to be X-rayed (Shi'ite tribesmen would never dare interfere with emissaries of the Ayatollah, even if they did carry only a copy of the map). Then the picture was to be delivered as Courtney had instructed Kloster. To a PLO representative in Paris and by anonymous messenger. Courtney would be led to believe that Harkness had somehow managed to send the painting on to the PLO man before he was killed.

But Thiele's agents in Bonn should have telephoned the code phrase "*Das Ende vom Lied*" to indicate success no later than seven o'clock. Of course, there may have been unavoidable delays, Thiele thought. Late airplane departures or arrivals. Harkness might have insisted on setting a later time for the meeting.

Thiele took the Koran in his bony, liver-spotted hands again, turned to the second *surah*:

". . . slay them wherever ye find them, and drive them out . . ."

He fervently hoped that the long-lost True Koran would prove to be equally ferocious in its murderous exhortations to the faithful.

The telephone rang a few minutes later. Thiele dropped the Koran, seized the receiver, and scowled when he heard Heinrich Kloster identify himself.

"Watch your words," Thiele warned. There was no scrambler in the hotel room. They would have to speak in the clear, but they were both masters of two-tiered telephone conversations.

"I regret that the athletes from Bonn failed in the competition."

The connection was poor. Thiele missed the stress in Kloster's voice. "Perhaps there can be another match tomorrow."

"The athletes were permanently disqualified."

Now Thiele understood. "What of the other team?"

"Its members have gone from Paris." Kloster paused. "With the trophy. However—"

"Get on with it!"

"I have reported the trophy stolen. Every police force in Europe has been notified. The thieves cannot go far."

No, they could not, Thiele thought. Not with a leading Swiss banker spurring the police in their search. He said:

"If you made the report, it is you who will be notified when they are apprehended."

"Yes."

"Then you must have someone reclaim the trophy and take it to Bonn."

"A roentgen examination can be made almost anywhere."

"It is to be taken to Bonn."

"But C. expects—"

"He will soon cease to exist as a factor."

"What?" Heinrich Kloster screeched.

No wonder he screeches, Thiele mused. Now he knows what he did not even dream before, and will have to scramble to salvage some profit for himself.

". . . not in our original agreement," Kloster, close to panic, was babbling. "Your people were to have the . . . the trophy for only an hour or two. I cannot permit them to take it—"

"Kloster!" It cracked out like a parade-ground "*Achtung!*" and there was instant silence at the Zurich end of the line. "Do you also wish to cease being a factor? Do as I've told you!"

Old reflexes die hard: "*Ja wohl, Herr Sturmbannführer!*" Kloster wheezed.

Thiele was satisfied and replaced the receiver. Hunch told him the painting would be recovered and all would be well.

Carlos Lozano flicked on his turn signal, slowed for the turnoff to the grounds of the Marbella Club.

"*Dar un rodeo,*" Marisa Alarcón said, reaching across and neutralizing the turn indicator.

"*Dicho y hecho*—no sooner said than done." Carlos shifted into second gear. "We shall detour. But where?"

Sexual tension, palpable since they left Broadmoor, intensified as she replied: "I want to see Urbanización Las Palmas." It was the name of the large Cabo Verde apartment complex where Carlos lived. Marisa had obviously cast herself in the role of Modern Spanish Girl playing the aggressor. But Carlos had to be absolutely certain for a hundred and one reasons ranging from the press of centuries-long tradition to the fact that she was Vivian Dixon's house guest and, apparently, her friend.

"Urbanización Las Palmas," he repeated, and glanced at Marisa. Oncoming headlights added a luminous quality to her dark Spanish beauty. "It is where I have my apartment."

"Yes. You mentioned it during dinner." They had been using the second-person familiar *tú* all evening. "And Vivi told me you live there alone." She erased the last wisps of doubt, and certainly made Carlos feel elated—and playful. He pretended surprise and puzzlement.

"Strange that she said nothing about my family."

Marisa gave a disappointed start. Could she have heard wrong, or had Vivian deliberately misled her? Worse, Marisa Alarcón, despite modernity and liberation, was still a prisoner of prejudices ingrained over countless generations. She suddenly visualized a typical Spanish middle-middle-class family. A plump mother bustling about serving coffee and *pasteles* and making a sharply critical assessment of her as potential daughter-in-law material. A father—a shopkeeper, perhaps—overwhelming her with clumsy gallantries. Assorted brothers and sisters . . .

"Your family?" She managed to keep her voice even. "There are many people in it?"

"Only two. Max and Solange."

"They are not Spanish names," Marisa blurted inanely.

"Because they are not Spanish. Max is German—*pues bien,* Alsatian. Solange is Asian. Siamese."

Comprehension dawned, and Marisa laughed—more with relief than amusement. Then, lips parting, head uptilted, she leaned close to Carlos. He braked the car, pulled off onto the shoulder of the road, tapped the stick into neutral. The engine idled quietly as their mouths met and locked. Tongues probed, and they embraced, hands exploring. The nipples of Marisa's braless breasts were sharp points that Carlos could feel pressing into his chest, even through the fabric of his shirt.

A heavy truck came from behind, lumbered by. Its headlights sharply silhouetted the two figures that were as one, and the driver blatted his horn in what might have been a cheer or a jeer. The figures moved apart. Carlos shifted into gear and eased the Seat onto the highway in the wake of the truck.

Carlos' condominium apartment was on the fifth floor of a

tower in the Las Palmas complex located at the eastern edge of the Cabo Verde Pueblo. There were three rooms, spacious enough, all with a clear view of the Mediterranean and furnished in good, subdued-masculine taste. It was anything but the stridently macho-male bachelor pad Marisa expected. And Marisa, despite impatience to have their lovemaking begin, realized there was an engaging charm to the *ambiente* and took the time to look around her and enjoy it.

Max, a big and fierce-fanged German shepherd, greeted his master delightedly, then planted himself on his haunches in front of Marisa. He studied her intently, critically for a few seconds. Obviously she met his criteria, for the dog stood up, tail wagging, and licked her hand. Solange, a matriarchal Siamese, rubbed herself against Carlos' leg, purred, then glared malevolent female feline jealousy at Marisa and vanished under a low-slung denim-covered sofa.

Marisa stroked Max's head and neck; the dog seemed ready to swoon with rapture. She looked around her at the paintings on the living-room walls. They were contemporary works by Spanish artists, and while by no means priceless masterpieces, of excellent quality. One wall was almost entirely covered with simply framed sketches and drawings. They were exceptionally good, but unsigned.

"Whose are those?" she asked.

"Vivi's," Carlos replied. The note that crept into his tone and the expression that came over his face spoke entire libraries of volumes, and Marisa read them all at a glance. They reaffirmed what she had intuitively sensed when they first met on the beach at Broadmoor. He was in love with Vivian Dixon.

Marisa felt no twinges of jealousy or resentment. Indeed, it eased her mind. She wanted Carlos, yes—wanted to have a sexual adventure with him. That and nothing more. No prolonged affair, least of all any degree of emotional involvement. And the apartment, its surprisingly warm and homey atmosphere, the affectionate Alsatian, cranky vanishing cat—and Carlos himself—had already begun to stir feelings that Marisa was determined should remain unstirred and unfelt. The clear reminder of his total emotional absorption in Vivian brought everything back into proper focus. Two dimensions only. Length measured by degree of pleasure obtained; the breadth no greater than that of a one-night liaison; no depth, emotional or cerebral, that might entangle, enmesh, trap.

"Would you like to have a drink?" Carlos asked, switching to English. "Or some music?" he nodded toward his stereo.

She laughed, also spoke in English, her tone taunting. "Is that a conditioned reflex, Carlos? Have you had so many foreign women that you can't get on with it in Spanish any longer?" Marisa thought she knew the real answer. He had been reminded of Vivian Dixon, and although Vivian spoke flawless Spanish, she and Carlos usually conversed in English. It was reassuring in a way, Marisa reflected. Carlos would have sex with her while in his mind making love to Vivian. Good, very good, she thought. That would make it all the more exciting and satisfying for them both.

The line of thought was cut short abruptly as Carlos, his smile knowing, spoke, replying to her jibes, and in the process, displaying remarkable keenness of insight.

"Foreign women don't want sex in their own language. When in Spain, they want it in Spanish—whether they understand it or not." He moved across the room toward her. "It's an exotic turn-on for them." He stopped a pace or two away from Marisa and held her eyes with his.

"And you don't want sex in Spanish. It makes you think of too many things. Of when you were a child. Maybe even of when you still went to confession and studied your *catecismo*."

Marisa flinched inwardly at the truth in what he said. Whenever she had been to bed with a Spanish male, unbidden mental images of herself in First Communion dress and fragmented lines of the rosary whirled through her brain. But only when she was with a Spanish lover. She had never given the phenomenon much thought before, but saw it now for what it was—guilt feelings created by a centuries-old heritage.

Carlos took another step, put his hands on her shoulders, kneaded them gently. His look mesmerized her—an improbable blend of understanding sympathy and raw carnal desire.

"Other languages don't bring you such memories," he went on, "and I think French is not right for you—too flowery. No, you are one who prefers English in bed. It is for sex. There are so many words . . ."

Marisa had seldom been with a man who could see through her. The effect was overpowering. She flung herself into his arms.

He led her into the bedroom. He began to undress her.

Her breasts were as lovely as any he had ever seen. He had never seen Vivian Dixon's bare breasts. Even so, he knew them to be the most beautiful of all. He held the image—it increased his desire for Marisa even further as they lowered themselves to the bed.

Carlos was an experienced—many women had said magnificent—lover who knew that sexual pleasure increases in ratio to that given. He would have given pleasure on any night to any partner. But this was a very special night with a very special partner—and not merely because Marisa was beautiful, desirable, and avid. He had met her through Vivi. She was staying at Vivi's home. Scarcely more than an hour before, he had been sitting at the dinner table with Vivi and Marisa. He was as close as he would ever be to realizing the impossible, Carlos told himself, and, fantasy seeming to take on the substance of reality, he made love to Marisa Alarcón as though making love to Vivian Dixon.

He brought her to orgasms such as she had never experienced—again and again. Her moans of pleasure rose to loud cries, then—as he continued—subsided to whimpers of ecstasy. And when they reached simultaneous orgasms, he did not—could not—stop. Marisa did not notice that visions of herself in white Communion dress failed to materialize as she neared the peaks and that her mind failed to form disjointed phrases from the rosary. Nor was she aware of the words she gasped or cried out when reaching climaxes. They were jumbled, disjointed—and Spanish words. Addressed to Jesus Christ, to God, to Mary, holy and immaculate.

It was after four in the morning, and they lay side by side, sated. Sated but basking in the kind of afterglow that transmutes physical exhaustion into languor and enables thoughts to evade conscious barriers and be voiced.

"Carlos," Marisa murmured. Her hand found his, held it. "I have been with many other men."

"And I with many other women," he said, hand not tightening on hers, and waited warily.

"When I was with a man, I could always remember the others who were good. I can't now."

Carlos remained silent.

"It was never like this for me before." She turned her head, gazed at his profile.

Carlos knew she wanted to hear him say, "Not for me, either," and although in one sense it would be true, in all others it would be a lie. Marisa had been largely a surrogate. He sensed it would not require much for her to wrongly interpret whatever he said, imagine herself infatuated. Best to reestablish the rules and limits, he thought, saying:

"We're lucky. We both know how to fuck." He spoke in English, his tone good-natured, and finally gave her hand a squeeze; it, too, was good-natured, conveying nothing more than a pleased and satisfied casual lover would.

Unwanted feelings had been stirring inside Marisa again, much more strongly than they had earlier—almost as though they were no longer unwanted. She bit hard at her lower lip, forcing them to retreat, bury themselves once more in some remote corner of her brain. They refused to remain there, reemerging as she moved her body closer to Carlos—who had drifted off to sleep—and stared up at the ceiling.

Leslie Grenville had managed to maintain his usual unflappable facade since speaking to Rashid el Muein and being told that he was chopped from the Arab's bribe rolls. Behind the facade, Grenville had been making agonizing reappraisals.

He was a mercenary at heart, and the dividing line between mercenary and double agent is often invisible. Especially for one embittered by loss of manhood who sees risks and dangers as the sole compensations to help fill the void. Not that selling his services to Rashid el Muein had been all that risky and dangerous, at least at the start.

James Courtney's megalomania was, in itself, protection. He believed himself to be supreme on the Costa del Sol. Rashid el Muein's estate was but miles from Montemar. Courtney was unable to conceive that any adversary, no matter how formidable, would dare direct a counteroffensive against him from what was virtually next door. He had not even taken el Muein into account.

Rashid's initial requests of Grenville had been modest, and he paid generously in advance, promised to be yet more generous in the future. He wanted only information on the Velázquez—when, where and by whom it was to be taken from Montemar. Grenville obtained these details, passed them on, was liberally rewarded. Once in, he had been willing to go deeper, as much for the excitement derived from double-dealing as for the money he was paid.

Then he had seen the helicopter and recognized its pilot, a former comrade-in-mercenary-arms with whom he had fought in Angola, Kyle Dunne. A total psychopath, Dunne had specialized in helicopter strafings of native villages in Africa, and then gone off to join the almost legendary Gruppe Thiele, a shadowy organization made up of aging former Nazis, younger neo-Nazis, and hired guns like Kyle Dunne. Gruppe Thiele had liaison offices and subheadquarters in many European cities. These carried out routine acts of extreme-right-wing terrorism. More complex operations were conducted by members of a hundred-man strike force based in Saudi Arabia, where Horst Thiele had lived since fleeing from Germany a week after Adolf Hitler's suicide.

Grenville had immediately deduced what was in the offing. El Muein had retained Gruppe Thiele to assault Montemar and assassinate Courtney. The helicopter had been on a reconnaissance mission, filming grounds and buildings to acquaint the assault force with the terrain, entrances, exits, locations of guard posts. He had thought Rashid would offer him a fortune to remain silent, but the Arab had summarily dismissed him over the telephone, saying—quite rightly—that he dared say nothing to Courtney.

Grenville added up the knowns and the almost-certains. The effort would be made soon. Doubtless in a matter of days—even tomorrow was a distinct possibility. He could not begin to guess what form it would take. If it succeeded, he would have no employer at all, and the chances were at least even that Thiele's men would have orders to remove him, too. If it failed, Courtney would at last trace the source of his troubles to Rashid el Muein and, in the process, learn of Grenville's involvement. Leslie Grenville harbored no illusions; were the latter the outcome, Courtney would have him killed, or if he fled beforehand, have him followed remorselessly and then murdered.

There has to be an answer, an out. Grenville battered at his brains as he paced the floor of his Montemar bedroom. Thus far, he had been able to think of one possibility, and it was extremely risky, but time was running out—his bedside clock read 10:55—and he would have to chance it. He stopped pacing, patted the bulge of the .357 Magnum under his coat, and went to the potted Dieffenbachia plant on his windowsill. The briar pipe was hidden there. He slipped it into his right-hand coat pocket, lifted his telephone, switched through to the private line Courtney kept open when in his study.

"Yes, Grenville?" The line light was color-coded.

"May I see you, sir? It might be important."

"All right." Courtney disconnected, checked his trouser front, glanced at the documents shredder, unlocked the *estudio* door.

Courtney looked oddly haggard, Grenville thought when he entered, took it as an encouraging sign. He might not be too alert.

"Sit . . . what's it about? Lippmann?"

"No. As a matter of fact, it was all that business with Lippmann that made me forget to tell you before." Grenville took a chair, put his right hand on its arm, poised, if necessary, to reach under coat front or into side pocket. "I think—I only think, mind you—that I might have seen Horst Thiele on the street when I was in Cabo Verde."

Courtney half-rose out of his chair. Horst Thiele had been among the earliest Nazi getaways. He had bought his way out by marching the remnants of his SS *panzer* battalion into the hands of the Russians. Thiele had been thoroughly despised by the members of Gemeinschaft Orff. Although he established a respectable power base in Saudi Arabia, even Odessa had refused to have anything to do with him. He was highly regarded in some Middle Eastern quarters, often photographed in the company of Arab dignitaries. But as Artur Hinze had warned a few months before he died in 1969 and turned total control of Gemeinschaft assets and CVI over to Courtney:

"When dealing in the Middle East, beware of Horst Thiele. Avoid him. He is poisonous. More dangerous to us than the Jews."

Courtney glared at Grenville. "You *think* you *might* have seen. Did you or didn't you?"

"Couldn't be certain. We passed a cream-colored Rolls going in the opposite direction. Man in the backseat was seventy or so with a thin, desiccated face and an erect, soldier's bearing even while he sat."

"Why would you notice Horst Thiele?"

"He came to see me in the hospital after Angola. Offered me a slot in his crew."

"Then you should have been able to make positive identification."

"I only saw the man for minutes." Grenville was lying throughout, but making the lies plausible. "I was still under sedation."

Courtney's eyes narrowed to slits. "Let's assume it was Thiele. What significance do you think his being here would have to me?"

Grenville knew he would have to tread with extreme care, but sometimes being bold and assertive is a form of caution in itself.

"Very well, sir. Let's assume. You're currently in the midst of activities in the Middle East. You have enemies there—and elsewhere. I'm surprised *you* didn't take Gruppe Thiele into account long before. Now that I think of it, Thiele would explain the attempt to intercept Harkness and Fischer—and what finally happened to Fischer."

Something clicked in Jim Courtney's brain. "That chopper!"

"Good Lord!" Grenville feigned astonishment. "Never occurred to me. There could be some connection"—he paused—"no, it must have been coincidence. Or we're becoming paranoid." He said the last in a tone that indicated he believed that Courtney was paranoid, and the billionaire exploded.

"Who the fucking hell are you to tell me—?"

"No one, sir." Grenville stood up. "My apologies." He was setting the hook—his safety hook—firmly. "I should never have mentioned—"

"Sit down, sorry." Courtney held spatulate fingertips to his cheek, pinching hard at the old scar. "It may be Thiele, it may not," he mused aloud. "The chopper might be what you say—a coincidence. Still, we should increase security here."

"Shall I ask for cooperation from police, Guardia, or the *gobernador militar?*"

"Christ, no! We can't have any of them looking into my affairs. We'll put our own men on double shifts, starting at midnight. Take care of it."

Grenville stood up again, content. Courtney had swallowed the story whole, reacted as Grenville hoped he would. No suspicion attached to him, and he would be safe.

"Shall I give the men any explanation, sir?"

"Extra pay is all the explanation they'll want." Courtney took a deep breath, exhaled it. "Oh, Grenville. If there is anything to . . . to our paranoia, it'll be more like your old line of work. I'd like you to oversee things."

"Gladly, Mr. Courtney." You'll never know *how* gladly—I hope.

"You'll receive extra pay too, of course," Courtney said in an odd tone.

"That's not necessary, sir."

"Oh, yes, it is, Grenville. Oh, yes, it is."

The tone was odder still, and it sent a chill of doubt through Grenville.

The International Criminal Police Organization—Interpol—has its headquarters in the St. Cloud quarter of Paris. Supposedly it deals evenly with the official police bodies in the 122 countries that are members of the organization. But the secretary general and key officers are Frenchmen, attuned to the nuances of internal French politics. The wine-and-vegetable war between France and Spain was continuing. French vintners and farmers were up in arms over imports of Spanish wine and fresh vegetables. These were available to consumers at prices a third or more below those charged for domestic *vin ordinaire* and farm produce. Politicians responding to the clamor of lobbies had passed the word through bureaucratic mazes—even to St. Cloud—that Spain was to receive less than full and wholehearted cooperation from French government agencies. Or even those that were purportedly international but directed by loyal Frenchmen.

Bureaucratic minds being what they are, the Interpol functionary who crossed Spain off the list of countries to be telexed the wanted-fugitive-criminals notice believed he was striking a blow for the honor and economic well-being of La Belle France. Thus Neil Harkness and Kenneth Dixon were able to disembark at Málaga airport and breeze through the immigration check. They claimed their baggage and went outside the terminal to hire a taxi.

"Too late to have a showdown with Courtney," Neil said. "Anyway, I want to clue Sybil in first. I'll drop off at her place, and you go on home—okay?"

Ken had drunk only one double gin on the flight from Madrid, but his face was alive, glowing. As he had told Harkness repeatedly on the plane, he was eager to go home, felt like a different person, and, as he now said:

"Jesus, with everything that happened, I should be nervous as a pregnant fox in a forest fire, scared shitless. But I'm not. I know everything's going to be okay—better than ever." He stopped, embarrassed. "I've been over that . . ."

"Like often." Neil grinned, lit another Celta. He had bought a carton of his favorite Spanish brand at Barajas, had been chain-smoking ever since. "I believe you."

A taxi drew up in front of them. The driver stowed their bags in the trunk, strapped the skis to the roof rack.

32

Sybil Pearson, wearing shorts and halter, listlessly sipped chilled *rosado* and watched/not-watched an American dubbed-into-Spanish telefilm on the Segundo Programa. The film, something about a bank heist, must have been dull in English, lost considerably more luster in translation. One of the characters was pointing to a gaping hole in a brick wall.

"*Abrieron paso*," he said, rather unnecessarily enlightening police, newly arrived on the scene, that the robbers had "forced their way through."

It was enough to make Sybil turn off the TV set.

The silence of her apartment closed in. Empty silence, she thought, drank the remainder of the wine in her glass. "I'm lonesome," she said aloud to the blank screen. "Bloody lonesome." She turned the set on again, wanting it to make some comment.

". . . *inventó muchas mentiras*." A detective was declaring that "he"—whoever "he" was—"made up a pack of lies."

"He hasn't," Sybil said to the detective, and blanked him out with another flick of the switch. "Wish he had, though," she said, speaking to her empty glass this time. "It'd be better than not hearing anything at all."

She missed Neil, longed for him. "I'm in love with the big ape," she confided to the glass, which she rewarded for listening by refilling it from the ceramic wine jar nested in an ice bucket. She went into the kitchen to finish delayed washing-up of her dinner dishes.

The wineglass was on the drainboard and she was holding a salad plate high to inspect it when a key was thrust into the front-door lock. The salad plate dropped from her hands, breaking as it struck the drainboard and knocked the wineglass to the floor, where it shattered. Neil Harkness had the only other keys to the apartment, and Sybil trampled shards of china and glass under her espadrilles as she ran from the kitchen.

"Hi, honey." He had the door open and was juggling what looked like—what were, Sybil realized—pairs of skis partially wrapped in what at first glance appeared to be old sacking. He dumped the skis on the floor. "Home is the sailor." She wanted to rush into his arms, but he ducked outside into the corridor, brought in an overnight bag, dropped that beside the skis, and closed the door. "Now I can say hello."

He held her close, his kiss as hungry as her own. Sybil had happy visions of being led into her—*our*, really, she thought—bedroom immediately. The visions were shattered. He eased her away from him, patted her bottom.

"Horny as I am, we gotta establish priorities. A long busy night stretches, duchess. Start by running a greedy eye over this while I make myself a drink." He took a pamphlet-sized booklet from his jacket pocket, gave it to her, and strode to the table on which there were bottles and glasses. He scooped bits of ice from the bucket, dropped them into the glass, dumped Scotch in after.

Sybil was thoroughly baffled. He had given her what seemed to be a passbook from some bank in Switzerland. But there were only numbers written into it. The figures 4711/1174 were at the top. Below, in the section showing transactions, there was a date and a single deposit entry: $US 500,000. She was, of course, familiar with numbered Swiss accounts—her employer, James Courtney, had scores of them. But this could not be Neil's.

"What on earth?" was all she could think to say.

Harkness held up one hand while he gulped Scotch, cracked a gargantuan smile. "Getaway money."

Her face fell. It *was* Neil's account—where and how had he made a half-million dollars?—and he would be leaving again. For good.

"Disappointed?" Major surprises in life were made all the better by suspense, even if the suspense was a form of torment.

"It's . . . it's a shock." Sybil had always known she could not expect her relationship with Neil to be permanent. But she had never expected him to announce its end so abruptly and crudely. But Sybil Pearson had been raised in the British stiff-upper-lip tradition. She blinked away the tears forming in her hazel eyes, said: "I'm very happy for you, Neil. Even though I'll miss you—"

"Turning me down?" Harkness said, relenting. "It was a proposition, not a proposal. Still . . ."

She flung herself across the room, held him, jarring the whiskey glass from his hand. She heard the crash, thought: If this goes on, the whole flat will be a mass of broken glass; said: "You rotten bastard," and wept. With joy.

He kissed her cheeks, made a thing of licking at the tears and pushing her away to arm's length, held her there. "Priorities," he said with mock sternness.

"I want to know everything—no, I want to make love first."

"Uh-uh. You always sleep after."

Sybil always did. Harkness sated—drained—her, and she would rest her head on the immense expanse of his shoulder and sleep like a contented child.

"You'll have to stay wide-awake, probably till morning." He released her, went to his overnight bag, opened it. "Take that long for you to read and listen." He fumbled out the thick pack of typescript that was Ken Dixon's research material on James Courtney. "Your boss is a monster, baby—"

"Not *that* again!" Sybil protested. Although Neil frequently did work for Courtney, he had repeatedly urged her to quit her job with him. She could not bring herself to believe any of the things at which Neil had hinted in the past. Instead, she believed that Harkness, as her lover, felt the classic jealousies and feelings of inferiority because she worked for a man of wealth and power.

"Remember the fat Swiss with the tin tube?" Neil asked, holding the pack of typescript out to her. She took it.

"Fischer," she said shortly, not looking at the large bundle of papers bound with metal fasteners.

"We found him dead—strangled—in Venice."

"We?" Sybil had thought Neil was alone.

"Ken Dixon and I found him."

"*Ken* was with you?" Sybil asked in consternation.

"Uh-huh." Neil was undoing the sacking around the skis and spoke over his shoulder. "Nearly had his head blown off along with mine, thanks"—he snorted—"to your favorite folk hero. You'll hear it all tonight." Well, maybe not all, Harkness thought, turning back to the bundle on the floor. I can't tell her that I shot somebody, at least not until we're hell and gone away from here. "Hey, put that stuff down and come over here."

Sybil laid the typescript on the table beside the bottles, crunched two steps across broken glass, saw that what she had thought to be sacking was canvas. Neil was unrolling it, moving the skis diagonally across it to keep it flat.

He laughed. Baggage handlers, travel in aircraft cargo bays and atop the taxi roof rack had wrought more havoc. Fully half of the impasto was gone.

"Don't you recognize it?" he asked. "May look like the portrait of Dorian Gray in the last stages—but it's not. Used to be—"

"*Horse and Rider!*" Sybil exclaimed, dropped to her knees beside Harkness, her eyes wide, disbelieving.

"Never really was," Neil said. Now that so much paint had peeled off, he could see larger segments of the map. He studied them silently for a moment. "Rugged terrain—probably desert of some kind."

"You're talking gibberish."

"Honey. This is what Fischer had in the tube. A goddamn map, with a fake Velázquez painted over it." He slapped a huge hand against what had once been the horse's head. "Fischer got strangled, and Ken and I almost got killed because of this fucking thing."

"Why . . . what kind of map?" Sybil stammered.

"Beats me." Neil stood up, lifted Sybil to her feet, Dutch-rubbed knuckles against her close-cut auburn hair. "Let's brew a gallon of coffee. We're going to have a long session."

He talked, pointed out key portions in Dixon's outline, let Sybil read them, answered those of her questions—dismayed or horrified—for which he had answers. There was still a great deal left to tell at five A.M., but Neil was afraid of causing overload, for Sybil was badly shaken, and, it appeared evident, totally disenchanted with James Courtney.

"I'll quit—I can't stay after this. And you—you meant it? About going away?"

"Sea scout's honor. I'll settle with Courtney today, and we'll leave fast. Pick the *Deirdre* up in Split and go on from there." Neil plucked at a string of her halter. "Still want to make it?"

"Believe it or not, I still do. More than ever."

But when they went to bed, her body began to tremble uncontrollably. Neil understood and held her close, calming her. At last she nested her head on his shoulder but did not sleep.

The Serrania de Ronda is a range of rugged mountains that walls the Costa del Sol off from the main—and inland—portion of Andalusia. There are modern highways through the mountains, and even the most remote of the scattered villages are accessible by good roads. But there are even more remote areas, sere, with volcanic rock and red clay predominating, and they are uninhabited. Some of these forbidding regions lie no more than thirty airline miles from Costa cities and towns, yet they might as well be on the other side of the moon. They can be reached only via rutted dirt tracks that wind and juke insanely through wild and hostile badlands.

If they avoided observation from the air by overflying civilian or military aircraft, hundreds of men could remain hidden for months in the tangled mountains and boulder-strewn valleys. However, it was necessary to conceal only eight men and two Bell helicopters for less than a day. The men were experienced, hardened veterans who could stay comfortable through the night in their Guardia Civil uniforms without building fires or showing light. The choppers, newly and brightly painted, were covered by mottled camouflage nets that made them invisible at ten feet even in broad daylight—and it was dark.

Kyle Dunne ducked under one of the camouflage nets. A Civil Guard flashed a blue penlight on his face, switched it off.

"Want to check your chopper?" the *guardia* asked in English that had a strong Polish accent.

"Going to sleep in it," Dunne replied, patting the pilot's wings emblazoned on his own Spanish Civil Guard uniform. "One of the perks—don't have to lie on the bloody fucking ground."

"When do we go?" the other man asked.

"When we're told—sometime during the siesta." Kyle Dunne chuckled. "When the real *guardia* knocks off for lunch and a kip." He unslung his Uzi submachine gun and put it aboard the copter, clambered up into the pilot's compartment.

Vivian Dixon heard the crunch of automobile tires on the graveled drive that led to the front entrance to the house. She put *Gusher!* down, looked at her bedside clock, saw it was not yet eleven, and uncertain whether to frown or smile, swung off the bed. She assumed the sound meant that Carlos was bringing Marisa back—much, much too early. It must have been either a comedy of errors or a grisly failure, Vivian thought, putting on her sandals. Not wishing the servants to be disturbed, she hurried downstairs.

She opened the door, recognized the car as a taxicab from its regulation blue-and-white paint scheme and the green lights mounted on its roof. Must have been bad if Marisa came home alone in a taxi, she thought, and prepared to be sympathetic. Then a male figure, indistinct in the darkness, came around from the boot with an overnight bag dangling from one hand.

"Ken!" She hurried toward him. "Why didn't you call? I would have come to meet you." She stopped. "I don't even know how you came in."

"By air . . . and hello, sweetheart." Ken paid the driver, who climbed back into his seat, rattled off the requisite *gracias/adiós/buenas noches* lines, spun the wheel, and drove off, his tires spewing crushed gravel into the air.

The warm tenderness of Ken's kiss took Vivian by surprise. It was unlike any kiss he had ever given her.

"Glad to see me?" he asked.

"Very," Vivian said, thinking of Marisa, then, remembering why he had gone, was uncertain. "Should I be?" She lowered her voice. "The book hasn't been officially published yet."

"I don't have to give a shit anymore." They were moving toward the open door. Ken paused, turned, squinted out at the front-of-the-house parking area. "Christ, don't tell me you bought a Porsche!"

"Belongs to a house guest."

"Who?"

"Spanish girl. Marisa Alarcón. One of your admirers."

"Get rid of her."

They entered the house. Vivian closed the door. "Easier said than done. She wrote wanting to do an article about you. The idea must have appealed. You wrote back inviting her to come and stay with us."

"I must have been drunk." Dixon, bag still in hand, was looking around him as though he had never before seen the interior of Broadmoor—and liking what he saw. "She here now?"

"No. Out with Carlos."

"Lozano? A little fuckee-fuckee maybe?" He flung the bag onto a chair, clapped his hands, did a time step on the terrazzo floor.

"Maybe. I hope so, for their sakes." Was Ken drunk now? Vivi wondered. She looked at him closely. No, she realized. He wasn't drunk. He was elated. Why?

Ken stopped tap-dancing, held out his arms to Vivian, began waltzing. She laughed. He released her, grinned. For the first time, she noticed that he was wearing hideously wrinkled cheap slacks and an eyesore ski jacket. She tugged at its bottom edge.

"Where did you find this—in a flea market?"

He ignored her, dug in one of the pockets. Like Neil—even more than Neil—he wanted to show his Swiss bank account, produced the booklet, held it open for Vivian to see.

"We can tell everybody to fuckee-fuckee—themselves. No more asses to lick. Between what you make at Galerías and this in the bank, we don't have to care if anyone knows I'm ghosted."

"Ken—"

"Another dance, lady?" He stepped close to her, not to dance, but to embrace and kiss her. "A lot's happened, Vivi. Maybe I'll be able to write again. Maybe I'll even be able to . . ." His voice broke, went hoarse. "Let's go upstairs. Let's try. Please."

"You don't have to say it like that, Ken. I do love you, you know, and if—"

"I think yes. I feel different." He paused. "What about you?"

"Maybe not at the start." Vivian smiled at him, the smile loving, maternal. "But if you can, I'll be able to one of these days."

His face reddened.

"It could even happen tonight," Vivian said hurriedly, and

thought: I'll pretend I'm enjoying it, pretend an orgasm—anything to help him. "I want to try."

"Your bedroom or mine?"

"You tell me." Let him be the assertive male, make the decisions, Vivi thought. It'll build his confidence—and God, how I hope it's going to work for him.

"Yours, sweetheart."

They went to her bedroom. Ken was understandably hesitant, awkward. His hands fumbled as he undid the zipper fastener of Vivian's dress while they stood in the middle of the bedroom floor. He slipped the dress off her shoulders. His fingers were chill, unsteady. He tried to avert his eyes from her breasts, failed, cupped them in his hands. "Christ, but they're beautiful," he murmured. Then he saw the faint traces of bruises, pulled his hands away. "I'm sorry," he whispered.

"Don't be." Vivian reached for his hands, put them over her breasts again. He held them tenderly. She could feel her nipples rise, offered a silent prayer for herself as well as her husband. Her dress had fallen around her feet. She stepped out of it, kicked off her sandals. She reached for his shirt buttons.

He stepped back. "No. I'll do it myself."

He had trouble removing his clothes, finally succeeded. His erection was only partial, but that was more than it had ever been without violence. Vivian took a step toward him. His penis grew a little more rigid.

Then the unraveling began.

Ken turned toward the bed, noticed the two books, *Gusher!* and *The Golden-Hearted*, on the table beside it.

"What the hell are those doing here?"

"I was reading *Gusher!*"

"And this piece of shit?" He seized the ghost-written *Golden-Hearted,* waved it at her. His erection was slackening.

"The girl—Marisa—wants to ask me questions about it," Vivian said. He could not bear to have her read the ghosted novels. She thought the excuse might placate him. It seemed to. He tossed the book halfway across the room, picked up *Gusher!*, stared at it as though mesmerized. "I was fucking women out of their heads when I wrote this," he said. He turned the book over, gazed at his photograph on the back of the dust jacket. "Write and fuck," he murmured. His penis was hardening once more.

Vivian felt her nipples flatten.

Dixon at last replaced the book on the bedside table. He

stretched himself out on the bed, beckoned to Vivian. ''Sit here—on the edge, facing me.''

She obeyed.

He fondled her breasts. The nipples remained flat. His erection grew. ''How did you like it most back when you did?'' he asked.

Vivian's gray eyes searched for some depth of feeling in his, found none. How did I ''like it most''? she thought, debating what kind of an answer to give him. It's surreal, insane, we've been married eleven years and haven't a clue about each other's sexual likes and dislikes.

''Well?'' Ken moved one hand from her breasts and tugged at a strand of her long coppery hair. ''How?''

''Inside me, I think.''

''That figures. You couldn't have gotten pregnant unless you did. How else?''

The gray eyes shut tightly. It slipped out, he didn't mean it, Vivi told herself. Please, God, don't let it be that he said it on purpose. She was dimly aware that his hand was sliding under her panties, fingers fumbling, one probing.

''You're dry,'' he said, pulling the hand free.

She nodded. ''I think we may have some Vaseline.'' She started to get up. He restrained her.

''Maybe if you think about other guys, fantasize . . .''

''I don't want to, Ken. It wouldn't do any good.''

''Can't tell unless you try. Shrinks say it's what turns women on when nothing else does.''

''They're wrong.'' She leaned toward him, hoping he would touch her breasts gently again, perhaps kiss her—anything.

''Oh, shit. Try. Listen, did you like to have a man go down on you?''

''Yes. Sometimes.'' Vivian knew she would have to give him answers. She wished she could bring what was rapidly becoming an ordeal to an end, but it wouldn't be fair to Ken. Obviously this is what he wanted—or thought he wanted—to regain his potency. His penis was already harder than she had ever seen it. He stared down at himself triumphantly.

''Did you give head, too?''

''Sometimes.''

''Like the feel of a prick in your mouth?''

''Ken, is that what you want me to do?''

''I want to keep talking awhile. Did you go down on Courtney?''

''Please, for God's sake, Ken.''

''*Did* you?'' He seized a handful of her hair.

The gray eyes closed again. It would be like it always was. He was merely using a different means to work up to a sadistic outburst. And I'll respond, because it's all I'm able to respond to—we're a pair of basket cases.

"Yes, I did." Vivian opened her eyes. Might as well hurry the process, she thought, get it over with—and use more cover-up cream to hide the bruises. "He was big on oral sex."

"Big cock?"

"Yes."

"Bigger than mine?" He patted his erect shaft.

"I really can't remember." It was the truth. She had blocked out everything she could about James Courtney. Unfortunately, she had not been able to block everything.

"Get rid of those pants."

She removed them, sat back on the edge of the bed. Would he hit her first or maul her breasts? She waited. He did neither.

"Lie down next to me, Vivi." His voice was suddenly gentle. "On your back, and spread your legs."

Vivian obeyed. He rolled on his side, right hand going to her pubes, fingers probing. "Shit, you're still dry," he muttered, tone no longer gentle and, rising to his knees, straddled her. Vivian flinched, an inner cold racing through her body.

Ken gripped his sex to guide it and thrust. Vivian's legs scissored shut and her vaginal muscles locked against him of their own accord. He forced her legs apart, thrust again. She whimpered. He tried once more, but blood was draining from his organ. His erection collapsed. He looked down at himself, then at Vivian, his face paling, then flushing almost black.

"Ken . . . please, I'm sorry," Vivian whispered. "I couldn't help it. I . . . I'm not ready yet. It's my fault—"

"Fucking right it's your fault. I was fine. I could have."

Then he did hit her, but as he had never struck her before. A clenched fist, swung with all his strength, crashed into the side of Vivian's face, stunning her. Then another blow. It cut open her lower lip, broke a tooth.

"My God . . . don't, Ken!" she begged, forcing herself not to scream because of the servants. She raised her arms to protect herself. He slammed them aside, struck her face again, and he was raving.

". . . did everything with Courtney. Went down on him. Let him get you pregnant. Whore . . . won't make it with me . . ."

The fists were battering. Vivian felt her nose break, blood pour from her nostrils. She had to scream, but another tooth was shattered, and she gagged on it and blood and the vomit that was welling up, and the scream came out as a ghastly gurgle.

He placed a knee on her stomach, placed his full weight on it, clubbed repeatedly at her head and face. The gray eyes were swollen shut, but Vivian was past feeling or knowing, unconscious and barely breathing.

Ken stopped. The fury had run its course. The wreckage of his wife's face came into focus. He saw the blood and saliva and vomit—some of it on his hands—became aware of wetness on his thighs. He got off the bed, stood beside it, examined himself. The head of his flaccid penis was wet, too. He had ejaculated. No wonder he felt calmed, Dixon thought, and went into his own room.

The sense of calm pervaded his being. He showered, scrubbing himself carefully, toweled, and dressed in a crisp white safari suit. There was a wad of peseta notes in his old trousers. He returned to Vivian's room, avoided looking at her, took the money, and went downstairs into the kitchen. There were fresh bottles of Tanqueray gin in a cupboard. He took one, opened it, drank deeply from the bottle, which he recapped and carried with him out on the portico.

He uncapped the bottle, took another drink, prowled the length of the portico, saw the parked Porsche. It gave him an idea. His own cars were garaged at the side of the house. God only knew where the keys were. Maybe, he thought, just maybe . . . He clambered over the ornamental iron railing of the portico, sauntered to the Porsche. He tried the door on the driver's side. Unlocked. He opened it, peered inside. The keys were in the ignition.

"Dumb Spanish cunt," he mumbled. "Lucky for me."

He got into the car, settled himself in the driver's seat. The lingering scent of whatever Marisa Alarcón wore mingled with that of the leather upholstery. Nice combination, he thought, taking another large drink and thrusting the open bottle upright between the bucket seats. Sexy as hell—just like all Spanish women. All sexy as hell, perpetually in heat. That's what I need, and then I'll make it. Really make it. He started the car, reversed, turned the wheels, knocked the stick into low gear, and drove off.

The road distance from Broadmoor to Puerto Cabo Verde was less than ten kilometers, but the Tanqueray bottle was empty when Dixon pulled up on the quay and parked opposite the Bar Espada. He knew the bar well, having drunk there often over the years, alone or with Neil Harkness. The Bar Espada was a favorite haunt for owners of the pleasure boats berthed in the marina and for those who worked aboard the vessels. It was because of the latter that the nighttime crowd always included some Spanish women, on their own, either outright professionals or semipros looking to earn two or three extra pesetas. The women were neither very young nor exceptionally attractive, and their presence was tolerated by Enrique, the owner, and the police because the *extranjeros* demanded it. And it's our money that keeps this goddamned Costa alive, Ken thought as he fought the car door open.

He started across the quay, weaving as he went, almost bumped into a deckhand off one of the yachts. The man avoided collision, smiled, offered a polite excuse—in Spanish.

"Go to hell!" Dixon growled.

The deckhand shrugged. Just another drunken *norteamericano*, he thought, and walked on.

Enrique, the burly mustachioed *patrón* of Bar Espada, recognized Dixon and greeted him warmly—but warily. He had been obviously drinking and there had been times when, *muy borracho*, he had caused disturbances.

Ken ignored the greeting, squeezed between two men seated at the bar, said: "The usual. Big one—*grande*. No ice."

Enrique produced glass and Tanqueray bottle, poured, and quickly moved down the bar. His publican's instincts warned that Dixon was in a foul mood.

"Beg pardon." The man on Ken's left, an English yachtsman by the look of him, shifted position on his bar stool. "It's a bit tight here. Would you mind—?"

"Yeah. I'd mind." Dixon gulped down his gin, rapped knuckles on the bartop to attract Enrique's attention and order another. Enrique came, refilled the glass, moved off once more.

Ken's eyes roved. Had any of his female admirers seen him, they would have said that the eyes were at their most intense and compelling. They fixed on a group of five people sitting at a table in the far corner, laughing. Two men. Three women. All Spanish. He picked up his drink, extricated himself, lurched toward the table.

The men were modestly dressed. More deckhands, Dixon thought. The women looked good. Especially the youngest of the trio—in her mid-twenties and wearing a V-necked blouse that displayed flashes of large, firm olive-skinned breasts as she moved her torso.

There was an empty chair at another table. He dragged it over, sat, leered. "*Buenas* and so on." The group was drinking *sangría* that had been served in a two-liter pitcher. "Cheap crap. I'll buy real drinks. What'll you have?"

The smiles on five faces were frozen. "*Nada*—nothing, *señor*," a man said. "Thank you, and please to leave our table."

"Balls. Public place. I'm staying. Buying, too—if you people tell me what you want."

"Sir. We want that you are to go. *Comprende*?"

"Nope." Ken knocked back his gin, put the empty glass down, and reached into his pocket. He drew out the wad of Spanish money—numerous thousand- and five-thousand-peseta notes—slapped it on the table in front of him. "Said I'm buying." He looked at the girl with the V-cut blouse. "What'll you have, *chiquita*?"

She swung sideways in her chair to avoid looking at him. The movement caused the V neck to yawn open. The two men were pushing their chairs back. Dixon chuckled, stood up. The men assumed he had decided to leave quietly, remained where they were. Ken poked at the money on the table, selected a five-thousand peseta note, leaned across the table, pushed it down the girl's blouse front. She stared, snatched it out, threw it in his face.

The men sprang from their chairs. One grabbed Dixon by the shoulders, whirled him around. The other seized the money and, holding Dixon's jaw open, stuffed it in his mouth. The picture of Orff crumpling after he smashed his head with a bottle flashed through Ken's mind. Shit! He was invincible. He tore himself free, spat out the money, grabbed the *sangría* pitcher. He sloshed the contents at the women, drenching them, and they shrieked. He swung it at the nearest man, who ducked. The other punched at Ken's belly, connected. Dixon doubled over. The first man rabbit-punched him. He slumped to the floor.

The bar was in an uproar. Enrique and a waiter pushed through the gathering crowd. The waiter gathered up what he could see of the money scattered on the floor and, when Enrique lifted Dixon, shoved the bills into his pocket.

Ken shook his head slowly, groaned. "Leggo," he muttered, making a weak attempt to get loose. "Spanish motherfuckers," he mumbled. "Bunch of pimps 'n' whores."

Enrique frog-marched him to the door, pushed him out. Dixon fell sprawling on the pavement. He lay for seconds, finally dragged himself to his feet, stood swaying. The Bar Espada entrance door slammed shut.

Harkness, Ken thought. They were a team. He'd go find Neil. They'd come back together and take the place apart. "I'll get the whore with the big tits, too!'' he croaked defiantly at the closed door.

A drunk in a torn and soiled white safari suit lurching down a quay is hardly an uncommon sight in any marina enclave, not worth a second glance. Dixon went to the right, toward Berth 21, where Neil Harkness moored the *Deirdre*. At last he reached it. The long dock thrusting out into the basin from the quay was dark, deserted. There was no one about.

''Neil!'' he yelled. The bastard probably has his lights out because he's balling some dame, he thought. He started out on the dock, took several steps, slipped, started to fall. He reached out for the hull of the *Deirdre* to steady himself. It was always snugged up against the dock. It was only after he had clutched at empty air and begun to fall toward the water that Ken Dixon remembered. Neil's boat wasn't there—it was in Split.

He started to scream, but only an instant before he struck the water. No one heard him or the splash as he went in. No one saw him go under—or that he did not come up again.

33

The stall shower was a tight fit, and they were tired from lack of sleep and tensed up for the day ahead, but neither of them could wait any longer. They allowed the needle spray to play over their joined bodies and made love.

Neil kept clothes at Sybil's apartment. He dressed in his customary outfit, khaki slacks and T-shirt, made more coffee, and they drank it in the kitchen.

''Got everything straight, honey?'' he asked. ''You show for work as usual—haven't seen or heard from me. I make my entrance later. When I'm finished with Courtney, you quit—and we exit laughing.''

Sybil's face was radiant with the afterglow of gratifying sex, said: ''You make it all sound so simple.''

''It is. I have more on him than he has on me now.''

Carlos Lozano was amused. Marisa Alarcón had reverted to traditional type. While he walked Max and Solange, she insisted on making breakfast. *Desayuno*—a Spanish breakfast, fresh bread, fresh fruit, *café con leche*. They were ready to leave at seven-thirty; he would drive her back to Broadmoor before going on to Galerías Vivi. Carlos noticed that Marisa did not have the thin shawl she had carried the previous evening. He asked her about it. She blushed, saying she had no idea where it could be. He began a search of the *sala*—Max joined joyously in the hunt, bounded around the room, then up on the blue-denim sofa. He flipped over the sofa cushion with his nose. The shawl was there, neatly folded.

Carlos picked it up. Marisa's blush became fiery red.

"You don't need an excuse to come back." Carlos laughed. "*Mi casa es tu*"—he emphasized the familiar "*tu*"—"*casa*."

The blush receded. "Even tonight?"

Carlos thought of the two tourist women who would be expecting him at their hotel for a threesome, but only for a moment. There would always be tourist women. "Even tonight," he said, and draping the shawl over his arm like a torero's muleta, bowed gallantly and escorted Marisa from his apartment.

Driving her to Broadmoor, he turned on the car radio. The speakers came alive in the midst of a newscast. The situation in the Arab emirate of Kuwait was suddenly stabilizing. Although sporadic fighting continued, the dispatch of troops to Kuwait by Saudi Arabian King Khalid—

"*Me aburro como una ostra,*" Marissa said, declaring that the news reports caused her to be bored as an oyster.

Carlos tuned to another station, gritted his teeth against blaring hard rock.

"*Mejor que mejor,*" she said, smiling contentedly.

Rashid el Muein listened to William Moore's digest of the latest news bulletins from Kuwait. They pleased him. Immensely. Although Saudi troops might temporarily shore up the Sabah regime, their presence would only create more internal dissent in Kuwait. And while that would benefit James Courtney's plan to dislocate Arab governments, today was the day that Horst Thiele would eliminate Courtney. After that, as he told Moore:

"I'll be the one to take charge."

Horst Thiele listened to the radio in his hotel room while he dressed. His interpretations of what the broadcasts signified varied from those of Rashid el Muein. In hours, Courtney would, as he had told Heinrich Kloster, cease to be a factor. Rashid el Muein next. After he had paid, of course. Then, Thiele mused, once the *verdammt* painting had been recovered, he would fly to

Iran. To Tehran and from there to the holy city of Qum. There the Ayatollah would welcome him with honor, as a fully participating partner in *jihad*.

"And the Jews will not be pleased with thee, nor will the Christians," Thiele quoted himself from the second *surah* of the Koran. Knotting his necktie, he thought of breakfast. The hotel restaurants? No. He expected telephone calls during the day. Important calls. Not the least of them one from Kloster, announcing that the Velázquez had been reclaimed and was on its way to Bonn.

Thiele lifted the telephone, asked for room service, ordered thick slices of ham, three eggs hard-boiled, an assortment of cheeses. He congratulated himself. Although he was seventy-two, he still awoke in the mornings with a hearty field soldier's appetite.

Marisa waited for Carlos to drive away, mounted the steps to the front door of the Dixons' house. She paused. Her Porsche was no longer where she had parked it. A servant had probably moved it into one of the garages, she thought, continued to the door, rang the chimes. Teresa, Vivian's maid, opened the door. Her pinched mouth said: "*Buenos días señorita*"; her ugly look said: You've spent the night in a man's bed, you rich slut.

Marisa was bursting to tell Vivi about her night with Carlos. Teresa said the *señora* was not yet awake. Unusual, Marisa thought. Vivi had been up and about by seven every morning. She went upstairs, stood in front of Vivian's door, knocked on it, waited, knocked again.

"Vivi!"

Silence. No, the faintest of faint sounds. Like a cat mewling. But Vivian did not have a cat. Ken did not like to have animals in the house, she had told Marisa. More mewling—or was it?

Marisa tried the door. It opened. She stuck her head inside.

"Vivi . . . good morning."

A sound that defied description.

Marisa stepped inside the darkened bedroom and went to the bed. Then she screamed.

Costa del Sol police—national and municipal—are noted for their efficiency and the speed with which they respond to calls for assistance. They are also accustomed to the high incidence of marital strife among foreign couples resident on the Costa. Alcohol, drugs, sexual infidelity, are among the elements that cause expatriate husbands and wives to quarrel, assault, and on some occasions even kill each other.

Vivian, barely conscious, unable to speak, was rushed by ambulance to the Hospital Marbella. Marisa wanted to accompany her. The police refused to allow it. They had questions to ask her and the servants. Mainly: "Where is her husband?"

They were dubious when told he was away and only Vivian knew where, and explored the next most logical hypothesis: "Does she have a lover?"

The denial was unanimous and vehement. The police were openly skeptical. Who but a husband or lover would have a front-door key and be able to enter the house and go upstairs into the bedroom, where, as even a blind man could see, the *Señora* had taken him into her bed. He had beaten her mercilessly. She had not cried out. He had gone into the husband's bedroom and taken a shower—even left old clothing behind. Since the servants declared that Señor Dixon had never possessed clothes of such kind, it must have been a lover.

Then someone found the overnight bag downstairs. Kenneth Dixon's wallet, passport, and other items Juan identified as his were found inside it. The husband had apparently returned in the night—and fled back into it.

Marisa was told she could go to the hospital. She asked Juan where he had put her car. It had not been touched, she was told. Wasn't it outside, in front? Marisa gave her car papers to a police officer—"I believe my automobile has been stolen"—and telephoned Carlos. She told him only that Vivian had been injured and asked that he come for her. They would go to the hospital together.

He arrived within minutes, pale and shaken. She began to tell him a little more on the ride. It was too much. He pulled the Seat over to the side of the road, unable to drive. Marisa took the wheel.

The Hospital Marbella is located on the fittingly named Calle Misericordia—which means mercy, compassion—and is, perhaps, as good as any such provincial facility anywhere on earth.

Marisa and Carlos were told flatly that although Vivian's condition was serious, she was in no danger of dying. On the other hand, after a week or so she would have to be transferred to Barcelona or Madrid and undergo extensive plastic surgery. Otherwise her face would be permanently disfigured.

"When can we see her?" Marisa pleaded.

"Come back late this afternoon."

"We shall wait," Carlos said. He took Marisa's hand—for support, she realized. He was faint, trembling violently.

Sybil Pearson saw that the guard at the Montemar main gate had been doubled. Either that or the shift change was running late, she thought, discarding that possibility after she drove through and saw extra security men patrolling the grounds.

Grenville met her at the side entrance to the house. "We're on red alert," he said. "Mr. C. received a threat last night. Probably a hoax, but no sense taking chances." The authorities had not been notified, he went on. Courtney preferred not to involve them when there was so little to go on. "So I'll have your tea sent in."

There had been similar alarms at Montemar in the past. Sybil had taken them in stride, accepting that a tycoon like Courtney was a potential target for terrorists of every stripe. However, that had been before. Now, with what she had learned from Neil and read in Ken Dixon's typescript, she was seeing with different eyes and was unnerved. Only the knowledge that she would be giving up her job the same day steadied her.

Even Paco had an assistant. The men offered the customary good-morning amenities curtly and were silent. Courtney arrived in his *estudio* at 8:45. He looked haggard. His otherwise fresh, clean open-throated sport shirt had a coffee stain on the breast pocket. Somehow that made Sybil uneasier than anything else had. It was the first time she had ever seen him wear a shirt that was soiled.

"Never mind the mail," he said. "I'll call when I want you."

"People over in the annex will be inquiring about the heavy security, Mr. Courtney. What shall I tell them?"

"That I received a threat. If they're afraid, they can go home—with no pay for time lost. That's all, Sybil." He was fingering the remote controls of his stereo set. Sybil felt a shiver run down her spine. She guessed what he was going to play. Her guess was correct. She heard the opening notes of *Carmina Burana* as she closed the studio door behind her. She had always thought his obsession with it a quirky but harmless hang-up. No longer.

Neil Harkness took his Citroën from the boatowners' parking lot in Puerto Cabo Verde and drove around to the Bar Espada. Like most of the waterfront bars, it had a bulletin board on which locals posted notices and messages. The two crewmen he had laid off at James Courtney's insistence before sailing for

Venice had no telephones in their homes and would be checking the board daily. He wanted to leave word that they could return to work immediately. They would fly with him and Sybil to Yugoslavia, go aboard the *Deirdre* at Split, and then leave on a long cruise.

Neil pulled up behind a silver Porsche parked directly opposite the Espada. A model 924 two-door with Barcelona plates, he noted, not caring. He got out, went into the bar. It was too early for Enrique to be at work. Neil ordered coffee and brandy from the barman, printed a message in Spanish on a slip of paper, asked him to post it on the bulletin board.

"Hi, Neil." An American who captained one of the larger yachts berthed in the *puerto* had entered and hoisted himself on the stool next to Harkness. "Heard about your buddy Dixon yet?"

" 'Morning, Stan. Nope, I haven't." Neil feigned indifference but snapped alert. What the hell could Ken have done in less than twelve hours to merit early-morning barroom gossip?

"I was here last night when Enrique had to throw him out. Bastard was crazy drunk. He thought some guy's wife was a whore and then wanted to fight every Spániard in the place."

So much for Ken's good resolutions and promises, Neil thought unhappily, asked: "Any idea where he went from here?"

"Home, if he had any sense left."

Neil made a mental note to phone Broadmoor and check on Ken. Later. He had too many other things to do first. He lit a Celta, slid from his bar stool. "Thanks for telling me, Stan. *'Luego*." He went outside. A port patrolman stood in front of the Porsche, a clipboard in hand, referring to it and studying the license plate. Harkness knew the man, waved an arm, got into his Citroën and made a U-turn on the quay.

James Courtney silenced the stereo at nine o'clock. Moments later he was on a scrambled line with Heinrich Kloster in Zurich, and growing steadily more irate at what he heard. Despite pressures Kloster had exerted on French police through influential friends in Paris, results had been negative. Kloster theorized that Harkness and Dixon had either gone to ground in France or left the country before he had notified the police. However, the Interpol alarm was out—

"You goddamned idiot!" Courtney barked. "Have the *Sûreté* search airline-passenger manifests, records of car rentals—"

"They would refuse so much effort for a theft, even a large theft," Kloster said.

"Then tell the *Sûreté* you have reason to believe the bastards were responsible for the incident at the hotel."

"It would serve no purpose, J.P." Kloster had received information from Paris less than half an hour before. It would soon be made public in the press. In any event, there was nothing to connect him with the Bonn organization—and who knew better than Courtney that he, like all men of the old Gemeinschaft Orff, loathed and despised Horst Thiele? "The victims have finally been identified." A pause. "As members of Gruppe Thiele."

Courtney gave what was half-groan, half-yowl of protesting rage. The theories Grenville had advanced now appeared to be verified. It must have been Thiele's men who were after the Velázquez from the start. They were still after it when they went to the Lutetia. And Grenville thought he had seen Horst Thiele himself in Cabo Verde.

"The police are calling it a political case," Kloster went on—freely, for he sensed he was in the clear with Courtney. "They say that neo-Nazi terrorists were attacked by terrorists of the extreme left."

"Heinrich." Courtney was almost pleading. "Spend any amount, move heaven and earth—but find that picture."

He disconnected and glanced at the Hals portrait. He looked away quickly. The chess player seemed to be laughing at him.

David Lippmann entered the outer office. The doubled guard did not surprise him. Ample evidence of increased security was visible everywhere, on the grounds, in the corridors. Nor, under these circumstances, was he surprised to see that Sybil Pearson had a taut, anxious look.

"What's up?" he asked. "The castle under siege by the proletariat?"

Sybil gave the stock answer she had been giving employees in the CVI annex—none of whom had elected to take the day off without pay. Someone—no doubt a crank—had made a threat against Courtney:

"If you'd rather leave Montemar for the day . . ."

"Thanks. No, thanks. I'll pick up where I left off in the files." He rubbed the flattened bridge of his nose. "Oh. I finally found out where the documents from the Prado experts are."

Sybil was holding a stapler as Lippmann spoke. She gave a start, dropped it. She is jumpy, he thought, leaning down to pick the gadget from the floor. He straightened, gave it to her, continued:

"Courtney told me he has them. Said he'd let me see them."

Interesting, Sybil thought. Neil had shown her the canvas. How could Courtney have authentic documents attesting to the destruction of something that hadn't been destroyed?

"Mr. C. actually promised you, did he?" she asked, going on a cautious fishing expedition.

"He wasn't definite as to when—but like 'one of these days.' "

Wonder how he'll stall and delay and for how long? Sybil mused. I'm glad I won't be around to find out and watch poor Dave become more and more baffled and frustrated. Perhaps it might be the kindest thing to take Lippmann aside and tell him some—not all, just a bit—of the truth, she thought. It would give him a chance to bow out of the cataloging project gracefully and return to the peace of academic life in California. But the decision was not one she wanted to make alone. She would have to talk it over with Neil. Then she remembered that Neil had never met David Lippmann. Perhaps the three of them could have dinner together that evening. She would ask Neil.

"Sounds like you and Mr. C. had a nice chat," she said, still fishing.

David grimaced wryly. "For the most part, I listened to lectures, like the last time. Same subjects, too. Jews, Judaism, Semitism—pro and anti—and last night, a quiz on Israel."

"They're things that interest him. Maybe he was trying to learn something from you."

"You're close. I've had the funny feeling all along that he's mining me for information. Can't figure what it might be, though."

I'm getting paranoid, Sybil thought. Suddenly everything has a . . . well, a sinister ring to it.

Lippmann went off to the annex and document files. Sybil made a pretense of working and counted minutes waiting for Neil to arrive.

Heinrich Kloster played a hunch and his own game. He ordered several employees of the Bauerkreditbank to drop whatever they were doing and make a telephone canvass of all airlines operating out of Orly and Charles de Gaulle airports in Paris.

"We must locate two of our important clients on a matter of urgency," he declared. "Here are their names and passport numbers. Use the bank's name—it is official business—and try to determine if they boarded any flight yesterday afternoon or evening."

Fifteen minutes later, success. The person calling Air France at Orly was told that Messieurs Harkness and Dixon had taken the 1605 flight to Madrid and were ticketed and reserved through to Málaga. Kloster knew he could make only one telephone call. He spent half an hour in silent debate with himself, weighing and evaluating. Then he came down on the side of the man to be feared most and placed a call to the Hotel Melià Don Pepe.

"They have returned to Spain," he told Horst Thiele. "You must conduct the search for them yourself."

"*Danke, kamerad*. You have made it simple for me."

"You will remember what you agreed? That you will make up what I shall not now receive from the other—from C.?"

"You can expect payment in full, Kloster."

"Before or after the *putsch*?"

"Before, *kamerad*. I believe in settling accounts quickly."

Thiele hung up, thought a moment, called a number in Bonn, West Germany. "Kloster," he said to the man who answered. "Send someone to Zurich tomorrow and settle the bill." The butcher's bill, he reflected, hanging up, and Heinrich Kloster would pay it. Apostasy had been Horst Thiele's own key to survival. No one knew better than he that a man who would turn one coat would never hesitate to turn another. Death alone would ensure Kloster's eternal loyalty.

Thiele reached for the *guía telefónica*. If the men had returned to Spain, they would go to—or be in touch with—their homes in the Cabo Verde area. Their addresses were certain to be listed in the directory. It would be child's play to zero in on their whereabouts.

A nursing nun led Marisa Alarcón and Carlos Lozano from the Hospital Marbella waiting room to an office cubicle. A soft-spoken business-suited man identified himself as an inspector from the Comisario de Policia. He told Marisa her car had been recovered in Puerto Cabo Verde. There was evidence to indicate it had been used—the word "stolen" was avoided—by Señor Kenneth Dixon, of whom no trace had yet been found. Since the *señora* was still unconscious, could he please ask them a few questions. To start, how well did they know Señor Dixon?

Marisa replied that she had never met him and explained the circumstances of her stay at Broadmoor. Carlos said he knew Dixon well.

"Where might he have gone?" the inspector asked.

"I do not have any idea. Anywhere." Carlos' voice and expression were heavy with hatred.

"Who are his closest friends?"

"Closest?" Carlos thought for only a moment. "Neil Harkness . . ."

The inspector nodded. "The *norteamericano* charter-boat operator." It was natural that Costa police would be familiar with Neil and his business. "Any others?"

"Harkness went often to Broadmoor with Señorita Sybil Pearson, but she is really Vivi's—Señora Dixon's friend."

Another nod of recognition. As secretary to the billionaire Courtney, Sybil often dealt with Costa authorities on his behalf. The inspector jotted notes in a memo pad, spoke. He said that while there had been no official notification of the press, rumors were spreading rapidly along both Spanish and expatriate grapevines. He warned that they might be "assailed" by *periodistas* and *fotógrafos* at any time and politely took his leave. Marisa stared after him, then turned to look at Carlos.

"What are we to say to the press? How much must we tell them?"

He ignored the question and stood up. His face was gray, and he was trembling again.

Marisa had never in her entire life known rejection. Idolized by her affluent parents, the darling of equally well-to-do aunts and uncles, she had never had to ask for anything more than once, and her wish was granted. It had been no different in the schools she attended. What charm and beauty did not accomplish, an intelligent and nimble mind did.

She had experienced rejection by Carlos that morning, but being the person she was, did not—simply could not—recognize, much less accept it as such. She found any number of rationalizations to explain his manner and actions. He, too, had been shaken by their night together. Then, of course, it stood to reason that Carlos, a salaried employee, probably felt intimidated by her wealth and social status. The rationalizations piled up, with Marisa accepting them as valid explanations, fully convinced that Carlos really wanted her as much as she wanted him and would have to acknowledge the utter futility of his love for Vivian. Even if he did not, she could make him forget—for however long the affair she now wanted to have with him might last.

Or so Marisa had been telling herself ever since the moment when she had said: "It was never like this for me before."

Telling herself until the present moment—when she suddenly found herself able to see into Carlos, share his thoughts, read his feelings. The shock waves struck. A part—a very large and important part—of Marisa Alarcón suddenly grew up, matured, learned for the first time that there are bitter realities which cannot be changed by wealth or beauty or charm or the most intelligent and nimble of minds.

Carlos was in love with Vivian, and the love was invulnerable. He was one with her. What she suffered, he suffered too. If she lived, he would rejoice and also live. If she were to die, he might continue to live on, but he would be dead inside.

"Sybil Pearson is Vivi's best friend," Carlos mumbled. He swayed on his feet, placed a hand on a wall to steady himself. "I should be the one to tell her, not the police or some stranger." He had recovered his equilibrium, turned, and went off toward the pay telephone in the hospital lobby.

Sybil was astonished. Carlos had never before telephoned Montemar, and if he had not identified himself by name, she would not have recognized him by voice, for it was hoarse and barely coherent. Then he spoke Vivian Dixon's name, and Sybil dry-swallowed nervously. The conversation was being recorded automatically. James Courtney might monitor the tape later—as he sometimes did—and there would be the devil to pay because his taboo against mention of Vivian had been violated. But Sybil remembered it was to be her last day at Montemar and relaxed—for a split second, until Carlos began telling her about Vivi, and she gasped with horror. The horror remained with her when he finished.

"I'll be at the hospital this afternoon—early, as soon as I can," she managed to say, and sat dazed after Carlos hung up.

There was a jolting aftershock from the intercom.

"Come in—immediately!" The voice at its harshest.

Seeing Courtney's face, Sybil knew why. He had obviously been using the device that monitored her outer-office telephone calls even as they were being made and taped. Added paranoia brought on by whatever had caused the security flap, she thought, bracing for the storm.

It did not come. Instead, he rapped out orders.

"Call the Banco de Andalucía. Tell the manager to set thirty million pesetas aside in a special account. Inform the *alcalde* and the provincial governor I'm posting it as a reward for Dixon's capture and arrest. Hurry it up."

Sybil left. Courtney congratulated himself. The decision to eavesdrop on office phone conversations that morning must have been prompted by some occult impulse, he mused. He now had information he had desperately sought elsewhere and new assurance that the situation which showed signs of sliding out of balance would be quickly redressed. If Kenneth Dixon had managed to slip back into Spain and Cabo Verde, Neil Harkness—and the Velázquez—also had to be nearby. He reached for the monitor-device control knob, turned it—but, in his preoccupation, failed to turn it far enough. He merely reduced the volume to inaudible minimum rather than a millimeter further to Off position. He then rang for Grenville, who appeared minutes later.

"Our intrepid sea captain," Courtney said. "I trust you haven't forgotten about him."

"Not likely, sir. Friend Harkness is very much in mind."

Sybil, having spoken with the Banco de Andalucía manager, was touch-dialing the Cabo Verde Ayuntamiento when she heard the men's voices over her telephone. She grasped the problem; it had arisen in the past. The monitoring equipment in the *estudio* had an inherent fault that technicians had not been able to correct. When turned down to very low listening volume, it became a transmitter. It picked up conversations inside the study, and these heterodyned in on the telephone line being used in the outer office. Her impulse was to call Courtney on the intercom and tell him to close the control switch. But she heard Neil mentioned, and with a furtive glance at Paco and his partner, listened:

Courtney: "I expect Harkness to show soon. Any day."

Grenville: "No change? I go with the pipe?"

Courtney: "Of course. It's foolproof. You'll have a full hour's leeway after. You'll be long gone when he . . . goes."

Grenville: "Quite tidy."

Courtney: "You understand the mechanism?"

Grenville: "Full right turn of the stem to prime. Full left turn and it delivers through the mouthpiece."

Courtney (laughing): "Make sure it's not in your mouth at the time."

Grenville: "Rather! I'll point at his—"

A tiny click and no more sound of voices. Courtney must have noticed the switch and flicked it full off, Sybil thought. Holy bloody Christ! she gasped silently as her brain worked to interpret what she had heard. It fought to reject the implications, lost the battle. But a pipe, a pipe stem, a mouthpiece? They could not have been speaking literally. She sat frozen as minutes passed, jumped when the study door opened and Grenville emerged. He closed the door, gave her a hard, searching look.

"You're white as the proverbial sheet, miss."

Did Courtney and he suspect that she had overheard them? "Terrible thing's happened to a friend of mine."

Grenville's expression eased. "His Nibs told me. The Dixon woman's in hospital. Put there by her husband. A pity, the poor thing." He smiled maliciously. "Old-hand domestic staff tell me His Nibs was very taken with her once. Got her pregnant and was heartbroken when she lost the kid." He studied his fingernails. "Elena"—an old crone who worked in the kitchen—"has a different version, though. She insists the lady in question miscarried and came a cropper after taking a climb up and down her *árbol genealógico.*"

"What—if anything—is that supposed to mean?"

"A reference to relations between relations, I should imagine. Well, I must get on with my labors. No pun intended."

Sybil gnawed at her lower lip. Thirty-million-peseta rewards. Talk of pipes. And of family trees. It took her several tries before she managed to dial the *ayuntamiento* number correctly.

34

Neil Harkness and his car were stopped at the Montemar main gate. The augmented guard force had no special instructions to let him through. He was forced to wait until a telephone call was made to the main house and clearance obtained from Grenville, who was (only temporarily, the guards hoped) in charge of security on the estate.

Grenville gave approval and rushed to James Courtney's study.

"I'll want to talk with him alone," Courtney said, "but stay close—in the outer office."

Grenville went out. He studied Sybil's face closely as he announced: "Mr. Harkness is back. He'll be here in moments."

Sybil exercised control, showed the right kind and degree of reaction: that of a woman delighted to hear that her man had finally returned from wherever he had been.

"Hope you don't mind if I grab and kiss him when he walks in," she said, beaming.

"You have my permission—and blessing." Grenville leaned against a wall. "His Nibs asked me to wait here."

Grenville was in normal civilian clothes that day, a lightweight gray suit, double-breasted. Sybil had assumed all along it was because of his newly assigned duty as security supervisor, paid scant attention. However, she now noticed the bowl of a briar pipe showing in his breast pocket, its dark sheen emphasized by the meticulously folded white pocket handkerchief. Everyone at Montemar knew that Grenville was a pipe smoker, but only in his own room, the staff dining room—over which he presided—or outside the house. She had never seen him carry a pipe while inside and on duty. She yearned to make some remark, ask to see it, but dared not.

"Hello, sorry to interrupt . . ."

Sybil looked eagerly at the doorway. The eagerness faded. It was David Lippmann.

". . . ran into a snag." He had a spiral-bound notebook in his hand. "Do you have a minute to spare, Sybil?"

"Wha . . . oh, yes. Sure."

Lippmann nodded to Grenville and to Paco and the other guard, then came to Sybil's desk.

"There's a cross-reference to 'Stored Art Files.' Nobody in the annex knows where they are."

Sybil wrinkled her brow. "I can't remember, either. I'll have to check." She pulled out the desk drawers, began rummaging through them.

Neil parked his Citroën next to Sybil's Seat. He got out and took the rolled-up canvas from the rear compartment. The roll was securely tied with twine. Holding it under his arm, he rang the side-entrance doorbell. The security man who opened the door had evidently been told to admit Harkness; he held it wide and even saluted.

Neil struck a pose in the outer-office doorway.

Sybil squealed, leaped from her chair, and did grab and kiss him.

"Grenville's pipe," she whispered urgently, pretending to kiss Neil's ear. "It's something else. To use on you. Get it away from him." She moved her lips, raised her voice: "You might have sent me a postcard, though."

Grenville may or may not have smiled at the scene. Paco and his partner chuckled; they envied Harkness as being the man for whom the *guapa inglésa* raised her skirts. David Lippmann glumly realized he had been wasting fantasies vis-à-vis Sybil, hid his disappointment behind an "I'm-waiting-to-meet-the-guy" grin.

Sybil introduced the two men. They shook hands, studied each other, and there was a quick spark of mutual liking.

"Dave's the art historian I told you about," Sybil said.

"My cue," Neil said, seizing the opportunity. He had warned Sybil he intended to go for broke, bulldoze Courtney, create as much turmoil as possible. "An art expert's just the person I want to see." He dropped the roll to the floor, snatched a pair of library shears from atop a filing cabinet, and knelt down, cutting the twine. "I could use a learned opinion." He opened the roll, exposed the canvas.

Grenville came alive at that, lunged. "Hold it!"

Harkness leaped up. He topped the butler by five inches, outweighed him by thirty pounds, but Grenville was tough, commando-trained, and scored the first point by straight-arming Neil away from the canvas. Harkness laughed, seized Grenville in a bear hug, waltzed him.

The guards tensed, waiting for orders.

"Naughty, naughty, temper, temper," Neil hammed it up, taking a dancelike step at each word. Grenville tried to knee him in the groin. He evaded.

Sybil pushed herself between the two men. "Stop it!" She turned to face Neil. "Leave Grenville alone!" she said, then whispered: "The *pipe*, you bloody idiot."

She moved aside. Grenville came forward again. Neil grabbed him by the jacket lapels, shook him. "Stop the heroics, friend. Just run in and tell J.P. I'm here."

He pushed Grenville away. The butler gave him a savage glare, hurried across the room, and disappeared into the *estudio*.

Neil hefted the briar hidden in his big hand. Maybe Sybil did know something, he thought. The thing was much too heavy for what it was—or was supposed to be.

"Are you hurt?" Sybil was standing close to him again. He made a show of patting her cheek, slipped the briar down the front of her blouse. "I'm fine." He signaled with a wink. She returned to her desk, stood behind it. The guards and Lippmann had their eyes on Neil. She dropped the pipe into her handbag without being noticed.

Harkness knelt again, spread the canvas. Her expression registering curiosity, Sybil went to stand beside him.

"What would you call it, Dave?" Neil asked. "I've titled it *Remnants of an Alleged Masterpiece*."

Sybil nudged the canvas with a sandaled foot. "We used to know it around here as *Horse and Rider*."

Lippmann gaped.

"The bastard has it," Grenville reported to Courtney.

"I expected he would."

"You don't understand. Most of the paint is gone."

"Jesus Christ!"

"He's letting everyone see it. What should I do?"

"The same as I will. Treat him as a conquering hero. Until I learn what he knows and I don't."

"But Sybil, and the Jew, Lippmann—"

"I'll find the answers. You'll only need to follow my instructions . . . and hints. Do you follow me?"

"I'm confident that you will . . . and I will, sir." Courtney had reactivated Grenville's Perfect Butler mechanisms.

Lippmann knelt beside Neil, his mental gears refusing to mesh. What remained of the picture did match descriptions of the Velázquez. It was an excellent forgery, but a forgery nonetheless—and it had not been destroyed as James Courtney claimed. Or could there have been two forged versions? Where did this one come from? What or whom could he—should he—believe? He stared at the mutilated picture and discerned evidences of underpainting: lines, whorls, tiny numbers, even letters of the alphabet. *Pentimenti?* No, impossible. Yet the apparent reality seemed even more impossible. A contour map. He bent nearer to the canvas, made out two words in the corner of a bare patch, read them aloud:

"Wadi Shahid." He stood up, frowning. "Arabic rendered in English. A place named after someone who died fighting for Islam—and you don't find wadis anywhere except in Middle Eastern deserts." He did a double-take, realizing what he had implied. The map was of a segment of desert in one Middle Eastern country or another.

Neil would have made some comment, but Grenville came out of the study in his newly reacquired character.

"My apologies for my outburst, Mr. Harkness. Mr. Courtney wishes to speak with you."

Grenville strode to the canvas. "Please go ahead, sir. I'll bring this in for you."

"Like hell." Neil knocked a reaching arm aside. "I've risked my ass hauling that thing all over Europe. I'm taking it the rest of the way—right up to God—myself."

"Sir, I only—"

"Blow it, buster!"

Harkness had the roll under his arm, started toward the study.

"Think I'll go back to the annex," Lippmann said.

"Sorry, sir," Grenville told him. "Mr. Courtney has asked that you remain here. He'll want to see you a bit later."

Sybil made certain that her handbag was zipped shut but left it in prominent view on her desktop. That, she thought, would help to avert suspicion. She flicked a glance at Grenville. He was hard at work regaining his composure for his own sake, and to reestablish authority over the security men. Neither of them liked Grenville; both were eyeing him with open amusement. His mind thus occupied, Grenville had apparently not yet realized that the briar pipe was gone from his breast pocket.

Harkness was prepared for a two-tiered reception, with James Courtney grateful and gracious at one level and mining furiously for information at the other. Neil dumped the roll on an Oriental rug where Courtney could see it from behind the Bureau Plat. He took some books from a shelf, and spreading the canvas, placed books at the corners to hold it flat. Courtney stared at the gangrenous painting, pale eyes sharp-focused, aquiline features devoid of expression, for a full minute before breaking into a smile.

"You couldn't make delivery, so you brought it back. I'm in your debt, Neil."

"Not the way I figure, J.P. The million paid you up in cash, and since I can climb all over your back now, you'll have to get off mine. That makes us even." He lit a cigarette, blew a lazy smoke ring.

Courtney picked up the Lucite cube that encased the B'nai B'rith medal and toyed with it. "Why did you think it necessary to strip off the paint?" he asked, the smile holding.

"Not I. It started to self-destruct when Fischer hid it under a rug, and it kept getting worse. Somebody did a cheap, crappy job, J.P."

Cheap, yes, Courtney mused, turning the cube in his hands. The forgers employed on the Meisterwerken Project at Gröss Rosen had received food, clothing, and a few more months of life. But crappy? He thought back over decades to what he had been told by Artur Hintze and the professor, Franz Josef Eichenbach. "Kirschwasser, the painter, was a genius. A Jew, of course . . ."

Of course, Courtney thought. The Jew must have cheated, adding adulterants to his paints so that the impasto would eventually crumble. He had to make certain, though, and got up, walked slowly to the canvas. He used a corner of the Lucite cube to prod and tap at the segments of still-intact impasto. Cracks formed. Perhaps sea air and the sticky humidity of Venice had caused a chemical reaction to set in, he reflected, and, returning to his chair, asked:

"Who's seen the picture in this condition?"

"With the map showing?" Neil grinned. "Kenneth Dixon." Might as well tell him now, he thought, and was surprised when the billionaire showed no reaction. Evidently he already knew. "Then the people in the other room. Sybil, your art expert Lippmann, Grenville, and the two thugs. Which reminds me. Why the oversized army today?"

"Never mind. Who else saw it?"

"No one." Harkness showed teeth. "Not even the clowns you sent after me in Paris."

Courtney blinked involuntarily. "I did not send—"

"Horseshit. You had Kloster set me up." Harkness dug the tape cassette from his hip pocket, flipped it onto the Bureau Plat. "Man who says he's Carl Orff gives me that, I'm to give him the picture. Bonehead play, J.P. You're the big *Carmina Burana* buff. Two and two makes, as they say. Of course, none of you figured I'd stay alive."

James Courtney went ashen as he examined the tape.

Neil took a gamble that Peter Osgood, the Colonel Blimpish character he and Ken had encountered at Barajas, knew what he was talking about. "And a happy Heil Hitler from Gemeinschaft Orff."

Bull's eye, he thought. Courtney dropped the cassette and his cheek muscles pulsed. But it was a reaction of rage rather than fear.

"Kloster," Courtney muttered. Kloster and Horst Thiele. No wonder his meticulous plans had showed signs of fraying apart. His hand reached for the telephone to call Zurich. He pulled it back. There were immediate, right-this-minute plans that demanded drastic revision. Fast. He looked at Neil, some color returning to his face.

"You were 'set up,' but not by me. Kloster evidently decided to go into business for himself." Courtney thought he would talk, hold Neil's attention to prevent him from leaving, and use the conversation as a screen behind which to formulate new tactics.

"Treachery in the bunker, *Mein Führer*?" Harkness jeered, but he was inclined to believe Courtney. Seen in that light, events did appear more comprehensible. However, it altered nothing. He had more than enough on Courtney. As soon as he made that entirely clear, he and Sybil could go wherever they pleased without ever once having to glance over their shoulders in fear.

Courtney ignored the last remark, said: "You've studied the map?"

"Looked at it, sure—what's visible."

"Do you have any idea what it represents?"

"Rough country." Neil remembered what Lippmann had said, bared teeth again as he added: "A piece of desert in the Middle East."

Worse and worse, Courtney thought, brain working to assemble a logical and safe set of interacting solutions. He said: "That isn't how I meant the question. The map represents more wealth than you could ever imagine, Harkness."

"Figures, but why tell me?"

"To explain why Fischer was killed for it, and why Kloster was willing to have you killed." To make you think I'm trying to regain some of your confidence, that I'm worried over the damage you can do me. To soften you a little, shape you for the next scenes in the drama. "The map leads to the greatest store of oil on the face of the earth," Courtney went on, allowing himself an inner laugh. It was a lie, which he expected Harkness to take literally—yet, in a sense, it was the gospel truth. The pun caused him to laminate a snicker on the inner laugh. The map led to the long-lost True Koran, Islam's holiest of holy books. Possession of the True Koran, dictated to Jewish slaves by Muhammad himself and written in gold, would confer absolute power in Muslim countries. Including those that produced half the entire world's supply of oil.

"Now do you begin to understand?" Courtney asked.

"No." Neil's blue eyes taunted with their open skepticism. "Oil maps don't have to be camouflaged as Old Masters." He waved a hand at the array of electronic gadgetry atop the Bureau Plat. "You're not a technological illiterate, J.P. You know fucking well that map could have been microfilmed down to the size of a comma printed by a typewriter. It could have been mailed out of here under the stamp on a postcard."

"Oh, you have theories?"

"A couple," Neil bluffed. "Interesting, too." He lit another Celta.

"Care to tell me what they are?" Courtney guessed it was bluff, but had to try to make sure.

"I'd rather hear your version."

Courtney mimed resignation. He had the new tactics firmly in mind. It was time to set the scene. "Maybe I do owe you and the others who've seen the thing a full explanation." He eyed Neil steadily. It was his turn to test for a reaction. "I'm only sorry your friend Dixon isn't with you—can't be with you, I should say."

"Ken's probably at home," Neil said with a casual shrug.

He had not heard yet, Courtney thought. Good. It provided a chance to rock him off balance, give him something to preoccupy his mind. It also suggested a fillip that could be added to Courtney's evolved scheme.

He sighed heavily, looked grim. "I hate to break bad news. Dixon beat his wife senseless last night and . . . well, vanished. There's a hunt on for him. I've even posted a reward for his capture. I did it for"—he almost choked on the name—"Vivian's sake."

Harkness started out of his Barcelona chair.

"No, stay where you are. I'll call in the others. Sybil can give you the details before I begin."

Courtney reached for an intercom key, touched but did not depress it as he raced through a final mental review. The thing would go off smoothly and quietly, he thought. But even if it didn't, the study was totally soundproofed. Doors and locks were impenetrable. No one could leave or enter unless he chose they should. Grenville could be relied on to read glances, gestures, obscure allusions, changes of inflection and intonation correctly and as instructions. Which he would carry out.

A spatulate forefinger pressed down the key: "Sybil, David, Grenville. Will you all come in, please?" He glanced at the tabletop chronometer: 12:37. He would allow half an hour or so for what was to follow.

Sybil entered first, then David, and finally Grenville. Courtney asked them to sit. Sybil and David took Barcelona chairs near Neil. Grenville sat in a chair Courtney indicated; it was drawn close to the Bureau Plat. He shifted it slightly so he could have a clear view of his employer and the others.

"I have some things to tell you about the painting," Courtney said, "but first, Sybil, will you please tell Neil about the Dixons? I'm afraid he's still in the dark."

Sybil swallowed hard and, in a strained voice, gave Harkness an account of what Carlos had said, concluding: "Haven't heard anything since."

Courtney spoke up, his tone pure silk. "Call the hospital—use my phone here. Oh, you and Neil want to see her, I'm sure. I won't take much more of your time. You can be there in . . . umm"—he looked, for no apparent reason, at Grenville—"in an hour or so."

Neil had caught the look, cocked an eyebrow at Sybil, who

nodded gratefully to Courtney, got up, and started out. "My handbag . . . tissues," she explained. "Afraid I might start blubbering."

The door was locked. Courtney had operated the remote-locking mechanism. Not right, not right at all, Sybil thought, apprehensions multiplying, and heard a faint click as Courtney released the lock. The handbag was where she had left it on her desk, the center compartment that now held the briar firmly zipped. She pulled some tissues from a side pocket of the bag, returned to the study, heard a click as the door was relocked.

"Sorry, everyone." Sybil dropped the handbag on the chair in which she had been sitting, dabbed at misting hazel eyes with the tissues. " 'Fraid I'm already sniffling." The apologetic smile on her pretty face was patently of the British stiff-upper-lip variety. She took the telephone Courtney maneuvered toward her across the tabletop, remembered the hospital number, and touch-dialed.

A nursing nun bustled into the waiting room, beaming. Señora Dixon had regained consciousness. The attending *médico* said she could have visitors, provided they did not upset the patient or stay too long. Marisa had reached for Carlos' hand. He ignored her and hurried after the nun. Marisa followed. With mixed emotions.

The private room was at the end of a second-floor corridor and almost dark inside. Shades and curtains were tightly drawn. Only a dim light burned in a corner. Its rays glinted on chrome-steel stands. IV bottles hung from them. Tubes from the bottles ran to Vivian's arms. Her head and face were swathed in bandages. There were breathing holes for her nostrils, another for her mouth, from which a metal tube protruded.

The nun maneuvered the two straight-backed wooden chairs through the forest of IV stands and set them at opposite sides of the bed, repeated her warnings, and withdrew. Carlos took the nearest chair. He reached for Vivian's hand. Marisa saw that he touched it gently, tenderly. He tried to speak, but his voice failed.

Marisa sat in the other chair, whispered: "Vivi. It's Marisa," then added hastily, "and Carlos. Marisa and Carlos," she repeated.

They could not see Vivian's bandaged eyes nor her lips move, but heard her say in a hoarse, barely audible whisper:

"Marisa. Please, I beg you. Don't write about this."

"No, Vivi. I won't write . . . anything." Marisa's horror at knowing that the novelist she had idolized was capable of such savagery had not subsided. It never would. Marisa Alarcón was aware that she could never bring herself to write a line about Kenneth Dixon.

"Vivi!" Carlos, filled with joy that Vivian had spoken, found his voice, and it was jubilant. "You will be well soon, Vivi." His fingers circled her wrist. She must have been aware of it, for she turned her head slightly and moved her fingers to entwine them with his.

The door opened. The nursing nun said there was a Señorita Pearson telephoning for Señor Lozano. Marisa, realizing that she was extraneous, and wondering if Vivian had been truthful about her feelings toward Carlos, volunteered to go out to the lobby and take the call.

Sybil did get tears in her eyes—tears of relief—when Marisa said Vivian was conscious and had spoken to her and Carlos. She dabbed at her eyes with tissues, said:

"Please tell her Neil and I will be there in about an hour."

Courtney exchanged glances with Grenville. So far, so good. There was now a witness to testify that Sybil and Harkness intended to drive from Montemar to the Hospital Marbella. The question was which of their cars they would use. Grenville excused himself, saying he had to check one of the guard posts. Courtney went through the door-unlocking routine, and Sybil noticed that he did not relock it. With Grenville gone, she was able to catch Neil's eye and pat the handbag she held on her lap. He gave a tiny nod and spread his hands as if to study their palms. She read his message: Okay, you've got the thing—but I don't have a clue what it is, except a briar pipe. Hang on to it, though.

"I'd like to clear up some of the confusion over the painting," Courtney said. He laughed. "There wouldn't have been any if Dave hadn't arrived when he did." He went into a brief account of what had led to his decision to have a catalog prepared.

Grenville needed only moments. The Citroën was faster, sturdier, more resistant to impact than Sybil's little Seat 124. He opened the valve on the right-front tire of the Citroën. Harkness would not pause to change tires if he was hurrying to the hospital. Satisfied that air was escaping slowly, silently, Grenville returned to the house and the *estudio*.

". . . I failed to remove the appropriate page from the inventory," James Courtney was saying as Grenville entered. He stopped speaking. Sybil saw his hand move. He was relocking the door once more.

"Then came Dave, with all the time in the world," Courtney said, gave another ingratiating laugh. "Still has it."

He circled thumb and forefinger of his right hand for a moment, as he would if holding a pipe.

Grenville understood. The Jew Lippmann, rather than Harkness, was to get the dart. Later on in the afternoon. Perhaps when word reached Montemar about the accident and Grenville asked Lippmann to accompany him to the scene.

Grenville's hand instinctively went to his breast pocket. Merely to reassure himself. But there was no reassurance. There was nothing in the pocket but the folded handkerchief. What the bloody hell? There had been the scuffle with Harkness. The pipe must have fallen out of the pocket then, or . . . No, what reason could Harkness have had to take it? But he would make certain.

"Begging your pardon, Mr. Harkness." Grenville whipped out the handkerchief, came to Neil's chair. "Could I ask you to stand up for a second?"

"Sure." Neil stood.

Grenville pretended to wipe at the chair seat. "Sorry, must've been light and shadow. Thought there were stains." He examined Harkness from the corner of his eye. No. The khaki slacks were skintight, no appreciable bulges showed. Nothing could be hidden under the T-shirt. Harkness had not taken the pipe.

"I must step outside again for a moment, Mr. Courtney."

"Go ahead." Courtney worked the remote lock, hid his concern and puzzlement over Grenville's obvious uneasiness, and picked up the thread of his time-wasting talk.

"All right, to the point. There's the picture, Dave," he said, nodding toward the canvas. "As you can see, it is a forgery. And it hasn't been destroyed"—a chuckle—"not entirely, that is. I had to claim it was in order to protect the original," he improvised.

"Then the genuine still exists?" David asked eagerly. It was his sole interest. The rest—mutilated forgery, map, the conflicting stories he'd been told—was extraneous.

Courtney, charmed by his own fiction, elaborated. "Oh, the real *Horse and Rider* is safe. Fabulous piece of work. You see, I had to take precautions because . . ."

Courtney had left the door unlocked for Grenville, who reentered, his sheeplike face registering consternation and anger.

"Problems, Grenville?" Courtney asked.

"Seem to have lost my pipe, sir—a lovely briar." Grenville

was fighting to keep his voice under control. "Must have slipped out of my pocket." He looked at Lippmann. No, again. The kike hadn't come near him. "Didn't happen to notice it, miss?" he asked Sybil.

"Sorry." She half-rose from her chair. "Be glad to help you search round, though."

"Did you ask the security men?" Courtney inquired softly.

"Yes, sir." Grenville's jaws worked. "Both deny seeing it. Deny it too much, I think." That, he thought, must be the answer. He whirled in very unbutlerlike fashion, ready to go out and have a showdown with the pair.

"Grenville." Courtney stopped him. Courtney knew how much Grenville was disliked by many members of both the domestic and the security staffs. The latter had a special resentment for him today because he had been placed in charge of security. Courtney guessed that Paco or his partner had taken the briar—out of spite, rather than to steal it—and ice blocks were forming in his stomach. The man who had it would sooner or later examine the pipe, twist and turn the stem. It might be pointed anywhere when he unwittingly hit on the correct combination. The idea of ordering a body search of the two men had to be discarded. Members of the security force, being Spanish and proud, might walk off in protest against the insult to their fellows. And if Horst Thiele and his *Gruppe* were in the vicinity, the guards would be needed. All of them.

Courtney realized that, with the CIA-pattern weapon gone—and God damn Grenville for having lost it!—he would have to make yet more changes in tactics. He fingered the old scar. Harkness had extorted a million from him, knew far too much—Jesus! even about Gemeinschaft Orff!—and was likely to deduce more. As Grenville had pointed out, Sybil Pearson had to be counted as one with Harkness. David Lippmann had connections with Israeli intelligence—of this, Courtney had convinced himself—and he had now actually seen the map.

All three would have to be neutralized. Today. At once. He dared make no further moves, take no other steps, until they were, and time was running out. Swift, summary riddance was the only option.

How—without risk?

The answer came to Courtney. He looked at the Hals portrait. The chess player seemed to agree and approve.

"Tell Paco and his *compañero* to go out and join the grounds patrols," Courtney said, speaking to Grenville. "They'll get the point, and your missing property will turn up mysteriously in a couple of hours. Come right back. I'll need your help on some matters."

Neil's animal instincts were operating. The session with James Courtney was not going as he had expected. It was wrong. All wrong. Get out—right now, an inner voice urged. Can't—unless I can stroll, not run, he talked back to it. There were forty, fifty armed guards on the estate. If Courtney wanted to stop him, he need only sound an alarm, and no one could leave Montemar. On the other hand, and by a related token, Courtney was severely limited in what he might do, Neil reasoned. The security men were tough, reliable, but they operated within the law. There were platoons of domestic servants in the house, the office employees in the annex—potential witnesses all, and thus deterrents.

Harkness recognized that the briar pipe was a key . . . To what? Sybil had been frantic for him to take it from Grenville. He had, and had passed it to her. They'd had no chance to talk privately since, but Grenville's great flap over its loss confirmed that it must be more than just a pipe.

It looked and felt like one—except for the weight, Neil reflected, which was half again that of an ordinary briar of like size. A disguised single-shot pistol? No, not heavy enough. A trick Mace sprayer, thousands of which were being sold in every conceivable shape and form? Improbable. Again, it was too light to contain a Mace canister that held enough gas to have much effect.

Sybil Pearson's instincts were also beaming out warnings. But she believed that whatever Courtney intended, it was for Neil only, and her rising fears were for him alone. She, too, pondered over the briar. She could feel the lump of its bowl in the handbag on her lap. She had gathered from the overheard conversation between Courtney and Grenville that it was dangerous. Perhaps, though Sybil found this impossible to believe, it could even kill.

David Lippmann appeared to be out of things, in another world, waiting impatiently to hear more about the original Velázquez. Neil glanced at Lippmann and promptly wrote him off. The academic mind is on its single track, Harkness thought, shifted his glance to Sybil. She smiled blandly, but patted her handbag as a reminder.

James Courtney spoke: "Ah, then. Where was I?"

"Forget it," Neil said, standing up. He decided to test. "Look, J.P. I told you before. We're even. You forget I exist, I keep my mouth shut."

Sybil rose to her feet. "I might as well tell you now, Mr. Courtney. I'm quitting."

Pale blue eyes crackled. "I suggest you both sit down."

A signal light flashed on Courtney's desk. He manipulated the remote-control lock, admitting Grenville. The door closed and was relocked.

"We're leaving," Neil said, reached for Sybil's hand—and obtained the test results.

"Really?" Grenville's right hand went under his coat, came out.

Instead of the .357 Magnum he usually carried, the hand gripped a .223-caliber Czech-made Ostrava automatic. Neil Harkness had seen weapons like it before. Deadly. Fifteen rounds in the clip. Used by professional assassins and hit men.

James Courtney smiled triumphantly. "Everyone knows I received an anonymous threat," he said, smile turning into a laugh. "Who would have dreamed it was made by the three of you acting in concert?"

"Or that I'd have to shoot when they attacked you, sir?" Grenville said, and advanced into the room.

35

David Lippmann's Robert Redfordish face registered terror, but Neil noticed that he stood up slowly instead of leaping from his chair, and he made a tentative reevaluation. The man moved like a trained fighter. "Please . . . not me!" He was begging. "I haven't—"

"Kike!" Grenville spat, shifted the gun to aim at Lippmann's chest. "Bloody coward, like all your kind."

David backed off—toward the Bureau Plat.

"What should they attack me with?" Jim Courtney asked Grenville calmly. "Have any suggestions?"

"Glad I thought ahead." Grenville reached into his coat pocket with his left hand, the automatic steady on Lippmann. He produced another pistol, a tiny .25-caliber model.

"That toy?"

"Certainly, sir. Easily hidden in a woman's handbag."

Sybil gave a start, shrank close to Neil, was stunned when his fingers jabbed at her side to move away.

"You're out of your head, J.P.," Harkness said. "Nobody'll swallow the story that we attacked you. Why would we?"

"For money." Courtney got up, went to the Hals portrait.

Neil caught the flicker of disappointment in Lippmann's expression.

"For money," Courtney repeated, pressing down on the bottom of the picture frame. A section of wall paneling slid aside. There was a large safe behind it. He worked a three-number combination, opened the door. There were banded packets of assorted currencies stacked on the shelves. He reached in, swept dozens of the packets out of the safe. They tumbled to the floor. He turned away, left the door gaping open.

"I'll give you the scenario now, Grenville," Courtney said. "Appearances will have to back it up." He made a wide detour around David Lippmann, returned to his chair behind the Bureau Plat, sat, and templed his fingers. "Started with a telephone threat. Blackmail. Something to do with a woman—the Spanish police will accept that and ask no more questions. The demand was for a million. I agreed to pay, then posted extra guards. But the blackmailers were people inside my own home."

Sybil wanted to scream, clapped a hand over her mouth.

Neil and Lippmann exchanged glances.

"They waited until I sent the outer-office guards away. Harkness had the gun . . . I opened the safe. When they saw how much money there was in it, they wanted it all—more than two million dollars. I balked. Harkness fired a shot—that *is* loaded, I assume?—and missed. The bullet struck the intercom, making it unusable."

"Right." Grenville raised the .25, aimed lazily, fired. The loud explosion could not be heard outside the soundproof study.

Lippmann screamed, cowered.

Sybil's stomach churned, and she swallowed back sour vomit.

"Last cigarette okay?" Neil's voice had a shaky edge as he lit a Celta, aware that Grenville watched him from the corner of his eye.

"Then Sybil and Jew-boy rushed to the safe, started clawing money from it. You entered. Harkness fired from there." Courtney pointed to a point midway between desk and safe. "Bullet buried itself in the door."

Grenville turned slightly, triggered a round at the door.

Courtney leaned forward, placed his elbows on the tabletop. 'Listen to this carefully. Sybil and the Yid hurled themselves at me—wanted to use me as a shield. Their clothing and mine will have to show signs of a struggle. Yours too, I think. You tried to pull them off me—after you'd shot Harkness."

"Who dropped his gun and Sybil took it," Grenville said. "She took a shot at me." He swung the .25 carelessly, fired, sending a bullet angling up toward one of the oak beams.

"Good."

"After that, I had no choice, did I, sir?"

"None."

"Move over where you belong, Harkness." Grenville slipped the .25 back in his pocket, gestured with the Czech automatic.

"For Christ's sake, leave Sybil out of this," Neil said, but took his first step, then another. He slid a look at David—who went to pieces.

"Don't . . . for God's sake!" he wailed, scuttling around the Bureau Plat and flinging himself to his knees beside Courtney's chair. He raised his hands as if to clasp them in prayer. Courtney swung the swivel chair sideways, kicked at Lippmann.

Grenville spun, cursed. The Jew was protected by the huge writing table, and he was too close to Courtney. He fired anyway, aiming wide. The .223 bullet spanged against the great Moorish fireplace, chipping stone. Lippmann shrieked his terror.

Neil leaped. One hand vised on Grenville's gun arm; the other, a balled fist, smashed into his stomach. Grenville staggered but kept his hold on the automatic. Harkness twisted the arm viciously.

Now it was Courtney screaming. Lippmann had seized his kicking legs and was pulling him from the chair. David had him on the floor, drew back one arm, punched for Courtney's jaw. But he was in a bad position kneeling, and Courtney's legs flailed. The punch missed.

Sybil, acting reflexively, rushed to aid Neil.

"Stay the fuck clear!" he bellowed at her. Pain exploded through his head as Grenville took advantage of the momentary distraction and karate-chopped him below the ear. He fought to remain conscious and maintain his hold on Grenville's gun arm. The gun went off. Neil felt the muzzle blast sear his cheek. His fist clubbed at Grenville's groin.

James Courtney had rolled free and scrambled to his feet with remarkable agility. He shoved the swivel chair at Lippmann, who was unable to dodge around it, and seized a heavy wrought-iron poker from the rack in front of the fireplace. He raised the poker. David moved toward him in a boxer's crouch. The poker flashed down, struck Lippmann's shoulder. He staggered back, groaning.

Sybil tore open the zipper of her handbag, took the briar, let the bag fall.

What had she overheard? Full right turn of the stem to prime. Full left and it delivers through the mouthpiece.

Neil had thrown himself backward on the floor, pulled Grenville on top of him. They rolled and thrashed. The gun fired again, but Neil was gripping Grenville's arm firmly. The shot went somewhere into the wall across the room. She saw that Grenville was weakening and Neil gradually subduing him. It was different with David, she thought. He was edging back, away from the poker that slashed at him.

She held the pipe by its bowl, used her other hand to turn the stem. "One full right," she said aloud. It felt as though something inside the stem had clicked into place. She started toward the Bureau Plat, hesitated. She had no idea what the pipe was supposed to do—what would come out of the mouthpiece. If anything.

Lippmann appeared to be in serious trouble. He was crouched very low, hard pressed to avoid the hacking, stabbing poker. Sybil looked over her shoulder at Neil. Grenville was going limp. Neil was twisting the gun out of his hand.

"Cocksucker!" That from Courtney. He slashed down again with the poker, missing David by inches.

Sybil bit blood from her lip as she went to the Bureau Plat. Courtney's back was to her. She pointed the pipe stem at him, turned it to the left. If she heard anything, it was only a tiny hiss of air. That was all. Courtney was unharmed, untouched. He did not even turn, but hacked again.

Lippmann saw that Courtney was sweating, tiring. He stayed in his crouch, bored in, fists hammering. The poker struck a glancing blow on one arm. He laughed, seized it, twisted it out of Courtney's grasp. Courtney stumbled back, recovered, made a flat dive across half the Bureau Plat, clawing for switches and buttons that would set off alarms, bring security men pouring into the study. Then he remembered the remote lock, clutched for the release first, howled rage as Lippmann dragged him off, went silent as David delivered a solid punch to his stomach, knocking him out.

"I've got the gun," Neil called from across the room. He was digging in Grenville's side pocket, brought out the .25. "Both guns." Grenville was moving feebly. Neil jerked him to his feet, held the Ostrava automatic against his spine, half-marched, half-dragged him to the Bureau Plat. "Dead?" Neil asked, staring at Courtney, who lay sprawled on the floor.

Lippmann shook his head. "He'll come to quickly. Now what, Neil?"

Sybil still held the briar. Grenville saw it. The stem was pointed in his direction. "Good Christ!" he croaked, terror-stricken. "Don't let her. Dart. Poison."

Neil began to comprehend. He gave the automatic to Lippmann, took the briar from Sybil, examined it. "One-shot, gas-operated?" he asked. Grenville nodded, eyes still wide with fear. "One of those CIA assassination gadgets I've read about?" Grenville nodded again.

"I . . . I used it on Courtney," Sybil stammered. "I don't think it worked—had no effect."

"You fired it?" Neil stared at her.

"Yes, I think so. Into his back. Turn right, then a turn left." She heard Courtney groan and saw his feet and hands move, said "Thank God, he's all right. He's alive."

"He has an hour," Grenville muttered. "One hour. Delayed-action poison."

David rammed the Ostrava muzzle against his head. "What else? Keep going."

"He'll have a stroke or heart attack. No trace."

"Antidote?" Neil snapped.

Grenville shook his head.

Sybil fainted. Neil lifted her in his arms, eased her down in a chair, returned to the Bureau Plat. He seized Grenville by the throat. "No trace—you're sure?"

"Certain." Grenville's face was turning purple. Neil eased his hold. "He's had it used before. There were autopsies. Nothing found. Natural death."

"Then you won't mind being with him when it happens." Harkness took the Ostrava from Lippmann, shoved the muzzle up into Grenville's nostril. It was Grenville's turn to plead.

"Don't kill me." The icy-nerved ex-mercenary had turned into a terrified wet blob. "I . . . I want to live, Harkness."

"You must be Jewish too," Neil jeered. He rammed the muzzle deeper. Blood spurted from Grenville's nostril. "Want to buy out?"

"Yes."

"In two minutes flat, what's with that map?"

"Sinai—" Grenville began.

"In Israel?" Lippmann exclaimed.

"Shut up," Neil rasped. "Let this bastard talk—and fast, bastard."

Grenville stammered out as much as he knew. It was enough.

Like Tinkers to Evers to Chance, Neil thought grimly. Map to True Koran to the whole fucking Muslim world blowing up in holy war.

"Neil, David . . ." Sybil walked unsteadily toward them. Her look was imploring. Lippmann read its meaning first.

"You were right," he said. "The thing didn't work." He somehow managed a grin. "You're not Lucrezia Borgia."

Neil quickly added his reassurances and pulled the automatic away from Grenville's nose. He reversed the gun, held it by the barrel, smashed the butt down on the man's skull. Grenville dropped. Harkness went behind the Bureau Plat. Courtney was sitting up. His eyes blazed hatred and rage.

"Take the money!" he said.

"Louder." Neil wanted Sybil to hear him speak, know he was alive and in command of his senses.

"I said take the money—all of it."

Harkness brought the gun butt down on his head. Courtney keeled over on his side. Lippmann crowded in, whispered: "Why did you bother?"

"Euthanasia," Neil whispered back sourly. "Let him pass away quietly in his sleep."

"How do we get out of this?" David was shaky beneath outward calm.

"We try." Neil straightened his clothing, combed fingers through his sandy hair. "Courtney's own lunacies give us an edge. Hang on." He picked up the Ostrava, emptied the magazine by firing the gun at walls and ceiling, put it in Grenville's limp hand. The .25 was next. He triggered the remaining rounds off at random. Déjà vu, he thought bitterly, remembering the hotel room in Paris, wiped the gun clean on his trousers, bent over Courtney, pressing and smearing his fingers over butt and barrel, left the gun beside him. "New scene," he grunted. "Butler and boss shot it out—their aim was lousy, though."

He picked up the briar, thrust it in a hip pocket, went to the safe. Lippmann was at his heels. "Nice touch—explains everything," Harkness said, looking at the packets of currency on the floor.

Lippmann was elsewhere again, staring in rapture at the Hals portrait. Neil shook him by the shoulder. "Wake up, the museum tour's over." He turned to Sybil. "Listen, honey. We'll have to create illusions." He spoke for a minute, asked: "You both with it?"

Sybil had pulled herself together, said yes. David, who was examining a Tintoretto over the fireplace, heartsick because a stray bullet had punctured a cherub's eye, said: "Sounds plausible."

Neil busied himself rolling up the canvas, left the books that had held the corners on the rug. This added to the impression of a struggle between Grenville and his employer. When he had the roll under his arm, Harkness stepped close to Sybil, kissed her. "You're the star, *querida*." David found the remote switch on the Bureau Plat, worked it. Sybil opened the door, went out of the *estudio*. Lippmann was next, then Neil, who held the door ajar with his shoulder.

Relief was apparent on all their faces. The outer office was deserted. Courtney's lunacies were working in their favor. So far. But there was still a very long way to go. Neil Harkness could only hope that he had allowed for all contingencies.

Sybil pressed a button on her desktop control console. The guard stationed at the side entrance door materialized a moment later.

"*Hola, Tomás.*" Sybil smiled at him, then turned, raised her voice. "Sorry, Mr. Courtney, I didn't hear you." She stepped to the *estudio* door, being held partially open by Neil, stuck her head inside, pretended to listen, said: "Yes, Tomás is already here, and I will tell him." She pretended to listen again. "Fine, Mr. Courtney. I'll see you in the morning. 'Bye." She drew her head back. Neil allowed the door to close.

Sybil spoke to the guard. "Don Jaime wants you to ride with Mr. Harkness to the gates. He's afraid the grounds patrols might stop and question him, and Mr. Harkness has to take a painting into Marbella right away. Paco will watch the entrance for you."

The ploy was precautionary. The security force might have been instructed to prevent Neil—or all of them—from leaving. Tomás could verify that Don Jaime had issued new orders, for by now he was believing that he had heard them himself.

They left the house. Harkness groaned when he saw the flat tire on the Citroën, guessed that Grenville must have released the air.

"We can take mine," Sybil suggested.

"No way. Both have to be gone."

Agonizing minutes passed while Neil, helped by Lippmann and the guard, changed the tire. They were made worse by a two-man security patrol that came by, stopped. Sybil broke into cold perspiration. Neil continued to work, let Tomás tell his colleagues that there were no problems. The men went off.

Tire changed, Neil eased the canvas roll into the backseat.

Sybil got behind the wheel of her Seat. Lippmann slid into the seat beside her. Neil leaned against the window on Sybil's side.

"You lead," he said, voice low.

"Where from here?"

"To the hospital to see Vivi. Nothing's happened at Montemar that we know of. We're all being very normal. Phone conversations are taped, right? You're on record telling Marisa what's-her-name that we'd be there."

David leaned across Sybil. "The map. It's like an H-bomb, Neil."

"You're not thinking, Dave. It's a life-insurance policy for the present. Lot of people want it. They may come after us, but no one will touch us until they know where it is. Let's go."

Harkness and Tomás climbed into the Citroën. Sybil pulled out of the parking area first. She stalled the car. "My mind's in a flat spin—so's my stomach," she told Dave, and restarted the car. "Too much input." She shifted into gear. "Not the nicest way to end part of my life—and I did like working for Courtney. Sometimes I even liked *him*."

There were tissues in the glove compartment. She took some. There were tears in her eyes.

The drive to the main gates seemed endless. Sybil braked. Neil pulled up behind her. Tomás dismounted and spoke to the men on duty. The gates swung open. Tomás and the other guards saluted.

Sybil drove off the grounds with Neil close behind. Both cars turned onto the Carretera de Cádiz only moments before a pair of helicopters skimmed in from the direction of the Serrania de Ronda.

36

Gruppe Thiele enjoyed unexpected luck.

Montemar security men were aware that some sort of threat had been made against Don Jaime and alerted to possible emergency. The fuselages of the two helicopters were emblazoned with Guardia Civil markings and insignia. The security men naturally assumed that Don Jaime had taken the next logical step. He had notified Spanish authorities and requested aid from the crack paramilitary national police force. He was an important man, a *billionario*. Madrid would give him whatever he asked. And, they told each other, the Guardia must consider the *emergencia* to be *muy grave*. The choppers were ignoring the helipad. They landed between the house and reflecting pool, in front of the main entrance. Their rotors continued to windmill.

Hatches swung up and out. Half a dozen uniformed civil guardsmen leaped to the ground. Their leather tricorn hats were set square. Some had submachine guns slung over their shoulders. They took up positions away from the air blast of the rotors, stood at rigid attention.

Then a *teniente* alighted. After him, a tall man of distinguished look and bearing. He was resplendent in the dress uniform of a *coronel*—peaked cap instead of tricorn, Sam Browne belt and pistol holster mirror-polished, white-gloved hands. Several security men started toward the copters. The colonel waved them back, spoke rapidly in the flawless Castilian Spanish to be expected from an officer of his rank.

Señor Courtney wished the Guardia operation be conducted in secrecy. Priceless objects stolen from him had been recovered. They were to be taken directly to him. The security men were to carry on as before, but stay away from the house and the helicopters.

Some of the guardsmen at attention broke ranks. They helped others unload some heavy olive-drab footlockers from a copter. The *teniente* and *coronel* marched to the entrance doors. The lieutenant rang. Although Kyle Dunne was Irish, he was Black Irish, with hair and eyes that could have been Spanish, and his face was deeply tanned. But he spoke little of the language. The talking would be done by Alfonso Fuentes, disinherited son of an aristocratic Madrid family who had served for many years with Gruppe Thiele and was, for the day, a colonel in the Guardia Civil.

A manservant opened the doors and, intimidated by the uniforms, pulled them wide. Coronel Fuentes and *teniente* aide entered. Behind them came men carrying footlockers.

"Don Jaime is expecting us," Fuentes said. "His *estudio* is that way, no?" The servant moved to lead him. "Remain here."

The footlockers were placed on the entrance-atrium floor. Three men followed the officers. The others stayed. They were silent and there was something odd about them, the servant thought as he shut the great doors. But it was none of his affair. He asked politely if the gentlemen wished anything, received curt negative headshakes and hand gestures of dismissal as a reply. Only fools failed to obey the Guardia promptly, he thought, and scurried off into the house.

"Thought he'd have more guards indoors," Kevin Dunne remarked. He had unholstered his sidearm, a Walther P-38 with a bulb silencer.

"Colonel" Fuentes had drawn his—an identical—weapon. "So did I." The trio of guardsmen accompanying them all carried submachine guns. They unslung them, held them at the ready.

They turned a corner. A Fragonard garden scene hanging on the wall caught his eye. "It will be a great pity," he sighed. He took pride in being a man of culture.

"We're only after one—*if* he has it," Dunne reminded him.

The outer office was empty. "Damned funny," Kevin Dunne muttered. There should have been a guard and a secretary. Or so Leslie Grenville had once told Rashid el Muein, who passed the information on to Horst Thiele. "Two of you at the door," Dunne said to the men. "You—come with us."

Fuentes was about to knock on the *estudio* door. Dunne stopped him. "We barge in, Fonso, like bloody commandos." He tried the knob, flung the door wide, burst inside with Fuentes and the man with the submachine gun on his heels.

"Good bloody Christ!" Dunne skidded to a halt. "A fucking shambles." Leslie Grenville, whom he recognized from old, lay spread-eagled in front of a huge writing table. Someone lay behind it. And there was money everywhere—strewn on the floor, piled inside an open safe. Dunne laughed. "We never saw the money, did we, Fonso?"

"Never." Fuentes also laughed. "Go find some sacks," he told the man with the machine gun. "Take it all—and everything else in the safe."

Dunne examined Grenville. "Out but alive," he said, and went around the writing table. "It's Courtney. Same for him."

Alfonso Fuentes was walking around the room, scanning it carefully. "I do not believe this," he said. "Two guns. Bullet holes. Neither man is hit. They could not have been such poor shots."

"Couldn't have knocked each other out, either," Dunne said. He had taken an ice-water carafe from the table and was pouring the contents over Grenville's face, trying to revive him. There was a feeble response, then nothing. He took a letter opener, held one of Grenville's hands, jabbed the point deep under a fingernail, causing pain that penetrates unconsciousness. Grenville's eyes opened. Dunne jabbed harder. The eyes began to focus.

"H'lo, Les. How's the cockless wonder?"

"Dunne . . . Kyle." Grenville tried to sit up. Dunne slammed him back to the floor.

"Don't waste time," Fuentes said. He had gone to Courtney, was slapping his face.

"I'm not . . . won't," Dunne said. Their orders were to do the job quickly but if possible find out if Courtney had a painting by Velázquez or knew where it was. Perhaps Grenville knew.

"Rest easy, Les, we're only after a damned picture," he wheedled as he nudged the bulb silencer under Grenville's jaw and wriggled the P-38 from side to side. "A Velázquez."

"Harkness."

"Stop talking the balls you don't have."

"Neil Harkness. An American. He took it . . . has it. He's here, Kyle. In Cabo Verde. No . . . no trouble finding him."

Kyle Dunne had much experience in breaking men, knew when they were broken and telling the truth. He was a little surprised that Leslie Grenville had broken so quickly—but then, he thought, maybe a man does lose his guts when he loses his genitals.

"Now let me up, Kyle."

"Sure, Les." Dunne's fingers tightened on the trigger. There was the sound of a finger snap, and the top of Grenville's head disintegrated. Blood and brain matter and bits of bone splattered against the underside of the writing table.

"This one can talk now," Fuentes said.

"Prop the bastard up in his throne."

They flung Courtney into his swivel chair. He was dazed, in pain, stared unseeing. "Thiele," he whispered. "You're from Thiele."

"Clever." Dunne slapped his face as Fuentes had. The pale blue eyes cleared.

"Grenville!" Courtney called out.

"He's no longer around."

"The safe," Courtney mumbled. His memory had gone back to the safe in which the Reverend Wendell Courtney—his father—kept his money. But he had his own safe, and money could buy safety. It always had. "Over two million in it. You can have it—"

"We already do." Fuentes turned the swivel chair so Courtney could see the civil guardsman stuffing packets of currency into one of the sacks he had procured somewhere or other. "We want the painting." It was wise to cross-check what Grenville had said.

"Painting . . . map." James Courtney closed his eyes. He had built a great pyramid, climbed almost to its apex. Almost. Not quite. And now the pyramid was crumbling. He was losing his footing. "Thiele knows I have hundreds of millions. Tell him I'll pay—"

Dunne snickered. "Should have told him yourself—before. You're a pig, Courtney—wanted it all for yourself. You and those stupid Pflegebrüder bastards should've worked with Horst from the beginning. He said I should tell you that."

Courtney felt another stone of the pyramid give way.

"Where is the picture . . . the map?" Fuentes slapped Courtney's face again, hard.

"Harkness."

"Checks." Dunne shrugged. "He's all yours, Fonso."

Horst Thiele had given precise orders. Courtney was not to die instantly. He was to see what Thiele had called "the final disintegration." And then he had quoted from the 111th *surah* of the Koran: "His wealth shall avail him not, nor what he hath gotten in fee. Burned in blazing fire shall he be."

Fuentes fired one finger-snap shot into Courtney's stomach, turned the chair so that he could slump against the Bureau Plat. He could live hours with such a gut shot—in excruciating agony. But Courtney did not feel pain yet. Only a numbed sensation in his belly. He did not slump, but placed his forearms on the tabletop to support himself. He watched the two men in uniform leave, pause in front of his safe—"Who opened it?" he wanted to ask—pick up what looked like sacks that seemed to bulge. Then he saw a third uniformed man. He had a submachine gun. He raised it. Not to shoot. He turned the weapon and in raw vandalism drew the front sight diagonally across the Frans Hals portrait, slashing through the canvas.

"No!" Courtney screamed. Now he could feel pain. Terrible pain. As though his own face were being cut open. His fingers fumbled to the scar on his cheek. It was intact. There was no blood. Yet he could feel the pain.

There were four footlockers. One was carried into the great dining hall, another up to the first landing of the main staircase. The third was pulled to the center of the entrance atrium. The fourth was carried into Courtney's *estudio*. The lids were opened, the ten-minute-delay time fuses activated.

Courtney watched the two men who brought the footlocker to the study. The pain in his face had receded, but a new pain was growing in his belly.

"What?" He could barely form the word. The men did not answer.

He did not see them leave the study, did not hear the helicopters lift off soon after. His fingers groped blindly on the tabletop. The million-dollar desk, he thought, and an inner smile curled around the pain in his stomach, easing it. I have millions, hundreds of millions, a fortune greater than any other, an organization unlike any other. A montage of successes, achieved against what others saw as insuperable odds, unreeled in his brain. College. The war years. Gemeinschaft Orff. Wealth amassed, multiplied. The pyramid isn't crumbling after all. Nothing I've built can ever crumble while I'm alive. And I've always outwitted them all. I'm still alive.

Fingers touched the Lucite cube encasing the B'nai B'rith medal. The inner smile became a laugh and the pain eased further. Jews. The Pflegebrüders. He had fooled the entire world—and was about to do it on a far grander scale. Before long, his greatest triumph would not only stun the world but also give him control over a very large part of it. With the map.

The cube dropped from his hand. He tried to remember. Yes. Harkness had brought the map back. All was well. Would be. Soon. Hand and fingers moved slowly, fumbled toward the intercom, did or did not touch and depress a lever.

"Sybil." He wanted her to do something. What? He'd think of it the moment she replied.

Silence.

"Sybil."

Nothing.

Wait a minute. Sybil was in . . . No, she was going to a hospital. Why? Memory banks faltered, recovered. Oh, Christ, my stomach! Sybil wasn't hurt. Who? Images spun, then a freeze frame.

"Vivian . . ."

William Moore hurried to the reception room. He told Rashid el Muein that Horst Thiele had arrived.

"He came in one limousine and brought two others."

"Send the servants to their quarters and usher him in."

The number of automobiles surprised Rashid, but when Horst Thiele entered, he chuckled. "You have a caravan—to carry away the money, perhaps?"

"Perhaps. We shall know in minutes."

The Guardia Civil helicopters were even more of a surprise, and for a moment Rashid almost panicked.

"My surgeons," Thiele calmed him.

They watched from a window as the craft settled on the lawn. Their engines stopped. Men got out. They were in civilian clothes, having changed quickly on the short flight from Montemar. Some went directly to the limousines. A few remained near the copters. Two—Fuentes and Dunne—strode toward the house. Rashid sent Bill Moore to meet them and, verging on panic again, asked Thiele:

"The use of Guardia helicopters was clever—but they won't be left here?"

"A most stupid question," the German said coldly, the nonanswer satisfying el Muein.

Moore escorted Alfonso Fuentes and Kyle Dunne into the room.

"My chief surgeons," Thiele said.

"Finished," Dunne reported, added details, went to a window facing the northeast. "You can see the smoke already."

"How can I be certain that Courtney—?" Rashid began.

Dunne whirled. "We could have cut his head off and dumped it in your lap—if you'd asked."

El Muein was in no position to quibble, not with Thiele's two men inside the house, others outside. "Bring the money," he said.

William Moore made three trips out of the room, returned each time with a leather suitcase, lined them up at Thiele's feet.

"Three million," Rashid said. "You can look—or even count."

Horst Thiele shook his head. "No time. Later. But I do not think you would cheat us. Do you, Alfonso?"

"No," was all Fuentes said, and drew the Walther from a holster under his civilian suit jacket. There were two finger-snap reports.

Rashid el Muein and William Moore toppled. Each had taken a bullet through the heart.

Kyle Dunne ran out to the main entrance, flung open the door, whistled. Two pairs of men, each carrying an olive-drab foot-locker between them, made a dash from the copters to the house.

"One in the room with the bodies, the other almost anywhere," Dunne instructed. "Five-minute fuse delays, three for the bombs on the choppers—and we're off."

Former SS *Sturmbannführer* Thiele sat between Dunne and Fuentes in the leading vehicle as the convoy of Mercedes limousines drove away from el Muein's estate. He was pleased with his men, congratulated himself on his masterful planning.

Montemar was in flames. Within moments, Rashid el Muein's house and the helicopters would also be ablaze. There was not enough fire-fighting equipment on the entire Costa del Sol to extinguish conflagrations fed by thermite, white phosphorus, and aviation fuel. The authorities would be completely baffled. They would trace as far as Rashid el Muein, of course, then run around in circles as they sought new trails to follow. For a full day, at absolute minimum, Thiele estimated. By then the limousines would long since have vanished, pushed off a cliff on the Málaga road and into the sea. The money—including the unexpected bonus brought from Montemar—and most of his men would have taken commercial flights to various countries, from where they would return to Riyadh.

Most of his men. Not all. Fuentes and Dunne would stay with him. "I know how to find Harkness and the map," he told them. "We shall have them both before the day is over. I guarantee you."

37

Marisa Alarcón felt better after speaking to Sybil Pearson. It would do Vivi good to have two more of her friends come to the hospital, boost her morale, if nothing else. A person who suffered was certain to feel better when surrounded by concerned and sympathetic friends, Marisa thought, but the thought turned slightly sour. She could not claim—not even to herself—that she was actually suffering. Certainly not physical pain, and the emotional hurt of rejection—so new and novel—was not sharp and localized, but rather a dull and oppressive overall ache of confused loneliness. And there was no one near at hand who could offer her comfort. She had formed close acquaintance only with Vivian and Carlos, and causes cannot provide balm.

No, that's not quite right, Marisa reflected, returning to Vivian's room. If Vivi were well, her normal self, she would ease the ache. By listening to Marisa with a soft smile, then perhaps with a sigh, perhaps with a sad shake of the head, telling her what she had before. That she liked Carlos, considered him a dear friend as well as an employee so trusted and valued that he was more like a business associate, but that she was not in love with him. It would have helped, for at least there would be the reassurance that Carlos was himself at the receiving end of rejection.

Marisa did not knock on Vivian's door—why should she? the girl asked herself. In any event, a knock could disturb the patient, and to prevent any noise doing this, she opened the door silently and stepped inside. She took only a single step and froze, her mind in a sudden turmoil of bewilderment, anger, resentment, and a sense of having been deceived.

Carlos sat where he had been sitting before, at the side of Vivian's bed. But his arms were around Vivian's hips, and he was bent over, whispering to her. Vivian was stroking his hair. Tenderly, lovingly, it seemed to Marisa, and she too was whispering.

Marisa listened. She could not help but listen.

"*Querida* . . . my love . . . always my love." Carlos jumbled Spanish and English. "Since the first—"

"Ssh. I know," Vivian was soothing him. The fingers of one hand tried to entwine themselves in his hair, lacked sufficient strength, failed, resumed the stroking motions of which they were capable.

"You know . . . you've known?"

"Yes."

"And you . . .?"

"Ssh, Carlos," Vivi tried to silence him. The stroking fingers groped for his lips feebly, found and pressed against them. He kissed the fingertips.

"Vivi, I will do anything . . . we can go away . . ."

"My dear, my dear." Vivian's murmur was a cry of anguish. The doctors had told her nothing except that she was out of danger. But she knew without being told that her face had been destroyed. "It can't be—ever. Try to understand—"

"No. I understand only that . . ."

Marisa at last retreated into the corridor, drawing the door closed silently after her. The ache was gnawing pain now. Vivian had lied to her. She was aware of Carlos' love, and whether they had ever been lovers or not, it seemed clear to Marisa that the feelings were not, probably never had been, one-sided. One part of Marisa's mind and personality had not been included in the abrupt maturing process—and probably never would be. Vengefulness rose within her. She thought of Vivian, her face disfigured, her body scarred—and if that was what Carlos still wanted, he was welcome to her.

Seething, Marisa went back to the waiting room and flung herself into a plastic-upholstered chair. Sybil Pearson and Neil Harkness were due to arrive in an hour or so. She would be there when they did. Good manners demanded that much. But no more. Once they had taken over the vigil, she would leave, retrieve her car from the police and her things from Broadmoor, and go home to Barcelona. Then, perhaps, a week or two on the French Riviera—where aches and gnawing pains can be made to disappear quickly. In light of what she had just seen and heard, Marisa desperately wanted to get away. And to forget. About the Dixons, Carlos, the articles she had hoped to write. About the entire series of experiences that had within a matter of hours become a nightmare.

Neil Harkness had second thoughts. He blew his horn, signaling Sybil to slow down, pulled alongside her car, and shouted: "I'm making a stop at the Puerto. You two go on. I'll only be a couple of minutes behind you."

Sybil stared back at him dubiously, but nodded. Neil fed gas to the Citroën, shot far ahead of the Seat, and took the Cabo Verde turnoff.

Harkness pressed the accelerator—and his luck—hard, going through the *pueblo* and on into the marina area, where he stopped outside the Espada. He left the motor running, dashed inside carrying the rolled-up painting. Enrique, the owner, stood just inside the door, and there was a large midday crowd in the bar.

"Keep this for me, Enrique"—Neil thrust the roll at him—"put it anywhere, as long as it's out of sight."

Enrique was accustomed to performing odd services for his regular customers, but wanted to talk about Kenneth Dixon. He took the bundle, passed it on to a waiter.

"The police are looking for Dixon. There is even a big *premio*."

"I know . . . have to rush . . . see you later. Thanks."

Neil burned rubber making a U-turn on the quay. As he drove through the *pueblo* to reach the main highway again, he heard sirens and Klaxons, slowed a little, glanced around him. Two columns of smoke—widely separated—were visible in the distance. The nearest was the larger, rising a hundred feet or more into the sky. His mind elsewhere, he assumed they were more of the brush fires that often plague the Costa. He had turned onto the highway and was speeding toward Marbella before impressions registered. The smoke was black, oily, unlike any given off by a brush fire, and the larger column rose from somewhere very near Montemar. He shrugged mentally. Black smoke or no, they were probably brush fires after all.

Bad ones, he thought. Oncoming traffic on the east-bound lanes of the divided highway was slowing, easing over to the far lane, being swept aside by more sirens and Klaxons. Police cars, ambulances, and the fire trucks of the Marbella *cuerpo de bomberos* roared by. A mile farther, instant replay—with ambulances and fire-fighting equipment coming from Torremolinos.

Harkness cursed. Drivers ahead of him, cowed by the sirens or merely curious to watch the emergency equipment go by, were reducing their speed. He saw a narrow gap between a *camión* loaded with hay and an Austrian-licensed Volks Rabbit, risked his fenders, made it through and past.

The first alarm had come from Montemar, a hysterical report that the Guardia Civil had attacked the mansion and blown it up. This was disregarded as the ravings of a lunatic. Then other calls poured in to police and fire departments. Although frantic, they sounded rational—and by then, billows of smoke were visible from many points.

Highway police were the earliest arrivals on the scene. They found the mansion ablaze and chaos on the grounds. Servants, security men, employees from the CVI annex milled about. Some babbled incoherently, some wept. Those able to speak sensibly recited the same impossible tale.

Two Guardia Civil helicopters had landed. Men headed by a *coronel* had gone inside. They took boxes—of Don Jaime's property that had been stolen and recovered—inside. Then they came out—with or without sacks in their hands—eyewitness security men differed on this point. The *coronel* declared that Don Jaime wished no one else to enter the house for fifteen minutes. The guardsmen—yes, yes, in uniform—had reboarded the helicopters and taken off. Then the mansion had erupted like a volcano.

Anyone still inside?

Don Jaime. Senor Grenville, the majordomo. One servant, perhaps two—no one could be sure.

All others out and safe?

Yes. It was believed yes.

The highway police were badly shaken. Not by the fire, but by the political implications. They remembered—as everyone in Spain remembered—the abortive *golpe de estado* on February 23, 1981. Several officers of the Guardia Civil were allegedly involved in the plot to overthrow Spain's democratic government and establish a military dictatorship. This might be the beginning of another attempt.

But why start a *golpe* with an attack on a *norteamericano?*

An easy answer presented itself. Large segments of the Spanish population resented the presence of ultrarich *extranjeros* and the economic power they wielded in the country. If the military wanted to stage a new coup, it could gain support from the working and middle classes by demonstrating its dislike for the foreigners.

The policemen radioed in their reports cautiously and with extreme delicacy. Such a matter as this required study by and decisions from the highest echelons of government.

The first *bomberos* who arrived declared it was useless to try to fight the fire. Their equipment was inadequate for a blaze of such magnitude. However, they hooked hoses to hydrants connected to the estate's private water supply, immersed others in the reflecting and swimming pools, and started their pumps.

By then the authorities were receiving reports of a second fire. On the estate of the Arab business tycoon Rashid el Muein. Again, it was being said that it was the work of the Civil Guard. However, something had evidently gone wrong for them. Their helicopters were also burning.

Now it was necessary to inform higher—the highest—authorities. There were top-priority conversations with cabinet ministers in Madrid. Government reaction was swift. The regular armed forces were placed on full alert. Civil Guard units were ordered restricted to their various headquarters and barracks until their loyalty could be determined. Emergency decrees were drawn up for signature by the Prime Minister and His Majesty Juan Carlos I, the nation's constitutional monarch. When signed, they would declare all Spain to be in a state of siege. What would happen after that, no one cared to speculate.

Neil more than made up the time lost by stopping off at the Bar Espada. He passed Sybil's Seat at the edge of Marbella without noticing, and pulled up in front of the hospital moments before she and Lippmann. He parked in a space clearly marked "*Reservado,*" sprang from the car, and vaulted up the Hospital Marbella steps. The lobby was in turmoil. Nursing sisters, attendants, clerks, and a handful of young doctors were all talking excitedly and at once. He made out words and phrases at random.

". . . *golpe . . . anarquistas . . . no, no, la Guardia! . . . el billonario . . .*"

He was still piecing it together when Sybil and David Lippmann came up behind him. Sybil touched his arm. He jumped.

"Insane, surreal," he stammered. "Civil Guard's on a

rampage—blew up Montemar and the place owned by that Arab. These people are talking revolution."

"The police and fire brigades that passed us," Sybil said.

"They'll probably have tanks out next," Harkness said. He reached for a Celta, saw the "*Prohibido fumar*" sign, decided it was a restriction with which he should comply, took a deep breath. "They say Courtney's dead . . ."

Sybil started to fold; Lippmann grabbed and held her.

"Honey, it wasn't you!" Neil exclaimed. "He . . . well, he didn't get out of the house."

Sybil stared at him a moment. "We did, though," she said, eased herself from David's hold, and stood—remarkably well, everything considered, Neil thought—on her own. But she had blurted the words and didn't know quite what she meant or how she meant it, and repeated, "We did, though." She realized that it was an expression of relief—and gratitude—that the three of them were alive. She felt a great need to embrace Neil, and did. She also felt an urge to cry, but fought it down. Harkness kissed the top of her head, tousled her close-cut hair.

"We're here to see Vivi," she reminded him.

"I can stay outside or wait in the car," Lippmann offered. "There's already enough confusion—"

"There'll be more if we separate and then have to look for each other," Neil said, and thought of the many reasons—best left unmentioned—why the three of them should stay very close together.

They made their way through the crowd in the lobby to the waiting room. There was only one person there, an attractive and well-dressed Spanish girl whose petulant expression changed to no expression at all as they entered. She had to be Marisa Alarcón, Neil decided, stepped forward, and introduced himself, then Sybil and David. Marisa eyed Lippmann quizzically. She had never heard of him before and asked:

"Are you also a friend of Vivian?"

"Afraid I've never even met her."

"Dave is a friend of ours," Neil interposed. "How is Vivi?"

"Carlos is with her." Marisa's voice was like the dry scratch of crumpled paper blown along a sidewalk by the wind.

"No doctors or nurses?"

"Since the first news of the *golpe*, there has been no one at all."

"Where is her room?" Sybil asked. Marisa told her. Sybil glanced at Neil. "Shall we go?" He nodded.

"I'll stay here—only be in the way," David said. He flashed

Marisa a smile, and her answering look, no longer quizzical, showed a glint of interest instead. "We can keep each other company."

Why not? Marisa thought. If there really was a *golpe*, there could be chaos—and worse—outside in the streets.

Neil and Sybil left. Marisa patted a chair next to her, and when David sat down, asked: "Are they lovers?"

Dave's interest was aroused by the blunt, first-off question. Her mind is where mine is, he thought. He had known sexual drought since leaving Los Angeles—scarcely more than a week ago, but it seemed like years. "They don't make a secret of it," he replied.

"You also like Sybil very much."

"Let's say I would have liked to like her very much." She played the are-they-lovers question for openers, Lippmann mused. Let's see what happens when I top it. "The result of congenital flaw. I'm subject to fits of heterosexual urges—think I'm having one now."

Marisa laughed, studied his face, frowned. "You look like—"

"It's the other way around. Robert Redford looks like *me*. We're almost identical twins. Except that our eyes and hair are different, I have a broken nose, I'm taller and weigh more, he's a good actor and I'm no actor at all"—get this next in fast so we have everything straight from the start—"and I'm Jewish." No negative reaction to that, which was good, promising. "Of course, he's married. I'm not. Otherwise, not counting hidden scars, marks, and blemishes, we're exactly alike."

She had listened, laughed again, leaned toward him. "Are you staying on the Costa long, Mr. . . . ?"

"Dave, okay? About"—he almost said "about a year," then remembered and corrected himself—"about as long as it takes to buy some new clothes and make a plane reservation." Luckily his passport, ticket, and traveler's checks were in his wallet. Otherwise—if Montemar had really burned down, and Dave was inclined to believe the stories that it had—he had nothing else left. No books, papers, personal effects, not even a clean pair of shorts or a toothbrush.

Marisa took what he said as some kind of joke, the point of which eluded her, but she was grateful to be amused. Especially by an attractive and clearly masculine male. Besides, he had told her that he was Jewish. Marisa counted numerous *judíos* of both sexes among her acquaintances. But, she reflected, never—at least to her knowledge—had she ever been to bed with a Jewish man. She found herself wondering if—as some women said—

they were highly sexed, sensual, different. She was already measuring David Lippmann as a possible windfall successor to Carlos, and moments later, they were deep in conversation.

Neil tapped on the door softly, and hearing Carlos' voice say "*Adelante*," opened it. He and Sybil entered. Carlos sat beside Vivi's bed, holding her hand. He remained seated, turned his head. His face was haggard, his eyes red and puffed from weeping. He looked a thousand years old.

None of this surprised Sybil or Harkness. They had long been aware of Carlos' feelings for Vivian. But they were horrified at seeing Vivi—or rather the bandage-shrouded figure that lay in the bed and might never again be the Vivian Dixon they knew.

"Vivi is awake," Carlos said hoarsely. "She wants to talk to you. You must listen to what she says. Please."

Neil went to the foot of the bed, stood. Sybil took the chair Marisa had used earlier, touched Vivian's wrist.

The bandaged head spoke with astonishing strength and clarity: "Sybil. Neil. Thank you for coming." A pause; then the tone changed. "Have you heard?"

"Uh . . . heard what, Vivi?" Sybil responded warily.

"That Jim is dead."

Harkness cursed silently. Who had been moron enough to tell her? Carlos supplied the answer without being asked.

"A nurse came in, very excited. I tried to stop her."

"I'm glad you couldn't." Vivian's fingers flexed—was it lovingly? Sybil wondered, noticing—against Carlos' hand, then made as if to grip it for support. Her voice turned harsh and unsteady. "I have to tell you. I should have told everyone. Years ago. Jim Courtney was my father."

Sybil had long suspected there were complex dimensions to the relationship between Vivian and Courtney, but never dreamed of anything like this. She gasped.

"Vivi's delirious," Neil said, stunned.

"No." The mummy-like head spoke clearly, steadily again. "I'm entirely lucid, Neil. I've already told Carlos." Vivi's fingers were making caressing movements on Carlos' hand once more. "I'm not sorry that Jim is dead. You should know that, too. He lived only to destroy others—everyone who came near him."

Amen to that, Neil thought, but wished she would drop the subject, because talking was certain to drain her strength, emotional and physical, and what she needed most was rest. Sybil seemed to read his mind.

"Let Vivi talk," she said. "It's catharsis. Best thing that could happen."

"Hold my other hand, Sybil," Vivian said. Sybil did, felt fingernails press into her palm, the fingers tremble. "Has anyone seen Ken or heard from him?"

"Uh . . . no, not yet." It was Neil who replied.

"Of course not. You see, Ken is dead too."

"Vivi—" Sybil began to protest. Vivian's voice stopped her.

"Maybe no one knows it yet, but I do. I know it inside."

"Easy—you're imagining things," Neil said. Where the hell are the fucking doctors? he thought. She needs a shot—something to make her sleep. But Vivian continued.

"Please, Neil. Ken and I were close—very close—in our own way. Two of Jim's victims who needed each other desperately because we were. Now he's gone. I can feel the emptiness where he was part of me."

Vivian released Sybil's hand, but not Carlos', and began to weep softly. Carlos, oblivious of the others in the room, leaned far forward, laid his cheek against Vivian's thigh, wept with her.

Sybil stood up, prodded at Neil's ribs. "Out—but like right now." Her lips formed a smile at once maternal and cryptic. "Vivi, Carlos, if either of you is registering, we'll be back later today." She all but dragged Harkness to the door, opened it.

"We've got to find a goddamned doctor!" he fumed as they stepped out into the corridor.

"Imbecile." Sybil closed the door, still smiling. "She already has the best doctor giving her the finest treatment any female patient could have."

"What in the name of Christ are you talking about?"

"Listen." Sybil patted his cheek as though he were a small and mentally retarded child. "Put your ear up to the door—go on."

He did, reluctantly, and heard:

". . . always, Vivi. Forever. I love you."

"Carlos, Carlos . . ." That also sounded like "I love you."

Neil could find nothing to say but "Well, I'll be goddamned," and meekly allowed Sybil to herd him down the corridor.

The Madrid government's fear of a *golpe* was erased in less than an hour. Even cursory examination of the still-burning helicopters sufficed to prove they were not of any make or type ever used by the Civil Guard or armed forces—and, in any event, all their aircraft were accounted for. As were all officers and men of the Guardia Civil, and thus none of them could have been involved. There was no shred of evidence of disloyalty, much less a plot to stage a coup. The conclusion was inescapable. A meticulously designed—and initially convincing—illusion had been created.

Obviously there had been—and probably still was—some kind of huge, dangerous conspiracy. But the most logical suspects—Basque terrorists, Catalan separatists, Red extremists, neo-*falangistas*—had to be ruled out. None possessed the resources needed to create the illusion. Furthermore, Spanish intelligence agencies had reliable informants planted in these groups. The conclusion was inescapable. The plotters and raiders came from some country outside Spain. The implications were harrowing. All the more so because the targeted victims were an ultrarich American and a super-rich Arab who held British citizenship. Already, the Embassies of the United States, Britain, and three Arab countries were threatening to lodge formal protests with the Spanish government. The President of the United States—no less notorious for grabbing headlines than for sleeping late—had been barely awake when informed of the incidents, but immediately issued an official statement. He was, he said, appalled by the lack of security provided for American citizens residing in Spain and hinted at taking the matter to the United Nations.

A member of UN and NATO and poised to enter the European Common Market, Spain could not afford diplomatic condemnation for failure to safeguard the lives of foreigners within its borders. Tens of thousands of expatriates resided in Spain, and tourists came there by the tens of millions each year. Like them or not—and many Spaniards, with ample justification, did not—the *extranjeros* were vital to the country's economy. Tourist spending alone accounted for almost nine percent of Spain's GNP.

New fears now hung over the Madrid government, and new orders were flashed to all military, police, and civil officials throughout the country. There had been no attempted *golpe de estado*. The attacks had been carried out by foreigners of unknown national origin who were clearly trained in commando-type operations. They were to be tracked down, found, and taken into custody . . .

". . . by whatever means and at whatever cost necessary."

Marisa Alarcón was feeling better. Much better. She would never have believed that an art historian could also be a boxer, an amusing companion, and a handsome man who radiated a palpable degree of animal sexuality. Then, she thought, there was the touch of the exotic. Yes, exotic, for he *was* Jewish, after all. But not religious—he told her that when she had asked. And she had made it clear that she was not, either, purposely not looking at the crucifix on the opposite wall while she spoke.

He was about to say something, but stopped as Neil and Sybil reappeared, and Marisa immediately asked:

"How is Vivi?"

"Amazing," Sybil replied. She had no reason to think that Marisa and Carlos were anything but casual acquaintances, and beamed. "Carlos is nursing her—and working miracles."

Marisa shifted her gaze, found herself staring at the crucifix, quickly shifted it again, angled for comment by saying ever so casually, "I think poor Carlos is in love with her." She meant it, of course, as an expression of pity for a man in love with ruined face and body.

Sybil missed the intent completely and, without thinking, blurted, "We can all omit the 'poor.' I think it's mutual."

Neil glowered at her. Bad enough that they had learned so many of Vivian's secrets. They should not be passed around to others. Whatever Vivi's intuitive feeling about Ken Dixon, Ken might well be (and Neil was inclined to think that he was) still alive. He could turn up at any time, and more than one battered wife had forgiven the husband who battered her and returned to him. If that happened and word got back to Ken that Vivi was in love with Carlos, God only knew what might result. Sybil read the message, looked apologetic, and was silent.

Marisa, having heard enough—too much—focused on David Lippmann, her expression unmistakable, an open invitation. Dave welcomed it. Beneath a surface he somehow managed to make appear calm, his nerves were in jagged shreds. Sex would mend them.

"Leave your car," Neil said to Sybil. "You and David can come in mine."

"Where are we going?" Sybil asked.

"Tell you later." Neil wanted to retrieve the painting from the Espada and go on to Sybil's apartment, where the three of them could decide what they should do next. Or *try* to decide, he thought gloomily.

"Please, may I come with you?" Marisa rose from her chair. "I'll leave a message for Carlos . . . and Vivi."

Harkness would have refused her, but Dave spoke up: "Sure" and Sybil said: "I can't see why not." At that point a number of nurses and hospital attendants boiled into the room, flung themselves into the chairs, and lit cigarettes. They had come to discuss the latest news bulletins about the attempted *golpe*. Neil did not want to risk starting an argument with his companions. It might be overheard—and their position was already risky. He would find a way of shedding Marisa—and soon.

"All right," he said bleakly, jamming a Celta between his lips.

Horst Thiele considered himself to be safe at the Melià Don Pepe—certainly until morning, when he would be leaving hotel, Costa, and Spain. The last guarded news reports he had heard half an hour earlier indicated that the Spanish authorities were still chasing their own, and he thought it hilarious. He had succeeded in making the Spaniards believe their Guardia Civil was attempting to take over the government. One "unconfirmed" report had it that the entire Guardia was confined to posts and barracks. This, Thiele was aware, neutralized the most potent and efficient of all Spanish law-enforcement agencies.

"We may move freely," he told Kevin Dunne and Alfonso Fuentes, whom he had brought to his room. Dunne was drinking straight Bushmill's, Fuentes *raki*, for which he had acquired a taste during a sojourn on Cyprus. Thiele sipped a *spritzer*, thought of the meeting he would have before long with Khomeini in Qum, and talked of Neil Harkness.

"Harkness berths his vessel in Puerto Cabo Verde," he was saying. "It is not there, but he is back. He has an apartment, but seldom uses it. He stays mostly with a woman—the late American magnate's secretary"—that was good for a chuckle—"and there is a bar he frequents along with many others who moor in the port." He gave Fuentes a sheet of paper. "The names and addresses are written down for you. If you cannot locate Harkness at any of the places, ask questions. He is well known. Someone will tell you where he is to be found."

"He might have cleared out when he heard . . ." Dunne said.

"No, he is certain to have stayed, because of the woman."

"Sybil Pearson," Fuentes read from the paper. "Is she worth it?"

Thiele shrugged. "I have never seen her." He sipped more of his watered white wine. "Threaten to kill her, and Harkness will give you the Velázquez. Of course, once you have it, they must both be removed."

The two men finished their drinks and Thiele gave them their final instructions. Another member of the *Gruppe* had bought a used and battered panel truck. It was parked on the Calle Ricardo—a one-block-long street in Pueblo Cabo Verde. . . .

"Here are the documents and the keys. There are workmen's

coveralls inside the van and tool boxes. Put on the coveralls, and you will be able to go anywhere."

Dunne and Fuentes went to Pueblo Cabo Verde by taxi. The van was where it was supposed to be. They changed into the worn blue Spanish workmen's coveralls they found inside the truck. Their first stop was Neil Harkness' apartment. It was deserted. Lugging his toolbox, Fuentes—now speaking rough, idiomatic Andalusian Spanish—made inquiries of the building *portero*. The porter denied knowledge of any remodeling *Señor* Harkness had ordered done in his *apartamento*. As a matter of fact, he had not seen *Señor* Harkness for many, many days. No, he was not authorized to open the *apartamento* to anyone—and *adios*. With all that was going on, the *portero* wanted to remain inside, in his own *apartamento*, and drink himself senseless on *vino tinto*.

The *portero* at Sybil Pearson's apartment building was no less worried over events that were being reported—and talked about—and he was only slightly more helpful. The *senorita* had spent the night home—with her *amante*—and gone to work as usual. The porter said—crossing himself—he hoped she had not been injured in the atrocity at Montemar and would return soon. Perhaps in the evening, also as usual—and, again, no, he could not allow the electricians into her home. It was a condominium, and each tenant was an owner. . . .

"The bar next," Kevin Dunne said when he and Fuentes clambered back into the van. "If we don't find him there, we'll come back and nail her here."

It was three P.M. and the crowd had thinned out at the Bar Espada. Alfonso Fuentes asked to speak with the owner. Enrique came out of the kitchen.

"We have been engaged to do some work by *Señor* Harkness."

Enrique said that Harkness had been there earlier and promised to return. The workmen said they would wait—if it was permissible—and drink some wine while they did.

"Permissible? Of course it is permissible," Enrique assured them.

Fuentes and Dunne were certain they could recognize Neil Harkness instantly. Horst Thiele had obtained excellent descriptions of Harkness from the men who had pursued the *Deirdre* after it set sail for Tangier and from those who played the role of customs inspectors there. Thiele had passed on the descriptions—so detailed they were as good as photographs.

Enrique saw the two workmen take a table near the front door, brought them a bottle of house red and glasses, which he poured full. The men sat, drank . . . and waited.

38

Neil kept the car radio on during the drive from Marbella to Puerto Cabo Verde. Marisa was in the backseat with Lippmann, Sybil sat up front beside Neil. Even so, he and Sybil made only innocuous comments about the endless news bulletins, which were sketchy. They wished to avoid arousing Marisa's curiosity, but in this they were less than successful.

"You must have left Montemar only minutes before the attack," she said—not once, but several times. And each time, one of them—Neil, Sybil, or David—would try to pass it off.

". . . oh, it must have been fifteen, twenty minutes later . . ."

". . . guess it was just our luck . . ."

". . . oh, hell—call it fate, kismet . . ."

But Marisa persisted with her questions. Weren't they all horrified by what had happened to James Courtney? How could they have gone on blandly to the hospital after hearing the first news flashes? Didn't they want to go back to Montemar and see for themselves?

The questions were fielded one by one.

"Sure we were horrified, but by then there was nothing we could do," Neil said. "Anyway, only damned fools would go rushing back to where people might still be shooting at each other."

Sybil said, "Vivi is my best friend. I had to see her."

Lippmann's offering: "Be useless to go out to Montemar now. The police would never let us near the place."

To this Marisa said: "They would if you told them who you were—how well you knew Courtney and that you were there just before."

I am going to ball you—and with a vengeance, Dave thought, and, teeth gritted, said: "Marisa. Going back there so soon would be traumatic for me—probably the most traumatic experience of my life." And it was true.

"Because Courtney and others were killed?"

"Because a great—a very great—art collection, one I was going to study and catalog, has ceased to exist, burned to ashes. Do you have the faintest idea what that means?" Lippmann knew only too well what it meant to him. The loss was catastrophic—for the whole world. Thinking of it made him want to bellow in pain, batter his fists against a brick wall, bawl like a baby.

If Marisa said anything further to that, it went unheard. A siren shrieked from behind them. Neil pulled to the right lane, slowed. A car packed with uniformed civil guardsmen roared past, verifying the most recent news flash that the Guardia was being deployed in an all-out manhunt. Another siren, another carload.

Neil pondered how long it might be before some official agency began a methodical interrogation of the servants and security personnel at Montemar. It would then be quickly learned that there had been three people in Don Jaime's *estudio* shortly before the helicopters landed. Their names were known to the staff, and the hunt for them would be on. We have to sit down and have a long talk before that happens, he mused grimly. The three of us. Without Marisa. The Cabo Verde turnoff was two kilometers ahead when he asked:

"Marisa, suppose I run you over to Broadmoor and drop you off?"

Sybil broke in before she could answer. "None of us have eaten, Neil. I know I shouldn't be hungry, but I am." She was uncertain when her stomach had stopped churning, but it had. A sense of resignation, I suppose, she thought. Can't undo what's been done, and can't think about what to do in the future if I'm starving.

Marisa declared she was also very hungry, and Dave said, "I didn't think I'd ever want to eat again, but I do."

Neil capitulated. He guessed it would take police another hour to crank up a hunt for them. With luck, they'd have longer, perhaps as much as two hours. And they did need to eat, stoke up. They could have a fast meal at the Espada, after that take Marisa to Broadmoor—whether she liked it or not—and go to Sybil's apartment.

Workmen, laborers? Enrique phrased the question in his mind and shook his head. The two men were still at the table near the door. One had done all the talking. The other had hardly spoken a word. Both had clean hands and manicured fingernails, even though their faded blue jumpsuit coveralls were soiled with fresh dirt and grease. Enrique continued to watch them from behind the bar. *Both* were talking now, he noticed—in low tones, their heads together—and drinking their *vino tinto* slowly. Much too slowly.

Police? No, Enrique decided. They did not have the look. *Contrabandistas*, smugglers?—yes, that had to be the answer. Many came to the Puerto—as to all ports everywhere—in many guises, seeking boat owners or crewmen who would take this or that here or there for a price. He shrugged burly shoulders. It was none of his business. His business was running the Espada—which, thanks to events of the afternoon, was filling rapidly. The Puerto crowd wanted to congregate, drink, wolf down *tapas* and discuss, theorize, argue. Spanish, Brits, *norteamericanos*, Dutch, or whatever, each would have his own theories to offer and rumors to spread—and some customers were already at it.

". . . always said the Guardia's crooked. Went after Courtney and the Arab because they wouldn't pay graft. . . ."

"Balls. It's another coup—and the King's behind it this time."

"I'm for it. Let the soldiers run Spain. We never had it so good as we did under Franco. . . . Hey, Enrique, another round here. . . . Everything was cheap, there wasn't any crime . . ."

"Know what I think? Courtney was into dope—had a factory processing cocaine at Montemar. That was the reason for his tight security."

And so it went, the babble growing louder, the calls for fresh rounds of drinks becoming more frequent and insistent.

General Diego Quintana was a slender, deceptively mild-featured and -mannered man of fifty-two whose most passionate love was for his country and its people. He would protect them at any cost, his own life being a negligible sum to pay if ever demanded. On active duty for thirty years, he had not worn a uniform in almost a decade, and his name was never mentioned in the press. Yet he was known and respected in the circles where it counted, feared and hated in those where he did not give *una mierda seca* whether it counted or not.

Disdaining partisan politics, General Quintana was fiercely loyal to duly constituted government and totally incorruptible. He headed a tiny ultrasecret agency that was above and apart from other official intelligence and security organizations. He reported directly—and only—to incumbent prime ministers and to King Juan Carlos I, the constitutional monarch of Spain. In normal times his agency worked invisibly behind the scenes as a stabilizing influence. But when the framework of the still-young Spanish democracy or the nation's security was threatened, the

Prime Minister could give General Quintana sweeping emergency power and authority.

The general was singularly qualified and equipped to hold a position of such awesome responsibility. He had a brilliant mind—unlike that of many military men, flexible and imaginative. He was a student of history, economics, philosophy, science, and technology—and a linguist fluent in a dozen languages. Within him was a steel core of devotion to duty, which he equated with ensuring the safety and welfare of Spain and Spaniards. Inside that core was a heart that could be—when given reason—warm and compassionate.

General Quintana and a quartet of aides—also in civilian clothes—had been flown from Madrid to Málaga by military jet transport. After landing at Málaga, a staff car with motorcycle escort took them to the Cabo Verde town hall. A makeshift command and communications center had been established there by temporarily evicting the *ayuntamiento* bureaucrats from their offices and sending them home until further notice. Officials—civilian, police, paramilitary, and military—already assembled there understood that the general had come to take overall command, and were glad of it. He had knowledge far beyond what they possessed—and the rare knack for instantly welding disparate and sometimes rival groups into a single smoothly functioning unit.

Quintana's first request was for copies of all reports made by those who had been to Montemar and the estate of Rashid el Muein. He went through the reports with customary and, to those who had not seen *el general* work before, incredible speed. Next he wanted the name rosters of all the people who worked or were present at either place. Scanning the lists took a bit longer, and he made tidy check marks beside the names of those he desired to see first. Since all those on the rosters were being detained for questioning, it was a simple task to locate and bring them in. Paco, the regular guard posted outside Courtney's office, and Tomás, the security man who had escorted three persons to the main gate minutes before the bogus Civil Guard helicopters landed, were of special interest to the general. From them he obtained three other names that interested him even more. He ordered that every document and report on them at local, provincial, and national levels be pulled from the files at once and their gists telexed to Cabo Verde.

Then he returned to questioning Tomás.

"Courtney was doing what when the people left?"

"He was in his *estudio*, Señor General. He spoke from there and said the painting had to be taken . . . to the Pueblo, I think."

"What kind of painting?"

"I did not see it, Señor General—only the back. It was wound up in a roll."

Harkness parked on the quay opposite La Espada, led the others inside.

Fuentes and Dunne started to rise from their chairs, dropped back into them. The party went past them, squeezing through the crowd.

"Bloody hell. Four." Dunne eyed the two women. "The small girl must be his—Sybil Pearson."

"The other is Spanish," Fuentes said, leered. "Succulent."

"I prefer Harkness's woman. The word for her is 'cute,' Fonso."

"Who is the man with her?"

"Haven't a clue." Kyle Dunne was drinking wine with one hand, scratching at his head with the other. "Never figured on four. Be hard to handle that many."

"Kyle. We sit. The owner will tell Harkness we are here waiting for him. He will come, by himself. One of us will start to talk, the other goes to the girl and says Harkness wants her to join us. When she is here, we're out the door with them."

"Hell of a mob here, and more straying in. Might be dicey."

"Mobs are helpful." Fuentes grinned. "Much noise, much movement. Who will notice what we are doing?" He patted the invisible bulge under the breast of his coveralls. "With this in his spine and yours in the girl's, they will be very silent and very obedient."

Enrique was in the kitchen, supervising, and did not see Neil Harkness enter. Neil made his usual slow progress through the crowd, for he was well known, had to exchange greetings and then extricate himself from further involvement at almost every step. A waiter took him and his party to one of the few empty tables in the restaurant section of Bar Espada. They seated themselves. Neil and Dave ordered large Scotches. Sybil and Marisa opted for chilled *rosado*.

"Let's make the food order simple so we can eat and leave," Harkness said. "*Paella*."

The drinks came. Neil swallowed his whole, lit a Celta.

"*Hola!*" Enrique had emerged from the kitchen, was making a good-host tour of his domain, saw Neil's big frame, came to the table. "You wish me to bring what you left with me?" he asked.

So this is where he stashed it, Dave thought, swallowing Scotch.

"No." Harkness signaled a shut-up signal with his eyebrows—which, by some process of association, reminded Enrique.

"There are two men waiting for you."

Neil assumed they were his crewmen, for whom he had posted notices on the bulletin board earlier in the day that already seemed to have gone on for a century. "Where are they?"

"First table by the door."

" 'Scuse—I'll be back." Harkness unfolded, went toward the bar, turned right toward the entrance.

Right table. Right number of men. But he had never seen them before in his life—a pair of *trabajadores*.

"Señor Harkness," Fuentes opened in Spanish. "We must speak. It is very important. Please join us, seat yourself."

Neil said he was sorry, he was with friends and not interested. He made to move away, stopped, his attention drawn by a sharp rap on the Formica tabletop. He found himself looking into a bulb silencer that barely showed over the edge. Kyle Dunne held the weapon to which it was attached in his lap.

Neil was glad it had happened before he ate. He might have lost his lunch all over the table. As it was, his empty stomach merely growled and knotted tight. He pulled one of the two empty chairs out, sat, said nothing.

"Fonso, you're elected errand boy," the man with the gun said in English, and Neil's gut knot tightened further.

"I shall be gallant"—also in English, and the first man left the table.

"You people have names?" Harkness asked, pretending a calm he did not feel.

"Today I'm Kyle Dunne, he's Alfonso Fuentes," Dunne replied. The names were real, permanent, but what the hell difference did it make? When he and Fuentes finally went on their way, neither Harkness nor his girl would be able to repeat names. Or anything else. The glint in Dunne's eyes mirrored his thoughts, enabled Neil to read them. The stomach seized up completely, but his mind raced.

"Okay, Dunne. Who asks the questions—you or me?"

"Me. Ready to deliver at last?"

"Deliver?" Harkness realized what it was about immediately, and that was a help. Not much of a help, but a help all the same.

"Picture. Velázquez. Map." The bulb silencer hadn't moved a fraction of a millimeter.

"I gave it to Courtney. Must have gone up in smoke with everything else. And speaking of smoke . . ." Neil grinned, fished for a Celta. Damn, he had left his pack on the other table. But, patting at his pockets, he felt the straight-stemmed briar. He had forgotten about it. "Guess I won't."

"I don't—they say it gives you cancer. You're a fucking liar, Harkness. You took the picture away. Grenville and Courtney both said so, and they were too scared to lie."

Then Dunne—and probably Fuentes—had been among those who fire-bombed Montemar, Neil thought. His muscles tensed. He was going to grab the table, fling it up against Dunne—and he would have.

But.

Fuentas returned. With Sybil, who appeared somewhat puzzled. "The *señor* here says you wanted to see me."

"I did, I did," Neil said, pulled out the other empty chair, grabbed Sybil's arm, and pulled her down into it. "Sit . . . join us." Their both being seated would gain a little time, make it a little more difficult for Dunne and Fuentes to get them moving and out—which, it was obvious, they intended.

"Motherfucker!" Kyle Dunne snarled.

Fuentes stepped close behind Sybil. He held a gun hidden in the roomy slash pocket of his coverall top, leaned so she could feel hard metal through fabric against her neck.

Dave Lippmann stared hungrily at the mountain of *paella* being served him, but he was frowning.

"What's the matter?" Marisa sat next to him and was pressing her thigh against his under the table. "Don't you like *paella*?"

"I'm thinking about the guy who came after Sybil. I don't know much Spanish, but I do have an ear."

"He spoke beautiful *castiliano*."

"Do many Spaniards in dirty workclothes speak that way?"

"Many speak good *castiliano*, but his was so perfect—that's why I noticed it. And he had such nice hands for a *trabajador*."

"That does it." David leaped to his feet. "Stay here."

Lippmann wormed through the now-three-deep babbling crowd at the bar until he had a clear view of the front table. The positions in which the four people—three sitting, one standing—held themselves told it all. He wanted to run away but instead strolled over to them. His first goal was to determine if the men in coveralls were undercover police. If not—first things first.

"Hi," he said, elaborately casual. He saw the silencer peeping over the table edge, dry-swallowed. Police officers did not carry silenced guns—or did they? "*Paella*'s getting cold." He glanced down at Sybil. The laborer who had been fool enough to speak perfect Castilian because he wanted to impress a pair of attractive women was holding something against the base of her skull through his pocket. Gun, what else? Lippmann thought, and that wasn't police style, either, but he had to be sure. He looked at Harkness. Neil's expression confirmed: they aren't police.

"We'll be busy awhile," Neil said brusquely.

"See you when you're finished if not before." Dave shrugged, turned, ambled until he was deep into the crowd, then rushed to find Enrique, almost collided with him, grabbed his arms, spoke rapidly.

"You're the owner?" Enrique nodded. "Call the police—quick. *Muy pronto*. Neil . . . Sybil . . . Those guys are thugs. They've got guns."

Enrique nodded again, knowingly. He had been right about the men in the coveralls. But if they had guns, and the police burst in and there was shooting, his customers . . . Very well, he would take the risks and telephone.

"And give me a bottle of white wine—the kind with the long neck," Lippmann said. "Unopened."

"Sir, I don't understand."

"Dammit, just give me a bottle!"

Enrique used his owner's prerogative to yank a bottle of *vino blanco* from a wall rack. He handed it to Dave and moved on to the kitchen, from where he could telephone in relative quiet.

Lippmann gripped the bottle by its neck, held it at his side, started pushing through the mass of people again.

"Dave!" Marisa had tired of being left alone and came into the bar looking for him. "Dave!" He did not hear her, but she recognized his back and followed after him, ignoring the pinches and fondlings she received from the men densely clustered at the bar.

Lippmann once more paused at the edge of the crowd, and his fears were realized. He could not hear the seated man speak—

". . . you'll both get up and walk out the door. I'll be behind you, Harkness. Fonso'll be lock-stepping your bird . . ."

—but it was obvious they were about to leave and take Sybil and Neil with them. Timing, he thought. Timing down to the millisecond. He took a firm grip on the bottle, a firmer one on his nerves, edged a step forward, just clear of the crowd. He caught Neil's eye, showed the bottle, received an answering eyelid flicker, and went into motion.

He leaped, swung the bottle against the wall. It smashed. Fragments of glass exploded, wine poured over him. The noise brought the man standing behind Sybil spinning around, his chest directly meeting Lippmann's thrust of the jagged broken bottle. Glass ripped flesh, scraped bone. The man bellowed. David threw himself sideways, away from the right-hand slash pocket. There were no sounds he could hear, but holes appeared in the pocket and the fabric smoked as it was charred by burning gunpowder. David went in low, jabbed once more.

Neil had swept Sybil out of her chair with a single powerful sweep of his arm, did what he had thought of doing before. He heaved the table up into Kyle Dunne's face. Dunne reacted. Bullets fired from behind the table tore through the Formica top, so close that Harkness could hear their whir through the air, feel them pass.

Someone screamed. Then others.

Dunne was disentangling himself from the table, coming out, Walther P-38 in the open. The bulb silencer swung toward Neil, fixed on him. But Fuentes, streaming blood from chest to groin, was rolling on the floor, and he slammed against Harkness's legs, knocking him off balance—and saving his life, for as he went down, Dunne's bullet creased through his hair.

There was an agonized shriek. The bullet had buried itself in human flesh elsewhere in the room.

Then a tide broke. Men and women stampeding toward the door trampled over Sybil, Neil, and the blood-drenched Fuentes. Dunne, obsessed with Harkness and trying to aim at him, was bowled over, trapped by running feet and pumping legs. He held the Walther up, fired blindly in hopes of turning the mob, but the finger-snap shots could not be heard, and when his last round struck a woman in the leg, she fell screaming on top of him.

"Dave!"

Lippmann had to shove Marisa away, for she threw her arms around him—and he still had Fuentes to worry about. No, he didn't, Dave saw. Fuentes had lost his gun—God only knew where it had slid or been kicked—and was holding himself, trying to hug his wounds closed.

"Dave!" It was Marisa again, and this time David let her hold him.

Neil lifted Sybil gently to her feet. There were trickles of blood on her arms where she had been cut by flying glass. Neil wiped the blood away with his fingers, kissed the cuts. Sybil clung to him and wept uncontrollably.

A Puerto patrolman was the first to respond.

Reinforcements started to arrive minutes later.

After them came the shiny official car bearing General Diego Quintana. An aide singled out Neil Harkness, took him to the general—who was polite, soft-spoken.

"I had just issued a search order, Mr. Harkness. For you, Miss Pearson, and Mr. Lippmann."

"Am I . . . are we, under arrest?"

"Quite to the contrary. Is there any place you prefer where we can all talk—privately?"

Sybil stepped forward. "We were going on to my apartment—before."

"I shall be grateful for your hospitality." Quintana saw Marisa Alarcón standing beside Lippmann. Sybil introduced them.

"You were with your friends?" the general asked.

"Yes."

"Then, with Miss Pearson's permission, I ask that you join us."

39

The aides remained outside in the corridor. Sybil, whose cuts had been bandaged by a doctor in one of the ambulances that came to the Bar Espada, offered drinks, coffee. Everyone refused.

"Pretend this is a classroom," the general said. He seated himself in an armchair. Sybil and Neil, Marisa and David, made pairs, sitting close to each other on sofas.

"There is much else for me to do," Quintana began. "I shall have to hurry—and, I'm afraid, be blunt. You shall have to listen to me and answer whatever questions I ask. Truthfully, for I already know most of the answers."

He turned to Neil. "You and Mr. Dixon are wanted by Interpol. For the theft of an extremely valuable painting from a Herr Heinrich Kloster in Zurich. Are you aware of that?"

"No."

"Mr. Harkness, we know what that painting is. What we do not know is where you have hidden it."

"General, it's deadlier than an H-bomb."

"Not if it is destroyed—as I will order done, and before your eyes. Once it no longer exists . . . well, there will no longer be any validitiy to the Interpol notice, will there?"

"You'll have to trust him, Neil," David said.

"Enrique has it at the Espada."

"Open the door, please," the general requested. Neil complied. Quintana told an aide to go to the Espada and bring back the painting Señor Harkness had left in the care of its owner. The door closed; General Quintana resumed.

"Spain is grateful to you. Unfortunately, it must show its gratitude in ways that may not appear very friendly."

"Anything short of a life sentence appears friendly at this point," Neil said. "You could throw the book at me."

"At all of you—except Señorita Alarcón." A good-natured smile. The smile was bogus. Inwardly Diego Quintana felt sad—and bitter. He believed that certain standards and values were—or should be—constant, permanent, and he sorrowed because they were decaying. Marisa Alarcón was a product of the trend, personified it, member of a breed with which the general was all too familiar. Their kind were speeding the decay, dulling the once-bright promises of Spanish democracy to extinction.

The breed had sprung into being with the generation that spawned Modern Spanish Youth. Parents, suddenly affluent, casting aside integrity and dignity. Quick to adopt and ape new fashions and fads, even quicker to discard them when newer ones appeared. Doting on their children, giving them everything, refusing them nothing. Sending them to expensive schools at home and abroad. To schools where teachers prated liberty and freedom while mass-producing conceited snobs with no sense of responsibility toward themselves, much less to others, their sole purpose in life the relentless pursuit of pleasure.

Parents and children a shallow breed. One-dimensional cardboard figures richly decorated to hide their shallowness. But their scent could not be hidden, Quintana mused. It was a compound of many odors. Money, arrogance, pretension, hypocrisy. Self-indulgence. Sex as a form of self-love expressed in casual, meaningless encounters. Underlying all, the stench of undefined yet perpetual discontent and of formless fears. He could not change the breed, Quintana thought with a weary mental shrug; he could only do his duty. His counterfeit smile held.

"Señorita Alarcón, whose direct involvement was negligible,

is to have only a page or two of the book—as you put it—thrown at her. As I shall explain soon. However, first things first."

Neil offered a Celta. Quintana accepted graciously and lit both their cigarettes with a disposable plastic lighter. Neil had somehow expected he would use a gold Dunhill at the very least, as most generals would, and was favorably impressed, respect for the man increasing.

"Permit me to begin by speaking of Gruppe Thiele, an organization of terrorist mercenaries. Once its members were all fugitive Nazi war criminals. Now only its founder, and still its leader, Horst Thiele, remains of the original group. The ranks are filled with younger murderous scum from many countries. With such men as the Irish Kyle Dunn and—I regret to say—the Spaniard Alfonso Fuentes, both of whom were identified minutes after we arrested them at the Bar Espada."

Quintana gave Neil a conspiratorial grin, continued.

"Two others have been identified as Gruppe Thiele members by the French Sûreté. By odd coincidence, they were attacked in a Parisian hotel, the Lutetia, while you and the now-missing Mr. Dixon were staying there, and succumbed to their wounds. I might mention that the Sûreté takes the view that the only good terrorists are dead terrorists and has closed the case. No further investigations of it will be made."

Thank God, Neil thought; asked: "Who hired the Thiele bunch—Courtney?"

"No. The group was retained to take the painting—the map—from Courtney, then kill him. They failed to do the first, thanks to you, but succeeded in doing the latter. Then, because Horst Thiele had his own plans, they killed Rashid el Muein, the man who had originally retained them. Unfortunately, they also created an exceedingly dangerous situation—a crisis—in Spain by making it appear that the Guardia Civil was attempting to topple our government, stage a coup d'etat."

"It didn't fool anyone for very long," David Lippmann said.

"True. However, while one set of fears receded, others rose immediately to take their place. Our Spanish authorities were baffled, and, I must admit, terrified. There were no clues, there was nothing—absolutely nothing—to indicate who or what we faced, what forms the next outrages might take." The general stubbed his cigarette butt into a ceramic ashtray. "That is why Spain is grateful to you. The incident at the Espada snapped all the pieces into place, provided all the answers."

The doorbell sounded. Quintana raised his voice: "*Adelante!*"

His aide had returned from the Bar Espada and entered carrying the rolled canvas. The general told the man to lay it on the floor, dismissed him, and addressed Sybil:

"I see there is a portable barbecue grill on your terrace, Miss Pearson. Do you happen to have a pair of strong scissors?"

She blinked puzzlement but nodded. "I have some heavy shears."

"Excellent. The picture can be cut into pieces and destroyed—by being barbecued."

Dave was opening the canvas roll. He examined it, nodded. "It's okay, the genuine fake. Nobody's slipped a ringer in on us."

Sybil had found the shears. She knelt down beside David and they started to hack at the canvas. Marisa stifled a bored yawn. Neil grew alert as Quintana took a deep breath, shifted position, and spoke:

"I have said Spain is grateful . . . and hinted of a rather unpleasant side to that gratitude. It is this. You must all leave Spain. Señorita Alarcón for only four or five weeks. The others, perhaps two years."

"Gratitude? It's a goddamned kick in the fucking teeth!" Neil's angry outburst expressed the shock and consternation of all.

"Listen to me!" Quintana's tone carried authority. "What happened today must be swept under the rug until it is forgotten. There are far-reaching implications, domestic and international. The doubts and suspicions of foreign governments—American, British, those of Arab countries and others—must be allayed. Some thirty million foreign tourists visit Spain each year. They must not be afraid to come. Nor can we afford to lose the confidence of the foreign expatriates who live in Spain. These are but a few of the reasons why much of the story must be buried."

"What are you going to tell the world?" Neil sneered. "Fairy tales?"

"The truth—but only up to a point. That the outrages were perpetrated by mercenary terrorists. Beyond this, the truth will blur. The terrorists tried to extort huge sums from Courtney and el Muein and took their revenge when the two men refused to pay. Then the terrorists fled the country. Except for Dunne and Fuentes, who were taken into custody by local police after staging a savage barroom fight, and who"—Quintana glanced at his wristwatch—"despite heroic efforts to save their lives, have by now expired. Such will be the official—the *only*—version."

"And the rest go scot-free?" Sybil demanded indignantly.

"Miss Pearson. Gruppe Thiele has its base and bolthole in Riyadh. There has already been a telephone conversation between Madrid and the King of Saudi Arabia. Gruppe Thiele—and its leader—will soon cease to exist."

"You didn't offer the map to the Saudis?" Dave was suspicious again.

"My friend, the Saudis are the last people on earth to want a fundamentalist Muslim *jihad* and the first to want the map destroyed. Now, please permit me to explain why it is imperative that you leave Spain."

He leaned forward in his chair.

"You three"—he indicated Sybil, Neil, and David—"were very close to the affair and know far too much. Some of our less responsible politicians and journalists might seek you out, investigate, and capitalize on what they are able to learn." He looked at Marisa. "You have little firsthand knowledge and we could easily discredit anything you might say. However, it is still best that you be away from Spain for a few weeks."

"I'll tell the story—write it myself—when I return!"

"An empty threat, *Señorita*. Within forty-eight hours my office will have compiled detailed dossiers on you, your family, and all your activities and personal lives. Do I make myself clear?"

Marisa glared at him sullenly.

Lippmann was scornful. "You make me laugh, General. Once any of us is in another country, you can't stop us from talking our heads off."

Quintana's eyes hardened. "The world is filled with paradoxes. One is that agencies such as that I have the honor of heading enjoy infinitely greater latitude of action when operating outside the borders of our own countries."

"Riddles?" Dave jeered.

But Neil Harkness got it. "General Quintana just dropped another hint, Dave. About what the CIA supposedly calls organic operations—wet work. I don't think he's kidding, either."

"It would be a last resort, of course . . . and, no, I am not kidding," Quintana said. He saw that Sybil and David had cut the canvas into roughly foot-square pieces, spoke again. "Before we begin our barbecue, while I am aware that you all have valid passports, I do not know if you all have adequate money. I am prepared to furnish—"

"We have plenty," Dave said, speaking for all.

Quintana said, "You are to leave tonight. Reservations will be made for you on flights to your chosen destinations and your first-class fares paid."

"A minute, General," Neil interrupted. "Sybil and I have our apartments, cars, furniture—and then there's my charter business."

"I shall give you my address in Madrid. Write me submitting round-figure claims. My government will honor them in full, without question, by same-day telex transfer of funds to whatever bank designated."

"General," Sybil spoke up. "I have a friend in hospital—at least let me run into Marbella and see her."

"It is impossible. There might be journalists there who would recognize James Courtney's private secretary. You may telephone or write Mrs. Dixon—oh, yes, we know about her and your friendship, too—when you are abroad. I will even permit you to make a brief—a very brief—telephone call to her from here a little later."

I should be allowed as much, Marisa thought, and, self-confidence resurgent, said: "You must allow me to speak with my father in Barcelona. He is an important man with many important friends. He'll be furious at you—"

"My adjutant in Madrid has spoken to your father, and he is not at all furious at me, *Señorita*. He is, in fact, very . . . docile, shall I say? My adjutant jogged his memory. About some recent foreign currency transactions that he forgot to report—by accidental error, of course. No, you may not telephone him until you are out of Spain."

Quintana rose from the chair, took the pieces of canvas, nodded to Neil Harkness. They went out on the terrace, pulled the glass sliding doors to a tight close behind them. There was an ample stock of patented, warranted-to-light-instantly charcoal and a quarter-liter can of inflammable fluid. But it still took almost twenty minutes for the fragments of forged Velázquez—and the map that led to the hiding place of the True Koran—to burn into ashes. The smoke was heavy, the fumes acrid, evil-smelling. General Quintana and Neil coughed and choked frequently as they tended the funeral pyre on the portable barbecue grill. Between coughing fits, they talked. Harkness was curious about many things, and the general was, within limits, willing to answer questions.

"What'll happen to Courtney Ventures International and el Muein's business interests?"

"The licenses and permits they had to operate in Spain will be revoked. If their subsidiaries survive, it will be in other countries, not here."

"Their personal properties—Montemar and the Arab's estate in Marbella?"

"*Quién sabe?*" An arch grin from Quintana. "It is possible—just barely possible, mind you—that some government clerk will run across old filing folders. In them he may discover documents such as the French are wont to unearth in more or less comparable cases—Kreuger and Stavisky, for example. These will prove that the deceased never held legal title to the properties. Or they may be like those of which the Italians are so fond—showing that the lands had been deeded over to the local authorities for use as public parks. Or . . ." The general spread his hands, shrugged.

"God, what a cover-up!"

"It is necessary—an imperative."

"General, what's really the point . . . and what do you get out of it?"

"The answer to both questions is the same. My country is spared domestic and international problems and its economy is spared heavy blows which would cause grave hurt to its people. That is the point and that is what I get out of it."

You're quite a guy, General, Neil thought, stirring dying ashes with a barbecue skewer; said: "Sybil and I will be going to Yugoslavia."

"There is a flight tonight for Vienna. You can go on from there in the morning."

"A last question. My crew—"

"They are Spaniards and totally ignorant of the true events. It is best they remain here. I shall drop a word so they may find employment without delay."

They went back into the apartment and to the bathroom, where they washed soot from their hands and faces. Sybil, who had been packing suitcases furiously, blocked their path when they emerged.

"My phone call to Vivi—Mrs. Dixon . . ."

"Very well." The general nodded. "But it must be short, and be most careful what you say."

Sybil remembered there was no private telephone in Vivi's room. She dialed the hospital, asked that Carlos Lozano be called to the phone. Minutes passed. Quintana was growing impatient. At last she heard Carlos speak.

"This is Sybil, Carlos. Neil and I have to go on a trip—it's very sudden and urgent. Please tell Vivi and give her our love—"

"Sybil, there are things I have to tell *you*!" Carlos' voice sang. "Vivi and I—"

"I think we already know, Carlos. Bless you both . . . and we'll write. Soon. Within a couple of days. Now I simply must run."

Quintana, eager to tie up loose ends and be on his way, ticked off points with crisp efficiency. A staff car would come for Sybil and Neil in half an hour. Until then, an aide would remain posted outside the apartment door and would accompany them not only to the airport but also on the flight to Vienna. Another car and aide would take Marisa to Broadmoor so she could pack, go with her to the Málaga airport and on to . . .

"You have not yet told me where you wish to go, *Señorita*."

Marisa had no answer of her own, gave David Lippmann a searching—and hungry—look.

David's mind worked. He had been granted a full year's sabbatical. It was not his fault that there was no longer any collection to catalog and no chance that the Wyler College Art Museum would be given or bequeathed a thing by James Philip Courtney. Wyler's bigwigs would probably suffer cardiac arrests, but they would have to accept the official story. And he, Dave Lippmann, could goof off at full pay for eleven-months-plus. He eyed Marisa, weighing pros and cons. The pros won a landslide victory. She would, he knew, become a pain in the ass after her prescribed "four or five weeks." But until then, she would be fantastic in bed—and that, he reflected, blood pumping, was what it was all about.

"London is always fun," he said.

"Air Iberia has a direct flight at nine," Sybil volunteered. "You can make it with hours to spare."

"Oh, we'll make it—together," Marisa said, the double-entendre so heavy it was leaden. "We'll be making it, won't we, Dave?"

General Diego Quintana thought of the affairs he had had in his life—and there had been more than a few, all of them containing at least some degree of human warmth and feeling. It was a new and to him alien Spain, he mused, and for a split second wondered what it was he sought to preserve and why. The doubt vanished. There were still breeds of Spaniard other than that of the Alarcóns and their kind.

"Please, we must leave now," he said.

There were embraces and handshakes, and Quintana departed with Marisa and David.

"We'll have a ball," Neil said when he and Sybil were alone. He held up the Swiss bankbook that showed the half-million-dollar balance. They smiled broadly at each other, but the smiles faded as both felt the rush of void pangs that come with eviction.

"I wish I knew where Ken is," Sybil said, turning away and pretending to be wholly engrossed in closing up another suitcase.

"Weird—like mental telepathy," Neil said, and fumbled in his shirt pocket for a Celta. "I was just thinking of him myself."

Kenneth Dixon's body floated to the surface in the Puerto Cabo Verde yacht basin three days later. His death was listed as an accidental drowning. Out of deference to his widow, no mention was made of the fact that he had been wanted by the police for assaulting her.

The newest Kenneth Dixon novel, *The High Rollers*, was, by coincidence, officially published on the day of his funeral. Because of his death, it received an enormous amount of publicity, immediately went to the top of all the best-seller lists, and became the most successful of all Ken Dixon blockbusters.

For more than two years Vivian Dixon could not bring herself to look at the ghost-written book. By then she and Carlos Lozano were living in Lugano, Switzerland. Plastic surgery had restored her face—not exactly as it had been, but she was still attractive, and the frigidity barriers had long since crumbled. Sale of Galerías Vivi and Broadmoor and the 500,000 dollars in the numbered Swiss account had left Vivian wealthy, and she had resumed painting. Carlos operated a small but profitable art gallery in Lugano.

It was Carlos who found a used hardback copy of *The High Rollers* in a bookshop and brought it home one evening. The photograph of Ken on the back of the dust jacket was the same as the one that had been used on his first novel, *Gusher!*

Vivian and Carlos did not make love that night.

ABOUT THE AUTHOR

Jonathan Black was born in Cleveland and raised in Los Angeles. He has held a wide variety of jobs in many different places and served in the U.S. Army during both World War II and the Korean War. Since 1956, he has resided in Europe and currently lives in Spain. Black has written well over a hundred books, fiction and non-fiction. His novels enjoy a brisk sale abroad as well as in America. He devotes most of his time to writing but manages to travel extensively—combining, as he says, "the business of firsthand research with the pleasure of frequent change."